DANCE WITH THE DRAGON

DANCE
WITH THE
DRAGON

DAVID HAGBERG

A TOM DOHERTY ASSOCIATES BOOK
NEW YORK

DANCE WITH THE DRAGON

Copyright © 2007 by David Hagberg

A Forge Book
Published by Tom Doherty Associates, LLC
175 Fifth Avenue
New York, NY 10010

www.tor-forge.com

Forge® is a registered trademark of Tom Doherty Associates, LLC.

Library of Congress Cataloging-in-Publication Data

Hagberg, David
    Dance with the dragon / David Hagberg.—1st hardcover ed.
        p.cm
    "A Tom Doherty Associates Book."
    ISBN-13: 978-0-7653-0834-4
    ISBN-10: 0-7653-0834-7
    1. McGarvey, Kirk (Fictitious character)—Fiction. 2. Chinese—Mexico—Fiction.
3. Americans—Mexico—Fiction. 4. Terrorism—Prevention—Fiction. 5. Intelligence officers—
Fiction. I. Title.
    PS3558.A3227D36 2007
    813'.54—dc22

                                                                        2007018764

First Edition: September 2007

Printed in the United States of America

0   9   8   7   6   5   4   3   2   1

This book is for Lorrel.

. . . we must pass through solitude and difficulty, isolation and silence, in order to reach forth to the enchanted place where we can dance our clumsy dance and sing our sorrowful song—but in this dance or in this song there are fulfilled the most ancient rites of our conscience in the awareness of being human and of believing in a common destiny.

PABLO NERUDA
TOWARD THE SPLENDID CITY

THE
BEGINNING

ONE

CHIHUAHUA STATE

The foothills of northern Mexico's Sierra Madre were bathed in the cold silver light of a full October moon as Louis Updegraf stopped a moment behind a stand of pine trees to catch his breath. Somehow everything had gone horribly wrong over the past two weeks, and this evening he was running for his life because of what he'd learned. The job was no longer a game.

At thirty-three he was a tall man, well built, with a dark complexion and a large Gallic nose. Not so long ago, someone he thought was a friend had told him that he could be Gerard Depardieu's twin bother. He'd thought the French actor was good, but not very handsome. But that was the story of his life; there was always something not quite right.

He had come west, just below the crests of the hills, and he figured by now he was at least three miles from the compound. The city of Chihuahua was spread out below in the valley, and as he took out his 9 mm Beretta 92F and ejected the magazine to check the pistol's load for the third time, an Aeromexico 727 took off from CUU Airport in the distance and headed southeast toward Mexico City. He was supposed to be on that flight, he reflected bitterly. From here it was a long walk. But if he could get into town he could call for help, though how he would explain his presence up here he hadn't figured out.

First things first. He had to stay alive long enough to reach a telephone.

He stepped out from the shelter of the trees and continued west, angling down into the valley where he thought he could intercept the highway to Cuauhtémoc. From there it might be possible to get a ride into Chihuahua, provided the Doll's people didn't catch up with him.

In high school in Madison, Wisconsin, he had been an all-star quarterback on the football team, and he had gone to UW to study political science on a four-year football scholarship. In his senior year he had taken the school to the Rose Bowl, and in the eleven years since then he'd not let himself get out of shape. It was one thing in his life that he was proud of, one thing that no one could take away from him.

He was dressed lightly, in blue jeans, T-shirt, and windbreaker, sneakers on his feet, and although the mountain air was chilly at this hour he was sweating by the time he reached the power lines two hundred meters southwest. The high-voltage lines came down to the city in a broad swath cut through the trees.

Once again Updegraf halted up in the shelter of the forest. It was possible that no one was coming for him. But it was equally possible not only that they were somewhere behind him, but that they may have doubled around and gotten ahead of him. It was possible that Roaz's shooters were right now waiting in the woods across the fifty-meter grassy lane that was lit up like day.

He nervously switched the safety catch to the off position, and then on again. It would be just his rotten luck to stumble on a rock and shoot himself. Save the opposition the trouble.

Cocking an ear, he held his breath to listen for something, a snatch of conversation, a rustling branch, a dislodged rock tumbling down the hill. But except for the sounds of a hunting bird in the distance, perhaps a hawk or a screech howl, and the light breeze in the treetops, the hillside was silent.

Updegraf weighed his chances. Miguel Roaz and the people working for him were smart, but then they had been trained by Chinese intelligence, so they knew their jobs well. On top of that they were highly motivated. There was a lot of money involved. A fabulous amount of money. More than any of them could possibly grasp.

"Señor, please to put down your weapon," someone called from across the clearing.

Updegraf's heart lurched. He stepped back, and as he switched the safety catch off and started to raise his pistol, someone was right behind him, the muzzle of a gun pressed to the base of his skull.

"Don't do anything foolish," a man speaking English with a heavy Mexican accent warned.

Louis didn't recognize the voice, but he could have been any one of the dozen security people from the compound. He didn't know them all. But the fact that he and the other one were here meant that they knew he'd gone over the wall almost immediately after he'd tried to drive into town and been turned back.

"What do you want?" he asked.

"The camera. It wasn't in your car, which means you must have it with you."

"Then what?" Updegraf asked. There wasn't a chance in hell they would let him leave here alive even if he gave them the digital camera that had been used to snap pictures of the guests, especially the new one whose presence had come as a total surprise. He had to survive to call this home.

The Mexican laughed softly. "Then you can either come back to the house for your car, or continue with your hike in the woods."

Updegraf weighed his chances, which didn't seem very good. The muzzle of a pistol was pressed firmly against the back of his skull. If he tried to duck or turn suddenly so that he could bring his own pistol to bear, he would most likely get a bullet in the head. But he had no other options. What he'd learned was too important.

"Okay, you win," he said. He started to reach into his jacket pocket, but the Mexican jammed the pistol even harder.

"First drop your gun."

Updegraf suddenly felt calm, the same way he had just before every key play in a football game. All he could do was his best. "You're going to shoot me anyway—," he said, and he suddenly turned away as he brought his pistol up over his left shoulder.

A thunderclap burst inside his head, and for an instant he saw a billion stars all cascading one over the other. The sight was the most beautiful thing he'd ever seen.

MEXICO CITY

CIA station chief Gilbert Perry parked his smoked silver Mercedes 500SL in his spot behind the U.S. embassy on Paseo de la Reforma a full hour before his customary time of nine in the morning, and took the ambassador's elevator up to his suite of offices on the fourth floor. Tom Chauncy, his number two, had telephoned at six this morning telling him to get his ass to the embassy. Something so big was up that it could not be discussed on an open line.

"We goddamned well might have to shut down the entire operation until we get this shit straightened out!" Chauncy had shouted.

Perry, who'd prided himself on his cool demeanor under fire—he'd spent three months in Kabul and a full thirty days doing dirty duty at Baghdad's Abu Ghraib—was irritated. He damned well was going to have it out with Thomas. Gentlemen simply did not lose their heads in a crisis, and they certainly did not speak to a superior officer in such a peremptory fashion, no matter what the reason. A report of this incident would be placed in Chauncy's personnel jacket.

At six three, with a slender build, penetrating blue eyes, a narrow angular face, and a thick head of hair parted down the middle that had turned gray when he was in his freshman year at Harvard, Perry was called "the Judge" by friends, a sobriquet he discouraged, but one that he secretly enjoyed.

His cover as special assistant for cultural affairs gave him the opportunity to mingle socially with President Ricardo Sabina and other high-ranking Mexican government officials, as well as with the upper echelons of the foreign diplomatic corps here. Symphonies, operas, ballets, fine restaurants, hunting lodges in the mountains, lavish fishing retreats along the Gulf and Pacific coasts, and a nearly endless stream of cocktail parties, receptions, and full dress balls, all were exactly his cup of tea. He'd confided to a friend in Washington that at thirty-eight he was young for this sort of duty, but being here was preparing him for the eventuality of becoming the deputy director of Central Intelligence. It was a position he felt he'd been born for.

When Perry got off the elevator, Chauncy appeared at the end of the corridor, at the door to the secure room that they used as a conference center. Other than the communications center in the basement, the conference room was the safest spot in the entire embassy. It was electronically and mechanically shielded from the outside world. Whatever was said or done there was perfectly immune to any means of surveillance.

Except for humint—human intelligence, Perry thought as he walked down the hall. "What's all this fuss about?"

"Glad you're here, finally," Chauncy said. He stepped aside. "Inside."

Perry followed him into the windowless room, the first glimmerings of doubt entering his mind. At forty-five Chauncy was too old, too overweight, and too much of a blue-collar man ever to rise higher in the CIA than he already was, but his was generally a steady hand in a situation. But this morning it was plain that the man was concerned, even frightened.

Chauncy closed the door and flipped the light switch that operated the door lock and activated the electronic countersurveillance equipment. "It's about Louis," he said.

Perry's stomach did a slow, sour roll. "What about him?" he asked, careful to keep his voice level.

"He's dead. Took a bullet to the side of his head."

"Good Lord," Perry said softly, and he sat down at the long conference table. "Where?" he asked.

"I said a bullet to the side of his head."

Perry looked up. "No, I mean where was he found? Who found him? I hope to God it wasn't Janet." Janet was Updegraf's wife. She and Louis had a trendy apartment in the city's La Condesa neighborhood. She was a cow who stupidly trusted everything her husband told her, but nobody deserved to find her husband lying in a pool of blood.

"It wasn't Janet. Someone from the Red Cross up in Chihuahua called the switchboard a couple hours ago, said they needed to talk to someone in security. It was about a dead American whose body had been dumped in front of the hospital's emergency-room entrance. So the locator called me."

"Good heavens," Perry cried. "What was he doing all the way up there?"

"I haven't a clue," Chauncy admitted. "I was hoping that you might know something."

Perry felt as if he was going to be sick at his stomach. "Are we absolutely positive that it was Louis?"

"It gets worse, Gil," Chauncy said. "The people at the hospital found his ID. They didn't know what to do with it, so they turned it over to the Red Cross along with his other belongings."

"What do you mean, his ID?"

"Just that," Chauncy said. "His CIA identification card."

CIA officers in the field *never* carried anything that could link them to the Company. It just wasn't done. "That's not possible," Perry said.

"They gave a good description."

Perry closed his eyes for a moment to give himself time to think. The entire CIA operation in Mexico could easily unravel over this incident. If that happened it would be the chief of station who took the fall.

"I want you to get up there right now and put a lid on it," Perry said. "This hits the media and we're dead. In the meantime I'll do what I can here to put out any fires that might develop."

"What about Louis's body?" Chauncy asked.

"I don't care," Perry said, but then he changed his mind. "No, get it out of Mexico. Fly it up to the Air Force hospital in San Antonio and have it autopsied." He shook his head. "Tell them that Louis did not commit suicide. He was murdered, and I want the proof."

TWO

U.S. EMBASSY
MEXICO CITY

It was nearly noon, local, which put it about one in Washington, before Perry was able to call his boss, Deputy Director of Operations Howard McCann, at the Building. He'd sent a very brief classified cable around nine, after Chauncy finally left for Chihuahua, reporting only that a CIA officer was dead, presumed assassinated. In Perry's estimation the DDO was not only a consummate professional, but also enough of a gentleman to allow his local station chiefs to handle their own shops without interference from headquarters.

McCann's not bothering him all morning had given Perry a few hours to make a couple of phone calls, and to figure out what his next moves would have to be. Most, though not all, CIA officers operating under cover legends out of the embassy did so with the tacit approval of Mexico's intelligence apparatus, the Centro de Investigación y Seguridad Nacional. So long as the CIA was not spying on Mexicans, but only on the intelligence operations run from the embassies of other governments, nothing was said at the official level. But every station chief's first job on arriving in Mexico City was to make his contacts within the CISN. Perry's was Colonel Luis Salinas, in charge of counterterrorism operations. So long as Perry kept him informed, the colonel would not press the matter, and would do what he could to keep it out of the media.

"This is a bad business, when FSOs are murdered on Mexican soil," Salinas said. "Do you think it was guerrillas? The EPR?" The EPR was the Popular Revolutionary Army, formed in 1996. The organization wanted Mexico for Mexicans, which meant all foreigners were to leave or be killed.

"It's possible, but we're just not sure yet," Perry said. "When I find out something I'll call you."

"Yes, please do, my old friend. And if there is anything else I can do to help, let me know. I have some friends in Chihuahua."

"Thank you," Perry said. "I might have to cancel the reception and concert this weekend."

"Duty calls, I understand," Colonel Salinas said. "Good luck."

Perry's secretary buzzed him. "Mr. McCann is on the secure line."

"I've got it," Perry said. He picked up the red handset, and a powerful quantum effects encryption algorithm automatically kicked in, lending an odd tone to human voices. "Good afternoon, sir," Perry said.

"What the hell is going on down there?" McCann shouted.

Normally McCann ran the DO with a steady, if sometimes overly cautious hand, and Perry had never heard the man raise his voice. This now came as something of a surprise. "One of my people was probably shot to death up in Chihuahua last night. That's in the mountains about one hundred fifty miles south of the Texas border."

"I know where it is," McCann barked. "What the hell was he doing up there that got him killed? I haven't seen a damned thing in your operation reports."

"Frankly, I don't know," Perry admitted. "But I'm going to find out."

The line was silent for a long moment. "I would hope so," McCann came back sarcastically. "What are your people at the CISN saying?"

"They knew nothing about it, but they've agreed to keep it out of the media as long as possible. In the meantime I've sent one of my people to take the body across the border to San Antonio for an autopsy."

"What about his wife?"

"I haven't talked to her—"

"Well you goddamned well better do it pronto. If she finds out about it from someone else, she could start screaming her head off, and we'd be up a creek. Are you clear on that?"

"Yes . . . sir," Perry said, keeping his temper in check. His estimation of McCann's gentlemanly attributes had sharply lowered. But he needed to stay on the DDO's good side on this one. "I'll talk to her this afternoon and then have her brought to Washington, where we can get her a couple of babysitters until the issue is resolved."

"Good thinking," McCann said, somewhat calmer. "I don't want to interfere in your shop, but when one of my people takes a hit I need to know who, what, why, when, where, and how. I'll expect you to get on with it."

"Consider it as good as done, sir."

"I have a better idea. I want you to bring his wife up here yourself on Saturday. Gives you three days to figure out what happened. Once you get her settled, you can brief me on what progress you've made. Hopefully the situation will be resolved by then."

Perry closed his eyes. Three days. It was impossible. "Yes, sir," he said. "I'll see you on Saturday."

After he hung up he turned his chair so that he could look out the window toward the modernistic Torre Mayor skyscraper, which at fifty-five stories was one of the tallest buildings in Latin America. It was supposed to represent Mexican progress into the twenty-first century, and Mexican engineering. It had been designed to withstand even the strongest of earthquakes. But knowing what he knew about Mexico and Mexican engineering, Perry had long ago decided he wouldn't want to be anywhere near the skyscraper in even a minor quake.

In fact at this moment he didn't want to be anywhere near Mexico, but since he couldn't run away from this business, he would have to deal with it.

He asked his secretary to find Gloria Ibenez and have her come to his office. Surprisingly, she was in the building for a change, and she showed up five minutes later, dressed in a very short khaki skirt, sandals with no nylons, and a white peasant blouse that left little to the imagination. He'd warned her repeatedly about dressing suggestively, but she'd completely ignored him. "If you don't like what I'm wearing to work, don't look," she'd once told him, actually laughing in his face. She was a Cuban-born American, and had been with the CIA seven years. Mexico City was the perfect assignment for a Spanish-speaking woman who was beautiful, intelligent, and experienced, and had good contracts. Her father was General Ernesto Marti, who was an adviser to the CIA on Cuban affairs, and just last year she'd been involved on an assignment with Kirk McGarvey when they finally tracked down and eliminated Osama bin Laden. She was a pain in the ass, and Perry had wanted to get rid of her within the month after she'd arrived, and now he saw his chance.

She sat down across the desk from him, a bright smile on her oval, dark face. "Good afternoon, Judge," she said brightly, which Perry was sure she did to needle him, as if she were making fun of him. "What's up?"

Perry studied her for several long seconds, as if he were examining a bug under a magnifying glass, but then he shoved Updegraf's personnel file across the desk to her. "Louis was shot to death last night up in Chihuahua."

Gloria had reached for the file, but she stopped, the smile fading from her lips. "My God," she said softly. "Are you serious?"

"I'm always serious," Perry replied drily. "I sent Chauncy up there to take charge of the situation, and I've talked to the Mexican authorities, who've agreed to keep it out of the media for the time being."

"What about his wife?"

"I'll take care of her," Perry said. He laid a thin buff folder stamped TOP SECRET on top of Updegraf's dossier. "It's what we have so far, which isn't much. Louis's body was dumped outside the hospital early this morning. But we don't have any idea what he was doing up there, except it may have involved Chinese intelligence."

Gloria's eyes narrowed. "Their intelligence presence isn't very strong in Mexico. Anyway, I wasn't aware that we were running any ops against them."

"Neither was I until I opened Louis's safe this morning."

"What'd you find?"

"I don't know what it means yet, I'm still working on it," Perry said. "But I know enough to think that he was trying to turn an embassy clerk. Someone in their communications section."

"What do you want me to do?"

"Run his background. Find out what he was doing with the clerk, and find out if he'd ever approached anyone else over there."

"I'll need to see Louis's encounter sheets so I can get the name of the clerk," Gloria said. "That'd at least be a start. But what about Chihuahua?"

"Chauncy is taking care of the situation up there. At least for the time being, I want you right here in Mexico City."

Gloria gathered the files and rose to leave.

"I need to see something in writing on my desk no later than eighteen hundred hours Friday," Perry told her.

She laughed. "You're dreaming."

"Eighteen hundred hours, Ms. Ibenez. Let's see just how much of a hotshot you really are."

THREE

□

Chauncy had returned from San Antonio late Thursday with the results of the autopsy on Updegraf's body, and Gloria Ibenez had turned in her brief report exactly on time yesterday afternoon. And then the weekend had turned into an absolute disaster.

As Perry drove out to the Building in a rental Taurus a few minutes before five on a stiflingly hot and humid afternoon, his palms were sweaty and his stomach was sour. Handling Updegraf's widow was one of the worst jobs he'd ever had to accomplish. Even with the help of Dr. Carol Zywicki, a Company shrink who'd flown aboard a private Gulfstream IV down from Andrews Air Force Base Friday morning, the evening had been a mess until Zywicki had sedated the blubbering cow.

"God save us from hysterical women," Perry mumbled to himself. His own wife was no mental giant, but she'd come from good Ivy League stock—her father was a prominent Boston attorney and her mother was still a society maven—and she knew when to keep her mouth shut. Being the wife of an important CIA officer demanded her discretion, as well as an ask-no-questions-expect-no-lies attitude when it came to her husband's extracurricular activities.

Janet Updegraf, on the other hand, had begun screaming bloody murder at the top of her lungs the moment she'd found out that her husband had been shot to death in the line of duty sometime late Tuesday night or early Wednesday morning.

"You son of a bitch!" she'd screeched. "You knew all this time and yet you didn't have the common decency to tell me." She'd come off the couch in their expensively furnished downtown condo and physically attacked Perry, slamming her fists into his chest and trying to slap him in the face.

On the way up to Washington, the cow still sedated, strapped in one of the rear seats, Perry had debated putting the incident in his situation report. In the end his good sense had won out and he'd written a complete Sitrep with the recommendation that the Company be more thorough when it vetted the wives of its field officers. If she hadn't been brought under control she could have created a potentially embarrassing incident for everyone involved.

It was one time in which Perry had been totally at a loss trying to figure out a way to turn a situation to his advantage. And he had to admit to himself that he was becoming concerned. If they took another hit, the situation in Mexico could very well unravel.

A pair of babysitters from Security had met them at Andrews with an unmarked van that was set up as an ambulance, and had taken Janet Updegraf off his hands. The strange thing was that Dr. Zywicki had refused to shake his hand when they parted. It was damned odd, he thought.

And, if dealing with Louis's widow wasn't enough, he had to face McCann when all he wanted to do was return to Mexico City and do his job.

He presented his credentials at the main gate and was directed to the Visiting Employees parking lot. On the drive up he could see himself coming this way each weekday morning. Only, as the deputy director of Central Intelligence, he'd be riding in the backseat of a chauffeured Cadillac limo, and he would be dropped off inside the underground garage at the VIP elevator. It was a happy thought just now.

He wasn't carrying a weapon, but he was required to step through the security arch and on the other side open his attaché case for a security guard. But he didn't mind. These sorts of routines were a comfort.

Upstairs on the seventh floor, McCann's secretary put him in the small conference room to wait until the DDO was finished with his afternoon briefing to the DCI. "We'd expected you much sooner, Mr. Perry," she said. "I'll tell Mr. McCann that you're here."

"Thanks," Perry said, but the woman was already out the door. "Bitch."

The DDO's conference room was furnished with a table for eight people, a credenza on which was a carafe of water and glasses, and a couple of seascapes on the walls. Perry opened his attaché case and laid out copies of Updegraf's personnel file, Chauncy's initial report and the autopsy results, Gloria's one-page summary of her legwork, which contained absolutely nothing of value, and his own brief summary of the events subsequent to Updegaf's assassination.

Slim pickings, but it was to be expected given the delicacy of the situation in Mexico and the ridiculous time constraints he'd been given.

He was just pouring a glass of water when the door opened and Howard McCann breezed in. The DDO was a short man, with a round face, narrow glasses, and thinning light brown hair. But he was dressing better these days, though certainly not Armani or Gucci, and he was clean-shaven even at this hour of the afternoon.

"I had to brief the director without your report," McCann said, taking a seat at the head of the table.

Perry put down the glass. "Sorry, sir," he said. "I was delayed taking care of Updegraf's widow." He sat down to McCann's left.

"How is she?"

"You were right to be concerned about her. She became hysterical—"

"Something you should have anticipated," McCann interrupted. "I expect my station chiefs to show some initiative."

"Yes, sir," Perry replied, biting his tongue. McCann was a DDO to be admired because he ran a tight operation. But he was being unfair just now.

"What's going on in Mexico that got one of my people murdered?"

Perry laid the files in front of McCann. "It's not much yet, but it's all there."

McCann didn't bother looking down. "I'll read these later. For now I want you to tell me what the hell is going on. Why did you send him to Chihuahua? If something important is going on up there, why didn't you send him some backup? You know my drill, goddamn it. When you send assets into the field, you send them in pairs."

"I didn't send him to Chihuahua," Perry said. "The first I heard Louis was up there was when my assistant COS called to tell me that his body had been dumped at the emergency-room door of the hospital."

McCann sat back. "You're telling me that you have no control over your people?"

"I'm telling you, Mr. Deputy Director, that I have no control over a field officer who has his own agenda. Perhaps if he had been better vetted before he was sent—"

"He was your man, and you got him killed," McCann interrupted.

"Yes . . . sir."

"Are you one hundred percent confident that Updegraf didn't commit suicide?"

"The Air Force doctor who performed the autopsy said the entry wound was at an impossible angle to be self-inflicted."

"Continue," McCann said after a moment.

"We still don't know what he was doing in Chihuahua the night he was killed, but we think that he may have been running an operation to burn a communications clerk in the Chinese embassy."

"Where's the connection?"

Perry spread his hands. "We don't know yet. But my people are backtracking Louis's movements for the past ninety days, although his encounter sheets are turning out to be almost useless. He was lying to us."

"Why?" McCann demanded.

"I don't know," Perry said. "I think he was trying to make a mark for himself. The big score. He wanted my job."

"Is anyone else on your staff working a Chinese connection?" McCann asked.

"Not that I know of," Perry said evenly. "Unless it's another rogue operation."

McCann pursed his lips, but then nodded. "I suggest that you return to your station and find out," he said. He got up, gathered the files, and left the conference room without another word.

For a long minute or two Perry sat stock still, staring across the room at nothing in particular. *The big score. That's what it was all about, what it had always been about.*

Finally he closed his attaché case and left the room to catch a commercial flight back to Mexico City. First class.

F O U R

□

OFFICE OF THE DIRECTOR OF CENTRAL INTELLIGENCE

It was seven o'clock and dark as Richard Adkins stood slump-shouldered at the floor-to-ceiling Lexan windows in his seventh-floor office looking out at the lights toward the Potomac. He was stumped, and the problem was that he didn't know anyone to call for help. The only man who might have the answers, or know how to get them, was finally retired with his wife in Florida, and had promised in no uncertain terms: "Retired means retired!"

Something was coming at them, he was sure of at least that much. Perhaps another 9/11, perhaps something even bigger, but all the signs were there. Otto Rencke, the director of Special Operations, was talking lavender, which in the CIA's resident genius's lexicon meant that we were on the verge of taking a major hit.

At fifty-four, Adkins was a slightly built man with a pale complexion, small blue eyes, and wispy light hair. He'd lost his wife to cancer a few years ago, and since that time he'd thrown himself into his job first as deputy director of Central Intelligence under Kirk McGarvey, and then as DCI when McGarvey had retired. His Senate confirmation hearings had taken only two days, and had been the least rancorous of any nomination in recent history. It had been anything but a lovefest, but the media had dubbed the proceedings the "Senate Sleep-in of the Decade."

He'd done nothing of note when he'd served as number two under McGarvey, and he'd done nothing of note since then. Even the media, which post-9/11 had practically camped out in the press officer's briefing room, rarely showed up now. The Company was quietly going about its business, there were no new wars or crises looming on the horizon, and for once the CIA was not being blamed for doing nothing.

Rencke was a flake, but he was never wrong. This time his lavender had to do with the Chinese Ministry of State Security, Guojia Anquan

Bu, Guoanbu for short, especially with one of its senior intelligence officers, who had been spotted in Mexico City recently. Rencke had only
stumbled across a hint that the man had been recorded making a telephone call to Beijing from the Chinese embassy.

There'd been nothing in the daily reports from the CIA's station
down there, which Rencke had found odd because Army General Liu
Hung was one of China's most important intelligence experts on Western affairs. Over the past few years General Liu had conducted operations from the UN and from the Chinese embassy in Washington, and it
was believed that under his leadership the Chinese had practically gone
on a military-technology shopping spree right under the noses of the
FBI.

He had dropped out of sight for more than a year, presumably back
to Beijing, until he'd shown up in Mexico City. Rencke had confirmed it
four days before by repositioning a KH14 satellite to watch the Chinese
embassy, where he caught a clear, face-up shot of Liu getting into a Mercedes limousine at the rear of the compound. Two days later the satellite
caught another shot, this time of Liu standing on a rear balcony of the
embassy.

This too had been a clear picture, with Liu looking directly up as the
satellite passed overhead. "Like the guy knew when our bird would be
there, and went out to look up and say, 'Hiya, guys, I'm here,' " Rencke
said. He had been hopping one foot to the other, something he did
whenever he was excited and had a bone in his teeth.

"Any doubt that it's Liu?" Adkins had asked hopefully.

"Nada," Rencke said. "How about giving Perry the heads-up? He's
got some pretty neat people down there. Someone could take a quick
pass."

"That's exactly what we're gong to do, but first I want some more information. Anything you can dig up on Liu. They wouldn't have put one
of their best people into an embassy operation unless something important is going on."

"Bingo," Rencke said. "The sixty-four-dollar question: What are the
Chinese doing in Mexico?"

That had been four days ago, and this afternoon Gil Perry had flown up with the widow of one of his officers who had been trying to turn a communications clerk in the Chinese embassy and had gotten himself shot to death in Chihuahua.

Rencke had gone home early. He and his wife, Louise Horn, who was director of photo analysis for the National Security Agency, were leaving on vacation in the morning, the first either of them had taken in years, and Adkins hadn't the heart to call him back with the latest news.

Someone knocked at the open door to his outer office and Adkins turned around, expecting it was his bodyguard to tell him that it was time to go home, but Rencke stood there, his red hair flying all over the place, a Red Sox baseball cap askew on his head.

"I just heard," Rencke said. He was gaunt looking, arms and legs too long, head impossibly big for his frame, wide green eyes and a broad forehead. He looked and acted the part of an eccentric genius, which was exactly what he was.

"About what?" Adkins asked.

"Louis Updegraf. One of my computer programs caught it and called me."

"You're leaving on vacation."

"It's the Chinese connection," Rencke said. "I called Louise and she understands." He began hopping foot to foot. "Oh, boy," he said. "You oughta see the shade of lavender now."

PART

ONE

Ten days later

F I V E

□

CASEY KEY, FLORIDA

A cold front from up north had been unable to penetrate as far as Florida's west coast, so the summer pattern of very warm, tremendously humid air hung over Sarasota County like a damp wool blanket in a sauna.

But it wasn't tourist season, and the locals knew enough to stay indoors with the AC on, which suited Kirk McGarvey just fine. He had the beach all to himself for his early morning five-mile run along the water's edge.

His wife, Kathleen, had gotten up with him while it was still dark and brought a bottle of water to the downstairs exercise room, where he began his morning routines on a weight-training machine. She'd been in one of her patient moods, which she used whenever he was irascible and feeling cooped up. As he had been for the past few weeks.

"Are you ready to talk about what's eating you?" she'd asked.

He knew the tone of voice, and he wanted to snap at her for being patronizing, but he managed a thin smile because she was right. "Pretty soon," he said.

He was pulling two hundred pounds behind his shoulders from above, and his body glistened with sweat. He was a couple of years over fifty and in superb physical condition because of a daily regimen of exercise that had begun more than thirty years ago when he was in the Air Force, and had continued through his years with the CIA, where he finally rose to the seventh floor as DCI, a job he hated. He was about six feet tall, with a pleasant face and gray-green eyes that never missed much.

He had started and ended his career as a field officer, an assassin on the few occasions when such a black operation became absolutely necessary, and he exuded an air of supreme self-confidence. He was a man who could take care of himself. The few people who had gotten close to him, and were perceptive enough to understand what he was, felt an aura of safety around him. When Kirk was nearby, everything would work out. He would make sure of it.

"How about right now?"

He finished his last three reps and took the water bottle from his wife. "Have I been that bad?"

"Yep," she said. "You've been a real poop."

McGarvey took a drink of water, then put the bottle aside and toweled himself off, the muscles in his shoulders and back in a pleasant slow burn. He shook his head. "I wish I knew, Katy. Maybe it's teaching again. I guess I've lost my taste for it." One of his loves was the writings of the eighteenth-century French philosopher Voltaire, about whom he'd written a book that was critically acclaimed. He was teaching the subject on a part-time basis at the University of Florida's New College in Sarasota. They were less than two months into the semester and already he was bored. Voltaire had maintained that there was nothing less common than common sense, and he was seeing the lack in many of his students, but then he supposed he was being a little hard on them because of his dark mood.

"Quit," she said.

He smiled. He was a lucky man, married to a beautiful, intelligent woman whose short blond hair framed an oval face, high cheekbones, a finely formed nose, and full lips, and whose complexion was nearly flawless even without makeup. She was tall for a woman and slender, and it was impossible to guess that she was the same age as her husband. "That's not really an option, Katy. I'm committed at least until spring."

She had given him an odd look that stuck with him as he ran on the beach. It was as if she knew something about him that he didn't, which possibly had something to do with his dreams. They'd started again a couple of weeks ago, as they had from time to time over the past ten or fifteen years, and always began with the same one. He was in the catacombs beneath a castle outside Lisbon. The tunnels were flooding and it was almost totally dark. His escape would be cut off at any second, yet he could not leave until he finished what he had come to do. Before he left this place he had to kill Arkady Kurshin, a KGB intelligence officer and assassin whose operations were as brilliant as they were bloody.

In his dreams, McGarvey could see life fading from Kurshin's eyes in the tunnel. Then the faces of the other men, and a few women, he had killed swam into view. All of them had the same expression of surprise that they were dying. They had been bad people, some of them murderers of innocent women and children, but human beings for all that, with mothers and fathers and people who saw good in them and who loved them.

He thought that he may have cried out in his sleep. He'd done it before when he'd had the dreams. But if Katy had heard him, she'd said nothing about it.

A hundred yards from the path to his house across the road, McGarvey pulled up short to catch his breath and walk it off. In the distance, hull down on the horizon, a sailboat was slowly making its way south. The hurricane season was nearly done, and cruising sailors were already coming down from the north, heading for the Keys and across to the Bahamas.

Maybe his mood was nothing more than a reaction to being cooped up, with the prospect of the entire winter—Florida's good season—to be more of the same. But this was the life that he had chosen for himself and Katy. He was retired. He was no longer in the field. No longer on the hunt.

He didn't want to be a part of that life any longer. Or did he?

He stopped a moment to consider realistically his present mood and his options. This now was almost like it had been when he'd run to Switzerland to hide from a past that had already begun to catch up with him. It was about that time that his dreams had started. He and Katy were getting a divorce, for reasons that he could no longer understand, and Marta Fredricks, the Swiss cop who'd been sent to keep a watch on him, noticed his volatile mood swings. By then she had fallen in love with him, and in the end her feelings had gotten her killed.

The newspaper had finally come; he picked it up, entered the house from the garage, and tossed it on the counter. He got a bottle of water from the fridge and headed upstairs to take his shower and get dressed. The house had long overhangs and a broad veranda around all four sides. From the bedroom French doors he could look across their backyard to the gazebo and dock on the Intracoastal Waterway. Katy was sitting in the gazebo having her morning cup of tea. It was her retreat when she was troubled about something, where she could watch the sparse boat traffic at this hour, listen to the birds, and smell the incredibly fragrant sub-tropical air. She especially liked to sit out there alone when her husband was running on the beach, and wait for him to finish. When he came out to her they would talk.

McGarvey took a quick shower, then got dressed in white linen trousers, a short-sleeved Izod, and boat shoes without socks. Down in the kitchen he made a thermos of Earl Grey and took a cup for himself and went out to her.

"Truce?" he asked, kissing her on the cheek.

"I didn't think we were fighting," she said.

He poured tea for her, and sat down. "We weren't, but you're right, I've been a shit lately. Sorry."

"Apology accepted," she said. "How about taking a break for a couple of weeks? Your students can get along without you for that long, can't they?"

He nodded. "What do you have in mind?"

"We can fly up to Washington and visit the kids and Audie. Maybe see a few old friends." Their twenty-four-year-old daughter, Elizabeth, was married to Todd VanBuren. Both of them were CIA field officers, and for the last year or so they had been running the Farm, which was the Company's training facility on the York River outside Williamsburg. They had one child, Audrey Kathleen, who was just two and who had her parents and grandparents wrapped around her little finger.

"We're going up for Thanksgiving, remember?"

"We could take the boat down to Key West, maybe out to the Dry Tortugas if the weather holds—which it's supposed to do. Late mornings in isolated little spots, short day sails, maybe tuck into a gunkhole for a swim, an early dinner on the grill, and whatever else might come up when the stars are out."

Six months ago they had taken delivery on a forty-two-foot Island Packet sailboat, which they kept in downtown Sarasota at Marina Jack. The boat had been Katy's idea, and McGarvey had named it the *Kathleen*. So far they had taken only day sails, mostly around Sarasota and Tampa Bay, but now with the better late-fall and early winter weather just around the corner they had planned on much longer trips.

But something nagged at the back of McGarvey's mind. It was as if something had gotten into his brain with a feather and was stirring around. He wasn't sure what it meant, but he had a fair idea, and he didn't like it. Years ago a Company shrink had told him that he had a soul filled with demons, and only he could drive them out. But only if he wanted to.

They were still there, usually buried where he didn't have to think about them, but coming to the surface when he began having his dreams. Or because he was having the dreams.

"We're about two weeks early in the season. I don't want to push it."

"We could grab our passports, pack a few things, and fly over to Paris. The weather's been good lately."

McGarvey looked up as a man and a young boy in a small outboard-powered boat passed by. "Too many memories."

"Maybe take one of the canal cruises on a barge. Eat four French meals a day and get fat."

"Maybe in the spring," McGarvey said absently.

"Well then, how about Vladivostok? I hear it's lovely this time of year."

McGarvey looked at her and smiled. "Go ahead and buy the tickets." He got up and gave her a kiss. "We'll leave first thing in the morning. Promise."

"Where're you going?"

"The college. I have to get a book."

"It's Saturday."

"How about meeting me for lunch on the Circle. Crab and Fin?"

Katy looked up at him, her eyes wide and filled with concern. "Will you be there?"

"Guaranteed," McGarvey said. "Noon?"

"I meant *all* of you," she said to his retreating figure.

SIX

☐

From the window of his small, cramped office on the second floor of the Humanities Center McGarvey could look across the campus and just see Sarasota Bay one block away. The school was quiet today, not many students or staff out and about, and the heavily planted grounds looked like a scene from a deserted tropical island. Watching a V formation of a half dozen pelicans gliding just above the tops of the palm trees heightened his sense of isolation.

He'd been in the business far too long to ignore his intuition, yet everything within him wanted to turn away from whatever was coming. Maybe take Katy to Paris, or to Vladivostok. He had to smile. He had caught her little joke, but at that moment he hadn't had the energy to give her an answer that made any sense to him.

McGarvey spotted Otto Rencke coming up the walk from the front parking lot at the same moment his telephone rang. His home phone number came up on the caller ID. He knew what had happened. He picked up the phone. "Otto's in town. Did he call you?"

"Yes," Katy said a little breathlessly. "I told him you were at the college. Is he there already?"

"He's on his way up."

"He said he wasn't here on vacation. He wants to talk business. You're not going back, are you?"

"I don't know," McGarvey answered, and it was the truth. "But I don't think so." Otto Rencke was truly a friend, and even more than that, he was practically a part of the family. A few years ago, during an operation that had gone bad, Otto had saved Katy's life. It was a debt that was impossible to repay except by friendship. And on top of that, McGarvey had a great deal of respect for his friend's big heart and vast intelligence. Rencke was an eccentric genius, but a good and loyal man.

"Right," Katy said, and McGarvey could hear the resignation in his wife's voice.

"I mean it."

"Well at least promise me that you won't do anything until we talk about it. Okay?"

"I'm just going to listen to what he has to say," McGarvey told her. "Honest to God, sweetheart."

"It has to be something worth your while, you know," she said. "Worth *our* while."

"Lunch is still on, but Otto will probably tag along."

"Call and let me know when you're done."

"Will do," McGarvey promised. He hung up the phone, and took the stairs down to the front entrance just as Rencke was coming through the door.

The Company's director of special operations was a mess as usual. His long red hair flew in every direction, his high-top sneakers had no laces, his jeans were faded and ripped, and the logo on his dirty T-shirt was the hammer and sickle under the letters CCCP. But he was smiling. "Hiya, Mac," he said. He gave McGarvey a large bear hug. "Nice to see you, ya know."

"Katy said you called the house. She's worried that you've come down here to ask me back."

Rencke's eyes widened. "Honest injun, nobody's wanting you to go back into the field." He raised his right hand with three fingers up. "We just want you to meet someone, listen to what she has to say."

"Let's go for a walk," McGarvey said, and they went outside and headed down one of the paths that meandered through the campus and toward the bay.

A boy and a girl were sitting on a blanket under a tree, and they waved. McGarvey waved back and managed a smile even though he was troubled. Rencke had *the* look written all over him.

"Maybe I should come down here and teach," Rencke said.

"What color is it?" McGarvey asked.

Rencke gave him a sharp look. "Oh, wow, it's lavender, and it's gotten a lot deeper in the past few days, ya know," he gushed. He was a mathematical and computer genius, at least on a par with guys like England's Stephen Hawking, but he had chosen to stay away from academia for a lot of not so savory reasons out of his past, including a dalliance with a dean's wife.

But he was a good man too. A number of years ago he had tried to explain color to a blind mathematician friend of his from the Sorbonne in Paris. Using a series of tensor calculus equations, the same mathematics that Einstein had used for relativity, he had managed to convey the entire range of sensory perceptions and emotions that a human saw and felt for every color from just above infrared to just below ultraviolet.

Shortly after he had come to work for McGarvey at the CIA, he had developed a second use for his equations. Using a set of sophisticated search engines that scanned the continuous streams of data coming into dozens of computers, from the Defense Intelligence Agency and the State Department, the National Security Agency and the Department of Homeland Security, as well as from the CIA's own mainframe, he was able to come up with very accurate threat assessments that showed up as colors. Toward the infrared range, the particular threat level was low, the world was at peace; toward the ultraviolet it was high, the U.S. was on the verge of an all-out thermonuclear war.

Lavender was about as bad as it ever got; it had been the same color in the weeks leading up to 9/11. But it hadn't been until *after* 9/11 that the CIA took Rencke's threat assessments seriously.

Something clutched at McGarvey's gut. "Is it the Middle East again? Saudi Arabia?" Last year McGarvey had gotten close enough to Osama bin Laden to put a bullet into the man's brain. Since then the terror organization al-Qaida had been relatively quiet. But he'd never thought the peace would last. The next step, he'd always believed, would come from Saudi Arabia, where some members of the royal family were siphoning money out of the country to finance Islamic militants and terrorists around the world. And that problem would be a tough nut to crack, nowhere as easy as Afghanistan or even Iraq had been.

"That's coming, I think, but this time it's Mexico," Rencke said. "We've got a problem down there that we'd like you to take a look at."

"I'm retired, Otto, remember?" McGarvey said. John and Mabel Ringling's mansion Ca d'Zan was off to their left, on the bayshore, and as they got closer to the water the morning breeze was noticeably cooler.

"Dick's not asking you to come back, I already told you. He just wants you to listen and give us your opinion."

They walked for a while in silence, an operation he'd been involved with in and around Mexico City about ten years ago coming back to McGarvey in living color. A KGB general by the name of Valentin Baranov had set up an exquisitely complex plot out of the Russian embassy down there that had resulted in the deaths of a former U.S. senator and of Donald Suthland Powers, who was arguably the best director that the CIA had known before or since. The senator, Darby Yarnell, had killed Powers, and McGarvey had killed Yarnell. It had been one of the worst hits that the CIA had ever taken, even worse than James Jesus Angleton's devastating witch hunt.

"Is it the Russians again?" McGarvey asked.

Rencke shook his head. "It's the Chinese, if you can believe it, and they've all but shut down our operations. The chief of station is in over his head, one of his people was assassinated, and McCann is screaming bloody murder. He wants to run a full-court press, but for now Dick has managed to hold him off."

They stopped at the water's edge, and Rencke began hopping from foot to foot.

"What?" McGarvey asked.

"You ever hear of a Chinese Guoanbu guy by the name of Liu? General Liu Hung?"

"Vaguely," McGarvey said. "He was one of their stars a few years ago. His uncle was somebody, maybe the interior minister. We pegged him to head the agency eventually, but he was recalled to Beijing for some reason."

"The Bureau had the idea that Liu had been involved in some rapes and murders in New York and again in Washington. They couldn't prove it, but there was enough heat so he had to get out."

Across Sarasota Bay, Longboat Key bristled with condominium towers.

The island had been vastly overbuilt in the past ten years, which was one of the reasons McGarvey and Katy had chosen the relatively rural Casey Key.

"The thing is, when Liu was in New York and Washington we were being hurt pretty badly," Rencke said. "We didn't know it at the time, but the Chinese were making big jumps with their military technology because of a series of networks that Liu had set up. The guy is a bloody genius."

"What's he doing in Mexico?"

"Bingo," Rencke said, clapping his hands. "You just asked the sixty-four-dollar question. We don't know. In fact, we didn't even have a clue until two weeks ago when Louis Updegraf, one of our guys, was found shot to death up in Chihuahua. Apparently he'd been trying to burn a communications clerk in the Chinese embassy."

"What was he doing in Chihuahua?"

"No one knew. Not even the station chief. At least not until a couple of days ago, which is when we were able to connect General Liu to the situation. And it's got Dick plenty worried, ya know. He doesn't know what to put in the NIE or how to brief the president." The NIE, or National Intelligence Estimate, and a weekly document called the Watch Report were generated by the CIA and the other thirteen intelligence agencies in Washington under the umbrella of the national director of intelligence. Both were distributed to the National Security Council, and outlined every place on earth where fighting was taking place, and attempted to identify and warn about every threat that the U.S. was facing. "Whatever Liu is up to in Mexico has gotten one of our people killed, and it's not going to get any better unless somebody stops it. We need to know what he's doing before it bites us."

"I'm retired, Otto," McGarvey said.

"All Dick wants is for you to listen to someone," Rencke said. He nodded toward Longboat Key. "And she's right over there."

SEVEN

□

Traffic on the South Trail was heavy especially when they reached the turn for the Ringling Bridge over the ICW. It wasn't quite the start of the tourist season, but plenty of locals spent their weekends playing on the islands and having lunch on St. Armand's Circle.

Rencke was driving a Toyota van with deeply tinted windows that he'd rented at the airport when he'd arrived last night. "It was too late to call you," he said. "Anyway, we wanted to get settled in first."

McGarvey used his cell phone to call his wife. She answered on the first ring.

"Tell me that you're taking me to lunch and I'll be a happy camper."

"No," McGarvey told her. "But listen to me, Katy. They don't want me back in the field. Dick just wants me to talk to someone this morning. Give him my opinion."

"About what?"

McGarvey let it hang for a moment. "I'll call as soon as I can."

"Today? Tomorrow? Next week?" she asked. She was brittle. "Any clue on that score you'd care to give? Or should I just expect you when you walk through the door?"

"Today," he said. "Look, I'm okay. I don't want you to worry."

"I've almost always been worried about you," she said. "Didn't you know? You tend to attract the bad guys like flies to honey. I've seen you in action, remember?"

"It'll be fine, Katy. Trust me."

"Right," she said, and broke the connection.

McGarvey thought about calling her back, but then shut off his cell phone and put it in his pocket.

"Ms. M okay?" Rencke asked.

"She doesn't trust us."

Rencke had to laugh. "I don't blame her."

Driving over the high bridge onto the chain of barrier islands that began with Bird Key and ended twenty-five miles north on Anna Maria Island in Tampa Bay was like coming from the real world into a cross between a South Seas paradise and a sophisticated European setting of palm trees, sidewalk cafés, and beaches. The islands had always reminded McGarvey of France's Côte d'Azur on the Mediterranean.

"Who're you taking me to see?" McGarvey asked.

"Her name is Shahrzad Shadmand. She's an Iranian belly dancer who worked in one of the clubs in Mexico City."

They made it through the traffic around St. Armand's Circle, which was a trendy area of shopping and sidewalk cafés much like Rodeo Drive in Beverly Hills and Worth Avenue in Palm Beach, and headed north to the New Pass Bridge and Longboat Key. McGarvey felt a twinge of guilt because of his missed lunch date with his wife, but his unsettled feeling had spiked the moment Rencke had shown up, and had continued to grow driving out to the islands.

"Is she Iranian intelligence?" McGarvey asked.

Rencke gave him a sidelong glance. "We don't think so. She's been freaked practically out of her skull, and she'd have to be pretty good to fake that. Anyway, she's a walk-in, and that type usually doesn't do things that way." A walk-in was someone who showed up out of the blue at a U.S. embassy or consulate somewhere with information, usually in trade for something, most often money or a visa to the U.S., or both.

"Does she know who killed Updegraf? And why?"

"It's more complicated than that, Mac," Rencke said. "You just gotta hear her out." He shook his head. "Gil Perry, the station chief, is convinced she's legitimate. In fact he brought her up here on Dick's okay without letting McCann know anything about it."

"What are you talking about?"

"This girl came to the embassy four days ago. Said she wanted to talk to Perry, by name. Anyway, after all the delays and security hassles—you know, there's no one by that name here—Perry finally agrees to see her. After one hour he's impressed enough to call the seventh floor direct 'cause he's scared shitless and he doesn't know who to trust."

"Evidently Dick agreed with him," McGarvey said. "What does she want?"

"That's just it, she hasn't asked for anything except for you."

McGarvey was startled. "Me?"

"Yup. She told Perry just enough to prove that she was legitimate, and convince him that we're facing a bigger problem with the Chinese than we can possibly imagine, but she wouldn't say anything else to anyone except you."

"I've never heard of her," McGavey said.

"Well she's heard of you," Rencke replied. "And you're going to see her face-to-face in about five minutes."

EIGHT

LONGBOAT KEY

Two thirds of the way up the long, narrow island, Rencke pulled off the road and stopped at a security gate, where he entered a code on the keypad. From the entry the roofline of a very large house was just visible right on the beach, but not much else was, because of the dense foliage.

"This is Tommy Doyle's place," McGarvey said as the gate swung open. Until his retirement a couple of years ago Doyle had been the CIA's deputy director of intelligence. He'd come from East Coast money, and with his inheritance and shrewd investments over the years he was a multimillionaire. McGarvey had had almost no contact with him after they retired. "Is Tommy in on this?" he asked.

"No. He's over in Baghdad doing some consulting work. Said we could use his house for as long as we needed it." Rencke glanced over at McGarvey. "We wanted to make it as convenient as possible for you."

"Thanks."

They drove through the gate and down a long driveway that seemed as if it had been hacked out of a very carefully tended jungle. Doyle, like a lot of men who'd held big jobs within the intelligence community, valued his privacy above almost everything else.

The lane opened up to a large area at the sweeping front entrance of the three-story glass, concrete, and massive-wood-beamed mansion, which McGarvey figured had to be at least fifteen thousand square feet. Tennis courts were off to the left next to an Olympic-size pool with a high diving platform. An eight-car garage was off in the trees to the left near what was probably a three- or four-bedroom guesthouse. Doyle had done very well for himself.

"Who's here besides the woman?" McGarvey asked.

"Gil Perry brought her up, along with a babysitter."

"Any house staff?"

"A gardener, a cook, and husband-and-wife caretakers," Rencke said, pulling up in front of the house. "She cleans the place and he's the handyman. Tommy vouches for them."

"What I don't get is why some woman in Mexico City asked to talk to me by name," McGarvey said. "Did you do a background check on her to see if there was ever any connection between us?"

"Nada," Rencke said. "She left Iran a few years ago to be on her own because, she says, it's no place for a modern woman."

"Are we sure she's not a double?" McGarvey asked. The Ministry of Intelligence and Security was among the top agencies in the world, and it had tendrils on every continent.

"Not so far as I could find out," Rencke said, shutting off the van's engine. "But if she is, she's a lot better than I think she is. I only got to talk to her for a few minutes last night, but I got the impression that she's just a scared kid, and we're her last resort."

"How old is she?"

"She says twenty-five, but her birth records in Tehran say thirty."

McGarvey nodded. "There's one lie anyway."

"Just listen to her, Mac, that's all," Rencke said. "We gotta find out what the Chinese are doing down there, and if she has some of the answers maybe you can get them from her."

They got out of the van and went up the broad steps to a wide veranda, planked with teak. "Before you meet her, Gil wants to have a few words with you. Give you some background."

"What's your take on him?"

"He doesn't get along with McCann," Rencke said. "Of course nobody does, but beyond that his file is clean. He's got ambition. Wants to be DDCI some day. Says he's a spy, pure and simple. No messy politics for him."

"God save us from pure spies, whatever they are," McGarvey said.

"Amen."

The CIA babysitter, a pretty young woman named Toni Dronchi, let them in and directed them through the soaring stair hall back to the great room, which looked out over the Gulf of Mexico. "Your daughter Liz and I are friends, Mr. Director," she told McGarvey. "I'm getting married in a couple of months and she and Todd are going to stand up for us."

"Next time I talk to her I'll tell her I saw you," McGarvey said.

"Yes, sir."

"What's your impression of your guest?"

"I think I should feel sorry for her, but she's been doing a fair amount of lying. I don't know if it's because she's scared or she doesn't trust anybody, or she's just confused, but she's told some really stupid whoppers."

McGarvey had to smile. "For instance?"

"She says she doesn't speak Spanish, but she has a Mexican driver's license, and when we picked her up she had a copy of La Crónica de Hoy in her carry-on bag. That's Mexico City's main newspaper. I asked how long ago she'd left Iran, and she told me she'd been gone only a few months. But she told Mr. Perry that she'd left Iran four years ago. And that's just some of it."

"Thanks for the heads-up," McGarvey said.

"Any idea how long we'll be on this assignment, sir?"

"I guess that'll be up to Gil Perry," McGarvey said. "I'm only here to find out what the woman has to say."

"I'll go up and get her," Toni said, and left.

Perry, dressed in a white linen suit with a dark shirt and tie, despite the warm weather, came bounding into the great room right behind them from the stair hall. "By God, am I glad to meet you, Mr. McGarvey," he said effusively. "Maybe we can finally get this nasty mystery resolved and get back to business."

They shook hands, and McGarvey got the impression that Perry was a politician looking for votes, not a station chief who'd lost a man and whose operation was apparently in shambles.

"I'm just here to listen."

"Well, she mentioned you by name, so I should hope so," Perry said. "I mean, we can use the help." He glanced at Rencke with obvious distaste. "Have you been briefed?"

"Only that one of your people trying to burn a Chinese code clerk was found shot to death nine hundred miles north of Mexico City, and that this girl you want me to meet probably knows something about it."

"There's a lot more," Perry said.

"I'm sure there is. Probably even more than you know yet, and probably more than this dancer will want to admit. But she does want something. She didn't walk into the embassy with our names on her lips for a reward. Or has she asked for money?"

Perry shook his head, and McGarvey could almost see the man's thoughts generating in his brain and slowly making their way past his eyes to his lips. Plodders had always driven McGarvey nuts. He wanted to finish their sentences for them. But he could also see something else in Perry's face. The man might be slow, but he was a thinker. Right now he was figuring the angles, whatever they might be, that would help advance his career out of this apparent mess.

"She's asked for nothing, except you. She keeps telling me that you're the only one she'll talk to. You're the only one who'll understand." Perry shook his head again. "Do you two know each other from somewhere?"

"Never heard of her."

"If you want, I'll brief you before we begin."

McGarvey glanced over Perry's shoulder as Toni Dronchi appeared with a young, slightly built, exotic woman with a beautiful tawny complexion, very high delicate cheekbones, and devastatingly foreign dark eyes of a perfect almond shape, all framed by long, flowing black hair that seemed to shimmer with a light all its own. She was dressed in sandals, a long white peasant skirt, and a lace, off-the-shoulder white blouse, and wore a gold chain around her tiny neck.

"You're too late," McGarvey said.

Perry turned around, vexed. "We were having a conversation here," he told Toni.

"Sorry, sir, but I thought Mr. McGarvey would want to get on with it as quickly as possible."

"That's all right," McGarvey said before Perry could order the girl to be taken away. "I don't believe we've ever met."

The girl's eyes met McGarvey's, and the slight smile that had formed on her full, rich mouth slowly died and she looked away. For just a moment he'd seen something there, some hint of recognition followed by a flash of fear, as if she had been taught to be an animal trainer, and the first time she entered the cage she realized that she might just be in the wrong place at the wrong time.

"Well, for goodness' sake, you wanted to talk to him, and we've brought you all this way," Perry shrilled. "Shahrzad Shadmand, this is Kirk McGarvey. So why don't we all get to it and begin."

NINE

LONGBOAT KEY

It was nearly eleven o'clock by the time they'd all settled down around a teak table beneath a green market umbrella on the expansive back veranda that looked out across a white sand beach to the swimming-pool blue of the Gulf. McGarvey and Rencke sat across from Perry and Shahrzad, as if they were on opposing teams. The woman from the house staff had brought them a large pitcher of sangria and cold glasses, and then she and Toni had withdrawn. Perry and especially the girl seemed nervous.

"Well, let's just get started then, shall we?" Perry said. "Let's not keep the good man waiting."

"Who gave you Gil Perry's name as chief of station?" McGarvey asked.

"Louis," Shahrzad replied in a small voice.

"Louis Updegraf," Perry put in. "He's the officer who was assassinated in Chihuahua, though what in heaven's name he was doing all the way up there is beyond me."

"Spying," Shahrzad shot back.

"Who gave you my name?" McGarvey asked.

When she had flared she'd turned to Perry, but now she looked back at McGarvey, and this time she did not avoid his eyes. "My father told me about you fifteen years ago."

"In what context?"

"My father was General Razed al-Deyhim," Shahrzad said. "Is this name familiar to you?"

"I know that name," Rencke said. "He was chief of the American desk for the MOIS in Tehran until about two years ago, when the Revolutionary Guards decided he was overstepping his mandate by getting himself involved with the nuclear issue, and they had him shot as a traitor. I did a paper for an NIE."

"He wasn't a traitor," Shahrzad cried. "He loved his country."

"Did you marry?" McGarvey asked. "Is that why your last name is different?"

Shahrzad shook her head. "I changed it when I left Iran. My mother and sisters went to Paris afterward, and they wanted me to come with them. But the Guards have people there, and I figured it would only be a matter of time before they found me."

"What do they want with you?"

"I know things," she said. "My father talked to me like a son. He always did. He told me stuff."

"Secrets," McGarvey said. "That's how you first heard my name?"

"It was the Russian general who came to our house and stayed for a weekend. I was a teenager, and I think he liked me. We went horseback riding along the river outside Tehran, and afterward he sent me some nice presents from Moscow." She looked at McGarvey, almost pleading for him to understand. "It's not what you're thinking. I'm not a whore."

"I never said that you were," McGarvey told her, intrigued despite himself. Seeing her now, and listening to her, he could just imagine what the riverside rides had been all about. But Toni's assessment of the girl was probably spot on. None of what McGarvey was hearing made any real sense. What the hell was she doing in Mexico, if not spying for the MOIS?

"My father had just been promoted and assigned to the American desk, and General Baranov came from Moscow to brief him. He was an important man."

All the air left the room, but McGarvey was careful to hide his reaction, and he noticed out of the corner of his eye that Rencke had caught it too. If it was the same Baranov that McGarvey had dealt with in Mexico City and had eventually killed in East Berlin, then whatever he'd been doing in Tehran had to have been important.

"What did he have to say about me?" McGarvey asked.

"That you were a dangerous man," Shahrzad replied. "He had a great deal of respect for you. He told my father that unless someone were to put a bullet in your brain, you would probably run the CIA someday. And he said that would be a disaster for us. I think he was planning on killing you, and he might have wanted my father's help. I didn't hear that part."

"What did you call him?" McGarvey asked.

Shahrzad was confused. "What do you mean?"

"How did you address the man? General Baranov? Sir? What?"

"At first, General, but later he asked me to call him by his Christian name, Valentin."

"How old were you?"

"Fifteen," she said.

"Didn't your father raise any objections about you riding off into the wilderness with no one else but the general? I would have."

Shahrzad's eyes lowered. "The general told us about you, and I remembered your name, that's all. I didn't know who else to talk to. With Louis gone I was alone down there, and I wanted to get out."

"Why not go to your family in Paris?" McGarvey asked.

She looked away and didn't answer.

"Maybe because your mother kicked you out of the house?"

"*Merde*," she said softly. "I wanted to come here, to the United States. This is where I wanted to live. But since bin Laden and the al-Qaida attacks I couldn't get a visa."

"Arabs are not well liked," Perry suggested.

"I'm Persian, not Arab."

Perry hid a slight smile. "Whatever." He waved her off.

"There is a difference," she said sadly. "Louis knew it."

It came to McGarvey that the woman was battered. Some turn of fate had knocked her down, and she was having a nearly impossible time getting back up. She was like the victim of a brutal rape who believed she would never get clean again. The question was what she wanted.

"Why did you go to Mexico?" he asked. "Were you planning on sneaking across the border on foot?"

"I don't know what I was thinking," she said. She fingered the heavy gold braided chain around her neck. "When I left Tehran I had only a few thousand French and Swiss francs, and a few pieces of jewelry—this necklace my father gave me on my twenty-first birthday."

She was wearing a diamond ring that looked to be four or five carats on her right hand. "Your father give that to you too?" McGarvey asked.

She dropped her hand and said, "No," but then thought better of it. "It wasn't for my birthday," she added.

"One of the presents from the general?"

She opened her mouth to say something, but then shook her head in a gesture of irritation. "It's none of your business."

"Do you know who killed Louis Updegraf?" McGarvey asked.

She just looked at him.

"Why he was killed?"

She said nothing.

McGarvey pushed away from the table and got to his feet. "Sorry, Perry, but she's all yours. I'd suggest that you take her back to whatever Mexican sewer she crawled out of and dump her."

"Wait!" she cried.

"Let's go," McGarvey told Rencke. "We can meet Katy for lunch."

"Please wait, you *salopard!*" Shahrzad screeched, tipping over the edge for just a moment.

McGarvey looked at her. She seemed lost, and vulnerable, completely strung out, at wit's end.

She sat stock still for several seconds before she lowered her eyes again. "I'm sorry," she said. "I've been telling lies for so long that I'm not sure if I know the truth."

"You came to us," McGarvey said. "You wanted to talk to me. Here I am."

"I don't know who killed Louis, or exactly why, but I have my ideas."

McGarvey glanced at Perry and then looked out at the Gulf. The water this morning was almost flat calm, and there wasn't a cloud in the sky. Katy was right, it was time finally to retire all the way. Sail their boat, travel, work on another book, take long naps on weekday afternoons, play golf or tennis. Yet when Otto had shown up on his doorstep he hadn't turned his old friend away. He'd insisted that he was retired, yet he had come out here to listen to this woman, and find out what was going on in Mexico that had gotten a CIA field officer shot to death. And now that he had come this far he was back in the game.

He turned back to her. She was lying to them, and he was going to find out why. "How old are you?"

She started to speak, but then held off for a moment. "Thirty," she said.

"Who gave you the ring?"

"General Baranov."

"Did you have sex with him when you were fifteen?"

Her nostrils flared, and her eyes darted from Perry to Rencke and back to McGarvey. "It's none of your business," she said.

"Yes it is," McGarvey told her. "Because I suspect that you were having sex with Updegraf, and I want to establish a motive."

"I was in love with Louis. It's something you have to understand from the beginning."

"Did you have sex with Baranov?"

Again her eyes darted to Perry and Rencke. Then she nodded. "Yes," she said in a small voice. "He raped me."

TEN

□

Rencke poured a glass of sangria for Shahrzad, and after she'd taken a sip, he gave her a sad smile. "It must have been terribly difficult for you, all alone in Mexico City, not knowing a soul."

She nodded. "Mr. McGarvey was right. I figured that I could find work, and as soon as I had saved enough money I could head north, maybe to the Texas border, and get into the States. But I wanted to do it right, I wanted to have the correct papers, and my green card."

"And did you find work so that you could save some money?" McGarvey asked.

"Yes, but it wasn't easy."

"Easy enough so that you weren't forced to sell your necklace or ring."

"I didn't have anything else," Shahrzad flared. "Once they were gone I'd be stuck." She looked away for a moment. "It was degrading. All the men were just like you; when they looked at me they thought I was a whore."

McGarvey wanted to feel sorry for her, but he wasn't convinced that it was anything more than a very good performance. "Belly dancing?"

She started to answer, but Perry cut her off. "Not quite belly dancing," he said. He gave Shahrzad a disparaging look as if he were examining a bug under a microscope. "I believe the euphemism for what she did is exotic dancing, though I don't believe it has any connection with either."

"It paid good money," she said.

"Downtown is filled with those sorts of establishments," Perry said. "Especially in Polanco and Zona Rosa. Strip joints. Lap dancing. Massage parlors. And much worse."

"That's where you met Updegraf?" McGarvey asked.

She nodded.

"Did he tell you that he worked for the CIA?"

"Not at first."

"But you spotted him in the audience, and you danced for him in particular," McGarvey said. "I just want to get this part clear in my mind. Why him?"

"He was sort of handsome. And he was very nice. A kind man."

"He was a rich American who could help you get to America," McGarvey suggested. He was getting a pretty fair idea where this was going. But he wanted to hear the details from the girl's own mouth.

"That too, at first," she admitted. "But he didn't hit on me, which I really appreciated, you know. He was a gentleman in that respect."

McGarvey refrained from asking in what respects Updegraf *hadn't* been a gentleman, because he thought he might already know the answer. Anyway, the subject was going to come up soon. "How often did you dance at the clubs?"

"It was the same club," she said. "The Wild Stallion in Zona Rosa. I danced five nights a week, Tuesday through Saturday, from eleven until three in the morning."

"How often did Updegraf show up to catch your act?"

"After the first couple of times, he was there just about every night I danced."

"Did he ask you to sit with him at his table, buy you drinks?"

"At first."

"Did he give you presents, like the general had done?"

Her jaw tightened. "It wasn't like that," she said. "It was never like that."

McGarvey turned to Perry. "What the hell was one of your field officers doing there? Or was that where his code clerk hung out?"

Perry spread his hands. "I don't know. There was nothing in any of his encounter sheets that he was doing the club scene. Supposedly he was meeting the code clerk at a coffee bar just around the corner from the embassy."

"Sounds to me like he was playing with fire," Rencke suggested.

"Was General Liu also one of your admirers?" McGarvey asked, taking a stab in the dark.

Shahrzad was about to take a drink, but her hand suddenly shook so badly she nearly dropped the glass. "I didn't know anything about him until much later," she blurted. She turned to Rencke as if she wanted help. "The club was always packed. It was almost impossible to pick someone out of the crowd. They all looked the same to me."

"Except for Updegraf," McGarvey said.

"He stood out."

"I'll bet he did," McGarvey said drily. "When did you start having sex with him?"

She took a moment to answer, and when she did she hung her head, the gesture almost theatrical. "It was about a week or so after I first saw him that I started doing lap dances for him in one of the private rooms."

"I assume that he paid you for those sessions, and you had to share the money with your boss."

She nodded. "But then I fell in love with him," she said. "He was kind and gentle, and he had a good sense of humor."

"You knew that he was married," McGarvey said.

She nodded again. "It's why we never could go to his place. And my apartment was a dump, so we had to use the club." She smiled with the memory. "It was perfect at first. He liked to watch me dance, and afterward we would make love." She looked up. "He was a sweet man. I'm going to miss him."

"I'll bet you are," McGarvey said.

"It wasn't like that," she replied softly. "I loved him."

"He gave you money for the dancing. Did he pay you for the sex?"

Her eyes suddenly filled. "I was in love with him. And I think that he was in love with me."

"But he gave you money," McGarvey persisted. He was almost certain where this was going now, and he was disgusted. Updegraf had recruited her by playing the role of the perfect gentleman, and it would have been easy for a woman in Shahrzad's state to believe in him. "I want to be clear on this point before we continue."

She glanced at Rencke and Perry, who were offering no help. "He knew that I wanted to go north, and he promised to help me."

"In exchange for what?" McGarvey asked. They were finally coming to the point. "I mean other than the dancing and the sex."

This time she managed to take a drink with a steady hand, and

McGarvey had to admire her resilience and her ability to compose herself. She must have been a dream come true for Updegraf, who was a field officer with at least as much ambition to make his mark as Perry. The girl was not only bright and beautiful, but also vulnerable, willing to do whatever the man she'd fallen in love with told her to do.

Yet there was more than just that. He could see in her eyes that she was embarrassed by some of what she was telling them, and she had to look away. And he could see it in the way she held herself, as if it had been so long since she had truly relaxed, and perhaps shared a laugh with a friend, that she had no idea that such a thing was even possible.

Solitude and difficulty, isolation and silence. We all bore the burdens at one point or another. McGarvey's was in the early morning hours, when he would awaken from his dreams bathed in sweat. Sometimes Katy would be awake, and she would hold him until his heart stopped pounding. But most of the time she was sound asleep and he would be alone. Shahrzad never had someone to hold her close, and tell her that she was loved, and be telling the truth.

"It was a Thursday night when the club usually wasn't so busy that I had to sit with too many other customers, when Louis and I went back to our room and I started to dance for him," she started. "He wasn't himself that night. He was watching me, but I don't think that he was really seeing me, you know."

Rencke nodded, encouraging her to continue.

"It was the same when we made love. It was as if he wasn't there with me. He was someplace else. And it hurt. I thought that it was probably the beginning of the end for us, which made me really sad. Like I said, I was in love with him, and for goodness' sake, I thought he was in love with me. But right then I wasn't so sure.

"Afterward when we got dressed he liked to have a cigarette and a bottle of champagne. I had never smoked before, but I smoked with him. Because of him." She was looking inward now. "I don't think he realized that I was making little sacrifices like that for him." She shrugged. "But it didn't matter as long as we were together."

"And he was paying you so that you could get to the U.S.," McGarvey said sharply, not sure why he was baiting her, except that he still wasn't sure if she was genuine, or an MOIS double.

She ignored the gibe. "Sometimes we would talk, mostly about little things. You know, about baseball, about Ghirardelli Square, about South Beach, places I wanted to visit."

"But not that night," McGarvey prompted.

She shook her head. "No," she said. She looked up as if she were coming out of a daze. "Not that night. He said that he wanted me to help him with something. 'Anything you want, Louis,' I told him. And I meant it, and he believed me, because he admitted that he was an American spy."

"God in heaven," Perry blurted.

"He wanted me to find out about some people. If I did that for him, he would make sure that I would get a real visa to come to America, and that I would never have to worry about money again."

"The bastard lost his mind," Perry muttered.

"No," Shahrzad cried. "He said this was very important. The most important job of his career. More important than I or anyone else could possibly imagine. And we were going to be the heroes."

"You were to become a spy for him," McGarvey said.

"That's right."

"The Chinese?"

She went a little pale and her hand shook as she reached for her glass. "That's right," she said. "But mostly just one man. An important man. General Liu."

ELEVEN

LONGBOAT KEY

They took a short break. Toni was summoned to escort Shahrzad to the bathroom, and when they were out of earshot McGarvey was the first to speak.

"If she's here of her own free will, why the babysitter?" So many things weren't adding up in his mind that he didn't know where to begin.

"One of my people was shot to death, after all," Perry said earnestly. "I'm not taking any chances."

"Beyond the ones that you've already taken," McGarvey said.

Perry's eyes narrowed. "I don't know what you mean. What chances?"

McGarvey had to wonder if anyone told the truth. "Updegraf had to be a busy man, running a one-man show with just the help of the girl."

"I didn't know anything about it. We've already established that much." Perry waved his hand in a sweeping gesture toward where Shahrzad had been sitting. "All of this is news to me."

"I understand," McGarvey said. "But your field officer was a busy man. Gone all hours of the day and night. You must have noticed something."

"He was going after his code clerk."

"A lot of work for a code clerk, wouldn't you say?" McGarvey asked rhetorically. "But you had to be taking a big chance that with all that activity, something else might have been going on. Something that as station chief you would be responsible for."

A sudden shrewdness came into Perry's eyes, a sudden understanding of what McGarvey was getting at and how best to respond. "Every chief of station worth his salt has his own philosophy. My method is to allow my senior officers the latitude to develop their own sources without hindrance. If they strike gold, or even if they catch a glimmer, they come to me and we put our heads together. Come up with a winning strategy. Heavens, man, I'm a spy, not a paper pusher. Surely you of all men can understand."

"But Updegraf wasn't playing by the rules. I'd say that a senior Chinese intelligence officer was something more than just a glimmer."

"What was I supposed to do?" Perry cried, throwing his hands up.

"Something, I suppose." McGarvey shrugged. "It was your man who got himself killed. Is there anything else about Updegraf that I should know about? Anything that's not in his jacket or his OPR?" McGarvey asked. An OPR was an Officer Performance Report that was written every year by an agent's immediate supervisor.

Perry shook his head. "No."

Shahrzad came back and took her seat, and Toni withdrew. "Could we maybe stop and have some lunch? I'm starved."

"Later," McGarvey said. "You were in love with Updegraf, so you agreed to become a spy for him."

"That's right," she replied defensively. "It's what people who are in love do for each other. Without sacrifices there is nothing. It's a special bond that maybe you don't understand." She glanced at Perry. "Well, I understood, and so did Louis."

It occurred to McGarvey that this little girl had no idea what love was. She was merely spouting some cliches that sounded good to her, wrapping up her feelings for a man she couldn't have known well in a tidy little package that made sense, that gave her a sense of self-worth. If this American spy she was having sex with loved her, then she was validated as a woman.

He had to wonder what her life had been like in Tehran with a father who as a spy had set her up with a Russian general old enough to be at least her father, and possibly her grandfather. The same thing had happened to her again in Mexico City. A man she loved was setting her up with another general, and for the same reasons.

McGarvey felt a genuine pity for her, yet was wary. She may have been misguided, but she was playing a dangerous game that her father had taught her, and which General Baranov had perfected.

"How did it happen?" McGarvey asked.

"The first thing I did was quit dancing at the Wild Stallion and become Louis's full-time girl," Shahrzad began. She smiled wistfully, which made her appear to be all the more vulnerable.

"But that didn't last long."

She shook her head. "Just a few days. Then we made the rounds of all the clubs, mostly right there in Zona Rosa and Coyacan and Condesa, but we finally wound up at a place called the Doll House in Polanco. It was fancier than most of the others, and more expensive, so there was a better class of clientele who showed up."

"Heavy hitters," Rencke suggested.

Shahrzad smiled uncertainly. "I never heard that term before."

"Rich guys with lots of power."

She nodded. "They were mostly heavy hitters in that place. And the acts were better. You know, prettier girls, younger mostly, and white mostly, although there were a couple of cute Japanese kids. The average age was maybe fifteen or sixteen. I felt ancient.

"The third night we were there General Liu showed up with a couple of women, and Louis got all excited. 'It's him,' he told me. 'It's our mark.' We were going to target the general, and once we had him we could write our own ticket. We would be the emperor and empress of the moon."

"What happened next?" McGarvey asked.

"Louis said that we would have to take it easy, let the general come to me," Shahrzad explained. "If I came on too strong he'd know he was being set up. Liu got the VIP treatment whenever he was in the club. Miguel Roaz, the owner, would personally escort the general to a table right in front of the stage where they did the dancing and the sex shows. He always drank champagne, usually Krug but sometimes Dom Pérignon, and he always had a couple of women with him. Sometimes they would go into one of the back rooms with him, and the Doll—that was Roaz's nickname because he had a baby face—would send one of the dancers back to entertain them."

"And have sex?" Rencke asked.

Shahrzad seemed embarrassed. "Sometimes. That's the whole idea of these clubs. And there're a lot of them in Mexico City. Clubs for gays and lesbians, for the S&M freaks, even a few clubs for men, and some women, who liked to do it with animals. Big dogs, Shetland ponies, snakes."

"But the Doll House was for the straight crowd," McGarvey said.

Shahrzad nodded. "I never liked the other sort of places. They made me nervous."

"I'll bet they did," McGarvey said, but she didn't catch his sarcasm. "Didn't you wonder why an important Chinese man such as the general would take the risk of going to such a club? If he were to be seen and reported to Beijing he'd be in big trouble."

She shook her head, and her soft lips pursed in disgust. "Anyway, in between the acts couples could dance on the floor, and sometimes it was like an orgy. The music was wild, the place was practically pitch black except for a spotlight that moved around the floor, and by the time they were ready to start the next show everyone was all but screwing their brains out."

"You and Louis?" McGarvey asked.

She looked away for a moment. "He wanted me to try to seduce him, but he said everything from now on was for the general's benefit. That night I was half naked, rubbing against Louis's arm, when the spotlight came to us. Louis shoved me back and hit me in the mouth. I never saw it coming, and it hurt more than you can imagine. I fell down on the floor, and the next thing I knew the bouncers had grabbed Louis and were throwing him out." Shahrzad appeared to be on the verge of tears. "I thought they were going to toss me out too, but Roaz helped me back to the table, and the waiter brought me a bottle of Krug. 'From an admirer,' the Doll told me. I was welcome to stay as long as I wanted."

Perry was staring at the girl, an intent, almost admiring, look on his face. He caught McGarvey watching him, and flushed. The exchange lasted only an instant, and neither Shahrzad nor Rencke noticed, but McGarvey thought the station chief's reaction to the girl's story was odd. Something was out of place.

"I tell you that it felt strange to be sitting all alone in a place like that," she continued.

"The admirer was General Liu, of course," McGarvey said. "You were in."

"Not quite. He didn't speak to me that night, which Louis said would probably be the case. So I was to ask the Doll for a job dancing in the show. But he just laughed at me, at first. Said I was too old and the wrong color. Unless I had what he called 'special talents.'"

"Which were?"

She hesitated.

"He wanted to know if you were good in bed, and willing to service perhaps the admirer who'd sent you the champagne."

She held her silence.

"That's why Louis seduced you, to see if you were any good. And when he found out that you were, he made you fall in love with him so that you'd do whatever he wanted you to do."

"You can't *make* someone fall in love with you," Shahrzad flared.

"But you fell in love with Louis, and he asked you to seduce General Liu. He asked you to become his whore, and you agreed."

"It was important," she said weakly. Now her eyes *were* filling with tears.

"How long did it take before the general asked you to his table?"

"It was the second week," she said. She shook her head. "I just wanted someone to love me. Is that so terrible a thing?"

TWELVE

LONGBOAT KEY

They had talked for nearly an hour and a half when the woman on the house staff wheeled in a serving cart laden with Cuban sandwiches, black bean soup, and small salads, along with iced tea. McGarvey asked for a beer, and while the others were serving themselves he stepped to the edge of the veranda and looked out to the horizon. The sky was cloudless, the day was warm, but the humidity had dropped. It was what the locals called chamber of commerce weather.

He could hear Rencke behind him talking to the woman in quieting tones about her early days in Iran when she was just a little child, how happy she must have been. Gardens surrounded their house, she said. Fruit trees, flowers, a topiary where she would play hide-and-seek with her older siblings. And tall grasses grew along a winding creek that was cool in the summer. Rencke was trying to calm her nerves so that she would better be able to face up to the next part, which would probably be difficult.

Updegraf had apparently done his homework on General Liu, figuring that the general's weakness was women. But if Updegraf had done *all* his homework he would also have learned that Liu had been suspected of brutally murdering several women in New York and Washington and possibly again in Mexico City. He was sending the woman he professed to love to become his whore so that she could seduce the general and then spy on him, and for that there was a very good chance she would be murdered.

For this job, Updegraf had been paying her, with the promise that if she was a success he would guarantee her a U.S. visa and the prospect of a future in which she would not have to worry about money. The sad part was that if Updegraf had done a proper job of his due diligence he would have realized that merely loving the girl would have been enough.

It was the one statement she'd made that McGarvey believed wholeheartedly. All she wanted was for someone to love her. It's all she'd wanted ever since her father had sent her to General Baranov's bed.

After her father had been assassinated and her mother had fled to Paris, there had been no place for Shahrzad to go. Her family would have rejected her because in places like Iran, women were always blamed as seductresses. If a young girl was raped, she would be held responsible. In some not very remote villages, she would even be put to death for her crime. It was almost never the man's fault.

The woman came with his beer. McGarvey thanked her, went back to the table, and sat down. Shahrzad was to be pitied. But she wore the diamond ring that Baranov had given her as a mark of accomplishment, not a brand of shame. And it was she who had sought out Louis Updegraf; it was she who had willingly agreed to be his whore and seduce General Liu. At least on the surface just about everything she'd told them so far seemed to be a lie. And yet there was something there, something in her eyes and in her mannerisms, that McGarvey couldn't quite get a handle on.

"Tell me about your contact procedures with Updegraf," McGarvey said. "You were dealing with a high-ranking ministry officer, so I assume you were told to be careful."

"The general was the new generation. A real modern guy, according to Louis. So we were going to use *old-fashioned* tradecraft."

McGarvey's anger spiked. The girl knew the terminology. He had to wonder if it had been her father who'd taught her how to be a spy, or if it had been Updegraf. He could not fathom such men. Yet his own daughter had followed in his footsteps, though not at his urging.

"There was a telephone kiosk two blocks from my apartment in Zona Rosa that I had to pass by whenever I went to the market for groceries. Louis gave me two pieces of chalk, one white, one black. If I had something for him, I was to make a white mark, and he would meet me in the park across the street from my building. I sometimes went there to run."

"The black was if you were in trouble," McGarvey said.

She nodded. "If I used the black chalk I was to wait for him at the market and he would come for me right away."

"Did you ever have to use the black chalk?"

"Once," she said softly. "Everything was out of control by then. I mean totally out of control, and I was frightened. I wanted out."

"Did he come for you?"

"No."

"By then Louis was dead," Perry said. "Shot to death."

Shahrzad lowered her head, tears coming to her wide, dark eyes again. "I didn't know yet. I thought he'd just abandoned me. I waited for three days and nights in a hotel, hoping that I was wrong about him and that he would come for me. But he never did. So I went to the U.S. embassy."

Through all of her telling, including her tears, she had continued to wolf down her lunch as if it were her first meal in a week. As sad as the memory was of her assassinated lover, her appetite had not been affected. McGarvey didn't know what it meant, except that perhaps there was something even worse she hadn't come to yet.

"Let's go back to the beginning," McGarvey said. "Louis sets you up at the club where you catch General Liu's eye. After the first week he invites you over to his table for some champagne, and finally he takes you to his bed."

She put down her spoon and dabbed the cloth napkin to her lips, a sudden wild, even insane expression coming into her eyes, as if she'd just remembered something that was so surreal she didn't know whether to laugh or scream.

"It took ten days," she began. "I did as Louis told me, and let the general seduce me. He would have expected the honey trap otherwise. I was supposed to play hard to get." She shrugged. "And it worked. He was the perfect gentleman, at first."

"Did he know who your father was?" McGarvey asked.

"There was no reason for him to know. But I tell you that I was plenty scared at first."

"You did wind up in his bed after all," Perry said.

Shahrzad looked at him as if he were an idiot. "Yes," she said. "At first I just sat with him, drank champagne, and watched the shows. Then sometimes we would dance. And it was great, he really knew what he was doing."

"Were the other women with him at the club?" McGarvey asked.

She nodded. "At first, but one night he came alone, and he never brought them back."

"Did you ever see them again?" Perry asked. "Could you identify them?"

"Sure. They were part of his crowd at the house. And at the compound."

"We'll get to that," McGarvey said. "You had sex with the general. Was it at the club? Did he pay you?"

"We went to one of the rooms in back and I danced for him. This time he asked me to do the *raqs sharqi*."

"That's the traditional belly dance," Perry interrupted unnecessarily. McGarvey let it go.

Shahrzad nodded. "When I was finished he took my costume off and laid me down on the cushions." She was looking inward, the almost maniacal expression on her face again. "It was hot in that place, but I was shivering. I didn't know what to expect."

"Oh I think you did—" Perry said, but this time McGarvey cut him off. "Shut up."

Perry was startled, but he held his silence.

"He got undressed then, and I almost laughed at him." Shahrzad was blushing. "He wasn't a man . . . down there. He was just a boy. He couldn't get it up, and I didn't know what to do." She looked up at McGarvey, willing him to understand her predicament. "He had seen me completely naked onstage before, I had just done the dance, and I was lying on the cushions waiting for him." She shook her head. "I didn't know what else to do."

"Continue."

"That was all," she said.

"You didn't have sex with him?"

"In a manner of speaking."

"What in heaven's name is that supposed to mean?" Perry blurted.

Shahrzad turned to him, acutely embarrassed that she needed to practically draw him a picture. "He lay on top of me, did a couple of bumps, and came on my thigh."

Perry looked away, embarrassed. "Oh," he said in a small voice.

"What was Liu's attitude afterward?" McGarvey asked. "Was he embarrassed?"

"That was the scary part," Shahrzad said. "He was mad as hell for a couple of minutes, maybe less. I don't know for sure. But I do know that I thought he was going to kill me."

"Did he hit you?" McGarvey said.

"No. In fact when he calmed down he made some little jokes while I was cleaning up and getting dressed. And before I left he gave me five hundred dollars, which he said I could keep for myself, he would take care of the Doll. And he said that he was busy tomorrow, but that he would see me on Friday."

"The next day you went to the market, left a white chalk mark by the telephone, and met Louis in the park," McGarvey said. "Did you tell him about the money?"

"That wasn't important—"

"It must have given you some satisfaction," Perry suggested. "Here it was, two men paying you, with one of them promising to get you to the States. You were on the fast track to get everything you'd wanted."

"The general was crazy in the head. Some of the other girls heard there were rumors that he'd killed a girl in New York. He liked to strangle them during sex. They were only rumors, Louis told me, but I was just about out of my mind. I wanted to quit. All the money in the world wasn't worth the risk I was taking."

"But you went back," McGarvey said.

"You don't understand what it's like to be in love," Shahrzad said, her voice rising. "Of course I went back, and about a week and a half later the general invited me to move out to his house, and Louis agreed."

"Let me explain about General Liu's house," Perry cut in. "It's really a palace with its own lake and floating gardens down in Xochimilco, about fifteen miles south of the city. Apparently he holds big parties for all the heavy hitters, most of them high-ranking Mexican politicians and military officers."

"Were reports made to Langley?" McGarvey asked.

"Yes, finally," Perry said. "As soon as Ms. Shadmand walked in and gave us a few bits and pieces that we could verify. I sent two of my best people out there on a surveillance operation and we hit pay dirt the very first night."

"That was just a few days ago?"

"Unfortunately, yes," Perry admitted.

"Nobody down here was given the heads-up," Rencke said. "It was Dick's call. He wanted a little more information before we mounted any sort of an operation."

Perry perked up. "Here, what are you talking about?" he demanded. "Heads-up about what? Were you aware of General Liu's presence in Mexico City?"

"We caught him in a couple of satellite shots," Rencke said.

"Why wasn't I informed?"

"We'll discuss it later," McGarvey promised.

Perry wanted to say something, but he thought better of it, and slumped back.

"Roaz was out there most of the time," Shahrzad said. "Sometimes before things heated up downtown, everyone would come down to the general's house and we'd all go to the club together. And almost every night, after the clubs closed, there'd be a crowd until dawn. There were a lot of drugs that Roaz was supplying. And everything was free."

"But there was a price," McGarvey suggested. "For you especially."

"Isn't there always?" she asked.

THIRTEEN

□

LONGBOAT KEY

A couple of Roaz's people from the club helped load up Shahrzad's apartment and take it down to "the House," as everyone called General Liu's place. She didn't have much, but as soon as she was settled, the general insisted that she return to her dancing job. There was a very good reason, he told her. All she had to do was trust him, and whatever she wanted would be hers.

"Which was just as well," Shahrzad continued her story. "Louis had been worried about our contact procedures, but with me in town four nights a week he arranged for a drop box with one of the taxi men."

"Not cabbies," Perry explained. "Parking is impossible downtown. So a taxi man, actually they're entrepreneurs, stakes out a half dozen parking spots on the street that he mans twelve, sometimes eighteen hours a day. No one parks without paying him first, unless you want to come back and find that your car has been totally trashed, and there were no witnesses. Everybody's happy. Customers find a safe place to park, the taxi men make a living, and the bribes help the cops to survive on lousy pay."

"It took nearly a week before I could make an excuse to get out of the club for a couple of minutes," Shahrzad said. "I was smoking pretty heavily by then, so sometimes I would got out the back door and grab some air. Roaz didn't care, and there were some nights that the general sent his driver to take me to the club early, and he wouldn't get there with his crowd until much later, usually after midnight.

"My contact was an old man with long white hair and only one good eye; the other was milky and horrible looking. Anyway, he walked up to me and handed me a pack of Marlboros and a small gold Zippo lighter. 'From an admirer,' he told me. I gave him a few pesos, and back in my dressing room I found out that the lighter worked, but it was also a miniature digital camera. Before I'd moved out, Louis had told me that once I was in at the house he would get the camera to me. I was supposed to take pictures of everything and everybody. The camera could hold up to one hundred pictures, but no matter how many I had taken I was to exchange it every Wednesday and Saturday with the taxi man for a fresh one."

"Weren't you worried about getting caught?" Perry asked.

"Petrified," Shahrzad admitted. "But every time I lit a cigarette I'd use the Zippo and take a couple pictures. After the first few times right in front of the general when nothing happened, I relaxed a little." She gave McGarvey a wistful look. "By then I don't think he was really seeing me. We had sex only the one time, and after that I was just another one of the women he always surrounded himself with."

"But you were doing this for Louis, so you didn't mind," McGarvey suggested.

"Exactly," she said. "Anyway, I was afraid of the general." She looked away. "Sooner or later everybody became afraid of him."

"Was Louis happy with your snapshots?"

She smiled. "After the first week he was over the moon."

"How in heaven's name could you possibly know that?" Perry asked. "You didn't pass love notes via your taxi man, did you?"

"One night Louis was in one of the parking places. We kissed through the open window and he told me that I was doing fabulous work. 'Won't be long now and we'll be able to write our own ticket,' he said. His own words. I was to keep taking pictures, but now he wanted me to find the general's desk and his computer and take pictures of whatever I could. It was going to be a lot riskier, he said, but rock-solid necessary."

"Well, if he was getting such rock-solid product he wasn't sharing it with me," Perry complained bitterly. "This is the first that I've heard about any of this."

"He kept repeating that this was going to be the big score," Shahrzad said. "But I told him that I was scared out of my skull. He looked into my eyes and promised that when it was over, not only was he going to get me up to the States, but he was going to divorce his wife and we would be together."

Perry started to snicker, but Shahrzad turned on him.

"You don't understand how it was with us. I believed him. I believed in him."

"We understand," Rencke assured her. "Ya know we're just trying to do our jobs here. We want to find out why your Louis was killed. Maybe we can figure out what went wrong, what Liu's been up to. Maybe stop this from happening to someone else."

Shahrzad closed her eyes for a few moments, as if she were collecting her thoughts. "A couple weeks after I moved down to the House, the parties started in earnest. Every weekend there'd be a huge crowd out there, live music, every kind of food and booze you could imagine. Champagne, oysters, and truffles flown over from France, caviar from my country, lobsters from Maine, you name it, and of course Roaz with his stash. They were called 'hospitality bowls,' and they were filled with coke. Practically everywhere you looked someone was dipping into one of them."

"You too?" McGarvey asked.

"It would have looked pretty odd if I hadn't," she said.

"This also is news to me," Perry said petulantly. "Did you know these people? Can you identify them for us?"

"I knew some of them from the newspapers. Senator Trinidad Lopez showed up at least once a week, usually with Carlos Huerta, whom I was told was assistant chief of police for Mexico City."

"Jesus," Perry said softly. "Were you able to take pictures of them?"

"Sure," Shahrzad replied. "That was easy. And so was getting the camera to Louis. I was still working four nights a week at the club."

"Did Liu ever come back to the club after that?" Perry asked.

"Just once. He wanted me to dance for a friend of his. I don't remember the name, except that he was an Air Force general, and he smelled like a donkey."

"Did you have sex with him in one of the back rooms?" McGarvey asked.

Shahrzad looked away for a few moments. "Yes," she admitted in a very small voice. "It was horrible. The whole time I kept thinking about Louis, and wondering how I was going to tell him about this."

"Why didn't you refuse?"

She gave McGarvey a bitter smile. "When General Liu asked for something, nobody refused."

"Did he threaten people? Did he do anything to you?"

She shook her head. "No. But everyone knew it would be for the best if they did what he said."

"Did you talk to the other women about him?"

"No."

"But you did talk."

"Of course. About the guests. Who was the most generous, who was roughest, who were the pigs and who were the gentlemen."

"All Liu's women were whores?" Perry asked.

Shahrzad bridled, but after a moment she nodded.

"Including you."

"I was working for Louis," she shot back. "I was a spy."

"What did you learn from your spying, then?" Perry asked. "I mean other than the photos you were busy snapping? Did the Air Force general whisper secrets into your ear as he was boffing you? Or maybe he slept afterward and you went through his pockets?"

"Just the pictures," Shahrzad said. "But not only of people. I got into General Liu's office one night and used up an entire camera taking shots of his diary, his calendar, his phone books. Stuff like that."

"Did you learn anything useful?"

"I just took the pictures," Shahrzad said. "You must have seen them."

"No," Perry admitted. "Even if I did, it'd be a moot point, since I don't read Chinese. But did Updegraf say anything about a translator?"

"Did you know that Louis could speak and read Chinese?"

Perry was startled, but for just an instant. He shook his head. "No, as a matter of fact I wasn't aware of it."

Rencke stiffened almost imperceptibly, but McGarvey caught it, though Perry and Shahrzad apparently had not. Something that the station chief had said wasn't sitting right with Rencke.

"Well he could, and he told me that I was hitting the jackpot. The 'veritable gold seam,' he said. He promised that he would pull me out very soon. In a few days, maybe a week. And I was glad because I didn't know how much more I could take."

"Are you talking about the sex?" McGarvey asked.

She nodded. "The general wanted me to go to bed with just about every guy who came to the house."

"What was it he wanted you to find out?"

"Nothing. I wasn't supposed to ask them about anything."

"I don't understand," McGarvey said, although he did. But he wanted to hear it from her own lips, and he wanted to watch Perry's reaction.

"I didn't at first either. But just before it fell apart, I saw some of the tapes that he'd made. They showed everything."

Perry kept a straight face.

"He couldn't have been using them for blackmail," McGarvey said. "A guy having sex with a woman doesn't carry much weight nowadays."

"There were videos of everything, not just the sex," Shahrzad said. "The parties, the drugs, and the money."

"Liu was paying these guys?" Perry asked. "For what?"

"I don't know, but it was a lot of money."

"Some of which went to you," McGarvey suggested. "Louis was paying you to spy on Liu. The general was paying you to spy on his guests. And his guests were paying you to have sex with them. How long were you together?"

"A couple of months. It was all I could take. It was getting too strange and dangerous."

"What about Updegraf? Did you tell him that you wanted out?"

"That's why I used the black chalk."

"By then Louis was dead," Perry said, unnecessarily.

FOURTEEN

LONGBOAT KEY

The woman on the house staff cleared the table, and Toni took Shahrzad to the bathroom again, giving them all a little break. To this point the story was moving along in a predictable progression of events. Updegraf's tradecraft was just about SOP, except that McGarvey couldn't figure out why the man hadn't kept his boss informed, and how it was that Perry had missed the entire operation.

Something was wrong, not only with Perry's account, but with Shahrzad's.

When Toni brought her back out to the veranda and they had all settled down, McGarvey took up the questioning.

"I'm not quite sure that I understand what happened at the end," he said. "The parties, the drugs, the sex, the spying, all of it got to be too much for you, so you dropped everything, made your black chalk mark, and checked into a hotel to wait for Updegraf to come rescue you. Is that right?"

"It was more complicated than that," Shahrzad said. "A lot more complicated. And in the end I didn't know what to do. I had to get out of there, and despite what had happened, Louis was my only contact. He was my lifeline, even then."

"Continue," McGarvey prompted.

"There was supposed to be this party for some big shot—" Shahrzad stopped.

"Go ahead," Rencke coaxed.

"They said he was from the States. I think it was probably about a drug deal, because there were also some guys from Colombia."

"Did you get the American's name?" Perry asked. "Did you snap his picture?"

Shahrzad was suddenly very nervous. She nodded. "I took his picture."

"You must have been anxious to get back to Mexico City and give the camera to Louis," Perry said.

"No," Shahrzad said, her voice small. She looked directly at McGarvey. "I didn't know if I'd ever see him again after Chihuahua at the compound. That's where the party took place."

"Jesus Christ," Perry said, but McGarvey gestured for the man to stop right there, and Perry shut up.

"Explain how that happened, please," McGarvey said. Whatever her real motive was for getting out of what had become a lucrative business deal was coming now.

"The general told me about the party, and said he wanted me to dance for a couple of guys. We were flying up in a private jet, and he'd only need me for that afternoon and night, and I'd be flown back to Mexico City first thing in the morning."

"More money," McGarvey suggested.

"I didn't want the job, and I told him so," Shahrzad said. "The whole deal felt wrong. Anyway, by then I was already spooked. I didn't want to leave the city. My life was rotten, but at least I knew my way around, and I had Louis." She looked away for a moment. "The general insisted, of course. In the end he got really mad, so I said yes. He promised to pay me five thousand dollars for the one night's work. I figured with what I had already saved up, and with the work I'd done for Louis, I could finally get up to the States."

"Were you able to contact Updegraf to tell him where you were going?" McGarvey asked. "Maybe he followed you up there."

She shook her head. "I didn't get the chance. It wasn't my club night, and after I packed a few things we went directly from the general's house to the airport and flew up to Chihuahua. It was about three in the afternoon when we got to the compound, which was behind a tall wall up in the foothills."

"Was it one of Liu's houses?" Perry asked.

"I don't think so. Maybe it was Roaz's. He was there when we arrived, and he acted like he owned it."

"Nice house?" McGarvey asked.

Shahrzad shrugged her narrow shoulders. "It was a nice place."

"When did the Colombians and this American show up?" McGarvey asked.

"Later that afternoon."

"You were supposed to dance for the American?"

"Just him."

"You didn't get his name?" McGarvey asked.

"The general called him Robert, but I don't think that was his real name. Anyway, I only heard it once."

"Did they use your real name?" Perry wondered.

Shahrzad nodded, but she had drifted off somewhere. She was looking directly at McGarvey, but he didn't think she was actually seeing him at that moment.

"We had a barbecue out back, by the pool. A lot of other people were up there, in addition to the house staff and some guys who carried machine guns or something like that, and watched the fence and the front gate. There were some girls, mostly Oriental and very young, and all of them were naked by the time it was dark. Finally Robert took me to one of the dressing rooms on the side of the pool across from the house, and I danced for him. But it wasn't long before we had our clothes off and were having sex." She shook her head, lost in the memory. "He was the biggest man I'd ever seen. And he was rough, but when he was done he got dressed, threw a few hundred dollars at me, and left."

She suddenly focused on McGarvey and the others. "He never said a word to me the entire time. He didn't even make any noise."

"Did you rejoin the party?" McGarvey asked.

"I got dressed, and as I was leaving the cabana I saw something that practically made my heart stop. It was the general with his arm around a man's shoulder like they were old friends. They were going into the house with a third man, but they never saw me. I waited until they were gone, then went through the kitchen and up to my room. I stayed there until morning, when the general's driver came up for me and took me to the airport so I could get back to Mexico City. Two days later was a club night for me, and I just walked away, made my chalk mark, and checked into the hotel to wait."

"What about your money?" McGarvey asked.

"I left it at the house," Shahrzad told him.

"For heaven's sake, who was the man so chummy with Liu?" Perry demanded impatiently. "Did you find out his name?"

"It wasn't necessary," Shahrzad said. "It was Louis."

All the air left the veranda. Suddenly the afternoon was still and hot.

"Updegraf and Liu knew each other?" Perry asked incredulously. "Are you sure it was him? Absolutely certain?"

"It was him," McGarvey answered for her. And it made sense. Updegraf had conducted a full-court press on Liu, sending Shahrzad to spy on him, and then insinuating himself into the Chinese general's inner circle.

"I didn't know what to do."

"When Louis didn't answer your chalk mark, you went to our embassy, but you asked for Mr. Perry, but not Updegraf," McGarvey said. "Why?"

"Louis would never have left me hanging like that unless something had gone wrong."

"Did you know that he was dead?"

She shook her head. "Not until Mr. Perry told me."

"Why me?" McGarvey asked. "What do you think I can do for you?"

"Find out who murdered Louis and why," Shahrzad flared.

"He was spying on a Chinese intelligence officer. Most of them don't take kindly to such a thing."

"We needn't get into that now," Perry cautioned.

"When you went to the embassy and asked for me, you didn't know that Updegraf had been murdered," McGarvey said.

"No, but I knew that he was probably in big trouble. And I think he knew it, too, because the last time I saw him, before Chihuahua, he told me that if I ever got into a really big mess with Liu, and if for some reason he wasn't around, I was to contact you."

"I don't remember ever meeting him."

"He knew you. Said you were the best the Company ever had," Shahrzad insisted. 'Talk to Kirk McGarvey' was the last thing he ever said to me." Her eyes filled and she looked away.

"Why did you leave your money behind?" McGarvey asked.

"I didn't want it," she answered. "Don't you see, all I ever wanted was Louis."

"Who was the other man with Louis and the general?"

Shahrzad's nostrils flared and she glanced away for just an instant. "I don't know," she said, and McGarvey figured she was lying.

Perry went into the house to summon Toni to take the girl upstairs.

"Will you help me?" Shahrzad asked.

"I don't know yet," McGarvey said. "I need to find out a couple of things first."

"I'll do anything you ask, just find out who killed Louis and why."

"Did he ever tell you what the big score was? Or what he thought the Chinese were up to in Mexico that would be so important to us?"

"No. But he was plenty scared, just like me. And he promised that when he had his proof we could write our own ticket."

Toni appeared in the doorway and Shahrzad got to her feet. "Please, Mr. McGarvey. Just consider it."

When they were gone Perry sat down at the table. "It's simply too fantastic a story to believe."

"Why's that?" McGarvey asked.

"High-ranking Chinese intelligence officers don't involve themselves with the drug trade."

"It's been done before," Rencke said. "But I think there's the possibility that whatever General Liu is doing in Mexico has nothing to do with Beijing."

"Are you saying that he's a rogue?" Perry demanded. "Working on his own?"

"He's done that before too."

"I should have been told that he was there," Perry said. He focused on McGarvey. "What do you think?"

"I think that we should find out what Liu is doing in Mexico, for starters."

"I'll get my people on it immediately," Perry said. "What about the girl?"

"Who knows that she's here?"

"Dick Adkins; Tom Burns, who's our new chief of security; and us," Rencke said.

"How about in Mexico City?" McGarvey asked the station chief. "What'd you tell your staff when you left with the girl?"

"Nothing," Perry said. "It was none of their business. But my question remains, do you believe her story?"

McGarvey had asked himself the same question. "Some of it," he said. "But I don't know why she got involved in the first place. I understand how and why Updegraf recruited her, but I don't see why she accepted so willingly."

"Maybe she actually did fall in love with him," Rencke suggested. "Things like that do happen to people, even in this business."

"There's more," McGarvey said. He glanced at Perry. "Keep the girl here for the time being. Toni can watch over her. I want you to go back to Mexico City and continue investigating Updegraf's assassination as if you'd never heard this story. Your man was working on something in Chihuahua that you knew nothing about. Let the Mexican Federal Police help you. Keep it out of the media, but make a few waves. Maybe you'll turn up something."

"How do I reach you?" Perry asked.

"Through me," Rencke said.

FIFTEEN

SARASOTA

It was past three in the afternoon by the time McGarvey and Rencke headed back to New College across the bay on the mainland. St. Armand's Circle was even busier with tourists than it had been when they'd come out to the island before lunch.

McGarvey was deep in thought, and neither of them spoke until they reached the Ringling Bridge.

"Something's going on," Rencke said, breaking the silence. "Perry was lying to us."

"Yes, what was that all about?"

"He told us that he didn't know Updegraf was fluent in Mandarin. But he had to know, it's in the man's personnel file. There was even a joke about it when he got reassigned to Mexico. Someone in Ops included a note in the transfer file that it was a good thing Updegraf didn't speak Spanish, or he probably would have been sent to China."

"Why would he lie about something like that?" McGarvey asked. "He'd have to know that we'd find out."

"Maybe he's running scared, just like Shahrzad."

"Of what?" McGarvey asked.

"Now that's the sixty-four-dollar question, kemosabe. So what're you going to do about it?"

"I'm not sure," McGarvey said, and he was trying to mean it, at least for Katy's sake, but he was intrigued despite himself. "Liu is up to something. But why Mexico? Has there been anything in the NIEs or Watch Reports about China's involvement?"

"That's one of the first things I checked when Liu's name popped up on one of our Beijing telephone intercepts. A couple of my search programs started getting into the lavender range over the past few months. There've been some serious shake-ups in the military high command, as well as the government. When that happens it usually means there's some kind of a serious argument going on that's polarized everyone. Survival of the fittest. The weak guys get the boot.

"The biggest thing from the China desk, other than the trade issue, is their space race, but my programs were getting twitchy, so I played around a little. When we picked up Liu's call on the Beijing circuit we found out it had probably originated in Mexico City. It was encrypted— pretty good algorithm too—and he used a sat phone, so it was tough to track. Took me a few days of sniffing around until I caught a couple of high-res shots from one of our KH14s. It was Liu all right, in Mexico City, looking right up at the camera as if he were posing for the birdy."

"Maybe he was," McGarvey suggested.

"That's what we thought," Rencke said. "It's got Dick pretty worried. He wanted to call you, but he held off because you're retired. And he really respects that, ya know. But when Shahrzad showed up on Perry's doorstep and asked for you by name, he didn't have a choice, so he had the girl brought here and sent me down to talk to you."

"Lavender?" McGarvey asked.

Rencke nodded. "Pretty solid, and getting a shade deeper every day."

"No mistakes?"

"I don't think so, Mac. Not this time."

McGarvey had to ask himself how many times he'd been at this same juncture over the past twenty-five years. More times than he wanted to count. And in each instance blood had been shed, sometimes a lot of it. His operations were the reasons for the nightmares he sometimes had. But he was already putting those thoughts away and getting ready to go back into the field, where everything other than the task in hand had to be blotted out of his conscious mind. It was more than a matter of trade-craft; it very often became a matter of survival.

"I'll need to see the personnel files for everyone at the embassy, including Perry's."

"I brought them with me," Rencke said. "When are you leaving?"

"As soon as I can convince Katy not to shoot both of us."

Rencke smiled, but it faded as quickly as it came. "Gloria Ibenez is in Mexico City," he said.

McGarvey had not kept track of her, but he knew that she'd been assigned to the station in Mexico City, where Cuban intelligence maintained a large presence. It would have been a waste of her Spanish language skills to send her anywhere else. She was a good field officer, inventive, steady under fire, and very bright. She'd had a serious crush on him last year, which was the only blemish on what had turned out to be one of the more satisfying operations of his career. He had tracked down Osama bin Laden and killed the al-Qaida leader. But there'd been very little fallout throughout the Arab world. Bin Laden was dead, and just about everyone knew it, yet just about everyone accepted the bin Laden double who'd sent the occasional taped message to al-Jazeera.

"How's she doing?"

"Perry wants to get rid of her. Thinks she's a pain in the ass. His OPRs won't win her any promotions."

Another thought suddenly crossed McGarvey's mind, and he nearly dismissed it out of hand, but he couldn't. It had glue. "Has Perry involved her in investigating Updegraf's murder?"

Rencke nodded. "He's got her looking down Updegraf's path. Supposedly he was working as a code clerk in the Chinese embassy, but no one else knew about it."

"Who's up in Chihuahua?"

"Nobody right now. But Perry sent Tom Chauncy, his assistant COS, to claim Updegraf's body and get it across the border for an autopsy at the Air Force hospital in San Antonio. But apparently he's back in Mexico City, and Perry hasn't told us how he's deployed his people."

"Sounds like a mess," McGarvey said.

"A cluster fuck," Rencke agreed.

"What do we know about Perry's background?"

"Old-money East Coast family, ambitious—wants to be DDCI someday—pretty much does everything by the book."

"Is he any good?"

"There've been no official complaints, so far as I could find," Rencke said. "But I talked to a couple of people who've worked for him. It was no lovefest."

McGarvey had seen a lot of guys like that in the Agency, pompous, arrogant three-piece-suit assholes who very often did land the promotions to a big desk at the Building even though they were lousy field officers, because they were good administrators.

"Makes you wonder why Updegraf took the chance of hiring an outside gun when he could have partnered with Gloria to go after Liu," McGarvey said.

Rencke was a bit shocked. "I didn't think she's that kind of a woman."

"I don't mean go to bed with Liu and the others the general was spying on, but she could have gotten into the club scene, and when Liu picked her up—which he would have—she could have played hard to get. He could have had someone else as his whore, and Gloria would have been one of the hangers-on."

"I never thought of it that way," Rencke admitted.

They pulled into the New College parking lot and Rencke drove over to where McGarvey had parked his Nissan Pathfinder.

"Apparently neither did Updegraf," McGarvey said. "What do we know about him?"

"He and Perry had to be like oil and water. Perry comes from a well-to-do family, while Updegraf was Midwest blue collar, Wisconsin, but he was just as ambitious as his boss. I talked to an old friend of his who's working the Middle East desk, said Updegraf fancied himself as the new James Bond. They were stationed together in Riyadh a few years ago, and eighteen months into the assignment Updegraf had to boogie out of Dodge in the middle of the night because he'd been caught in flagrante delicto with one of the wives of a prince he was trying to burn."

"A lady's man."

"Yeah," Rencke said. He took a small DVD player out of the glove compartment and gave it to McGarvey. "The personnel records of Perry and the people in his shop, plus everything we could dig up about Shahrzad, and what little we know about General Liu's presence in Mexico City. It's a one-play-only disk that erases itself as you watch it. It'll also erase automatically if someone tries to play it without the password, which is your Social Security number backward, every third digit deleted."

McGarvey had to grin despite the situation. "Who dreams up this stuff?"

"I did this one," Rencke admitted, a big smile on his face, his red hair even wilder than normal. "Do you want us to take care of your travel arrangements? Perry could have someone meet you at the airport. We could fly you down military."

"I don't want anybody except for you to know that I'm in Mexico," McGarvey said. "At least not for the moment. Not Dick, not McCann, and not Perry. Especially not McCann or Perry. And keep the housekeepers out of it too." Housekeeping, which was part of the Directorate of Operations, kept track of everyone working in the field with or for the CIA. It was an extremely sensitive section that had been completely devastated by Angleton a number of years ago. In its new form no one person had control over the entire list. Still, McGarvey did not want some suit in Langley looking over his shoulder.

"You going to carry, or do you want me to arrange something down there?"

"I'm going in on a diplomatic courier passport with a sealed pouch," McGarvey said. "If Katy calls, tell her what you can without worrying her too badly."

"Do you have a time frame?"

Once he had decided to go down there and take a look, he had asked himself the same question. He shook his head. "Not a clue."

"Take care," Rencke said.

"In the meantime I want you to dig as deeply as you can into whatever MOIS database you can hack. I want to know if there's even a hint that the woman might be a double. Her story has so many holes, it's bound to be at least partly true. I want your best guess."

"Anything specific you want me to look for?"

"She left her money behind," McGarvey said. "After everything she went through it's kind of odd, unless she doesn't need it. Maybe she's rich after all."

"Anything else?"

"Yeah. The other guy with Liu and Updegraf. Whoever he was scared the hell out of her. See if you can come up with any connection between Liu and someone who knew Shahrzad or her family."

"You're thinking about an Iranian connection down there, too?"

"Anything's possible."

SIXTEEN

CASEY KEY

Katy wasn't in the house when McGarvey got back from town, but when he went up to their bedroom he spotted her through the window. She was sitting reading a book in the gazebo, waiting for him. He watched her for a minute, marveling at his fantastic luck for having her in his life.

She had picked the wrong man to marry, though to hear her tell it she'd never had a moment of doubt. She was proud of him for what he had accomplished, even though in her heart of hearts she wanted to disagree with a world in which violence was sometimes a necessary evil with which to combat an even larger, mindless evil.

Her biggest complaint was his leaving her. She once told him that it was at times like those when she thought she might be losing her mind with worry. She'd been around long enough as the wife of a CIA officer to read about and attend more funerals than she ever wanted to. "One of these days it might be me wearing black with someone like Dick Adkins holding my elbow at graveside," she said. They were having after-dinner drinks at a trendy Georgetown restaurant. "Frankly, my dear, I don't look good in black."

He remembered that particular conversation just at this moment because of his answer. He'd been on the trail of an al-Qaida agent who'd planed a terrorist strike on the U.S., and at that moment he was fairly certain of what and whom he was up against, and of how he wanted the operation to play out. "No black for you this time, Katy," he said.

"Kathleen," she replied, a hint of crossness in her voice. But then she forced herself to relax. "Hell, I've just got the vapors seeing you off again."

He reached across the table for her hand. "I won't tell you not to worry. But I'll be back. Promise."

"I'll hold you to it," she said.

This time around, however, McGarvey wasn't as sure of what he was getting himself into. They'd already lost one man down there, and there was no knowing at this stage just how entrenched Liu and the Guoanbu were. There was a great possibility that whoever went up against the Chinese next could be running into a buzz saw.

And there was something else. Something that McGarvey couldn't quite get a handle on. Yet it was there, just over the horizon, watching, waiting, expecting someone like him to come.

Katy suddenly looked up, then turned and spotted him in the window. She waved, put the book down, and started to get to her feet, but he opened the French doors and went out onto the veranda.

"Stay there," he called to her. "I'll be right down."

She shaded her eyes. "Okay."

"Do you want anything?"

"Just a good explanation why I missed lunch," she replied, a touch of wariness in her voice.

He went across the room to his walk-in closet, slid a set of hinged drawers aside, and opened the small floor safe, from which he took a small black leather bag of the type diplomatic couriers usually carried strapped to their wrists aboard commercial air flights. It was his field operations bag, what in the old days he'd called his "go-to-hell kit." Inside were several passports, U.S., Canadian, and French, all identifying him under work names as a diplomatic representative. The bag also held ten thousand dollars in cash, in U.S. dollars and euros; credit cards to match the passports; and his pistol, a Walther PPK in the 9 mm version, two spare magazines of ammunition, and a quick-draw holster that could be worn at the small of his back or at the inside of his left ankle.

On the inside of the satchel, a fine mesh lead alloy screen had been sewn between the fabric lining and the leather, which made airport screening devices useless. In most instances traveling under a diplomatic passport excused him from body and baggage searches. The mesh was just another precaution.

He took the case down to the garage, where he added the DVD player Rencke had given him, locked it, and put it in the backseat of his Nissan. The he got a bottle of good Pinot Grigio from the wine safe in the kitchen pantry, opened it, got two glasses, and went down to the gazebo.

She'd put her book aside, and when she saw her husband coming with the bottle of wine and glasses, she looked away for a second, vexed. "Whenever you show up down here with wine and that look, I know something's up that I won't like."

"Am I that obvious?" McGarvey asked. He kissed her upturned cheek, and poured a glass of wine for her.

"Transparent," she said.

"Sorry about lunch, sweetheart," he said. "Couldn't be helped."

Her lips compressed and she nodded. "When are you leaving?"

"In the morning."

"Maybe I should fly up with you," she suggested hopefully. "While you're out at Langley doing your thing I could see Audie, and take Elizabeth shopping or something. Afterward you could join us and we could make a nice minivacation out of it. What do you say?"

McGarvey shook his head. "Not this time, sweetheart."

Her face fell. "Washington is just a way point."

He nodded.

"You promised that you wouldn't get involved with anything unless it was important to both of us. Is it?"

"I don't know," he admitted. But his gut feeling was as strong as ever, and Rencke's programs were lavender and deepening. "I'm just going to take a closer look, and maybe turn around and come home."

"Any hint where you're going?"

He shook his head.

"How long you'll be gone?"

"With any luck only a few days," McGarvey told her.

"And without any luck?"

He shrugged. "I don't know, Katy. Could be a week, maybe longer. Maybe even a lot longer."

"Goddamn it to hell!" Katy shouted. She jumped up, threw her glass away, shattering it against the railing, wine flying everywhere, and stormed out of the gazebo and down the thirty yards to the wooden dock.

It wasn't often she had these outbursts because of his profession, but he'd learned the hard way that when she did it was best to let her work it out on her own. She would calm down, and they could talk it out.

Early in their marriage he'd been sent to Santiago, Chile, to assassinate a general who'd been responsible for the torture and deaths of thousands of people, and who, if he had lived, would possibly have become president of Chile and would have killed even more of his people.

When he'd come back to Washington he'd learned that the operation had been called off at the last moment, but it had been too late to stop him. It had been a setup to get rid of him, and he'd been fired from the Company.

That afternoon when he walked through the front door of his house, bag in hand, Katy had been there in the stair hall with an ultimatum.

She'd had no idea where he'd been or what he had been doing, but she'd had enough of him running around the world at a moment's notice, leaving her to sit at home half out of her mind with worry and fear. It was her or the CIA. He would have to make the choice.

He'd been mentally fried at that moment. Not only had he killed the general, he'd been forced to kill the man's wife, putting a bullet in her head when she and her husband were in the act of making love, lest she sound the alarm and bring the guards down on him. It didn't matter when he stood just inside the door facing Katy that the general's wife had been just as responsible for the killing and torture as her husband, because he didn't know it then. All he knew was that he had gunned down two people, one of them a woman, in cold blood, he'd been fired from his job, and the one person on earth whom he desperately needed to make it right was treating him as if he were a criminal who needed to change his ways or get out.

His marriage was new enough that he hadn't learned how to react when his wife threw a tantrum. He'd turned around without a word and walked out the door. By the next morning he was on an Air France flight to Paris, and then to Switzerland.

He and Katy had been separated for a lot of years as their only daughter was growing up. And looking back, those wasted years made no sense to him. They had always loved each other; they'd just not been able to keep in step. They hadn't learned how.

After a few minutes he went down to the dock and stood beside her, watching a snowy egret fishing for its dinner on the opposite bank.

She looked up and smiled wistfully. "I was thinking about the time when you came home after one of your . . . trips, and I told you it was me or the CIA."

"I was thinking about it too," McGarvey said. "We were pretty stupid."

"I'm not that dumb anymore, Kirk," she said, turning to him.

"Neither am I," McGarvey said, and he took her in his arms.

"It was a long time ago."

"Yes, it was."

Katy looked deeply into his eyes, and after a moment she nodded. "I wonder what would happen if I threw down the gauntlet now?"

"I'd probably turn down the trip," McGarvey told her.

"Thank you for that much," she said. "Please be careful and come back to me."

SEVENTEEN

MEXICO CITY

McGarvey had booked a pair of first-class seats on a United Airbus A320, leaving Dulles at 3:00 p.m., just forty minutes after his flight from Sarasota had touched down. His diplomatic passport identifying him as Thomas Higby had not been given a second glance, and he'd been allowed to step around the security arch with his leather bag in hand. At the counter he'd checked one hanging bag with his clothes, which was tagged with a diplomatic status, and since he'd booked two seats he wasn't bothered with a neighbor.

As soon as they were in the air and had reached cruising altitude the captain turned off the Fasten Seat Belt sign and announced that portable electronic devices including cell phones would be okay to use. McGarvey ordered a Martell cognac neat from the stewardess, and after she'd brought it he took out Rencke's DVD and powered it up.

The personnel files on Gil Perry and the people working for him out of the embassy didn't contain much of any interest besides what Rencke had told him, and from what he'd gathered from Perry himself and from the woman. The entire station seemed to be composed of field officers who had their own agendas. Everyone was looking for the "big score," as Updegraf had called it. Perry was looking to make his mark so he could take the next step toward becoming DDCI. Chauncy wanted his own station, and he was willing to push Perry at every opportunity, hoping that his boss would make a career-busting mistake. Updegraf had been up to something that no one else knew about. And the only reason Gloria Ibenez had apparently made no splash was because Perry hated her for some reason.

It was one piece of the puzzle that McGarvey didn't quite understand. The Gloria he knew was an extremely ambitious woman, who had never let anyone or anything stand in her way. She wanted big things for herself—though what exactly those were wasn't quite clear—so why she wasn't demanding a transfer out of a station she had to know was a dead end for her was puzzling, unless, like Chauncy, she was pushing Perry into making a big mistake. It was possible that she was hoping for a COS whom she could work to her advantage.

The dossiers on General Liu and Shahrzad contained almost nothing of any use beyond what McGarvey had already learned at the Longboat Key interview, except that the FBI had twice reported its suspicions of the general to the government in Beijing through the Chinese embassy in Washington. The first time was in New York, when Liu had been working with the Chinese delegation to the UN. Within a few days he had been recalled to China, only to surface one year later in Washington at the Chinese embassy. The Bureau again sent a warning to Beijing that Liu was suspected of being a murderer. This time the general left the U.S. apparently without being recalled.

McGarvey looked up from a photograph of the general displayed on the tiny screen. It made no sense. If the Bureau had twice suspected Liu of being a murderer, and both times had been able to convince the State Department that there was enough of a case that a warning should be transmitted to Beijing, why hadn't Liu been declared persona non grata and kicked out of the country? The balance-of-trade issue had been on the table, and it was possible that the White House had not wanted to add any fuel to the firestorm over something so relatively minor as a suspected killer. Liu hadn't actually been *proved* guilty of anything.

Updegraf had probably been assassinated by the Mexicans on Liu's orders. It was also likely that Updegraf had found out something about the general and what he was doing in Mexico. It was this last business that apparently worried Adkins enough to send Rencke to Florida to ask for McGarvey's help. Perry and his crowd were evidently incapable of finding out what was going on, and if Adkins sent a flying team down there to help out, even a half-blind man watching our embassy would know something big was in the wind.

McGarvey stared at Liu's image on the small screen for a long time. Shahrzad had seen him and Updegraf together at the compound in Chihuahua, and more than anything else that had frightened her enough to bail out, leaving her hard-won money behind. He had to wonder what she'd expected to say to Updegaf when they met again.

He skipped back to the beginning of the disk, but the files had been erased and the screen stayed blank.

"Would you like another drink, sir?" the pretty flight attendant asked at his shoulder.

He glanced up at her. "Sure, why not," he said. He had a feeling he was going to be away from home a lot longer than he'd first guessed.

Aeropuerto Internacional Benito Juárez was a madhouse when McGarvey cleared passport control a few minutes after seven in the evening local. Mexicans referred to their capital city as D.F., Distrito Federal, just as many Americans referred to theirs as D.C., and the main airport was every bit as busy as Dulles usually was on an early weekday evening. Once he retrieved his check-through bag, he paid his cab fare at the teller window just outside the customs area, and took his receipt out to the sitio at curbside, where he climbed in the backseat of the lead cab.

"Hotel Four Seasons," he told the driver, and settled back for the ride into the city. He had some serious history here with Russian KGB General Valentin Baranov. Although that had been more than fifteen years ago, nothing seemed to have changed; there were still the same cardboard and shipping-container slums to pass through on the half-hour trip into the city; the same burned-out hulks of cars and trucks lying along the road; the same frenetic pace; and nearly the same pall of exhaust and smoke of burning garbage thick in the air.

Despite the cab's air-conditioning McGarvey felt a little tickle at the back of his throat from the foul air, and a shortness of breath from the altitude. Twenty-two million people lived in the D.F., which sprawled across a dry lake bed above seven thousand feet and was ringed by snowcapped mountains, which tended to keep the pollution in place. The locals never seemed to notice, but most visitors did. At some tourist spots around town there were vending machines that sold a couple of minutes of oxygen for a few pesos.

At the hotel, McGarvey gave the driver a small tip, and checked in under his own passport. The arrival of another courier traveling under a diplomatic passport wouldn't be flagged, but if he'd checked into a hotel instead of going straight to the embassy a few eyebrows might have been raised.

He was given a small suite on the hotel's eighth floor that looked down into a pleasant inner courtyard with a fountain. From here he was only a few blocks from the American embassy in the city's historical downtown district.

When he was settled in, he took a quick shower, changed clothes, and went back downstairs, where outside the bellman summoned him a cab.

"Where would you like to be taken, sir?"

"I want to take a look at a house up in Tizapan San Angel," McGarvey told the bellman. "I want to make sure it's in a good neighborhood before I meet the agent tomorrow."

"That's a very nice neighborhood, señor," the bellman said as a taxi pulled up. He opened the door. "Do you have an address?"

"It's just off the Avenida Rio Magdalena," McGarvey said, giving the man a tip. "I'll direct the driver."

The bellman said something to the driver, and closed the door.

The cabbie merged with traffic, and a couple blocks later passed the modernistic U.S. embassy. Thirty minutes later they came to an area of graceful hillside homes in the Spanish hacienda style, many of them behind tall stucco walls, with winding cobblestoned side streets and far less traffic. The Chinese embassy occupied one of these upscale houses: four stories behind a tall stucco wall topped with iron spikes and secured by a tall wrought-iron gate.

"Slow down," McGarvey told the driver. "I think it's somewhere around here."

The cabbie did as he was told and they passed the embassy at a crawl. The roof of the main building bristled with antennae and satellite dishes. Lights were on in most of the windows, and perhaps two dozen cars were parked along the curb on both sides of the street. Evidently there was something going on inside, a diplomatic reception or party.

Passing the gate, McGarvey could see a second, much smaller, building to the right of the main house, and the edge of another, perhaps a garage, around back. A man dressed in dark clothing stood just inside the gate, and he raised something in his hand to point at the cab. McGarvey got the impression it might have been a camera or perhaps a Starlight Scope, because the man held it to his eyes.

McGarvey turned his face away from the window. "I was mistaken," he told the driver. "I'll just have to wait until morning. Take me back to the hotel."

"As you wish, señor," the cabbie said, and at the next corner he made a U-turn.

Back in his suite McGarvey ordered a light dinner and a couple bottles of Dos Equis beer from room service. While he waited he used his sat phone to call Rencke.

"I'm at 805 at the Four Seasons. I need you to send me a few things."

"Dick wants to know what you think about the girl," Rencke said.

"Does anybody know I'm here?"

"No."

"Tell Dick I'm still working on it," McGarvey said. "I'll get back to him in a couple of days. Are you and Perry still in Florida?"

"Perry left a half hour after you did, and I got home last night," Rencke said. "Toni knows what she's doing."

"Okay, this is what I want sent down here."

EIGHTEEN

□

D. F., COLONIA CUAUHTÉMOC

The D.F. was divided into sixteen areas called *delegaciones,* and four hundred neighborhoods called *colonias.* The U.S. embassy was on Paseo de la Reforma in the Colonia Cuauhtémoc, which was in the heart of the modern skyscraper and business district downtown.

McGarvey had spent the day arranging for a rental Toyota SUV and finding his way around the huge city, going to the Wild Stallion and some of the other clubs Shahrzad had mentioned, including the Doll House, where she had danced for General Liu.

Driving, especially downtown, was mostly a matter of nerves. Mexican drivers didn't understand or respect the notion of right of way, and most of them apparently believed they were immortal.

He was parked across the street from the chancellery at a quarter till five in the afternoon, as the first of the day-shift cars emerged from the embassy grounds through the tall iron gate manned 24/7 by armed security guards in black uniforms with bloused boots. But it wasn't until nearly seven thirty that Gloria Ibenez, driving a bright yellow Mini Cooper, roared through the gate, tossed a cheery wave at the guards, darted across three lanes of traffic, and flew up toward the Zona Rosa.

McGarvey managed to keep up with her, while staying two or three cars back, as she threaded through traffic, sometimes slowing down so that she would just make a light before it changed red, other times turning off the main boulevard for a few blocks before returning to it.

She was obviously trying to shake a tail, although McGarvey was pretty sure that she hadn't spotted him; there was just too much after-work traffic, and every other car seemed to be a gunmetal gray SUV of one Japanese make or another. But she was using tradecraft, which meant she was concerned that someone might be following her.

Gloria's apartment was in Lomas Altas, not far from downtown, but instead of going directly home, she pulled in to a small shopping center and parked in front of a supermarket.

McGarvey pulled in a few rows back, but left the engine running as he waited. The shopping center could have been in any city in the U.S. The Sumesa supermarket was flanked by a dry cleaners, a Postal Mart, a florist, a liquor store, a pharmacy, a martial arts studio, and a Hallmark card shop. On the corner, but detached from the mall itself, was a McDonald's. The shops were busy at this hour, men and women in business attire stopping after work.

The hill rose steeply behind the mall, and perched above were several modern-looking three-story garden apartment buildings that were surrounded by a riot of flowers and trees and vines. The balconies all faced back toward the city center, and McGarvey suspected the view was very good.

Gloria came back to her car fifteen minutes later with two bags of groceries. She was dressed in a very short khaki skirt with a white, scoop-necked T-shirt and sandals, her dark hair up in a bun at the back. She looked very fit: lithe, like an athlete or a dancer, with long, shapely muscular legs and well-defined arms from working out. She wore some sort of a heavy gold chain around her long neck that contrasted well with her dark skin.

She was a Cuban-born American who'd defected with her father and mother from Havana when she was only thirteen. Her mother had been killed in the escape and she'd been raised by her father, a former Cuban Air Force general, and then by an aunt and uncle in Miami. Her father had gone to work as a consultant for the CIA, the FBI, and several other governmental agencies, and after Gloria had graduated from law school and done a stint with the Navy's Judge Advocate's Office, she'd been recruited by the CIA.

Two years later, she met and married another Cuban-born American CIA officer, and they'd been stationed under deep cover in Havana. Six months into their assignment, her husband had been captured by Cuban intelligence and tortured to death. She'd managed to escape, but at thirty-three she still had not remarried.

She put her groceries in her car, and when she got behind the wheel

McGarvey caught a lingering glimpse of her thigh under the lights, and it came to him that she was posing for someone. Deliberately using her sex as a distraction. But so far as he could tell no one else had followed her here, so he wondered whom she was posing for, unless it was just a habit she'd gotten herself into.

Out of the parking lot she merged with traffic, and one block later she passed a large house situated behind a tall stucco wall, its driveway guarded by heavy iron gates. The writing on a brass plaque beside the gates was in Arabic and Roman script. The place was the Iranian embassy, and at the next corner Gloria turned to the right on a narrow road that wound its way up into the hill above the embassy and the shopping center to the garden apartments. She parked in one of the carports and took her groceries down a steep path to one of the first-floor apartments with an entry on an open walkway, and went inside as McGarvey pulled into the visitors' parking lot and shut off the engine.

By all accounts Gloria had stopped playing by the rules the day her husband had been killed. She was branded a troublemaker, who did not know how to work as a team player, but her father, General Marti, still had some influence in Washington, and she was good at her job. She'd been back to Cuba twice, at great personal risk, and last year she'd helped McGarvey find and kill Osama bin Laden. The Company owed her some slack, though Perry couldn't agree.

It was one of the reasons McGarvey had come here. He needed someone who was grounded in the D.F. He instinctively distrusted Perry, who, if there was any justice, wouldn't rise any further in the CIA, and he didn't think he could go to Chauncy, who had his own agenda—which left Gloria, the odd duck out.

But there was a darker reason he'd come seeking her help, one that he had skirted in his mind as Shahrzad was telling her story. But the thought had coalesced the moment Otto had told him that Gloria was here in the D.F.

He was startled out of his dark thoughts when a jet-black Porsche Carrera roared up the driveway and pulled into the carport. A handsome young man and attractive woman got out and went hand in hand to one of the second-floor apartments, their laughter trailing behind them. They were obviously very happy.

A deep sadness came over McGarvey all of a sudden, and he almost started the car and drove back to the hotel. He could get a flight to Tampa first thing in the morning and Katy could come up from Sarasota to get him, and he could return to being a retired sometime college instructor, sometime sailor, and full-time husband. He didn't belong here, because in order to unravel the mess Updegraf had left them, he was going to have to seriously meddle in some people's lives. When he was finished nothing would ever be the same for them again. They might never be happy again.

But there were too many things that weren't adding up in his mind, and the list kept growing. Like right now. Shahrzad was an Iranian, and Gloria's apartment was perched above the Iranian embassy. Coincidence? He didn't believe in them. Never had.

He got out of the car and took the path down to Gloria's apartment. But still he hesitated for just a moment before he rang the bell. He had a dozen questions in his mind, none of which he could ask her.

She came to the door barefoot but still in her khaki skirt and blouse, something in her hand behind her back. A host of emotions crossed her face in the space of an eye blink: total surprise, happiness, and for just the briefest of instants, perhaps fear.

"Hello," McGarvey said.

"My God, was it you in the gray Toyota?"

McGarvey was a little surprised. "You spotted me." He said it as a statement not a question.

She nodded, this time in plain wonderment. "Don't just stand there. Come inside." She stepped back to let him pass and reached up with her free hand to touch his shoulder.

Her apartment was open and very modern, with floor-to-ceiling sliding glass doors opening to a long veranda that looked down toward the city. Some good Picasso reproductions were hung on the wall, and several bookcases were filled with what looked like a mixture of Spanish novels and law books. The furniture was Danish modern teak, with thick faux fur rugs in white. A large flat-panel television was perched on a low stand that held several pieces of electronic equipment including a satellite receiver, DVD player, and surround sound.

"I saw you when I came out of the embassy." She smiled. "I thought I had lost you a couple of times, so I stopped at the mall to see who you were and what you'd do. But the windows were tinted so I couldn't make out your face."

"That was damned good work in that traffic. Were you expecting somebody?"

She nodded. She took her hand away from the small of her back to reveal a 9 mm Beretta. "We've all been on edge since Louis bought it. We still don't know why he was killed, or if one of us will be next."

"That's why I'm here," McGarvey told her.

"Thank God," Gloria said. She laid the pistol on the counter separating the kitchen from the main room. "Does Perry know you're here?"

"No, and we're going to keep it that way for now."

"Thank you for small favors. The man's a complete idiot, and Tom Chauncy has got his nose so far up Perry's ass it's a wonder he ever comes up for air. Louis was the only halfway decent officer we had down here."

She suddenly stopped talking and threw her arms around him, holding him very tightly, her face buried in his chest.

For just a second McGarvey felt an almost overwhelming sense of disgust with himself for what he was going to ask her to do, but then he put his arms around her and held her.

"My God, it's so good to see you again," looking up at him. "Will you please kiss me?"

"I don't think that's such a good idea."

She smiled. "I guess not. Just hold me for now. It's enough."

NINETEEN

COLONIA LOMAS ALTAS

McGarvey sat at the kitchen counter while Gloria opened a bottle of Don Julio Anejo tequila and made them margaritas with a lot of ice in tall salt-rimmed glasses. "While in Rome do as the Romans do," she said, looking at him from across the counter as she raised her glass.

"Good," McGarvey said, taking a drink.

"So, exactly what are you doing here?" she asked.

"Updegraf was working someone in the Chinese embassy that probably got him killed. We want to know why."

Gloria shrugged. "He was just a code clerk. The Chinese connection probably doesn't mean a thing," she said. "But what I want to know is what are you doing here at my apartment?"

"I need your help."

Her face lit up, but there was a hint of wariness in her eyes. "Okay," she said carefully. "But no one else at the embassy is supposed to know about it. Right?"

"That's right."

"But you're not here on your own. You're supposed to be retired, which means they sent Otto to ask you to come back, and he had a good reason. Who was it, Mr. Adkins?"

"You don't need to know that yet," McGarvey said. "In fact, you might never need to know. I want your help, no questions asked."

"Dangerous?"

"It got Updegraf killed."

She nodded without hesitation, her eyes bright, a half smile on her full lips. "But you knew I'd say yes before you asked me," she said, half teasing. "And what do I get out of it?"

McGarvey waited. Using a mark's fantasies against him or her was one of the oldest bits of tradecraft in the field officer's handbook. The shrinks called it transference, when the mark's fear of being discovered as a traitor turned into love for her handler. He became the savior.

Gloria had studied the book, but her knowledge was no defense. Her smile faded and she nodded again. "Okay."

"What did Updegraf tell you about the code clerk he was trying to burn?"

"I didn't know anything about it until Gil handed me the file with Louis's encounter sheets. But the guy wasn't worth any real effort. It's still bothering me. Louis shouldn't have been going after some small fry like that."

"He never said anything to you about it, about going to the clubs?"

Gloria's brow knitted. "I don't know what you're talking about. What clubs?"

"The sex clubs. Did he ever mention a place called the Wild Stallion?"

Gloria stifled a small laugh. "No," she said. "But I know about them, of course. Half the guys in the embassy, especially the married ones, hang out downtown. Usually in the Zona Rosa or Polanco."

"You've never been?"

She laughed out loud. "Of course not."

"What do you do for entertainment?"

"I certainly don't hang out at those kinds of places," she shot back. "The symphony orchestra here is world-class, and the ballet and theaters are first-rate. All in Spanish, of course."

"Dates?"

"Sometimes," she replied warily. "But if you're asking if I'm seeing anyone special, the answer is no." She started to say something else, but bit it off.

McGarvey looked away for just a moment, unable to take the next step with her. But if the notion he'd come up with had any chance of working, Gloria would have to become one leg of a dicey triangle that would be as disgusting as it was delicate.

"The code clerk is the key," he said, turning back to her.

"I told you that he's a small fry."

"You're probably right, but I think Updegraf wanted to burn him in order to get to a much bigger prize."

"Did you come up with something already?"

"He was meeting the guy at the Wild Stallion, probably buying him women."

"None of that was in the encounter file that Gil gave to me," Gloria said. "I'm supposed to be looking down Louis's track here in the D.F., but there isn't much to go on. According to his file he was meeting the clerk at a wireless coffee shop a block and a half from the Chinese embassy, but I haven't been able to confirm that. And Louis's wife went back to the States, so I got to toss his apartment, but I came up empty there too."

"The club is the next step."

"You want me to go to that place?"

"We'll go together. Tonight."

"And look for what?"

"I don't know," McGarvey admitted. "Maybe a reaction?"

COLONIA ZONA ROSA

From the carved oak front door, the Club Wild Stallion could have been the office of a group of high-priced lawyers, or a boutique selling haute couture to fashionable women, not a sex club. A very small brass plaque engraved with a plain CWS above a stylized stallion reared up on its hind legs and the number 84 was the only indication that the elegant three-story brown brick building was anything other than what it was.

They had driven over from Gloria's apartment in McGarvey's Toyota, and when they pulled up in front of the club a valet in a red vest came out to park their car.

"Do you think you'll see anybody you know here?" McGarvey asked her.

She had changed into a short black dress with almost no back and a plunging neckline. "It's possible someone from the embassy will be here."

"Perry or Chauncy?"

She laughed. "Not those two."

"Welcome to the Club Wild Stallion," the valet parker said. He gave McGarvey a ticket.

Just inside the door McGarvey paid a one-hundred-dollar club membership to a pretty receptionist seated at a desk. "This will be good for one year, sir," she said pleasantly. She was young, perhaps eighteen or nineteen, and she was Oriental, probably Japanese.

Through an inner door, they found themselves in a large, dimly lit room, with a long bar to the right, and small tables facing a stage across from a fairly good-sized dance floor. The hum of conversations from perhaps fifty or sixty people, most of them at the tables, nearly half of them scantily clad girls and women, was a low, underlying drone.

A pretty Mexican waitress in a topless costume and spike heels showed them to a table near the dance floor. "Welcome to the Wild Stallion," she said. "Our next show begins any minute. Maybe I bring you a drink?"

"Champagne," McGarvey said. "Dom Pérignon. A good year."

"Yes, sir," the waitress said, and she left.

"Do you see the age of most of these girls?" Gloria asked. "They're just kids. Let's get out of here, Kirk."

Most of the men were middle-aged or older, and although the majority of them were probably Mexicans, there were a fair number of gringos. All of them seemed to be prosperous. But the girls were mostly in their teens. It reminded McGarvey of some of the clubs in Taiwan where well-to-do Europeans went to have sex with young girls. The look on the men's faces was sickening.

"Have you spotted anyone you know?" he asked.

"Not yet," Gloria said. "What the hell are we doing here?"

McGarvey leaned closer. "This is one of the places Updegraf hung out. I want to see what goes on and who shows up, so keep your eyes open."

"You think Perry or Chauncy might come through the door?"

McGarvey shrugged. But it wouldn't have surprised him if either man had been there. His primary target, though, was General Liu. If Shahrzad had been telling the truth, this was one of the places the man liked to frequent.

Their champagne came, a minute later all the lights went out, and suddenly Debussy's "Clair de Lune" began to play from a piano somewhere to the left, and a soft red light illuminated the stage. A large bed had been set up in the middle of the stage, a mirror suspended above it at an angle so the audience would have no trouble seeing what would be happening.

A short, slender Japanese girl who could have been the twin of the receptionist came out onstage. She was dressed in a clinging silk nightgown that fluoresced in the dim light. She looked out at the audience and held out her hand as if she was lost and was asking for help.

After a beat, a man who looked as if he could be a gymnast, dressed only in a pair of tight-fitting jeans, his chest bare, came out onstage, spotted the girl, and went to her. She turned, hesitated for a moment before she gave the audience a big smile, and then fell into the gymnast's arms.

They embraced for what seemed a long time, and when they parted the gymnast ripped the nightgown off the woman's body with a flourish, shoved her back onto the bed, then pulled off his jeans to reveal an almost impossibly large erect penis.

Some of the girls in the audience cheered and a few of the men laughed and clapped as the gymnast mounted the Japanese girl and began to have intercourse, slowly at first, then with increasing speed and force.

"Do you think this is sexy?" Gloria asked across the table.

"No, not at all," McGarvey said. He was of mixed feelings thinking about Shahrzad in this place, doing these things. Her father had tossed her into the ring with Baranov when she was only fifteen, and ever since that time she'd apparently been used by a series of men, so that now she was probably hardened to such things. Yet she could have walked away long before she'd met and fallen in love with a CIA officer. For Updegraf, however, his feelings were anything but mixed. On the surface, at least, the man had been a son of a bitch, and quite possibly had deserved what he got.

But there was so much more that they didn't know. Whispers around the edges, coming from dark places with hidden meanings. Nothing was as it seemed to be.

One of the men from the audience got up and led a girl across the dance floor and through a door to the right of the stage, as the couple on the bed continued to have sex, and the woman began to moan.

"Louis was a bastard just like every other man," Gloria said under her breath. "Let's get out of here. I've had enough."

TWENTY

COLONIA LOMAS ALTAS

On the way back to Gloria's apartment she sat hunched in the corner silently watching the traffic, which had started to pick up. Mexicans usually started late: drinks around eight in the evening, dinner around ten, and then the clubs really came alive around midnight. It wasn't even ten when McGarvey drove up the hill to her apartment above the Iranian embassy and parked in one of the guest spots.

"I'd invite you in, but I know you'd refuse," Gloria said. She was subdued. "Let's go for a walk. There's a jogging path that runs just below the road. Nice view."

"Okay."

She slipped out of her heels and took McGarvey's arm, and they headed past the apartment buildings and started down a blacktop path that wound its way around the hills a few meters below the road. Every so often there was a park bench, and sometimes the glittering night view of the city stretched out below was fabulous.

"I've never met your wife," she said. "But if your daughter Elizabeth is any indication, she must be lovely."

"She is," McGarvey told her.

"Lucky lady."

They walked for a while in silence, but the evening was getting chilly, so McGarvey took off his jacket and put it around her shoulders.

"Thank you."

"You're welcome."

She stopped. "Look, I'm not sorry, you know."

"For what?"

"For falling in love with you. That'll never change. But I promise to stop throwing myself at you."

McGarvey smiled despite the situation, despite what he wanted her to do. Updegraf had nothing on him. "I was flattered," he admitted to her. "But this way is going to be a lot easier on both of us."

She laughed lightly, but then became serious again. "Growing up in Cuba my poor mother never knew what to do with me. She tried to teach me the proper manners for a lady, when all I wanted to do was fight with the boys. When I was twelve or thirteen, she took me to a beauty salon downtown where I got my first do. My hair had only been trimmed, never cut, so by then it was most of the way down my back. When we got home that afternoon, my father told me how beautiful I looked. He said I'd been transformed from a tomboy to a young lady."

Gloria looked across the valley toward the lights of the skyscrapers downtown.

"The next morning I got up early, before my mother, took a pair of scissors into the bathroom, and cut my hair so it was as short as a boy's. When I showed up at the breakfast table wearing jeans and a T-shirt, my mother almost fainted, but she didn't say a word about my hair. She never said anything about it, and after that I let it grow, started to wear makeup, and even went on chaperoned dates."

"But it was never the same after that, was it," McGarvey said. He'd had the same sort of falling-out with his sister. When their parents died, he inherited the ranch in western Kansas, which he sold over his sister's objections. They never spoke about it again; in fact, they hadn't spoken at all in years.

"A few months later the situation between my father and Castro had become intolerable, so my father stole a light plane and took me and my mother to Key West. Only we ran out of gas and the plane crashed in the strait just offshore. My mother drowned." Gloria's eyes were filling. "I never got to tell her how sorry I was that I'd disappointed her."

"Did you tell your father?"

Gloria laughed. "Oh, him. He was always too busy after that. For the first couple of years I was pretty much on my own, with just a house-keeper in the apartment in Washington. But then I was sent to live with an aunt and uncle in Miami. I don't know which was worse. The moment I could get out and go to college on my own, I left."

"Were you ever resentful?" McGarvey asked.

She looked at him. "What do you mean?"

"Your childhood didn't go the way you'd wanted it to go, your father uprooted you from your life and your friends in Havana, and because of it your mother was killed, and then when you got to the States you were all but left on your own. Maybe there were times when you just wanted to say fuck it."

She smiled wistfully. "You sound like the Company shrinks." She nodded. "Damned right I wanted to say fuck it, but I was usually too busy doing something whenever the idea came up."

"Why law school?" McGarvey asked. Nothing he'd learned about her background so far pointed toward a law degree.

"I never wanted to be a lawyer, if that's what you mean," she said. "But the French have a saying, Le droit mène à tout. The law leads to everything. Scratch a rich person in the States and you'll probably find a law degree."

"Is that what you wanted to be?" McGarvey wanted to know. "Rich?"

"We were rich in Cuba, relatively speaking. We lived in a big finca in the country, and I grew up having cooks and maids and gardeners and chauffeurs. And that was under Castro, so we did okay. Being poor, hav-ing to scramble for a living, never occurred to me until we came to Washington and I saw the black ghettos." She shook her head, remem-bering. "They looked at my dark skin and they thought that I was one of them. But when I looked at them, I knew that I could never be like that. I wasn't a black woman, I was cubana. There's a world of difference."

"There're plenty of poor people in Cuba."

"That's because of the regime. Anyway, I never noticed until Washington."

They walked in silence for a while, arm in arm, McGavey hyperaware of the warmth radiating off her. Whatever else she was or wasn't, she was definitely Latina. If she'd been a man she would have become a wheeler-dealer, probably a major player in the Cuban community in exile down in Miami.

"After law school why'd you go to work for the Navy?" he asked. "Nobody gets rich that way."

She smiled. "No, but you make contacts. Defense is what: a three-hundred-billion-dollar-a-year industry? I figured there'd be a place somewhere in there for me." She looked at McGarvey. "And before you ask me why I left the JAG's office to join the CIA, I'll tell you that I didn't know at the time except that I wanted to get back at the bastards who had made my father's life so impossible he had to defect."

"And kill your mother," McGarvey said softly.

"El hijo de puta," the son of a bitch, she said with feeling. But the moment of anger passed as swiftly as it had come, and again she smiled wistfully. "That was a long time ago, Kirk. And whatever my initial reasons were for joining the Company, I'm in it now for the long haul."

"Why?"

"Good question," she said, shrugging. "For the thrill of the hunt, maybe? Knowing stuff that no one else knows? Women love secrets. That's one of the things the Agency doesn't have right. They don't hire enough women spies. Why is that?"

"They don't show up at the door."

"Your daughter's a spy. Ever ask her why? Or is it just like father, like daughter? Or maybe she was rebelling against her mother for you not being there when she was growing up?"

McGarvey said nothing, wondering how she had gotten that kind of information. She must have talked to somebody or hacked the Company's mainframe. The fact that he'd been divorced from his wife all during Elizabeth's childhood was not something in his unclassified personnel file. There were damned few people still around who knew anything in depth about his background, but there were a couple.

"Or, why did you become a spy? And why have you come out of retirement again?" She stopped and looked up into his eyes. "It's really an unfair question. I am what I am for a billion separate reasons. It's the same for everyone."

"Was it the same for Updegraf?"

"Probably more him than anyone else. I don't think he really knew why he worked for the Company. At least not the real reason." She thought of something else. "Did they tell you how he was found in Chihuahua?"

"His body was dumped at the hospital's emergency-room door, an apparent suicide."

"That's a laugh," she shot back. "He had a bullet in his head all right, but that's all he had."

"I'm not following you."

"That's all that was left in front of the emergency-room door. His head. His body wasn't found until Chauncy got up there the next day. After they cut off his head, they wrapped his body in plastic and dumped it in a ditch outside of town."

"Drug dealers?"

"That's what it was made to look like."

"But you don't believe it," McGarvey said.

She shrugged her shoulders again. "I don't know what I believe."

"When we were leaving the club you said he was a bastard just like every other man. What'd you mean?"

"I don't know," she said, turning away for a moment. "But did you see the looks in those bastards' eyes? If Louis hung out there he was one of them." She turned back to McGarvey. "And what was all that about, taking me there tonight?"

"I may have to ask you to go back, alone."

"And become a whore?" she demanded.

"No. But I think we'll find some of the answers there," McGarvey said. "If you're willing to help."

"If it means being near you, yes, I'll help," Gloria said.

"Then go back to work in the morning, like usual, and don't say anything to anybody."

"When are you coming back?"

"I'm not sure. There're a few other things I have to take care of first."

"Are you hungry? I could fix us something to eat."

"Not tonight."

"A rain check?" she asked hopefully.

"Sure."

TWENTY-ONE

□

HOTEL FOUR SEASONS

It was nearly midnight by the time McGarvey got back to the hotel and took a shower while he waited for room service to send him up a sandwich and a couple bottles of beer.

He had dried off and put on one of the terry cloth robes when the waiter came up with his late supper. He signed the check and added a tip, and when the waiter was gone, he stood with a beer at the window looking out over the city, trying to put everything into perspective.

Shahrzad had been sucked into a trap of Updegraf's devising, but she hadn't gotten out until the last minute, when she realized that the man she loved had lied to her.

On the other hand, he'd come down here to devise a trap into which he was going to send a woman who loved him. She was a trained CIA field officer, but she would be leading with her heart this time.

The points of similarity between him and Updegraf made him uncomfortable, yet he could see no other practical way to get inside General Liu's circle. It was just like the old days when Darby Yarnell had surrounded himself with a lot of heavy hitters here: military leaders, senators, high-ranking intelligence officers, and the connections with the drugs and the young women. They were called "Darby's mob," and although Yarnell and everyone else figured they were the in crowd, the entire operation had been choreographed from behind the curtains by a Russian KGB general with his own very special agenda.

Maybe Updegraf had gathered his own mob, which was being directed behind the scenes by Liu. Or, possibly, it was the Chinese general who was being manipulated by someone else just offstage. Maybe the situation was like Russian nesting dolls: Open one to reveal another. Open it to expose still another, seemingly without end, the next one always concealed, always a surprise.

He had used a woman to get close to the mob that time too. In fact, it had been Yarnell's ex-wife who had burned him.

He focused on his own image in the window glass, remembering his last trip back to Soho to see how she was doing. But it had been too late by then. She had become so overwhelmed by all the horrible things that had happened to her that she had committed suicide.

Someone knocked softly at the door.

McGarvey put down his beer, got his pistol from the nightstand and, crossing the room, switched the safety catch off. Standing to one side, he looked through the security peephole. A man of average build, with thinning light brown hair, was standing back well away from the door. His jacket was open, his hands were in plain sight away from his sides, and he stood facing the peephole with a frank look. A large aluminum suitcase with wheels and a black handle was visible to his left.

McGarvey lowered his pistol, released the safety bar, and opened the door.

"Good evening, Mr. McGarvey," the man said. "Sorry about the hour, but Mr. Rencke told us that you needed this asap."

"ID," McGarvey demanded. The corridor was deserted for the moment.

The courier very carefully reached inside his jacket, pulled out a leather wallet, opened it, and held up his Washington Federal Courier Services Ltd. identification card, in the name Albert Stein. The service was one of the cover companies the DO used for covert deliveries.

McGarvey lowered his weapon and stepped aside to let Stein wheel the aluminum case in. "Anyone local know you're here?"

"No, sir," Stein said. "I checked in this evening under a work name. You didn't answer your door so I waited downstairs where I could watch the lobby entrance for you to come back."

"Good man," McGarvey said. "Anything else for me?"

"Mr. Rencke says, good hunting," Stein said. "The combination is eight, seventeen, twenty-four, thirty-five."

"Watch your back getting out of here," McGarvey warned. "There's a good chance the opposition knows I'm here."

"Yes, sir," the courier said, and McGarvey let him out, locking the door after him.

A double blind on the courier was the combination, which McGarvey had gotten from Rencke. The numbers were in reverse with one subtracted from the first and last. No one but a legitimate courier could have come up with that combination.

He put the case in the closet, then shut off the lights, put his pistol within reach on the nightstand, and stretched out on the bed. He had been hyper for the last week and hadn't been getting much sleep. Rencke showing up when he did had almost been a relief. At least he'd been able to put a reason to his unease. But now he was tired. First listening to Shahrzad's story and then being with Gloria had been draining. His thoughts were racing down a dozen dark alleys, none of which seemed to point toward any light.

Something else was happening here. Something that involved more than a high-ranking Chinese intelligence officer setting up shop. He fell asleep on that note.

TWENTY-TWO

XOCHIMILCO

In the morning after breakfast McGarvey left the hotel and walked a couple of blocks down toward the embassy, where he got a cab from the *sitio* in front of an office tower right on Paseo de la Reforma. He ordered the driver to take him to the American Airlines arrivals gate at the airport and sat back with his thoughts.

The morning was cool, the air unusually crystal clear so that the snow-capped mountains ringing the city stood out in sharp contrast against the deep blue sky and, closer at hand, the palm trees lining the traffic-choked boulevard.

He'd slept lightly, dreaming about sex all night. At first he and Katy were walking along a moonlit beach on one of the Greek isles, maybe

Santorini. They were completely alone, the evening pleasantly warm. And then she was in his arms, and they were taking off their clothes, and lying down on the sand, her legs wrapped around his waist as he entered her. A cloud momentarily covered the moon, and when it had cleared McGarvey could see that it wasn't Kathleen he was making love to. The beautiful dark-skinned woman in his arms was Gloria. He started to move away, but then she said something to him, which he couldn't make out, and they began to make passionate love. Only now they weren't alone. It was daytime and the beach was crowded with tourists, families and children all staring at the couple on the sand.

He had awakened with a start, his body bathed in sweat, the morning sun streaming through the tall windows.

The dream had been highly erotic, but he had been left with a sense that he was getting involved with an operation that was inherently wrong. His instincts after hearing Shahrzad's story at the Longboat Key house had been to turn his back on the affair and go home. Stay retired.

He'd had the same feeling last night walking with Gloria on the path below the road, and a third time this morning. He'd almost called Katy to let her know that he was on his way back to her. But something, some inner voice, had stayed his hand from picking up the phone.

Rencke said that the situation down here was going lavender. A deeper shade than before 9/11. Enough to scare a lot of people in Washington, including Dick Adkins and his number two, Dave Whittaker.

At the airport McGarvey got out of the cab at the American Airlines arrivals area, went inside, and walked over to the Hertz counter, where he rented a dark blue Saturn station wagon, and fifteen minutes later he was on his way back into the city. Gloria had spotted his Toyota yesterday, and if the opposition knew that someone had come down to poke around, they might also have noticed the SUV. It was just a simple bit of tradecraft that a man as busy as Liu might not even notice.

Instead of driving into the city center, he headed south along the Boulevard Puerto and then Rio Churubusco, both main highways in and out of the city, both heavy with traffic at this hour, especially through the numerous industrial parks.

From what he'd seen so far, the D.F. was a city at war with itself. Shiny new Mercedes and Jaguar sedans shared the roads with thirty-year-old junkers. Men in business suits, Louis Vuitton attaché cases in hand, sat at sidewalk cafés across from leftover American hippies with long hair and tie-dyed shirts playing music, their guitar cases open so that passersby could toss in a few coins. Gleaming glass-and-steel manufacturers head-quarters blocked the sun from shantytowns that sprawled just across dusty fields. And everywhere, it seemed, were women on foot, infants in their arms, trailing two or three other children behind, trudging along the side of the road. Nobody seemed to notice or care, but there was an underlying tension like the hum of high-voltage electrical lines shooting through the city that seemed as if it were about to explode into some-thing violent at any second.

In those respects at least, Mexico City had not changed since he'd been here last. The only differences were all the new skyscrapers down-town, and the even heavier traffic.

The industrialized areas started to give way to the desert until road signs directed McGarvey to the east toward the Jardines Flotantes of Xochimilco, which during the weekends was a busy tourist area, but on weekdays was very quiet. In pre-Columbian days the area was covered by a very large but shallow lake. The natives needed more land to grow crops, so they constructed barges that they filled with dirt in which they planted willows. The barges were taken out into the lake, where the wil-lows took root, right through the bottoms of the barges, to the bed of the lake. The barges became islands, on which the natives could grow their crops.

Liu's compound was at the foot of some hills that had once been the southern extremity of the barge-covered lake. Rencke had downloaded a map onto McGarvey's sat phone so the place was easy to find. The nar-row highway that followed the lakeshore ended at Liu's place, so McGar-vey pulled over to the side of the road across a narrow bay and got out of the car. The compound was about three-quarters of a mile across the water, and was guarded by white stuccoed walls, with a tall wooden gate in front, and a smaller gate at the rear, facing the lake.

It was impossible to see anything but the upper floor and red tile roof of the main house, but it was enough to tell that the compound apparently had its own generator; there were no electrical lines running from the town, and Liu was a very well connected man, because six satellite dishes, all generally pointing toward the southwest, were lined up like sentinels on the roof.

Since the road ended at the compound, any attempt to reach the front gate would be detected immediately. It might be possible to reach the place from the lake, but if he wanted to see what was going on inside he would have to either get through the rear gate or breach the wall. The best option, he figured, would be to climb up into the hills where, if he could get close enough to the walls, it would give him a vantage point to see down into the compound.

He hadn't brought binoculars with him, and it was too far to see if there were any closed-circuit television cameras or any other security measures trained on the walls or the gates, but he was certain they were there. A man in Liu's position couldn't afford to live unprotected. And there would be armed guards as well. Of that McGarvey had even less doubt.

He would find out tonight.

TWENTY-THREE

THE COMPOUND

It was a few minutes before eleven and the night was pitch black as McGarvey made a U-turn on the access road so that the Saturn was facing back toward town, the car partially concealed in some prickly brush. He was a quarter mile from the compound, which was lit up like a sports stadium. He could hear music and the sounds of people talking and laughing across the narrow bay. The general was apparently having one of the parties Shahrzad had described.

He opened the Saturn's tailgate and unlocked the aluminum trunk. He'd brought the car around to the back of the hotel, and had smuggled the suitcase down the service elevator just before ten. He'd been lucky; none of the hotel staff had spotted him. If they had, questions might have been asked. He wanted to keep his low profile as long as possible.

He took a set of black night fighter camos and hood out of the case and quickly pulled them on, transferring his Walther PPK, silencer, and two spare magazines of ammunition into one of the many zippered pockets. He blackened his face with camouflage salve, then stuffed the other pockets with a compact set of night vision stabilized binoculars, and an extremely lo-lux video camera that was capable of recording in almost no ambient light as well as in the near-infrared range. Finally he pocketed a little device about the size of a cell phone that Rencke had helped the Directorate of Science & Technology develop a couple of years ago. It was an electronic-surveillance-measures detector that was capable of picking up the signals from just about any surveillance equipment, including radar, low- and high-frequency radio ranging, and laser beams that were beyond human visual range.

If anyone at the compound was watching or listening for intruders, which was probably the case, Rencke promised his toy would detect it.

McGarvey secured the case, then locked the car and trotted across the road into the brush. Almost immediately he came upon a narrow path, probably used by small white-tailed deer, that led up into the hills, and he followed it for the next fifteen minutes.

He stopped frequently to make sure that no one was behind him and that the animal trail was still leading in the direction he needed to go. He kept low each time the path crested a part of the hill and started down into a narrow valley to reduce the chance of anyone below catching his silhouette against the night sky.

Although the night was cool, he was sweating lightly by the time he reached a spot directly above the compound where he could conceal himself in some low brush and yet have a clear sight line into Liu's stronghold.

The party below was still going strong. From his vantage point about eighty feet above the compound walls, and maybe two hundred feet out, McGarvey had a three-quarters view of the back of the house and a very large patio area complete with a huge pool. In a corner, a jazz combo with a baby grand piano played American big band favorites of the forties. Buffet tables and a couple of bars were set up here and there. Thirty or forty people were down there, some of them dancing to the music, others gathered in knots at the bars and buffet tables, and still others in the pool.

McGarvey took out the ESMs detector, powered it up, and pointed the receiving end of the device toward the compound. Immediately three small indicator lights began flashing: one warned that the area where he crouched was being scanned by a motion detector, the second had picked up the signal from an infrared receiver, and the third light indicated a low-power electronic signal in an ultrahigh frequency, the purpose of which the device could not identify.

Liu's security people would know that something was up here and would probably be sending someone to check it out. He figured he had another five minutes at the most before he would have company.

He pulled out the binoculars, powered them up, and slowly scanned the entire compound from left to right. Closed-circuit television cameras were trained on the perimeter outside the walls at intervals of fifty feet or so, so somebody inside the main house was also watching the approaches, as he had expected.

At least half the guests were young women, most of them naked or nearly naked, while the rest appeared to be older men, a couple of them in Mexican Army uniforms, their jackets open, their ties loose. Everyone seemed to be having a good time.

No armed men were in sight anywhere, nor had he been able to spot General Liu or anyone else who didn't appear to be Hispanic, except for the girls, most of whom seemed to be Oriental or white, and all of them very young.

In addition to the main two-story house with red-tiled roof and large sliding doors open to the patio, a line of open-front cabanas faced the back of the pool, and McGarvey could make out a man and woman having sex on a couch or daybed in one of them. Around the other side of the house he could just make out the corner of what probably was a garage, and possibly where the compound's electrical generator was located. He was also able to see a number of cars parked at the front of the house, all of them late-model Cadillacs or Land Rover SUVs.

Besides Liu's absence, McGarvey also found it curious that none of the guests had parked *outside* the compound's wall. They were locked inside, their freedom presumably at the general's discretion, though McGarvey was reasonably certain that none of them would see it that way. It was an interesting trait. Men in Liu's position, and perhaps *especially* him, almost always had a need to be in control of everything and everyone around them. Shahrzad had said as much, although by the time she'd gotten to the general she'd had stars in her eyes for no one other than Updegraf.

The general taking control of her would have been child's play. So easy, in fact, that Liu had gotten tired of her almost from the start. It was something that could be useful when the time came.

McGarvey took out the video camera and began shooting the entire compound, again scanning left to right as he had with the binoculars so as not to miss anything. He lingered on each face for a few seconds to make certain he'd recorded the features well enough for a positive identification. The women were like the combo and the buffet and bars, there for entertainment. But he had a feeling that finding out who the men were would provide a big clue as to what Liu was doing in Mexico.

When he was finished he pocketed the camera and, keeping low, started back down the path to where he'd left his car. He stopped every few yards to listen for the sounds of someone coming up from the compound, but except for the music from below and the insects and the hoot of a far-off owl, the night was quiet. There was an off chance that Liu's security people might believe that it was a deer or other animal on the path, and might not even come out to take a look.

Fifteen minutes later he came to the spot above the road where he'd parked, and he pulled up short. He smelled cigarette smoke. Someone said something and someone else replied, the voices too low to make out any words. He edged a little farther down the path until he could see his car. Two men were leaning against the hood, one of them smoking a cigarette. They were dressed in khakis and armed with what looked like Uzis casually slung over their shoulders. They didn't seem particularly worried that there would be trouble they couldn't easily handle.

McGarvey took out his Walther and screwed the silencer onto the end of the barrel. Switching the safety lever to the off position, he started directly down the hill to the car, stopping at the bottom when he came out of the brush onto the road.

The two men pushed away from the car and had started to unsling their weapons when McGarvey raised his pistol. "It wouldn't be to your advantage to try something stupid."

The man with the cigarette tossed it aside. He was tall and lean, just the opposite of his partner. But they were both olive-skinned and looked Mexican or Hispanic. "We don't like spies," he said. He moved a few feet to the left, his eyes never leaving McGarvey's.

"I thought my girlfriend was in there. From the Wild Stallion."

"Sí," the tall guard said. "Why don't you come back to the compound with us, and you can find out. No need for all this sneaking around in the dark."

"Maybe the general's killed her, like the others," McGarvey said. "I'll call the cops."

The tall one laughed. "I think that's a good idea." He moved a little farther to the left.

"But first you're going to drop your guns on the ground, and then you're going to walk back to the compound," McGarvey told them pleasantly. "And if you behave yourselves, I may not shoot you in the back."

"Not very sportsmanlike, is he, Miguel?" the shorter one by the car suggested.

"No," the tall one replied. He was smiling. "The trouble is, there are two of us. One of us is bound to get lucky." He edged even farther from his partner.

"You're right, of course," McGarvey agreed. He lowered his pistol and strode directly toward the man.

For just a moment neither man knew what was happening, and they were too late reacting, fumbling with their weapons, trying to bring them to bear.

McGarvey got directly in front of the tall guard, raised his pistol, and put one round in the man's left kneecap at point-blank range, dropping him where he stood.

The second guard had his Uzi nearly up and ready to fire when McGarvey switched aim. "Don't," he ordered.

The guard hesitated, his eyes flitting to his partner writhing in pain on the road.

"Drop your weapon and I'll let both of you live to go back to the compound," McGarvey said.

"You bastard," the man on the ground cried, but he made no move to reach for his weapon.

"How do I know that I can trust you?" the other one asked.

"You can't," McGarvey said. "But I want you to take a message back to the general. Tell him that I don't like him screwing around with my girl-friend. If I ever see them together I'll kill them both."

The guard was obviously weighing his odds. The muzzle of his Uzi was pointing vaguely but not exactly at McGarvey.

McGarvey took a step closer, his aim at the guard's head never waver-ing. "Your choice."

Slowly the guard lowered the Uzi, then slipped the strap off his shoulder and let the weapon slide to the ground. "What is the name of your girlfriend?"

"Shahrzad," McGarvey said. "I haven't seen her in two weeks. I want her back."

The guard started to say something, but then he nodded. "I will pass the message."

TWENTY-FOUR

HOTEL FOUR SEASONS

It was after two in the morning before McGarvey changed out of his black jumpsuit, cleaned his face, and got back to his suite with the alu-minum case. This time he didn't care if anyone spotted him. He'd thrown the gauntlet at General Liu's feet. There was no longer any need for stealth.

"I was waiting for your call," Rencke said when the sat phone connection was made. "Did you run into any trouble?"

"Some," McGarvey said. "Liu is serious about his security. A couple of his people were waiting for me at my car."

"The ESMs detector worked okay?"

"Like a charm. Gave me the heads-up so that I didn't walk into a trap."

"Send me that download first. I want to see what kind of shit they've got out there."

"Hold on," McGarvey said. He powered up the detector and plugged it into the sat phone's data port.

"Okay, I see it," Rencke said. The transfer of information took only a split second. "Wow," Rencke said softly. "They *are* serious."

"They must have picked up my body heat with their infrared detectors," McGarvey said.

"Yeah, they probably did, but they also nailed the ESMs detector. I'm showing absorption lines on several bands. Cool."

"What are you talking about?"

"They've got some state-of-the-art shit down there, kemosabe. Their equipment sent out surveillance signals that your ESMs detector picked up and identified. But in order to do the job the device had to absorb some of the signal strength. And their stuff detected it. Like I said, that's definitely some cool shit. I'll get this over to Jared soon as he comes in."

"Is there any way of telling the nationality of the equipment?"

"If it was radar or sonar, sure, but with this kind of stuff . . ." Rencke drifted off for a second. "I don't know. Maybe I'll try to figure something out. What are you thinking?"

"If it's Chinese gear, then Liu probably has the backing of Beijing for whatever he's doing here. But if it's something he bought off the shelf, Swiss, Japanese, German, maybe even Taiwanese, it could mean that he's pulling an independent op."

"I'll see what I can do," Rencke promised. He was the kind of person who when challenged with a problem wouldn't rest until he'd solved it. "Did you have time to get some pictures?"

"I got shots of just about everybody at the party, except for the general.

He was nowhere in sight, although I didn't have much time to hang around. The ESMs detector picked up on the surveillance signals soon as I turned it on. I figured I wouldn't have a lot of time."

"Okay, send them to me."

McGarvey powered up the video camera and plugged it into the sat phone's data port. "I want the names and backgrounds on everyone at the party, including the girls."

"Some of them might not have tracks, especially the women," Rencke said. "I'm getting the pictures now. Good stuff, Mac. Give me a minute."

"Be right back," McGarvey said. He put the phone down on the bed and went into the sitting room, where there were still a couple of beers in the bucket of melted ice. He opened one, but before he went back to the phone he looked out the tall windows at the lights of the vast city. The futures of Mexico and the U.S. were firmly tied together not merely because of a shared border, but because a significant percentage of the U.S. population was Mexican immigrants—legal and illegal. It made what Liu was doing here of extreme interest to Washington.

"Looks like a meeting of the UN General Assembly," Rencke said when McGarvey went back into the bedroom and picked up the sat phone. "Chinese, Hispanics, most of them Mexican, but at least two guys probably Colombian, and at least four of them Anglos, plus a couple I can't be sure of right now. The girls are Oriental, their features too long and delicate to be Chinese or Korean; I'd say Japanese. A few Mexicans, and the rest probably Americans. But most of them are just kids. Probably teenagers."

"Any familiar faces?"

"None yet, but I've just started," Rencke said. "It's the Anglos I'm worried about. Could be American."

"Or European?" McGarvey suggested.

"Nope, clothes and haircuts are wrong. Two of them are either American or Canadian. Anyway, I'll have to get back to you later today."

"Do what you can."

"I'm on it," Rencke said. "In the meantime, Adkins wants to know if you're going to help out. Perry is pressuring him from the bottom, and

Berndt calls every few hours." Dennis Berndt was the president's national security adviser.

"Stall him," McGarvey said tersely. "Has anyone taken an interest in Shahrzad? I assume she's still at Doyle's house."

"She's still there, and when I talked to Toni around ten last night, everything was quiet."

"Send some muscle down there. Go to the Bureau if you have to, but keep it quiet."

"McCann's not going to like it when he finds out."

"We'll deal with that when it happens. But this hasn't got a chance in hell of working unless we keep the need-to-know list to an absolute minimum."

"What do I tell the Bureau?" Rencke asked.

"Tell them she's in our witness-protection program. We're short staffed. They love it when they're asked to help us out. Makes them feel superior."

Rencke chuckled. "Do you want me to say anything to Mrs. M.?"

"Has she called?"

"No."

"Leave it for now. I may be coming back to the States in a day or two. Give Dick the heads-up. Tell him I'll have made my decision by then."

TWENTY-FIVE

□

CIA HEADQUARTERS

By four in the morning Rencke had isolated forty-three separate people from the photos McGarvey had taken at Liu's house. In many cases he managed to come up with multiple images, some full facials, others body shots from various angles.

Combining the best for each individual he started cross-matching them with the CIA's database of persons of interest, which contained more than one hundred thousand separate photographs of thirty thousand people.

It was a long process of first matching sex, probable ethnic background, probable age, and gross physical characteristics including height, weight, and body type against the data on file to eliminate obvious nonmatches.

When that first run was finished, the computer began matching facial characterstics—hairline, nose size and shape, eyebrows, eyes, cheeks, lips, jaw—again eliminating obvious nonmatches.

One by one, the computer spit out a series of possible matches that Rencke had to eyeball. Computers were marvelous tools, but even Rencke's programs sometimes couldn't match human intuition.

Within a few minutes the first two images were identified with better than 95 percent confidence, and Rencke could only stare at the monitor. One made sense, but the other was out of the blue, and for once in his life, Rencke was at a loss about what to do next. Mac would have to be told, but first he had to talk to somebody.

His wife, Louise, had been sound asleep at their apartment, but she woke on the second ring. "You're still at work," she said groggily. "What's wrong?"

"I want you to take a look at something."

"Are you okay, Otto?"

"I don't know. It's for Mac, but I gotta make sure I'm not dreaming or something."

"Just a sec," Louise said.

Rencke e-mailed the two images to the computer at the apartment. It took his wife less than a minute to get to the spare bedroom, open the e-mail, and download the attachment.

"All right," she said. "I don't know Thomas Alvarez, but it looks like your POI program has a high confidence that you've come up with a match. Where'd the pictures come from? They're lousy."

"Mac took them a few hours ago at a place outside Mexico City."

"The General Liu thing?" Louise asked. She and Otto never kept secrets from each other, even though it was against law. But from the beginning they had depended on each other's intellect and judgment.

"Yeah. Alvarez probably launders more South American cartel drug money than anyone else on the planet. The Bureau hasn't been able to prove it, but he's on their top twenty POI list. They'd like to talk to him in the worst way, but he dropped out of sight a couple of months ago."

"About the same time you think Liu showed up in Mexico City," Louise said, catching the point. "What is a top-ranking Guoanbu general doing with a moneyman for the druggies?"

"In Mexico, no less," Rencke said.

"Makes you think," Louise said. "But Jesus, Mary, and Joseph, no need for the computer to recognize the other guy. Fred is going to go nuts when you show him that one." Fred Rudolph was the FBI's chief of special operations, a position very much like Rencke's. Rudolph and Rencke had a history together, and a mutual respect.

"That's why I had to talk to you," Rencke said. "I don't think Mac's going to want to share this, leastways not right now."

"Does he know?"

"I don't think so. I had to do a lot of enhancements to come up with a reasonable image. He couldn't have recognized this guy from the viewfinder. He was too far out."

"Well you better get word to him soon, because there could be some shit going on down there that's even more serious than he thinks. The drug banker I can fathom, but Walter Newell is something else. A whole other universe. You have to ask what a U.S. congressman from Arizona is doing at a party hosted by a Chinese Communist intelligence officer."

"That's why I had to talk to you. What next?"

"Who else was down there?" Louise asked.

"A bunch of people, including some young girls they were using as whores."

"Any other IDs?"

"The computer is working on it," Rencke said. He explained the entire setup at Liu's house south of the city, including the sophisticated surveillance equipment.

"Before you tell anyone else, let Mac know what you've come up with," Louise advised. "In the meantime, take a close look in the dark corners."

"What are you talking about?"

"Logic, my dear," Louise said. "A party like that can be a dangerous thing for the wrong guy. Newell is not going to be a happy camper that he was spotted. But he's an amateur, unlike Liu, who you say was nowhere to be seen. Check the corners to see if you can spot him, or any other old odd bod who preferred to stay out of the limelight."

Rencke grinned. "I love you," he said.

"You're welcome," she replied. "Now I'm going back to bed. No need to ask when you'll be home."

"No," Rencke said absently, but even before his wife broke the connection he was bringing up the original digital images that McGarvey had taken.

In his first run he had isolated each person from every shot, enhancing the quality of the images and then combined them into an electronic photo album of the forty-three guests, including the girls.

This time he electronically subtracted all those images from the original shots Mac had taken with the digital video cam, leaving only the backgrounds—the buffet tables, the musicians' instruments, the back and sides of the house, the pool and chairs and lounges, and the cabanas.

Next, he divided each still shot into a grid of sixty-four squares, eight on a side. Taking one square from each of as many as a dozen shots of the same area, he stacked the individual images, averaging out the light, dark, and color values.

The morning shift was in full swing when he finished the huge task and sat back. He was tired, but his excitement acted like adrenaline on his system, and he was wired, scarcely able to keep himself from snapping his fingers, bouncing his feet on the floor, and rocking back and forth in his chair.

"Oh, boy," he said softly. "Oh, boy." Something serious was happening or about to happen in Mexico. Trouble was, he had absolutely no idea what it might be.

He had managed to catch the faint image of a man standing just inside the house, by a reflection in one of the sliding glass doors. The quality was terrible, but it was just luck that he was able to snag three separate images and stack them. It was almost impossible to get any kind of a clear identity, but he'd been able to extract enough information from the enhanced final shot to get his attention, and make him realize that something bigger, and probably even more sinister than anyone had first thought, was going on.

Sliding over to another monitor, Rencke brought up the program that was still sifting through the other forty-one images he'd lifted from the original shots, and identifying them from the CIA's database. So far a list of seventeen names had popped up with a confidence above 80 percent. Scanning the list, he wasn't surprised to find the names of several important Mexican Army and Air Force generals, plus a smattering of politicians and one aide to President Ricardo Sabina. None of the young women had been identified yet, but that didn't surprise him either. Chances were, none of them were in any of the databases that he could think of except perhaps the Mexican driver's license bureau, or something like that.

Back at his primary monitor he stared again at the stacked image of the man reflected in the glass door. Judging by the camera angle and the height of the door frame, Rencke guessed the man was short, probably five five or five six, and slightly built. He was wearing what looked like light slacks, perhaps khakis, and a regular button-up dress shirt, most likely white. The open collar and collar points stood out clearly. The man was looking out toward the pool, and slightly upward, possibly at the top of the compound's outer wall, so that some of the details of his face, though almost completely in shadow, were recognizable to a degree. He had narrow cheeks, an angular chin, and a long, hawkish nose. It was almost impossible to determine his skin color, though Rencke had to guess that it was dark, perhaps olive or maybe even tan, but definitely not African black.

Middle Eastern, Rencke thought. It had been his first impression once he'd looked at the stacked and enhanced image. Iraq, Iran, Syria, someplace like that. Not Afghanistan or Pakistan.

If he was right, what the hell was a guy like that doing at the same party with an American congressman, a drug money banker, and some important Mexicans, hosted by a high-ranking Chinese Communist intelligence officer?

McGarvey was just leaving his hotel room to go downstairs for breakfast when Rencke caught him on the sat phone. "Have you come up with some names?"

"Yeah, and you'd better be sitting down, kemosabe, I shit you not."

"What have you got?"

"I'll download what I've come up with so far to you in a minute, but something weird is definitely going on, so you're going to have to really watch your back this time."

"Continue," McGarvey said.

"Most of the people at Liu's party were about who you figured they would be, Mexican generals and politicians. But a guy by the name of Thomas Alvarez was in the thick of it. Does that ring a bell?"

"No. Should it?"

"Probably not, but the Bureau will be interested to know where he is. They've been looking for him ever since he disappeared a couple of months ago. The Bureau thinks that he's one of the major drug-money launderers. Does about six billion a year in trade."

"Sounds like Liu is looking for a money source," McGarvey said. "Could mean he's working independent of Beijing after all. Send me his file."

"Do you want me to give Fred Rudolph the heads-up?"

"Not yet," McGarvey said. "Who else did you come up with? Anyone interesting?"

"How about Congressman Walter Newell? Arizona?"

For just a moment McGarvey wasn't sure what to say. "Are you sure?"

"The computer is at ninety-eight percent, and when I showed the picture to Louise she recognized him right off the bat," Rencke said. "I don't like it."

"Neither do I," McGarvey replied. "I want you to put together something for Fred. Include what you have to about Liu, but don't mention me, or Updegraf's assassination."

"When do you want me to send it over?"

"Not just yet. I'll let you know," McGarvey said. "Any other surprises?"

Rencke took a deep breath and blew it out through pursed lips. "One more, so far," he said. He explained his wife's suggestion to look in the shadows for someone trying to hide, and the image he'd come up with. "Could be he's a professional intelligence officer trying to cover his ass."

"A Syrian or Iranian," McGarvey said with wonder. "Have you checked to see if Tehran or Damascus are running an operation down there?"

"I didn't find anything on a first pass, but I have a search program on it."

"Maybe it's just a coincidence, Shahrzad being Iranian," McGarvey said, but he didn't sound convinced.

"Yeah, right."

"Has your primary threat assessment color changed?"

"Still lavender, maybe a shade deeper," Rencke said. "But I haven't inputted the last bit yet."

"Okay," McGarvey said after a moment. "I'm going to have some breakfast, and then I'll go over to the Chinese embassy. There was something on TV this morning about a news conference at ten. In the meantime send me what you've come up with so far, and give Adkins the heads-up that I'm coming to Washington to talk to him about the assignment."

"Watch yourself, Mac," Rencke said. "I don't like this one very much. Too many warts."

"You have to admit, it's an interesting mix of people that Liu has gathered around him."

"Yeah," Rencke said. "Okay, hold on, I'm sending this stuff to you now."

It took only a second to download all the files to McGarvey's sat phone, and when the transfer was complete the connection was broken.

Rencke looked up as Deputy Director of Operations Howard McCann showed up at the door, a smirk on his round face, his eyes narrowed behind his glasses.

"Now why would my director of special operations be spending the night in the Building?" McCann asked. "Could it be he's working on something that he's not willing to share?"

"I'm working on a few things," Rencke admitted, sitting back.

"Give me a for instance," McCann said. "Like the lavender screen. That's one of your big ones, isn't it?"

"That's just something I'm dinking around with," Rencke said, and he idly hit the Escape button on his keyboard and the screen went to wallpaper, which was the logo of the old KGB.

McCann's expression hardened. "You're not a team player, are you?"

Rencke let his own expression fall. "No, I'm not, Mr. Deputy Director. Never have been. But now if you'll get the fuck out of here, I'd like to get back to work."

"I'll have your hide," McCann shot back. He was angry.

Rencke grinned. "Good luck," he said. "And don't let the door hit you on the ass on the way out."

McCann stood motionless for several seconds. It was obvious he wanted to lash out, but it was equally obvious that he was intimidated by Rencke. Just about everyone in the Building was, because just about everybody knew that if something or someone set Rencke off on a tangent he could bring down the CIA's entire computer system.

"You will fuck up one of these days, you and McGarvey, and I'll have you both," McCann said. He turned and got out without slamming the door.

As soon as the DDO was gone, Rencke brought up a small program and sent it to the computer in McCann's office and his PC at home, infecting both machines with a minor little virus that would last for only twenty-four hours, but would make both computers so temperamental, they'd be next to impossible to use. The virus couldn't be found or fixed until it ran its course. McCann would know that he was being screwed with, but he would not be able to prove it.

Rencke had to smile. Bothering the true assholes was one of the perks of working for the Company.

TWENTY-SIX

□

CHINESE EMBASSY
COLONIA TIZAPAN SAN ANGEL

Sitting alone at the restaurant at the Hotel Four Seasons, McGarvey scrolled through the images and identifications that Rencke had downloaded to his sat phone. There still was no sign of Liu at the party, but the presence of a U.S. congressman, a drug cartel banker, and a third man who was possibly an intelligence officer for a Middle Eastern country— though that was purely speculation at this point—was as intriguing as it was disturbing.

For the life of him he couldn't think of any scenario that would make sense of those three men being at the same place at the same time.

Darby Yarnell had surrounded himself with some fairly eclectic characters in his heyday down here, yet the mix was understandable against the backdrop of the cold war. The Russians had been looking toward a close relationship with as many high-ranking Mexican government and military officials as possible. Their long-range goal was to place offensive nuclear weapons on the desert less than one hundred miles south of the U.S. border. For that they needed the Mexican government to agree to a Russian-financed and -engineered agrarian-reform project. Russians were drilling a series of extremely deep wells, from which brackish water would be pumped. The water would be desalinated in massive facilities, and then used to irrigate the desert, which would come to life and bloom.

The facilities were to be used to hide the presence of nuclear weapons in silos.

The plan had failed in part because Yarnell, although he had been a self-serving son of a bitch, had turned out to be more of a playboy than a spy working for the Russians, and in part because of McGarvey's interference.

But the cold war was over now. The Russians, and presumably the Chinese, were no longer interested in threatening us with nuclear destruction. In this new era the battlefields were more up close and personal. The war was between us and the terrorists, mostly Islamic fanatics who were willing to bring the battles to our shores, and increasingly between us and China over natural resources and trade.

China wanted a lock on the world's supplies of oil and copper, with which to power its own nation's expansion, and the Chinese were well on their way to having a lock on world trade. Raw materials flowed into Chinese ports, and inexpensive manufactured goods flowed out to the world—but mostly to the United States.

It was something that the U.S. couldn't afford to let happen. The trade imbalance was pushing us toward bankruptcy. Our survival was at stake. Yet every administration that had tried to go up against the Chinese juggernaut had failed.

That would explain why Liu was hosting a party for the Mexican generals and ranking government people, and it might even explain Thomas Alvarez's presence if Liu was looking to finance an operation on his own. Beijing could very well want plausible deniability in case Liu was caught out. It would explain why Liu hadn't been brought to heel for his escapades in New York and Washington.

The Chinese government *wanted* Liu to develop the reputation as an out-of-control rogue agent. The entire past few years could have been an elaborate setup for whatever he was up to now in Mexico.

In McGarvey's mind, that went a long way toward explaining Liu's relationship with Alvarez and the Mexican officials. But he was still at a total loss as to why a U.S. congressman and a possible Middle Eastern intelligence officer had been down there last night.

The pieces weren't fitting together.

After breakfast, McGarvey drove the Saturn over to the downtown Hertz office in Colonia Juárez and exchanged it for a smoked gray Ford Taurus. The wagon was too big a car for city traffic, he explained, and after the Saturn was carefully inspected for damage he was given the smaller car. It was just an extra layer of tradecraft after last night outside Liu's compound.

He got out to San Angel around nine thirty, in plenty of time for the news conference, but it took another twenty minutes of circling before he was able to find a place to park. The Avenue Rio Magdalena on which the Chinese embassy was located was a mass of television trucks and print media people. The block had been cordoned off, and a podium bristling with microphones had been set up just outside the main gate.

A number of curious onlookers jostled for position, and as McGarvey approached on foot he got the impression that the newspeople were for real but most of the spectators were shills; too many of them appeared to be Chinese.

He took up a position just at the edge of the crowd directly across the street from the podium. At ten sharp the gate opened. A Chinese man dressed in a light suit and a young woman dressed in a dark skirt and white blouse came out to the podium, followed a moment later by three men, one of them much taller than the others.

McGarvey thought that by now in his life he had just about lost the capacity for surprise, yet seeing Congressman Newell emerging from the Chinese embassy, flanked by a short Chinese man dressed in a dark Western-cut suit, and another man, obviously Mexican, dressed similarly, he was taken aback for just a moment. And yet there was a symmetry between what he'd seen last night down in Xochimilco and what he was witnessing here this morning, and he knew that he shouldn't be surprised.

"Good morning," the first man said into the microphones, in English, his voice amplified.

"*Buenos días*," the young woman using a hand microphone translated into Spanish.

McGarvey glanced up and caught a glimpse of someone in one of the third-floor windows of the embassy building behind the tall wall. He got the impression of sunlight glinting off something, perhaps binocular lenses.

"Thank you for coming here," the man continued. "Permit me to introduce our deputy ambassador, Mr. Lee Chingkuo, who will make an important joint announcement this morning along with Mexico's director of economic development, Señor Juan Caro Fuentes, and United

States congressman the Honorable Walter Newell of Arizona. There will be a very brief period of questions afterward; however, a media package will be made available for those with proper credentials."

The young woman translated.

The man who was probably the embassy's press secretary moved aside, and Deputy Ambassador Lee stepped up to the microphones. He was a short, slightly built man with round glasses, dark hair combed straight back, and a serious manner. This was to be all business.

"My statement this morning will be brief," he said. "The People's Republic of China, in cooperation with the United States, has agreed in principle to create a joint exploration and utilization project to be called ChiMexAm Company, for the purpose of finding oil beneath the Sonoran Desert."

He paused for a moment as if he was expecting someone to challenge him, but the crowd was silent. The announcement had apparently come as a complete surprise to everybody.

McGarvey watched Newell for a reaction, but the congressman's expression was set in stone. It was rumored that he wanted the White House in three years, and if he had been looking to throw his hat into the ring with a splash, this morning was going to do it for him. Getting something like this through Congress, however, would probably be all but impossible. Right now most Americans didn't trust the Chinese.

"Many hurdles must be overcome before such a joint project can begin," Lee continued. "But of paramount importance is China's desire to share equally with its partners in the quest for oil. China cannot be viewed as seeking a world monopoly."

The young woman quickly translated Lee's comments into Spanish.

Fuentes came to the microphone, all smiles. He had come from one of the southeastern states, and was only one or two generations away from his mestizo heritage. It showed on his broad, weathered face. "I too will be brief, amigos," he said in English. "This is a great day for Mexico. In terms of economic development it will be a very good project for my country. In terms of cementing the bonds of friendship between the two great superpowers—China and our neighbor the United States—Mexico is proud to be the ambassador. And in terms of helping to alleviate the growing worldwide oil crises we stand ready to do our part."

His smile widened and he clasped his hands over his head. *"Gracias,"* he cried. *"Muchas gracias, amigos."*

He moved away from the podium, and the big, rawboned Arizona congressman stepped up to the microphones. He wore a western-cut suit, and his signature string tie and Stetson hat, which made him look like a young Lyndon Johnson.

"This morning's announcement is only the first step in what I believe will prove to be one of the most significant, far-reaching projects on the North American continent—good not only for our partners China and Mexico, but good for the world economy." He flashed his famous grin directly at the television cameras. "Forty-dollar-a-barrel oil," he shouted. "How does that strike you?"

McGarvey listened to the translation, and when the first of the questions was shouted from the media, he started back through the crowd toward his car in the next block in the parking lot of a small shopping mall. Almost immediately he knew that he was being followed.

Two of them had broken away from the media people and were jostling their way across the crowded street. They were Mexicans, and the first time he'd spotted them they'd had cameras slung around their necks, but they were not taking pictures. Now they had ditched the cameras, and seemed intent on keeping up.

McGarvey took his time so that they would not lose him. At the corner he glanced over his shoulder and made sure that they understood he'd spotted them, then hurried the rest of the way to the busy shopping center. Traffic here was normal, ordinary people going about their business on a pleasant weekday morning.

He crossed the parking lot, bought *Mexico News*, an English-language newspaper, from a kiosk, and sat down at a sidewalk café. The waiter came for his order at the same time the two men showed up around the corner.

They stopped to look around, spotted him almost immediately at the table, and headed directly across toward him.

"A coffee, please," McGarvey told the waiter.

"Sí," the waiter said, and left.

The two men, both of them short and husky, with broad faces and narrow eyes, walked over to where McGarvey was seated. They were dressed in jeans and short-sleeved white shirts, untucked. He figured they were probably carrying.

"Okay, get on your feet," the taller of the two said, his English fairly good. "Someone wants to talk to you."

McGarvey smiled pleasantly. "I'd be happy to speak with the general, but first I'm going to have a coffee."

The waiter came back and glanced nervously at the two men.

"Would you gentlemen care for something?" McGarvey asked.

The waiter set McGarvey's coffee down and hurried back inside as a black Mercedes SUV pulled up at the curb a few feet away.

"Now," the taller one said, and he reached for something under his shirt at the waistband of his jeans.

"If you pull out a gun, I'll break your wrist," McGarvey said politely. "Then someone will probably call the cops, and you'll have to answer some questions. I don't think your boss will be very pleased."

"*Bastardo!*" the man said, and he started to pull something from under his shirt.

McGarvey tossed the hot coffee at the man's face, jumped up, slammed the knuckles of his right fist into the second man's Adam's apple, then shouldered the first man back against the Mercedes' passenger door.

"Your friends will need a doctor," McGarvey told the gape-mouthed driver through the open window.

He slammed the gunman's arm against the car's window frame, the wrist breaking with an audible pop. The pistol, which McGarvey identified as a Glock, fell inside the car, and the man uttered a sharp scream of pain.

McGarvey pulled him close. "The next time I'll kill whoever he sends against me."

"You won't live through the day," the man said through clenched teeth.

McGarvey stepped away. "All I want is my girlfriend back, and then I'll leave Mexico. Tell that to the general."

He glanced at the driver, who was looking at him with a touch of fear, then at the second man, who had fallen to one knee and was trying to catch his breath through his badly bruised windpipe. He tossed a few pesos on the table, and walked away. Before he reached his car the two battered Mexicans had climbed into the Mercedes, and the driver peeled rubber getting out of the parking lot. They were pissed off, but he hadn't thought they would try to run him down or shoot him in the back. Liu would be getting nervous about who he was and what he was really doing in Mexico City. The general wanted to talk first.

TWENTY-SEVEN

WASHINGTON, D.C.

Dick Adkins lived in a pleasant three-story brick house that had been built on the grounds of the U.S. Naval Observatory shortly after the Civil War. It was in the woods not too far from the vice president's residence, and the only access was by a narrow blacktopped lane that was monitored 24/7.

Driving up from the main entrance off Wisconsin Avenue, McGarvey was reminded of other times he'd made this same sort of trip; in secret, with a sense of urgency, to tell a director of the CIA that bad things were coming our way, and that some tough choices would have to be made.

Not all DCIs had used this CIA-owned house back here, but several had during McGarvey's more than a quarter of a century with the Company, and he knew the way from long habit.

It was a Saturday morning and he passed two busloads of children on a field trip to the observatory before the driveway branched left into the woods. A man in a blue windbreaker and baseball cap marked SECURITY in gold letters stepped out of the guard box and motioned for McGarvey to pull up. He was armed with a Heckler & Koch M8 carbine.

McGarvey powered down the Ford 500's driver window and handed out his ID. He spotted a second security officer a few feet off the road in the woods.

"Good morning, Mr. Director," the security officer said. He handed McGarvey's ID back. "If you'll just head up to the house and park in front, they're expecting you. Are you carrying?"

"Yes, I am," McGarvey said.

"Thank you, sir," the security officer said, and as he stepped away he said something into his lapel mike.

Fifty yards farther the driveway opened to a broad lawn at the center of which was the house. The roof bristled with six redbrick chimneys, several radio masts, and three satellite dishes. A gunmetal gray Hummer was parked ahead of Rencke's battered old Mercedes diesel sedan in the driveway. As McGarvey pulled up behind Rencke's car an armed security officer came around the corner of the house and said something into his lapel mike. Another security officer, this one in a white shirt and tie but no jacket, was at the front door when McGarvey came up the walk. He wore a 9 mm SIG-Sauer P226 pistol high on his right hip.

"Good morning, sir," he said. "They're waiting for you in the study. If you'll just surrender your piece first."

"Fair enough," McGarvey said. He pulled his Walther PPK out, removed the magazine, cycled the live round out of the chamber, and handed everything over to the officer.

"Thank you, sir."

"Are we facing a security issue here?" McGarvey asked.

"No, sir. And we'd like to keep it that way."

"Good," McGarvey said. He crossed the stair hall to the left, knocked once on the double doors, and let himself into the study of the director of Central Intelligence.

The room was large, with high ceilings, floor-to-ceiling bookcases, a massive leather-topped desk in front of bowed windows, and a grouping of couch, chairs, and a low table facing a big fireplace in the corner.

Adkins was standing in front of his desk, and Rencke and Gil Perry, who'd been seated on the couch, got to their feet. They'd evidently been alerted to McGarvey's arrival. Adkins and Perry looked concerned, even a little frightened, but Rencke was fairly vibrating with excitement, stepping from foot to foot, a big grin on his face, his long red hair even wilder than usual. He had the bone in his teeth.

"Did you notice if anyone was interested in you at Dulles?" Adkins asked, almost breathlessly.

"No," McGarvey said. "And I assume that we're clean here."

"We are," Adkins said. "Did you see the news conference?"

"I was there. What's the president saying?"

"Nothing yet," Adkins said. "He wanted to see me first thing this morning. I stalled him until two. Promised that I'd have something for him."

"Well I certainly hope that Mr. McGarvey has brought something back with him after rambling around my station," Perry said. "But Newell came as a complete surprise to me, I can tell you that much."

"What have you come up with?" McGarvey asked mildly. There was no point leaning on the man yet, but he was the COS down there. He had to have found out something.

"Nothing of any substance, I'm afraid. But I don't have much to go on."

"One of your senior officers was shot to death and beheaded, and you have his Iranian girlfriend on ice. If you don't have any of the answers, you sure as hell ought to have come up with a few questions by now."

"We've pulled out all the stops, believe me."

"Updegraf was working the Chinese connection. According to Shahrzad he was trying to burn General Liu. Now, out of the clear blue sky the Chinese announce an oil deal with us and the Mexicans. Maybe that's what your man had turned over."

"Wouldn't have got him killed." Perry said indignantly. "They made it public themselves."

"Are you thinking another nuclear deal like the Russians tried to pull off a few years ago?" Adkins asked.

McGarvey shook his head. "I don't think so. The Chinese would have too much to lose and nothing to gain. Without us as a trading partner they'd have a tough time keeping up with their own growth."

"What Russian nuclear deal?" Perry demanded.

"It's nothing that has any bearing on what's going on right now," McGarvey assured him. But he hated coincidences. Shahrzad was Iranian. Her father had been an Iranian intelligence office who knew General Baranov. The shadowy figure Rencke had picked out at Liu's compound was possibly a Middle Easterner, maybe an Iranian. And in some ways even odder was Gloria's apartment, located in the hills almost directly above the Iranian embassy.

Rencke shot him an odd look. He was having the same thoughts.

"Heavens, you're not suggesting that the Chinese government is planning on putting nuclear missiles in Mexico?" Perry asked.

"No," McGarvey said. He wondered exactly what Perry was so afraid of that he was going to these lengths to cover his ass. As chief of station he had to have known at least something of what Updegraf was doing.

"Well, we're still faced with the nuclear issue in Iran and North Korea," Perry reminded them. "Thank goodness not in my bailiwick."

Nothing had changed since McGarvey had started with the Company. It seemed that a handful of good people did most of the real work, while a lot of the others didn't have enough imagination or daring to do much of anything other than cover their own asses. The problem was that there never seemed to be enough of the good ones to go around.

And the even bigger problem for McGarvey was that he needed Perry to backstop him, or at least make enough noise in the bush so that Liu and company might be distracted for a bit.

"What about you, Mac?" Adkins asked. Just then his eyes were wide as if he was expecting a nasty surprise. "You wanted us here in secret, so it's your call, but at this point it looks as if we're facing nothing more than a political problem. The Chinese want Mexican oil and we can't allow it. Something for the president and the diplomats."

That would have been the extent of it as far as McGarvey was concerned, except for the drug cartel banker and the third man at Liu's party. They didn't fit.

It always seemed to come down to whom to trust. It was why for most of his career McGarvey had worked alone. But on rare occasions it became necessary to use people, like now with Shahrzad and Gloria. He had to question if the ends really did justify the means, and wonder whether, if he were just a little brighter, a little more mentally agile, he could think of another way to get to the general.

But Liu's weakness was the women he surrounded himself with. They were his Achilles' heel. And McGarvey meant to find a way to use that flaw.

"You might be right, Dick, except that Walt Newell was at a party down at Liu's house in Xochimilco. Lots of drugs and young girls. Could be used against him."

"Do you know that for a fact?" Perry protested, which McGarvey found slightly odd.

"I was there. I have the pictures of Newell and of a guy by the name of Thomas Alvarez. Otto pulled up his file. The FBI thinks he's one of the major money launderers for most of the South American drug cartels."

"Good heavens," Adkins said. "Have you passed this over to the Bureau?"

"Not yet."

"Okay, you tell us, what does it mean?" Perry asked.

"You knew nothing about any of this?" McGarvey demanded. "No hints, nothing Updegraf or any of your other people might have mentioned? Any odd little bits that didn't seem to fit."

"No."

"Your office wasn't informed that Congressman Newell was in Mexico?"

Perry shook his head. He was clearly on edge.

"You don't have a watch on the Chinese embassy?"

"Not as a matter of routine," Perry said, his back up finally. "We simply don't have the budget for that kind of operation. Goodness, we would have to watch every embassy of interest. Certainly the Russians and the North Koreans."

"Or the Iranian embassy?"

"Yes, of course, them too. But unless there's a clear reason for such a surveillance operation we don't do it." He glanced at Adkins. "If I had been informed earlier of General Liu's presence in Mexico I would naturally have taken a look."

"Naturally," McGarvey said. "But Updegraf was watching the Chinese code clerk, and he was seen with Liu at the compound up in Chihuahua."

"He never told me any of that," Perry protested. "I trust my officers, but I'm not a mind reader."

"No one expects you to be, Gil," McGarvey said.

Perry was surprised by the sudden conciliatory tack. "We do our best. But sometimes even that's not good enough, and something like this slips past us." He looked to Adkins for support. "We're working the problem, Mr. Director. Believe me, we'll find out who killed Louis and why."

"General Liu had him killed," Rencke broke in. "That's fairly obvious."

"We have no proof," Perry shot back. "I'm not one to go off half-cocked, damn it! We have standard procedures."

Rencke started to say something else, but McGarvey held him off with a gesture.

"Louis was up to something that involved the Chinese, there's no doubt of that," Perry went on. "But exactly what it was, and if it had any bearing on the recent issue with Congressman Newell, is still to be determined. I will not run my station in a panic mode." He looked again at Adkins. "Until I'm relieved of duty, I will do my job as I see fit," he said, stiff-necked.

"No one is talking about relieving you," Adkins said. "We have a problem on our hands, and we need to keep our heads."

No one offered an objection.

"Newell's presence at Liu's house, along with the moneyman for the drug cartels, is nothing short of disturbing," Adkins said. "But I still don't understand what it has to do with us. We're talking about an issue for the FBI, not one of national security. At the very worst the oil business between the Chinese and Mexico does rise to that level, of course. But it's something that has to be handled in the political arena."

"Except for Liu's reputation as a maverick, and Updegraf's assassination," McGarvey said.

"He was beheaded," Perry said.

"You're suggesting that he was involved in the drug trade?" Rencke asked.

"That's how they deal with people who get in their way. Or people who double-cross them." Perry turned to McGarvey. "You mentioned spotting Thomas Alvarez at one of Liu's parties. There's your connection. Could be if we look closely enough at the good congressman's finances, we might find a skeleton or two in his closet."

"That's something for the Bureau," Adkins said. "Could be the president will suggest just that. In the meantime what else do I tell him? He's going to want some answers; what's going on down there and what are we doing about it?"

McGarvey had done little else but think about just those questions ever since he'd listened to Shahrzad's wild story. He shook his head. "I don't know," he admitted. "But between the woman's story, the assassination of one of our people, Liu's presence, and Otto's lavender, I'm not going to walk away from it."

"I'm glad that you're going to help, but the question remains what do I tell the president this afternoon?"

"I don't know anything about the oil deal. Could be a separate issue that Liu's not involved with," McGarvey said.

"You spotted Newell at Liu's house," Adkins pointed out.

"I said that it *could* be a separate issue. Tell the president that you've instructed Station Mexico City to put Updegraf's assassination on the front burner, and in the meantime if the president wants to know what Newell is trying to do, he should ask the good congressman just that."

"If Liu had Louis killed, for whatever reasons, it might be next to impossible for us to prove anything," Perry said.

"Doesn't matter, as long as you make a lot of noise trying to find out what happened."

"What if the media get onto the story?" Perry asked. "We've been lucky so far."

"Where's Updegraf's wife?" McGarvey asked.

"Here in Washington," Adkins said. "McCann wants her isolated until we find out what happened."

"Loosen the strings and let her go to the *Post*," McGarvey said.

"Christ, we'll have every network, every newspaper, and every tabloid on us like paparazzi on a bad-girl movie star," Perry protested.

"And I'll be called to the Hill to find out what the hell we think we're doing in Mexico," Adkins said. "It'll become a media circus."

"Exactly," McGarvey said.

Perry suddenly caught McGarvey's intent. "Leaving you completely out of the spotlight," he said admiringly. "I like it."

"I'm glad you approve, Gil," McGarvey said, unable to keep himself from the small sarcasm, which Perry didn't catch.

"What about the woman down at Longboat Key?"

"Leave her there for now," McGarvey said. "I'll let you know. Meanwhile I want you to terminate Gloria Ibenez. Immediately."

Perry smiled. "Nothing I'd like better, but it probably won't be that easy. She's a lawyer, and she'll probably sue."

"Just get rid of her," McGarvey said. "I'll take care of the blowback."

TWENTY-EIGHT

□

THE WHITE HOUSE

Adkins was shown into the Oval Office a few minutes before two in the afternoon. President Lawrence Haynes, in shirtsleeves, his tie loose, was seated at his desk talking on the telephone, while his national security adviser, Dennis Berndt, stood in front of a television set, the sound turned low, watching an ABC News report on Congressman Newell's oil-deal announcement.

Aides came and went practically on the run, laying files, documents, and what looked like press clippings on the president's desk, and rushing back out. The White House was in crisis mode.

Haynes put the phone down. "I hope you've got some good news for me, Dick."

Berndt looked away from the television. "Any news would be appreciated," he said.

"If you mean the oil thing with Newell, I'm sorry, Mr. President, but that part took us completely by surprise," Adkins said. "I've come over to brief you on the Updegraf situation. And frankly we're at a loss there as well, although we've stumbled across what could turn out to be even bigger news."

Haynes was a large man, he'd played some football in college, but he'd not let himself go. Despite his schedule he managed to watch his diet and maintain a rigorous routine of workouts every day except Sunday, even when he was traveling. *Air Force One* had been equipped with a small but complete workout center.

He gave Adkins a flinty look, but nodded. "Dennis, I want you to stay, but get everyone else out of here now," he said. He picked up his phone and told his secretary to hold all calls and visitors, no matter who they were.

As soon as the Oval Office was cleared and Berndt had the door closed, Haynes motioned for Adkins to have a seat in front of the desk. "You have my attention," he said coolly. No president liked to hear bad news, but this one, unlike a lot of others, never shot the messenger.

"So far we've been able to keep the story out of the media, but that's about to end," Adkins said. "Which itself isn't so bad, unless it gets out whose company he was in the night he got shot and beheaded. Evidently he was seen at a party held by a Chinese intelligence officer."

"The code clerk he was trying to burn?"

"No, sir. This was with General Liu Hung, who we didn't even know was in Mexico until last week. He's on the FBI's persons-of-interest list because of a series of murders in New York and here in Washington. There's no concrete proof that Liu was involved, but the State Department did send a back-burner warning to the Chinese ambassador, and last year Liu was pulled back to Beijing."

"Apparently Updegraf was aiming higher than a code clerk," Berndt said. "What's General Liu doing in Mexico?"

"We don't know that yet," Adkins said. "But there's more."

"There always is," Haynes said. "Continue."

"A few days ago Liu held another party, this one at his house a few miles south of Mexico City. Lots of young women, some of them only girls, booze, drugs, the whole thing. Lots of Mexican government people, a few high-ranking military officers. I've brought a partial list for you."

"And who else?" Haynes asked.

"Congressman Newell."

"Jesus H. Christ," Haynes said softly. He exchanged a look with his national security adviser. "How sure are we about this, Dick?"

"Kirk McGarvey was there. He took the pictures."

The president was stunned speechless for a moment. He and McGarvey had a history together that went back a few years. McGarvey had saved the lives of Haynes and his wife and daughter by stopping a terrorist attack in San Francisco, yet just last year Haynes had been forced to accept McGarvey's resignation as director of the CIA, over a sharp difference of opinion. But everyone in Washington, including the president, had a great deal of respect for McGarvey's judgment and abilities.

"You'd better start at the beginning," the president finally said.

Adkins nodded. "You remember Otto Rencke."

"Your computer genius?"

"Yes, sir. One of his analytical programs has been warning that the U.S. may be on the verge of another terrorist strike. Maybe as big as or bigger than 9/11, and soon, though he hasn't come up with a time frame yet."

"Why wasn't I briefed?" the president asked.

"I decided to keep it in the Building until we had something more concrete, which we didn't until just this morning, when Kirk came back from Mexico City," Adkins said. "Rencke's program warned that whatever was coming our way probably had something to do with General Liu, either as some sort of a government-sanctioned operation, or more likely as a rogue mission."

"I can't believe that Beijing would do anything of that sort," Berndt said. "China is not Syria or Iran."

"That's been our thinking from the start," Adkins said. "But Congressman Newell's presence at General Liu's house on the evening before he showed up in front of the Chinese embassy for the oil-deal announcement has got our attention."

"That's no coincidence," Berndt said heavily.

"No, sir, it's not likely."

"Whose decision was it to send McGarvey, and what was he supposed to look for?" Haynes asked.

"It was my decision, on Rencke's recommendation, but there's even more."

The president nodded tightly. "Let's hear it."

"Our people in Mexico City found out that Updegraf had a mistress, and he was using her to spy on General Liu. We have her in protective custody, and McGarvey has interviewed her. It's why he agreed to go down there to take a quick look at Liu's operation."

"What did McGarvey find out?"

"Liu is up to something, there's little doubt about that, but as soon as Congressman Newell showed up to make the oil-deal announcement, McGarvey flew back to Washington."

"He's here in town now?" the president asked. "He's agreed to help?"

"He's agreed to take this business a little further, but I don't know where he is. It's possible he's flown back to Mexico City already. He keeps in touch through Rencke."

"What can you tell us about Updegraf's mistress?" Berndt asked.

"That's the last part that no one understands," Adkins said. "It's just too big a coincidence to swallow. The woman is an expat Iranian belly dancer, whose father was a high-ranking Iranian intelligence officer until he was tried for treason and shot a few years ago."

"Good Lord," Berndt said softly.

"When she turned up at our embassy after Updegraf was murdered she said that she wanted to speak to Kirk McGarvey."

"By name," the president said. "Did they know each other?"

"Apparently not, but she said that her father had been warned about Kirk by a Russian KGB officer fifteen years ago. It impressed her enough so that she remembered his name."

"McGarvey is going after Liu and he'll use this dancer as the key, is that what you're telling me?" Haynes asked.

"Yes, sir."

"What about Walt Newell? Has any of this been turned over to the Bureau?"

"Not yet, Mr. President, that's your call," Adkins said. "But Kirk did suggest that you have a little chat with the congressman and ask him what's going on."

Haynes uttered a short, sharp laugh. "I'll do just that," he said. "In the meantime, let me know what happens, Dick. Everything that happens."

"You may want plausible deniability, Mr. President, if Beijing is involved with something."

"I don't want to hear the term," Haynes said. "Find out what's going on down there. If it's a threat to us I want it taken down, no matter who's behind it."

"I'll pass the word to Mac."

"Yes, do that," the president said. "And whatever help he needs, give it to him."

PART
TWO

The next day

TWENTY-NINE

XOCHIMILCO

Liu Hung awoke in a cold sweat, and for the first moments he was disoriented, with no grasp of where he was or what was expected of him next. All of his life he had lived with expectations. He'd never known a time in which he'd been totally free to be himself, to do what he pleased, when he pleased, and how he pleased.

And now he was backed into a corner that could very well result in his disgrace, his arrest and imprisonment, and possibly even his death.

That was his first coherent thought of the day as he opened his eyes in the predawn darkness and listened to the vagrant sounds of the house, and to the noises outside his open window, which faced the hills from where the intruder had spied on them.

He pushed the covers back and got out of bed, padded on bare feet across the tiled floor, opened the sliding screen, and stepped out onto a broad balcony, where he breathed deeply of the cold air, fragrant from the dwarf pines that grew here.

He was naked, and when he lowered himself to the balcony's bare floor his scrotum tensed from the cold. Nevertheless he sat cross-legged, his hands, palms up, resting easily on his thighs, his back erect, his head held high.

The Japanese warrior's code of Bushido rested on five moral principles that the Chinese master Confucius had laid down. They were the relationships between the supreme ruler and those he ruled; between a father and his son; between a husband and his wife; between older and younger brothers; and between friends.

He closed his eyes and slowly cleared his mind of his most urgent problems and expectations and chanted the three sounds of his om word.

He'd been born in late 1965 in Beijing just before the start of Mao Zedong's Cultural Revolution, which lasted until the Chairman's death in 1976. Liu's father was an important lawyer who had traveled, lived, and worked in Europe, in Great Britain, and for a time in Washington, D.C. He became an important behind-the-scenes voice of reason in Mao's government, and had been so well respected, and feared, that he and his family were bulletproof in the middle of the chaos. People across China were either starving or being tossed into reeducation camps, while the Liu family lived in quiet luxury behind high walls.

There were no brothers or sisters, no aunts or uncles or grandparents, only house staff and guards. The Lius, father and mother, lavished all their attention on their only son. From the beginning they convinced him that he was the golden one, that the sun rose and set on him, that he was and would always be the center of the universe. But with such high honors came expectations. In public he was to present a humble posture. In fact, the best path was for Liu to be seen as little as possible by the public, which was why after his education he'd enlisted as a major in the army and immediately gone to work for the Secret Intelligence Service. He'd been raised to be an honored shadow, so it was the world he was most comfortable in.

He was also expected to do his duty to his country, by way of which he would guarantee his survival.

"The mighty oak tree topples in the strong wind," his father impressed upon him. "But the willow, which knows when to bend, survives." This was in the early fall of 1976, when the Liu family attended Chairman Mao's funeral.

The metaphor had not been lost on the eleven-year-old boy, and at that moment he truly opened his eyes and his ears not only to what his father was telling him, but to what was going on in China and in the rest of the world.

Finally, and perhaps the most important lesson he'd learned from his father, was that he was expected to make his mark not only on China but on the world. It wasn't necessary for him to make things better, but simply to make the world a significantly different place.

Which he had done, spying on the U.S. for his country, sending back hundreds if not thousands of important military and civilian technology documents.

But all of that took money. His father and mother died in an airplane accident eighteen years ago, and Liu had gone through the family fortune within a few years. Ever since then it had been a struggle for him to keep up with the lavish lifestyle he'd been born into. It was a lifestyle he needed to maintain in order to continue his spectacularly successful espionage work.

In Beijing he was still the golden boy because his product trumped his indiscretions. But that status would not last much longer if he failed now.

From the beginning his father had trained him as a warrior, so naturally he had gravitated toward the ancient Japanese code of Bushido, a practice he'd always kept strictly to himself, for obvious reasons considering his nationality. And his meditations had always worked to calm him down in times of crisis, to make him see reason, to make him understand the path to success.

But it was not working this time, nor had it worked since the disturbing photographs they'd found on Louis Updegraf's body. He'd known that the CIA agent had targeted him through the stupid woman, and he'd allowed it to happen, merely to see how it played out. But he had not realized the extent of Updegraf's spying until he'd seen the digital images, some of them showing his computer files, and until the woman disappeared so suddenly that she'd left her money behind.

He stopped chanting and opened his eyes, his gut still tied in knots, his head seething with dozens of possibilities, most of them grim.

Shahrzad Shadmand had disappeared, and within a week the man had shown up and started snooping around.

He looked up toward the spot in the hills where the intruder had done his spying the first night. Liu had sent two of his Mexican security people to find him and bring him in. But they'd come back empty-handed, one of them with his kneecap destroyed by a single bullet.

"Allow me to take care of this business for you," Miguel Roaz had suggested that night. "They said he was an American, could be CIA. But their operation here is a joke, you know that."

"If there's a connection between him and Louis I want to know about it," Liu had insisted. "I don't want our operations jeopardized. Don't kill him, just find him and bring him to me."

"It's as good as done," Roaz had promised. "I have just the three men to do the job. Real professionals, not merely house staff."

Liu closed his eyes again and tried to conjure up an image of the only woman he'd ever loved, but he couldn't do it this morning. She was a figment of his imagination, a woman he dreamed of meeting, one he'd looked for all of his adult life, but one he'd never found, though in his mind's eye he knew exactly what she looked like—tall, slender, with large dark eyes, a pretty mouth, and a flawless body. He sometimes thought of her as his porcelain doll. She was intelligent, yet she knew how to be a wife and adviser without ever becoming a demanding shrew like all of the women he'd ever met. She was perfection, but right now he had too much on his mind, too much to worry about, too much anger, to bring up even the outline of her face.

It had been ridiculously easy to find the man. He'd shown up right outside the embassy when they'd staged that media circus, and he'd acted like an amateur, allowing himself to be tracked to a sidewalk café.

Yet the three "professionals" that Roaz had sent came back almost empty-handed, one of them with a bruised windpipe, the other with a broken wrist.

"Was he armed this time?" Liu demanded.

"I didn't see a weapon, though we were told to expect it," the one with the broken wrist answered. He had to be in a lot of pain, but all that showed on his broad Mexican face was anger. "But he knew how to handle himself."

"So I see," Liu shot back. "Get out of my sight," he told them. When they'd left he turned to Roaz. "Those are your best?"

"Yes, but had they been warned who the man was, they would have taken precautions, made a different kind of approach. Perhaps even killed him—it would be for the best, I think."

"What does it matter who he is?" Liu shouted. "I want to talk to him, and then you can kill him!"

Roaz stood his ground. "He works for the CIA, or at least he did at one time. He was probably sent to look into Louis's assassination. Since he targeted you, the connection may already have been made, or suspected."

Liu controlled his temper. They were in the kitchen just off the pool. Most of the house staff had the afternoon off. Something of what Roaz was telling him began to sink in past his irritation. "How do you know he's CIA?"

"Because you pay me to be your eyes and ears here in Mexico, and I make sure that my people do their jobs well. Salvadore was driving. On his first pass he managed to take several good photographs through a telephoto lens. A friend of mine who works for the Seguridad recognized the face as soon as he saw the first picture. And you probably know of him as well."

"Get on with it."

Roaz took several five-by-seven photographs from a manila envelope and handed them to Liu, whose stomach did an instant flip-flop as soon as he saw the face. He looked up. "There is no mistake?"

Roaz shrugged. "You tell me, General. I can see by your expression that you know who he is."

Liu had looked again at the digital photographs. There was no doubt in his mind who the man was sitting at the sidewalk café, the same man who had spied on them from above the compound. But he could not fathom why Kirk McGarvey, the former director of the CIA, a man with a very hard reputation—even if only a small percentage of what most intelligence agencies thought they knew about him was true—was doing in Mexico claiming that Shahrzad was his girlfriend and he wanted her back.

"You must kill him as quickly as possible," Liu said.

"It won't be easy."

"Nevertheless, it will be your highest priority."

"There will undoubtedly be serious fallout," Roaz warned. "McGarvey is an important man."

"When his body is found, it will be without his head."

Roaz saw the plan, and he nodded his approval. "Alvarez will take the initial heat, but because of the increased attention that will be placed on him by the FBI and CIA, as well as our own Seguridad, the cartel families will withdraw their support. It is a very delicate situation. If I were in Thomas's shoes, I would trade your head for mine."

"Exactly why you'll have to kill him as well," Liu said.

Roaz smiled. "It will be as you wish, General," he promised. "Perhaps there will be a dramatic shoot-out, in which Thomas is killed. Unfortunately, someone will be needed to take his place."

"I will put in a good word for you."

"Thank you."

Sitting in a modified lotus position on his balcony, Liu tried to calm his mind in order to believe that Roaz would arrange to kill Kirk McGarvey and Thomas Alvarez within a few days, and he would be free to continue without interference.

He could easily conjure up an image of McGarvey's face in his mind's eye, and he had the unsettling feeling that this business would spiral out of hand, and it would be him, not Thomas Alvarez, in a final shoot-out with McGarvey.

After a long time, the eastern horizon beginning to glow with the dawn, Liu smiled and opened his eyes, finally at peace. If it was his destiny to destroy the American CIA officer, or be destroyed himself, he would let the energy flow through his spirit and embrace the task with a loving heart.

THIRTY

CHINESE EMBASSY

Liu, dressed in an impeccably tailored Savile Row suit, driving his own metallic gray Range Rover, showed up at the Chinese embassy at his usual time of eight in the morning. He was admitted through the front gate, parked the car in back, and took the elevator to his small office next to the deputy ambassador's on the fourth floor.

He had no secretary or assistant inside the embassy; he'd always preferred to work alone. Nor was he connected in any way with Colonel Lin Hochin, the station chief for Guoanbu activities here in Mexico, and the seven-man, three-women staff, though Colonel Lin believed that despite their difference in rank, Liu actually worked for him.

The only man he reported directly to in the field was the deputy ambassador, and then only if whatever Liu was involved with had something to do with the relationship between China and the host country. Normally his intelligence product was sent directly to Beijing, where Lieutenant General Xiao Zhang, who headed Special Agency Eight of the Second (Foreign) Bureau, analyzed the material and saw to it that it was distributed only to those men in the government who had a need to know. The agency had been created solely to handle Liu's product, and Xiao, whose family had been a close friend of the Liu family since before Liu had been born, had naturally been picked to head it. Xiao was the only man on earth that Liu was close to, and even their relationship was troublesome at times. Liu often thought that Uncle Xiao was a meddling old fool, and Xiao still thought of Liu as a dangerous young boy who needed to curb his brash, intemperate ways.

But it was an arrangement that worked well. Fully one third of China's success at reorganizing and practically reinventing its armed forces could be credited to Liu's spy networks in New York and Washington, which had connections all the way from the Pentagon out to California's Silicon Valley and back. The Chinese Space Agency's manned missions to space owed their spectacular success in part to Liu's spying on NASA. And in the past eleven years Chinese industry had practically exploded because of its uncanny ability to home in on just the right consumer markets at just the right time, especially in the U.S., where Liu had surround himself with manufacturing and marketing people in the know.

He'd once admitted to his uncle that the real secret of his success was letting the enemy do the spying for him. "They *want* to tell me their secrets," he'd said. "And sometimes I have to listen even though the information is old and useless to me. When their trousers are down around their ankles they become stupid fools. It's as simple as that."

China's latest target was a lock on the world supply of oil, which had to be engineered in such a way that the U.S. would not know for sure what was being done, or how, until it was too late.

When he'd met with President Hu Jintao several months ago, Liu had suggested that Mexico's oil fields would make for an interesting exercise. At the very least it would keep the Americans very busy worrying about what China was doing so close to its border. "So busy, Mr. President, that they might not notice what we will do in Venezuela and elsewhere."

"How will you bring this about?" Hu had asked.

"That, sir, you can leave entirely up to me," Liu had replied.

"And your uncle," Hu had added.

Liu had smiled inwardly, his secret triumph sweet. He had found a way to solve his problem while still making it appear as if he were doing his country a great service. "Yes, and Uncle Xiao."

This early the embassy wasn't very busy, and getting off the elevator Liu was mildly surprised to see Lee Chingkuo standing in front of the open door to the secured conference room.

"Good morning, General," the deputy ambassador said warmly. "May we have a few minutes of your time this morning?"

"Of course," Liu said, a minor alarm bell ringing at the back of his head. Lee was a cautious man who wanted someday to be appointed ambassador to the United States. He felt that he was within eight or ten years of that goal, and he was doing everything within his power not to make a mistake that could embarrass Beijing. He seldom made a move without first clearing it with the ambassador, who himself was a shrewd old man adept at covering his own ass.

The Chinese knew how to play the game very well; they'd been doing it for more than three thousand years.

But Lee was also a man who wanted to know what was going on at all times in his embassy. His interference was a nuisance that Liu was usually able to sidestep. No one in the embassy, and not even Uncle Xiao in Beijing, ever knew the full extent of Liu's spying, and he intended to keep it that way. Some secrets, he'd decided long ago, were simply too important to share.

Liu followed the deputy ambassador into the conference room, where Guoanbu station chief Colonel Lin was seated at the long black lacquered table, several thick file folders stacked neatly in front of him.

"General Liu, congratulations on your tremendous coup," Lin said, looking up. He was smiling, but only with his mouth, not with his eyes. He had his nose so far up Lee's ass, Liu had to wonder how the man was able to breathe.

"I'm glad that my work meets with your approval, Colonel," Liu replied coolly.

"Of course, I don't like surprises in my shop. You could have warned me."

"I don't work in your shop, as you put it," Liu shot back.

"Gentlemen, please," Lee said. He was slightly built man with a small voice. He always seemed to be in perfect control of himself, precise. "The general is an independent agent within this embassy, and he enjoys certain freedoms until his efforts come in conflict with our mission." He smiled tightly. "I think we can have a consensus on at least that."

"Which efforts are those?" Liu asked, the alarm at the back of his head growing a little louder.

Lee closed the door and flipped a switch on a wall plate that activated the windowless room's sophisticated antisurveillance equipment. He motioned for Liu to have a seat across from Lin, and he himself took a seat at the head of table.

"The matter at hand, of course, is Congressman Newell's sudden arrival to insist that he take part in the deal memo we have with our Sinopec oil ministry and that of Mexico's Pemex."

"It was something I reported to Beijing more than a month ago," Liu said. "If the bureau sees fit not to notify you, then that is their decision."

"Yes, I understand this perfectly," the deputy ambassador said politely. "And we do understand the nature of your accomplishment and congratulate you."

"I don't see a problem."

Lin tapped a delicate finger on the top file folder. "Can you explain the exact nature of your relationship with Congressman Newell? He says that he was a houseguest of one of our deputy ambassadors. He meant you, of course."

"The little fiction was necessary—"

"But he's returning to Washington convinced that you are in fact a spy," Lee interjected sharply.

"How do you know this?"

"He telephoned me last night and told me that he was displeased. He claimed that he and his Mexican friends have been manipulated and that the oil deal is probably some manner of ruse meant to make him look bad personally and to damage the relationship between the U.S. and Mexico."

Liu managed to laugh. "The man is right, of course."

"You fool, have you any idea what President Haynes will say to our president the moment Newell returns to Washington with his report?" Lin retorted angrily.

Liu held his temper in check. "The next time you address a superior officer in such a manner, I will personally see to your return to Beijing for a court-martial."

"None of this bickering is necessary," Lee said. "But you have managed to put us in a potentially difficult position, which I will have to report to the ambassador, who will undoubtedly ask Beijing for a clarification. As soon as Newell goes public with his suspicions of you, the game will be over here for us."

"Newell will not go to the president or the FBI or the media with his suspicions."

"How can you be so sure?" the deputy ambassador asked.

"He's already made his announcement promising forty-dollar-per-barrel oil, which he hopes will leverage him into running for the presidency. He and Haynes are bitter political enemies, so he won't go running to the White House with what amounts to unprovable suspicions. Nor will he report to the FBI or the CIA, or especially not to the news media."

"He telephoned me," Lee said.

"He may have felt like a fool, and he was, as the Americans say, venting his anger on someone," Liu said. "But what would he tell the FBI or the media? That he had been a houseguest on numerous occasions with a PRC citizen who'd supplied him with young girls and cocaine?"

Lee paled visibly. "We shall proceed no further."

"I should imagine not," Liu agreed. Sometimes, he thought, a little truth was enough to convince the listener of a bigger lie. He got to his feet. "If there is nothing else, I have my Beijing report to attend to."

The station chief was looking up at him with a tight smirk. "One of these days, General, you will go too far, and despite your connections you will fall. I'd like to be there when it happens."

Liu nodded. "I shall include your sentiment in my report," he said, and he walked out of the conference room.

THIRTY-ONE

THE FARM

The CIA's field operations training facility 140 miles south of Washington sprawled across most of Camp Peary Naval Reservation on the York River. Established in 1952, shortly after the Company was chartered by President Truman, the facility nestled in the heavily wooded rolling Virginia hills had graduated thousands of field officers over its fifty-plus years of history. It was a boot camp where recruits were turned into agents.

The late-afternoon sun was low in the sky over McGarvey's left shoulder as he jogged along one of the footpaths that paralleled the river. He had driven directly down here yesterday after his meeting at Adkins's house, and his daughter had set him up in one of the rustic VIP cottages, the one farthest away from the camp's administration, classroom, and barracks area. As he'd explained to her, he needed to get back into shape by day and do his homework by night with as few distractions as possible. His only regular visitor would be Rencke.

"Do you want to tell me about it, Daddy?" Liz asked just after he'd arrived and been shown to his cabin. "Is it the thing in Mexico?" She was compactly built, with a pretty oval face and wide eyes like her mother's. This afternoon she wore a T-shirt and blue jeans, but as often as not she dressed in BDUs because she taught hand-to-hand combat in field exercises.

"Something like that," he'd said, unpacking his hanging bag.

"Does Mother know that you're back in the States?"

"No."

Liz was vexed, as she often was with her father when he was in the middle of something and wouldn't share it with her. She knew that for the most part he'd been a loner all of his career, but she loved him more than any man except for her husband, Todd, and she wanted to know what he was doing. And she was a spy—though for the past couple of years she and her husband had come in from the field to take over running the Farm—which meant she was naturally curious. She had a need to know everything.

"Are you going to call her?"

McGarvey stopped what he was doing and turned to her. "No, I'm not going to call her, because I'm in the middle of this thing and I have no idea where it's going to take me, or how long I'll be gone. She tends to worry less when she doesn't know what I'm doing."

"That doesn't make any sense."

"I'm sure it doesn't to you, but you're married to a field officer who knows the score. Your mother, on the other hand, has been involved, without training, in what I've been doing, and it's damned near gotten her killed four times."

Liz's eyes widened a little. "I only know of three—"

McGarvey held up a hand. "Later."

She wanted to press him, but she nodded after a beat. "What are you going to need?"

"A couple sets of training BDUs and a dining-hall pass, and spread the word that I'm to be left alone."

"Will you need to use the confidence course or situation ranges?"

"Not this time, but I'll probably need the indoor pistol range."

"How long do you think you'll be here?"

"I don't know," McGarvey told her. "Probably just a few days. Depends on what Otto can dig up for me."

She nodded. "Do you want some company?" she asked hopefully. "You could join Todd and me for dinner."

McGarvey had shaken his head. "Not tonight, sweetheart," he'd told her.

That had been earlier this afternoon, and since then she'd let him alone, nor had anyone from the nine thousand plus acres questioned him about his presence here.

The assassination of a CIA officer in the field was rare but nothing new, of course. When it happened a special investigating team would be sent to help the chief of station, but only if the COS requested help. Most of the assassinations had occurred in terrorist countries such as Iran, Pakistan, and Sudan, or in war zones such as Iraq, Afghanistan, and Somalia. Those kinds of affairs were understandable in the context of the war against America that had been raging for decades, especially ever since the U.S. proved that it was vulnerable in Vietnam.

But the killing and beheading of Updegraf in Mexico made almost no sense unless it could be proven that he'd gotten his hands dirty in the drug trade, and something had gone wrong. But everything Rencke had come up with so far, and almost everything he'd learned from Gil Perry and Gloria, pointed to a man who was a zealous but loyal field officer.

Only Shahrzad's story was different. If she could be believed, Louis Updegraf was more than a zealot; he was a man bent on some mission that involved a high-ranking Chinese intelligence officer, and possibly some of the shadowy figures General Liu had surrounded himself with. He had kept his true purpose from Shahrzad and from Perry his boss, and apparently had kept no encounter sheets or any other sort of a file or daybook or computer record of his mission. He had confided in no one.

That in itself was not terribly unusual. There had been plenty of rogue agents in the CIA who'd preferred to work on their own. McGarvey was one of them.

But it was the *where* and the *when* of Updegraf's assassination that were so worrisome, and that had moved Adkins to send for McGarvey. Mexico was directly on our border and therefore of vital interest to the U.S. A highly dangerous Chinese intelligence officer had been spotted in Mexico City. Rencke's search programs were coming up lavender. And shortly after his death, it had been alleged not only that Updegraf had been seen in Liu's company, right along with a drug cartel moneyman, a U.S. congressman, and a shadowy figure who was probably a Middle Easterner and possibly even an Iranian, but that he had been dirty: a double agent working for the PRC.

It was only one possible explanation for what Updegraf had been doing down there, but at this point it was a compelling one.

So in McGarvey's mind it came down to finding out what General Liu was doing in Mexico, and what skill or knowledge Updegraf possessed that the Chinese wanted that led finally to his assassination.

In order to do that he first needed to go back to the source—General Liu. But before he did that he needed to find out everything he could about the general's background and record, as well as the backgrounds, records, and personalities of as many people as possible who'd had dealings with the man.

The path angled away from the river and started up a slope that McGarvey took with an easy stride. He'd been retired for a year now, but he hadn't let himself go. He still had his wind and his muscle tone, assets he had a feeling he was going to need very soon.

Otto Rencke was just pulling up in his battered old gray Mercedes diesel when McGarvey topped the rise and headed through the woods to his cabin.

The Company's director of special operations, bedraggled as usual, his long frizzy hair flying everywhere, making him look like a redheaded Einstein, got out of his car and opened the trunk. He looked up when McGarvey came out of the woods and onto the road.

"Hiya, Mac," Rencke greeted his friend. But there was little enthusiasm in his voice.

The trunk was filled with plastic boxes of files marked "FORT A. P. HILL, ARCHIVES." The CIA stored its paper records dating back to even before the beginning of the Cold War in an underground bunker at the military reservation about eighty miles north of the Farm. With the Freedom of

Information Act, many of the files had been opened to scholars and historians, but that openness had all but ended after 9/11. Gaining access to the entire collection was not easy these days, not even for a CIA officer of Rencke's position, except over the signature of a deputy director or higher.

"Did you run into any trouble?" McGarvey asked.

Rencke shook his head. "Nah. They know me too well."

"What's wrong then?"

"I don't like lying to friends."

"Katy?"

"Yeah, she called last night, and again this morning. Insisted that I knew where you were and she wanted me to tell her." He shrugged his narrow shoulders. "I don't get it, Mac. Why not call her? She's worried, you know."

McGarvey stared at the boxes of files in the trunk. Something bad was coming. All of his instincts were humming like high-tension wires. And he knew that if he talked to his wife she'd sense that something was wrong, and want to come to him, or at least know where he was.

But there was no danger here, nothing to be worried about. He kept telling himself that; yet he had developed a strong look-over-your-shoulder feeling that someone was gaining on him. And each time he'd gotten that feeling, the people around him had gotten into some deep trouble. More than one of his bosses in the Air Force and the CIA had come to the conclusion that being around McGarvey when he was in the field was a dangerous place to be. People were going to get killed, and sometimes it was the good ones who got hit.

Not a day went by that he didn't thank the stars that his daughter had gotten out of the field. And he would do everything in his power to keep her there, and to keep Katy out of harm's way, even if it meant lying and completely distancing himself from them until he was finished.

He looked back at Rencke and shook his head. "Not yet," he said quietly. "Now, help me get this stuff inside. How long do I have?"

"It's gotta be back first thing in the morning."

"Maybe you'd better stay the night."

"That's what I thought. I brought a laptop—I thought I could do a little more snooping inside the FBI's mainframe."

"Louise going to be okay?"

"I told her I'd be with you," Rencke said.

"What does she know about this?" McGarvey asked.

"Everything," Rencke admitted. "I can't lie to her."

"I know what you mean," McGarvey replied.

THIRTY-TWO

□

THE FARM

It was a few minutes before dawn when McGarvey stepped outside and did a few stretching exercises to ease the cramp in his back from sitting at the dining-room table all night and reading the files that Rencke had brought down. He'd always liked this time of day; the air was sweeter and very few people were up and about. It gave him time to think in peace.

Last night he and Rencke had driven down to the dining hall to get something to eat. It was well after the normal dinner hour, so there were only a few stragglers, none of whom paid them the slightest attention, and after a quick bite they'd come back to the cabin—McGarvey to begin his reading, and Rencke to hack into the computers not only of the FBI, but of the law enforcement systems of half a dozen places where Liu had set up shop, including Paris and London as well as New York and Washington.

McGarvey had also asked Rencke to see what else he could dig up about Shahrzad and her father, especially anything out of the old KGB files about their relationship with Baranov fifteen years ago.

The first thing that became clear to McGarvey was Liu's position in Beijing. Despite the FBI's suspicions since his posting to the UN in New York that he had raped and killed at least one young woman, possibly more, the Chinese government had apparently dismissed the charges out of hand. Because of the general's family he was a favorite son, totally outside any normal channel of Chinese justice.

It wasn't just that, though. The CIA believed that Liu was probably a first-rate intelligence officer, possibly the best in the Guoanbu, and very likely the equal of the legendary Russian, Valentin Baranov, whom McGarvey had killed in what was then East Berlin. Like Baranov, Liu was always very transparent, or at least it seemed that way. He was a party boy who had inherited a small fortune from his parents, and starting in New York had begun to plow through it. He lived in very large, very expensive apartments or houses. He dressed in the best clothing—usually suits and shoes tailored in London—he drove expensive cars, drank the finest wines, had accounts at Sotheby's and Christie's, and whenever the need arose he seemed to have a Gulfstream or Lear bizjet at his disposal.

One CIA analyst, a Tommy Doyle–trained man, was tracking down the whiff of a rumor that a special agency within the Guoanbu had been set up for the sole purpose of dealing with Liu's product. If that was the case, it would mean that Liu was an even more important figure in the intelligence apparatus than anyone in the West had suspected. If true it would also mean that the intel Liu had provided was over the moon.

But almost all of that was purely speculation, based mostly on a lot of circumstantial evidence. Neither the FBI nor the CIA nor the Law Enforcement and intelligence organizations of the countries where Liu had worked had ever come up with a shred of proof. And although no one, including the U.S., wanted to see him come back, Liu was too important a Chinese citizen to deny entry.

Like Baranov, Liu operated mostly outside of the apparatus wherever he was stationed. He set up shop in lavish digs and created a social scene of his own that in New York, Washington, and Mexico City had taken only a few months to become the place to be.

And, like Baranov, Liu apparently stayed behind the scenes, for the most part, in order to allow the mix of people he surrounded himself with to interact among themselves.

It was actually a nifty bit of human chemistry that Liu was practicing. Almost from the start of McGarvey's reading he came to realize that Liu was probably not involved in the drug trade, at least not if his inherited fortune was still intact. But he'd pulled Thomas Alvarez into the mix to act as a catalyst. The drug cartel banker, with his finger on a cash flow estimated to be in the billions per year, had to attract a certain amount of fascination, especially among the power hitters in Mexico's government and military establishment. Yet just being near Alvarez placed them at risk. They were like moths to a flame, with Liu waiting in the wings to snag them with his net and killing jar.

McGarvey had also learned from his first night of reading that Liu would have no fear of bringing cops or intelligence offices into his inner circle. The general evidently thought of himself as bulletproof. The worst that could ever happen to him was to be declared persona non grata, which to his mind was a remote possibility. The FBI in New York and again in Washington had some pretty fair evidence that Liu had been involved in murder and rape, enough evidence to bring to the Department of State, which in turn had delicately brought it to the attention of a deputy minister of the interior in Beijing. The first time Liu had been recalled home from New York, but had shown up a few months later in Washington. The second time he had returned to Beijing on his own, and had popped up just recently in Mexico City.

Liu was not only brilliant, but also well connected, and apparently fearless.

In New York he'd probably set up spy rings to watch the other delegates, but he'd also surrounded himself with a lot of the upper-level managers and engineers who'd set up offices in New York to attract foreign business by working with the various UN delegations. As a Chinese millionaire who had the reputation as a deal maker, Liu had been like a magnet to the very people whose secrets he wanted to steal. The high-tech guys wanted to do business with China, and they were willing to do or say just about anything to get connected.

In Washington he'd done the same thing, working out of a big four-story brownstone in Georgetown, this time attracting a lot of middle-level managers from the Pentagon who salivated at the possibility of getting the inside story of China's reorganization and modernization of its military. A lot of aerospace reps had been regular fixtures at his almost nightly soirees, hoping to tap into the vast Chinese market. And many of them didn't go away empty-handed. From time to time Liu had apparently been authorized to leak a few of China's secrets in order to seed the pot. Put a little on the table in order to suck in a much larger return.

The general's failing, however, was his apparent penchant for young women, whom he used not only as bait at his parties, but for his own purposes.

One Directorate of Intelligence psychological analyst, using material supplied by the FBI in New York and Washington—all of it admittedly hearsay evidence—suggested that Liu might have a deep-seated need to dominate women by first drawing them into his circle and then humiliating them, perhaps even raping and killing them in the end. It could be that he was impotent and was lashing out, or it could be something out of his childhood, possibly involving his mother, or some other close female relative. He may have been psychologically scarred as a young boy, and now as a man he was acting out his aggressive fantasies.

At least that much of what Shahrzad had told them had the ring of truth to it, though Updegraf could have read the same DI report and shared it with her.

When it came to her, however, there was almost nothing in the CIA's archives or what Rencke had been able to find in the mainframe of the Sûreté in Paris, except that her mother and other family members had immigrated to France, where they owned a vineyard and château in Bordeaux and were wealthy, highly respected citizens.

Which raised the question why she had tried to earn money in Mexico as a dancer, a spy, and a whore. It made no sense unless there were unresolved issues between the young woman and her mother, or perhaps her actions were some sort of a legacy that her father had left behind for her.

McGarvey heard Rencke stirring in the cabin behind him, and he turned as the special ops director came out of the door, yawning deeply and scratching himself with one hand while tightly clutching his laptop with the other.

"I left the Homeland Security background file on Congressman Newell on the table, along with the personnel files for Gil Perry, Gloria Ibenez, and Louis Updegraf."

"Anything unexpected?" McGarvey asked.

"Nothing much. Newell wants to run for president, which is probably why he was screwing around with the Mexican oil deal, but he won't make it. Perry wants to become deputy director, and he'll probably make it unless he screws up. And Gloria, well, nobody knows about her. Her fitreps are all the same; she's a damned fine field officer, but she doesn't follow orders and she's a major pain in the ass."

"Updegraf?"

"A good officer across the board, and nobody knows what the hell could have happened to him down there. The fact that he was running an operation without reporting to Perry is right off the chart. Nothing in his file, including his psyche evaluations, could have predicted it."

"What about his wife?" McGarvey asked. "Has she gone public yet?"

Rencke shook his head. "Adkins convinced her to go back to Wisconsin and let us get to the bottom of what happened. Whatever it was, we'd let her know."

"Open the trunk and I'll help you load the files," McGarvey said.

Rencke put his laptop in his car and opened the trunk as McGarvey came out with the first box to be returned to Archives. It took them only a couple of minutes to finish the job.

"What else do you want?" Rencke asked.

"First off, I want all the Bureau's files on Liu," McGarvey said.

"I think I got most of them," Rencke said. "What're you looking for, Mac? Something specific?"

"I saw the files on the women whom the Bureau thought Liu had raped and killed. But there was no mention of the other women who hung around in New York and Washington. Someone must have interviewed them."

"If they'd known something it would have shown up in a Bureau report, and I would have seen it."

"Maybe they asked the wrong questions," McGarvey speculated. "Maybe there's another Shahrzad out there who had an affair with Liu but managed to get out before it was too late."

"I see what you mean," Rencke said. "I'll get on it as soon as I get this stuff back."

"Get some sleep."

"Yeah, right," Rencke replied. He looked like an unmade bed, all rumpled and bleary eyed, but then he always looked that way. "What else?"

"What about the guy in the shadows at Liu's compound? Have you come up with anything new?"

"Not yet," Rencke admitted. "But I've got one of my programs chewing on it. I'm using the assumption that he's Middle Eastern, with most of the weight on Iranian, and that he's either a businessman, specifically someone involved with Iran's oil ministry, or an intelligence officer. I'm betting intel."

"What the hell are the Iranians doing in Mexico?"

"Whatever it is, the prez ain't gonna like it," Rencke said. "I'll get what I can from the Bureau's files and anything else I can come up with and send it down with a courier. I don't think I want to trust the Internet with this shit."

"Make it early. I may be leaving tonight."

"Where are you going?"

"That depends on what you can come up with. But probably New York. I'd like to see if Liu left any pieces behind that the Bureau didn't pick up."

THIRTY-THREE

THE FARM

McGarvey had slept until noon and was just finishing reading the personnel files of Perry, Updegraf, and Gloria as well as Congressman Newell's Homeland Security jacket when a courier showed up around three with a thin manila envelope stamped TOP SECRET.

Rencke had gone back into the FBI's computer system in New York, where he had dredged up the very short encounter sheets for three women someone named Special Agent E. J. Charles had interviewed a couple of years ago. They'd apparently had some connection with Liu, and been part of the initial investigation. In each case the files had been stamped NO FURTHER ACTION AT THIS TIME.

The information was not very important, but Rencke always handled files he had hacked from other computers as top secret material. A number of people understood that their systems weren't secure from Rencke, but nothing could be proven and he wanted to keep it that way.

He had included a short note in his nearly illegible handwriting that a trace of the three women came up blank except for one of them. She was Monique Thibault, who had worked as a French translator at the UN and apparently had a brief relationship with Liu, though what sort of a relationship wasn't explained in the FBI file. Rencke had found her at an address on New York's Upper West Side.

In a brief postscript, Rencke had written that assuming Liu's mystery guest was an Iranian intelligence officer for the sake of his analysis program had deepened the lavender by two shades. "Keep in touch," he had added.

McGarvey looked up from the note. It was exactly what he had hoped for. Shahrzad had painted a picture of Liu that was in none of the CIA's files. Not even Tommy Doyle's people had guessed at the depth of the Chinese intelligence officer's weakness for women, as she had described it. If Monique Thibault could confirm even a part of the story, McGarvey would have two out of the three pieces of the puzzle he needed to unravel the mystery of what the Chinese were really doing in Mexico.

The third part, he suspected, was probably going to turn out badly for some good people, and he wasn't looking forward to forcing the issue, yet he knew that it could not be avoided. Just like Baranov, Liu had set up fail-safes for himself, much like the booby traps the VC had left behind in 'Nam. Pick up the wrong thing at the wrong time and it could explode in your face, killing you and anyone nearby.

He shredded the encounter sheets, Rencke's note, and the other files and sealed them in a burn bag. He thought about going over to the dining hall for a late lunch, but decided against it. Now that he had done his reading and Rencke had come up with at least one name, he wanted to get it over with, and the sooner he started, the sooner he would be finished.

He took a quick shower, got dressed, and packed his hanging bag, placing his pistol and extra magazines in a small diplomatic pouch, which he sealed, then called U.S. Airways to book a seat on the 7:05 p.m. Washington–New York shuttle, using one of his work name credit cards. He also booked a room under the same name at the Grand Hyatt, which was just a couple of blocks from the UN.

His daughter, Elizabeth, drove up in one of the Hummers as McGarvey was putting his bag and diplomatic pouch in the Chevy Impala he'd rented yesterday. She was dressed in camouflage BDUs and looked as if she had just come from a field exercise that hadn't gone very well.

"Were you going to say good-bye, or just drive out the gate?" she asked, jumping out of the Hummer and coming around to him. She was clearly unhappy.

"What's the problem, sweetheart?"

"Todd wanted to know if you'd have dinner with us tonight. We're going into town."

"I have any early plane to catch," McGarvey said. He went back into the cabin and Liz followed him.

"Have you finished your homework?" she asked.

"Just about," McGarvey said. He put on his jacket, and handed her the burn bag. "Take care of this for me, if you would. It's fairly sensitive material."

Liz boiled over. "Goddamn it, Daddy, you're getting too old for this kind of shit. We've got some capable field officers who can handle whatever it is you're looking for."

McGarvey faced his daughter and smiled indulgently. "That's the second time you've said something like that to me. Have I become that doddering?"

"Mother's worried about you."

He nodded. "She has every right to be worried."

"Well, goddamn it, can't you at least take the time to tell me what the hell is going on?"

"No. But Dick Adkins might talk to you."

She stamped her foot in frustration, and her eyes suddenly filled. She looked away, embarrassed by such a show of emotion. She was a woman, and sometimes, like at this moment, she was just a little bit ashamed of her sex. According to Katy, Liz had been a raging tomboy as a young girl, and more than one boy's parents had called to complain that Liz had beaten up their son. A glass ceiling existed for women in the CIA, even for the daughter of a former DCI, and Liz meant to break through, by being better than her male counterparts. In her mind that meant not getting emotional and crying.

McGarvey knew all of this, but she was his daughter. He took her in his arms. "It's okay, sweetheart," he said softly.

She stiffened and started to pull away, but then melted. "Oh, shit," she said. "Goddamn it to hell."

"You said that already," McGarvey said. "Now, do you want to tell me what's really bothering you, other than the fact that you have a father who had the bad grace to turn fifty-plus?"

"I don't know what's happening," she said into his shoulder.

"Neither do I, yet. And besides, you don't have the need to know."

She parted and looked into her father's eyes. "Have you talked to Mother? She called yesterday wondering if I knew where you were. If you were okay. I had to lie to her."

"It's better for now that she doesn't know. Believe me."

"Is it about Gloria Ibenez?" Liz blurted.

McGarvey had a sudden chill. He didn't like people, not even friends or co-workers, looking over his shoulder. "What about her?"

"She called yesterday too, looking for you, and I got the feeling that she knew or guessed that you were here. She says that you and she are working together again."

"That's true," McGarvey said. "What'd you tell her?"

"The same thing I told Mother; that I hadn't seen you and had no idea where you were. Then around ten this morning Otto e-mailed an update on Gloria's personnel record, asked that I bring it over to you. It's classified only confidential, so he didn't think it was necessary to send a courier. Anyway, he thought that you'd be sleeping."

"Where is it?"

"In the truck," Liz said. "I've got a right to know what's going on, you know. She's in love with you, and I don't think she's going to back off unless you force the issue."

McGarvey nodded, sad not only for Gloria's sake, but for that of his daughter, who was worried sick about her father and mother getting another divorce. She'd spent most of her childhood without her father, and now that she had him back she wasn't about to give up so easily.

"I know," he said. "And what I'm going to do won't be very pretty, and you might hear some things that'll be hard to swallow." He hesitated a moment for her to digest what he was saying. He could see the uncertainty and fear in her eyes. "But no matter what you hear, nothing I'm going to do will hurt your mother." He smiled. "I love her, too, you know."

Liz's eyes began to fill again. "Oh, Daddy," she blubbered. "I'm sorry." She came back into his arms, shivering.

"It's okay, sweetheart," McGarvey said. "I'm never going away again. You're going to have me around for the duration."

THIRTY-FOUR

EN ROUTE TO DULLES INTERNATIONAL AIRPORT

McGarvey picked up what at first he figured was a loose tail on I-64 at the entrance ramp just outside Camp Peary's north gate. Whenever the Farm came under someone's scrutiny the first thing the opposition put in place, after overflights and satellite views, was a tail on every car heading back to Washington or Langley on the interstate. He figured it was one of those operations. Lately the Russians had been taking a closer look at us.

It was late afternoon, and McGarvey wanted to get up to Dulles in plenty of time before his seven o'clock flight to turn in the rental car at the Hertz counter, have dinner, and look at the new material on Gloria Ibenez that Rencke had e-mailed. The black Toyota van a couple of cars

back wasn't much more than a nuisance, yet something at the back of
McGarvey's head was thinking coincidence. He was on the hunt, and
leaving the Farm someone was following him. Yet there weren't many
people who knew he'd been there, unless he'd been followed from Langley the day before yesterday.

He reached into the backseat with one hand and grabbed the diplomatic pouch. He opened it on the passenger seat, took out his Walther
PPK, loaded a magazine into the handle, and stuck the pistol into his belt
beneath his jacket. The black van was still two cars back, and McGarvey
concentrated on his driving, switching lanes now and then to pass a car
or truck, sometimes speeding up, sometimes slowing down, without
being obvious about what he was doing.

A half hour later on the outskirts of Richmond, I-64 split three
ways—straight into the city center, south on I-295 to Petersburg, and
north on the bypass highway to Washington. McGarvey waited until the
last possible moment to take I-295 North, but the Toyota driver easily
kept up. Apparently he had anticipated which direction McGarvey was
headed.

On the north side of Richmond traffic picked up, heavy at times,
the interstate rolling through the Virginia hills, the day pleasant and
mild. He'd thought about using his cell phone to call his daughter and
give her the heads-up that the Farm was being surveilled again, but by
now he was reasonably sure that whoever was behind in the Toyota
had targeted him specifically. It was an interesting thought, considering how few people knew where he'd gone for the past couple of days,
unless he'd been identified by Liu's people, who'd somehow found out
that he'd left Mexico City and returned to Washington. Could be the
general had laid on a fishing expedition, stationing people at all the
obvious places where a man such as McGarvey might reasonably be
expected to go. But that would take a lot of assets and, if nothing else,
at least the tacit approval of the Guoanbu chief of the Washington station. If that was the case it meant that Liu had definitely sat up and
taken notice. Which was a good thing because it meant that he had something to hide.

McGarvey bided his time for the next twenty miles, the van never far away, until he came to a rest stop about halfway to Fredericksburg. He took the exit and headed down to the car parking area in front of a pleasant-looking redbrick colonial building. There were plenty of people coming and going, including several families seated at picnic tables, a couple walking their dog, and three truckers over by their big rigs, the engines idling.

The van was just pulling into a parking spot twenty yards away when McGarvey got out of his car and walked up to the visitors' center. A corridor went straight through the building, past the vending machines and the restrooms, and out the back way to a paved path that meandered through the trees to several unoccupied picnic areas with concrete tables and barbecue grills.

McGarvey slipped out the back door and stepped to one side. Less than a minute later two men emerged from the building, obviously in a big hurry. They were young, probably in their early twenties, and they were Hispanic, probably Mexicans, which for an instant was a surprise. He'd figured they would be Chinese. But Liu had made a mistake; he'd just shown one of his hole cards.

"You've followed me this far, so what do you want?" McGarvey asked. He leaned nonchalantly up against the building.

The two Mexicans pulled up short and turned. The shorter of them reached inside his leather jacket, but the taller kid motioned him off. Both were neatly groomed, clean-shaven, and well dressed. They looked like professionals, unlike the ones McGarvey had encountered at Liu's compound and again at the sidewalk café near the Chinese embassy. Possibly ex-cops or military; they had the bearing.

"What makes you think that we were following you?" the tall kid asked. He spoke with a heavy Mexican accent.

"Just a guess," McGarvey said.

"Well, you're right, you stupid bastard," the kid said. "You should have kept your nose out of other people's business." He glanced down toward the picnic areas and the thick woods just beyond. "Down there," he said.

"The general must be getting nervous if he sent you guys after me," McGarvey said pleasantly, without moving away from where he was leaning.

"Move," the Mexican said.

"Or what?"

"You don't want a shoot-out up here, an innocent bystander might get hurt."

"Anyway, old man, don't you want to have a chance to take us down?" the short one asked. He was built like a fireplug, but his expression was bland, as if he had little interest in whatever would happen next.

"Okay," McGarvey agreed. He pushed away from the building and started down the path toward the last picnic area before the woods.

The two Mexicans were right behind him, and so far no one else had come out the back door. "Are you carrying?" the tall one asked.

"What do you think?"

"I think I'm going to enjoy seeing you beg for your life before I put a bullet in the back of your head."

"Like you guys did to Louis up in Chihuahua?"

"At least he was man enough in the end to try for his gun."

They reached the last picnic table, and McGarvey suddenly stopped and turned back to them. "Can you at least tell me what Louis was doing up there? He was a friend of mine, and I'd like to know what happened, before this goes too far." The short Mexican had taken out his pistol. It was a Glock with a silencer threaded to the end of the barrel.

"Keep going," the tall one ordered.

They were only a few yards from the woods, and no one else had come back here so far, but McGarvey didn't think it would last. "Okay," he said, and he turned and walked the rest of the way to the woods. "The next time I see the general, I'm going to recommend that he use Chinese intel officers," he said conversationally. "Not some stupid wetbacks like you guys."

"Fuck you," the short one said angrily.

McGarvey stepped down off the grass into the woods and suddenly slid to the left as he turned around. The short Mexican was pissed off and not thinking straight. He was shoving his partner aside so that he could bring his pistol to bear, but McGarvey was faster, grabbing the front of the tall Mexican's jacket and manhandling him into the muzzle.

The short Mexican fired on reflex, the 9 mm Parabellum round smashing into his partner's spine between his shoulder blades, dropping the man where he stood.

McGarvey stepped back, this time to the right, pulled out his pistol, and jammed it into the side of the short Mexican's head. "Move and I'll kill you."

For an instant it seemed as if the man would comply, but he suddenly lurched back and brought his pistol up. McGarvey fired one shot, hitting the Mexican in the forehead just above his right eye, and he crumpled in a heap, dead by the time he hit the ground.

"Goddamn it," McGarvey muttered. He'd wanted at least one of them alive to answer some questions. He shoved the pistol into his belt and glanced up at the visitors' center. Still no one had come out the back.

He dragged both bodies a few yards deeper into the woods so that they could not easily be spotted from the building or any of the picnic areas, then went through their pockets. Besides spare magazines for their pistols, they carried Mexican passports, a couple of credit cards and driver's licenses in the same names as the passports, and a few hundred dollars in American currency and about the same in pesos.

Unless the documents were fakes, the men had come into the U.S. quite openly, and possibly for just the one operation. But their wallets also contained photos of young smiling women, either sweethearts or wives, Mexican health system cards, car insurance IDs, and other bits and pieces, which made it likely the IDs were legitimate. Which also meant they probably weren't on any U.S. red lists.

Checking again to make sure that no one had come back to one of the picnic areas, McGarvey walked back up to the visitors' center and went to his car, where he used his cell phone to call Rencke.

"I have a job for housekeeping," McGarvey said, and he explained where he was and what had happened.

"Do you think Liu sent them?" Rencke asked.

"If he didn't, I don't know who else would have or why. But if it was him, he's made a mistake."

"Oh, boy, has he ever," Rencke agreed. "I'll get someone down there right away. But what about you?"

"I'm catching a flight to New York, see if I can get anything from that French woman the Bureau interviewed a couple years ago. In the meantime you might want to send someone down to Longboat Key to give Toni a hand. If Liu is sending people after me, it's possible he'll try to find Shahrzad."

"And anyone else connected with you," Rencke said. "I've got a couple of good people hanging around Casey Key, and they'll stay there for the duration."

"Thanks," McGarvey said.

"Oh, and I came up with some information on the French woman you're going to see. She was married when she first started working for Liu at the UN, but evidently her hubby didn't take kindly to her extracurricular activities so he dumped her and decamped to California. I can find him if you want, but I don't think he'd be much help."

"Don't bother," McGarvey said. "Does she still work at the UN?"

"No. She's translating novels for St. Martin's and a couple other publishers. Not much money. I'll send your phone a download of what I found out about her."

THIRTY-FIVE

□

NEW YORK

The cabbie dropped McGarvey on Broadway near West Eightieth, a couple blocks from the address Rencke had given him for the French woman. It was a warm early afternoon and the neighborhood just a couple of blocks up from the Hudson River was busy, though the pace was nowhere near as frenetic as it was in Midtown. Here were mostly apartments and co-ops for families, and the small grocery stores and businesses that served them.

He headed up to Eighty-third on foot, taking his time, stopping every now and then to look into a shop window while studying the reflections in the glass of what was coming up behind him. Twice he crossed to the east side of the avenue, walked back a block, and crossed again.

In twenty minutes he was reasonably certain that he wasn't being followed. The number Rencke had come up with was a shabby entrance next to a dry cleaner in a three-story building. Four buzzers for the apartments on the second and third floors were marked with the names of tenants, Monique Thibault on the third floor rear.

Born on a farm outside Lyon, Monique, whose maiden name had been Forcier, had attended the Sorbonne, specializing in languages. After graduation she worked for a number of French firms, including Michelin, where she met her husband, Pierre. After they were married he was transferred to Michelin's New York office, and within a few months of their arrival she went to work as a translator for the UN. According to what Rencke had been able to dig up, which was quite a bit more than what had found its way into the FBI's report, the Thibaults led very hectic, and most likely separate, lives. He traveled a lot, and her job entailed many night and weekend assignments.

McGarvey pressed the buzzer beside her name, then stepped back and glanced over his shoulder at the passersby. No one paid him the slightest attention.

He was about to ring again when a woman answered, her voice badly distorted in the tiny speaker. "Yes, who is there?"

"C'est moi, Monique."

"Qui?"

"Pierre, naturellement. Ouvrez la porte."

The door lock buzzed and McGarvey went inside to a dimly lit narrow hallway. Trash was piled in a corner, a narrow flight of steps was to the left, and a short dark corridor led to a door at the rear. The place stank of mold, dry rot, and plaster dust.

The FBI's file had identified Monique as thirty-one, which would make her thirty-three now. But the woman waiting for McGarvey at the third-floor landing looked twenty years older. Her narrow shoulders were hunched; her face, which had probably been pretty at one time, was bloated and splotched with red; and her long dark hair, shot through with gray, had obviously not been washed or brushed for at least a week. She was dressed in a dirty pair of painter's bib overalls and a T-shirt, her feet bare. A pair of reading glasses was perched on the end of her nose.

When she saw McGarvey, she stepped back into her apartment and started to close the door.

"No, please wait," McGarvey said, holding up a few steps from the top. "I'm a friend, Ms. Thibault. I don't mean you any harm."

"You're not Pierre," she shot back sharply. "Who are you? What do you want with me?"

"My name is Kirk McGarvey. I work for the Central Intelligence Agency, and I'm here to talk to you about General Liu Hung."

The woman was physically staggered and had to catch the door frame to stop from crumpling to her knees. "*Mon Dieu*," she whispered. She was gone for several moments, but when she focused again on McGarvey she shook her head. "Please go away. I don't know anything that can help you. It's been a very long time."

"We think he might be getting ready to kill another girl, this one fairly soon. I'd like your help to stop him."

She shook her head, her eyes vacant. She looked like a deer caught in the headlights. "He can't be stopped. He's too smart. He has too many connections."

"I'm going to stop him, if you'll help me."

"There's nothing I can do."

"All I want to do is talk to you, Ms. Thibault. Monique. Nothing more. I promise you." He raised his right hand. "*C'est vrai.*"

"You've already lied to me to gain entrance," she replied sharply.

"I couldn't think of any other way to convince you to open the door for me," McGarvey admitted. "It was a lousy trick to play on you, but here we are. I just need an hour of your time." He gave her a little smile. "I understand that you're translating books, so I would be cutting into your work. I could pay you."

"*Merde*," she said, and she disappeared back into her apartment, but she didn't close the door.

McGarvey waited for just a moment, then went the rest of the way up, crossed the landing, and stepped inside her apartment. The place was a mess. Books and magazines and newspapers competed for floor and table space in the tiny sitting room with piles of manuscripts that she was apparently translating. The sink and counter in the kitchenette were piled with dirty dishes and a frying pan. And through an open door he could see that the bed was unmade, and clothing was piled everywhere, along with more manuscripts, books, magazines, and newspapers. The tiny apartment stank of garbage.

Two windows looked down on Broadway, but both were covered with heavy brocaded red cloth that looked as if it might have been cut from stage curtains. The rooms were very dark; the only light other than what leaked from the windows and came through the open door came from a small floor lamp next to a broken-down easy chair in one corner.

Everything was old, shabby, neglected. It was the living space of someone who hadn't cared for a long time.

Monique stood beside the chair, beside which were piled a couple of manuscripts and a couple of French dictionaries. "Close the door, please," she said, gesturing. "And make sure the safety lock is in place."

McGarvey did as he was told, wondering for just a moment if coming here had been the right thing to do. The woman was so fragile, she was on the verge of completely disappearing in a puff of smoke. He hoped that she hadn't turned out like this because of her encounter with Liu, but he suspected that was the case. Just as he suspected that if he could get her to open up and tell her story, she very well might confirm Shahrzad's.

She brushed at her hair self-consciously. "It was a terrible truc you played on me," she said. Her heavily accented voice was small.

"*Je suis désolé.*"

"Do you know my husband?"

"No, I'm sorry, I don't."

She looked away momentarily. "He was a fine man. But the circumstances were *très mal* almost from the beginning. I'm sorry, but I have no tea just at the moment to offer you."

"It's all right," McGarvey said. "Why don't we sit down and talk? As soon as we're finished I'll leave and never bother you again."

An odd look came over her features. She smiled sadly. "It's already too late, didn't you know?"

"I don't understand."

"He'll know that you came here to see me," she said.

"He's in Mexico City."

"Yes, he's been there before, with me one time. But always he had his people everywhere, watching and listening." She glanced toward the covered windows, but made no move toward them. "Sometimes I think that there is a man watching me from across the street. All hours of the day and night, even in the rain or snow, he is always there." She turned back. "But that's impossible, isn't it? It would have to be a team of men. A relay surveillance, I think Liu called such things."

"I don't think he's interested in you any longer," McGarvey told her.

She smiled. "If he knows, or suspects, that you are on his trail, then he'll take steps to cover himself." She looked McGarvey in the eye. "He's a very smart man, you know. A genius, even, except that he's *fou*." She tapped a forefinger to her temple. "But he will almost certainly look over his shoulder to see what he has missed, and then send someone back to repair the damage."

"I don't understand," McGarvey said.

She seemed amused. "What is your name again?"

"Kirk McGarvey."

"Don't be dim, Mr. McGarvey. When he finds out that I have talked to you, he will send someone here to kill me."

"I can take you out of here and hide you—"

She waved him off. "Doesn't matter where I'd go, he'd find me. And if you do not comprehend that simple fact, then you don't know the man." She shook her head again. "I've lived under that fear for a very long time."

"The FBI came here to talk to you a couple years ago. Why didn't you ask for help then?"

"I'm what your media call an illegal alien. There is nothing for me back in France, and such as this was, I wanted to remain here, anonymous. Until now."

THIRTY-SIX

□

THE APARTMENT

Monique cleared a place on the couch for McGarvey to sit, then took her place in the easy chair. A mason jar on the small lamp table was filled with red, blue, and green pencils and a square magnifying glass on a long bone handle. It was where she did her translating, alone and frightened.

"When did you first meet General Liu?" McGarvey asked.

"Ten years ago," Monique replied. "But then he was only a major."

McGarvey was startled. "You told the FBI it was only two years ago, when he was here at the UN."

"That was the second time, and by then I had lost my looks and my figure, and he was no longer interested in me." She shrugged, the gesture Gallic in its indifference. "Pierre was gone, I was no longer working at the UN, and I didn't even know he was back in the city until I saw something online about a reception at the Chinese mission. His name was mentioned."

McGarvey glanced over at a table in the corner on which more books were piled. A surge protector was plugged into the wall, a telephone cable still connecting it to an outlet. Monique followed his gaze.

"Unfortunately my computer developed a problem, and when I could not afford to get it fixed or purchase a replacement, I threw it in the dustbin. In any event I work better by hand, and I needed the space."

"Why did you lie to the FBI?"

"I've already explained," she said. "Anyway, it was only one young man, and his manner was rude and irritating. I wanted to get rid of him, and he seemed to believe that Liu had only been here for less than a year." She smiled faintly. "I told him what he expected to hear."

"Are you being honest with me?"

"Of course."

"Why?"

"I've explained that as well. It is too late now. The damage has already been done by your coming here." Her eyes narrowed a little. "I lived with the man for over a year and a demi, I know how he operates, Mr. McGarvey. Do you?"

"No."

She sat forward. "Have you ever done something that you were ashamed of, even as you were doing it?"

"We all have," McGarvey admitted. "Do you want to tell me about it?"

She looked across the room at the window again, an oddly wistful expression on her puffy face, as if she wanted to rise, throw back the curtains, and finally revel in the clean sunlight.

The apartment was utterly still. No televisions or radios blared, no one's voices were raised in anger down the corridor; not even traffic sounds penetrated the thick curtains.

"You must understand how it was when I met him," Monique said, her thoughts and her voice turned inward. "I was young, just married for less than one year, and we were very ambitious. Pierre was a rising star with Michelin, and when I started work for the UN it was as if I had stepped into a maelstrom. Every day, it seemed, was some new crisis." She focused on McGarvey. "I have a natural gift for languages. English, Spanish, Italian, a smattering of Japanese and Russian and Arabic, plus of course Mandarin. It's what brought me together with Liu."

Rencke had not mentioned anything about Liu being here as long as ten years ago. But if the man had not been involved in any criminal or intel incident, his name would not have come to anyone's attention. It was either that or Monique was lying. But he didn't think that was the case. She was no Shahrzad; she was merely a sad woman whom circumstances had aged beyond her years.

"Captain Liu was the military adviser to Mr. Jintang, who was a deputy ambassador, and the first time I was called to translate Mandarin to Spanish it was at a meeting between Mr. Jintang and Liu and their counterparts on the Mexican delegation." She shook her head. "I don't remember the substance of the meeting—it didn't last very long—but

I'd done a god job, because Liu asked me to attend another meeting, this time between him and the Mexican military adviser and no one else, other than the translator the Mexican brought with him." She smiled. "They met the same night, this time at Liu's apartment just down First Avenue from the UN. There were dozens of people there, mostly Mexican and American military officers and diplomats, but a lot of women too. Some of them very young. And Liu kept introducing me as his secret weapon. He told everyone that I was a genius and beautiful."

It was the same sort of story that Shahrzad had told. Liu's methods had apparently not changed in ten years. "What did you think about that?"

"Nothing at the time, except that it was exciting," Monique admitted. "You have to understand that I was a young farm girl. All of this attention and glitter was new to me."

"And you loved it."

"Naturally." She looked inward again, a sudden dark thought coming to her. "It seemed as if Pierre was gone all the time, and when he was home and I told him what was happening he encouraged me. 'It is a way in which we will get ahead. In a few years we will be able to return to France and buy your parents' farm and vineyard. It will give us all a chance to rest.' I wanted to argue, but he convinced me that he didn't like his job any better than I liked mine."

"But you did like your job," McGarvey prompted.

"Yes," she said in a small voice. "At first. Was that so wrong for a young girl?"

McGarvey had no answer for her. Shahrzad disgusted him, but he felt nothing except pity for this woman. Yet, both of them had apparently been seduced by Liu, whom Shahrzad had described as an urbane, handsome man with money, power, influence, and impeccably good taste. Every woman's dream. What had happened to them wasn't strictly their fault, yet like a small child who reaches out to touch a flame and gets burned, they should have learned a lesson from the start.

"I think I got a little tipsy that night. Too much champagne. I have a weakness for it."

"Did you translate for Liu with the Mexican?"

"*Mais oui,* all evening," Monique said. "I think it amused him to have me at his side the entire time." She drifted off for a few moments; when she focused again on McGarvey, her brow furrowed and she scowled. "It wasn't what you're thinking. At least not then. He was a perfect gentleman, and so were all the other men."

McGarvey nodded understandingly. " 'At least not then'?" he prompted.

"I did a few other translation jobs for Liu, once with an Italian deputy ambassador, but usually with Mexicans, or sometimes Colombians or Venezuelans. He told me that he had been instructed by his government to open relations with Mexico and South America, which was foolish because he didn't speak more than a word or two of Spanish."

"I thought he was a military adviser," McGarvey said.

Monique nodded. "He was a major in their army, though I saw him in uniform only one time, and that was when he took me to Washington. There was a reception at the Mexican embassy for the new ambassador. But that was three or four months after he'd hired me to be his personal translator."

"How'd your husband react to that?"

"Pierre was over the moon. I was earning twenty-six thousand dollars a year at the UN. Liu was offering twice that. We were going to send the difference home to our bank in Paris. At that rate, Pierre figured, it would take only a few years to get everything we wanted."

"And what was that?"

She thought for a moment, but then shook her head. "I don't know if I remember what we were really working for, other than the farm. I don't know if I ever really knew. But it was important to my husband, and I felt important for the first time in my life."

"And then you fell in love with him," McGarvey suggested.

Monique closed her eyes and nodded. "Head over heels," she answered softly. "I'd never known a man like him. He was *chic, dans le vent, et très débonnaire*. Always charming, always thoughtful, pleasant." She opened her eyes and gave McGarvey a frank look. "He was the sun and moon to me for a long time."

"You must have been gone evenings and weekends."

"All the time."

"Your husband didn't object?"

"Not at first," Monique said. "But when he did, I no longer cared. Pierre became nothing to me. Just another Frenchman for whom a wife was nothing more than a business necessity. It's one of the reasons he left me, I think. I refused to go to his stupid cocktail parties that were boring."

"That was then. What about now?" McGarvey asked. When he'd identified himself at the door as her husband she had buzzed him in without hesitation.

"Ah, now," she said wistfully. "Now I understand what I gave up and can no longer reclaim." She smiled. "We wanted children. Two. A *fils* and a *fille*. Do you have children?"

"Did you sleep with him?" McGarvey asked, ignoring her question.

A spike of anger crossed her features, but then she shook her head. "I wanted him to make love to me, and I told him so every chance I could get. But he kept telling me that he didn't want to spoil our relationship just yet. It didn't matter. I loved him and I was willing to wait."

"What happened at the reception for the Mexican ambassador?"

She looked away. "It's where I discovered that Liu spoke perfect Spanish."

THIRTY-SEVEN

THE APARTMENT

At one point during the well-attended reception, Monique went in search of the ladies' room. When she was finished, she stopped in the hallway around the corner from the main room to take a glass of champagne from a passing waiter, and she heard two men speaking beautiful Castilian Spanish. One of them was Liu.

"It's the language of poets and scholars," Monique explained. "And if you weren't born to it, only a gifted scholar could speak so well."

"What'd he say when you confronted him with what you'd heard?"

McGarvey asked. Just as he'd done with Shahrzad, Liu had hid many aspects of his life from Monique.

Monique shook her head. "I never did." She shrugged. "If he wanted to hide from most of the world the fact that he could speak perfect Spanish, he must have had his reasons. In fact, I think I was a little flattered. He didn't need me as a translator, but he'd hired me at a very good salary. It made me believe that he found me attractive and that there was hope after all that I could make him fall in love with me."

McGarvey held his silence.

"I simply had to try harder."

"What do you mean?" McGarvey asked. "Try harder, how?"

"He was an extremely social man. Practically every evening either he was out somewhere at a party or reception for someone important, or he had a crowd at his apartment. But he was single. And at some of the important functions it was almost a requirement that a man bring a woman with him. I made it a point to be more than simply a translator. I became his companion when he went out, and his hostess when he entertained at his apartment."

"And you were getting paid to do it."

She smiled. "It was nice for the first few months. He'd laugh and say that he wasn't paying me a salary, he was just giving me an allowance. In fact, just before Mexico he gave me a credit card to use for household expenses. Food and liquor but not wine. He did that himself."

"All of this was ten years ago," McGarvey prompted when she trailed off. "But you said 'before Mexico.' "

She nodded. "That's when the honeymoon ended and the nightmare began. I still don't really know exactly how it happened, or why. Of course the rest of that year and most of the next are hazy in my mind, but I know the results because I still live with them."

"Had you moved in with him by then?"

"That never happened, though I wish it had. Maybe things would have turned out differently. Better." Her lips pursed. "Each night, no matter how late we were getting back from a party or how late into the morning the parties at his house lasted, and that was sometimes until dawn, one of his drivers would take me home."

"Didn't your husband ever question you, try to stop you?"

"At first he did, but not later. I think he was probably having an affair with a woman he worked with at Michelin." Monique shrugged. "But then after Mexico he was gone."

"Did you try to find out where he'd gone?" McGarvey asked. "Try to contact him?" He was trying to get a handle on exactly how strong Liu's grasp had been. For Shahrzad the relationship had been clouded by her love for Updegraf, who had forced her on Liu. But for Monique the opposite had been true.

She looked away. "If he'd left me *before* the first Mexico trip, I think I would have done something to find him. It might have been enough of a shock to wake me up. But after Mexico it was too late for us. It was too late for just about everything."

McGarvey figured he knew what had happened to Monique in Mexico, but what astounded him even more than the Svengali-like hold Liu apparently had on women was the timing. The Chinese had been setting their ducks in a row down there as long as ten years ago, and we'd had no inkling until recently. "Tell me about it," he said.

"I think it was a couple of months after my first translation job that he asked me to go with him to a meeting in Mexico City. We'd fly down in a private jet Thursday afternoon and be back in New York sometime late Sunday night. I was to pack evening clothes—there was going to be a soiree at the Chinese embassy—but he told me to pack casual as well, and to bring a bathing costume. We were going to be guests at an important Mexican's house up north."

McGarvey held himself in check. He was surprised but he didn't let it show. "Where was that?" he asked casually. "Do you remember?"

"Chihuahua," she said bitterly. "Just like the little dog."

"Do you remember the important Mexican Liu was meeting with?"

"He was a pretty guy. Miguel something."

"Roaz?"

She gave McGarvey a sharp look. "How did you know?" she demanded.

"Are you playing some fucking game with me? Because if you're a bastard like the others, you can get the hell out of here." Her voice was hoarse, just a little above a whisper, and she seemed to have trouble catching her breath.

"No games," McGarvey told her. "Liu is back in Mexico and he's still working with Roaz. We just had no idea it had been going on for so long."

She was only slightly mollified, not sure if he was toying with her for some dark reason. "All men are pigs," she said, and from her point of view she was right. "What is he doing there this time?"

"I can't tell you that, except that another young woman is involved with him and her life is in danger."

"You bet it is," Monique said. "But maybe I won't help you unless you tell me."

"I can't," McGarvey said. "But I can pay—"

She waved him off. "I don't want your money." She closed her eyes for a moment, and when she opened them it seemed as if she had come to a difficult decision. "Just promise me that what I tell you will help bring him down."

"That and more," McGarvey said. "And I'll also promise that whatever you tell me will be kept confidential. I'm not going to write any sort of a report, so no one else will know anything about this. Except for Liu when I tell him."

Monique's breath caught in her throat. "Are you going to kill him?"

"I can't say."

She sat forward, an intensity on her sagging features. "Kill him," she said with passion. "He's a monster. Do it!"

"Whatever happens to him, we'll make sure that he'll never hurt anyone again."

She said nothing.

"What happened to you in Mexico?"

She hesitated for another moment. But then she brushed a strand of hair away from her eyes. "The reception at the embassy was great. Nice people, some of them very important. And they all seemed to have a lot of respect for Liu, which at the time I thought was odd. He was only a major. There was champagne, and I remember afterward driving back out to the airport for the flight north. A car and driver were waiting for us, and we were taken to this nice house up in the foothills. It was behind walls, but inside it was like a palace. Big swimming pool, lot of people, including a bunch of young girls. Some of them were just kids. And more champagne."

"Did you know any of those people?"

"Liu introduced me to just about everybody, but I don't remember the names. It's been a long time, and by then with all the champagne I had to drink, I wasn't focusing real well."

"Were there a lot of men? Mexicans?"

She nodded. "Old men," she said. "Maybe your age or even older, pawing at the young girls. I thought it was disgusting, and at one point I said so to Liu. But he said things were different in Mexico than elsewhere, so I wasn't to be so quick to judge."

McGarvey suppressed a faint smile. It seemed as if half the world had been calling him old lately. "You weren't happy about the situation."

"No, but I didn't say anything else about the young girls that night. And later . . ." She hesitated for a beat. "Later it was too late."

"What happened that night that made it too late?"

"I was an attractive woman in those days. I had a nice figure, pretty hair, good complexion, and I took care of myself. The right diet, good makeup, a hairstyle, manicure, and pedicure every week. Chic outfits. So some of those guys were hitting on me, and when I complained to Liu he just laughed and told me to flirt with them, and that nothing would come of it. He'd make sure of it."

"So you did."

"Yes."

"Then what?"

"It got very late. I was tired and mostly tipsy on champagne. All I wanted to do was go to bed. But Liu talked me into staying up for just an hour or two longer, until dawn. When the sun came up, they would have a breakfast by the pool to celebrate the new day. They called it a 'survival party.' But I was dead on my feet, so Miguel offered to give me a little something to keep me going. A shot of vitamin A or E, or something like that."

"Did you take it?"

Monique nodded. "It worked. I was flying right through breakfast. It wasn't vitamins. I found out later that it was heroin, and I was hooked. But even that wasn't the worst."

"What was?"

"When I finally woke up the next afternoon, I was naked in bed and two of the girls from the party were making love to me, while a couple of Liu's old men were standing around watching." She looked away. "That was the lowest point of my life. But it got a lot worse after that."

THIRTY–EIGHT

□

THE APARTMENT

Monique stood up with some difficulty, as if she were having a problem with her balance. "I wish I had some tea, something to offer you."

"It's all right," McGarvey told her. "Are you okay?"

"Just have to use the *toilette*," she said. She went to the tiny bathroom between the bedroom and kitchenette, and without bothering to close the door, she unhooked her bib overalls, pulled them down around her ankles, then lowered her panties before she sat down on the toilet and peed. When she was finished she dried herself with some toilet paper.

She looked out at McGarvey, who had turned away. "You see I have no shame left. Liu burned it out of me."

"Maybe it'll come back," McGarvey said as she pulled up her panties and the overalls, and came out to the sitting room.

"I don't think so," she said matter-of-factly. "And when I've finished telling you everything, I don't believe you'll think so either."

"Have you told any of this to anyone?"

"No," she said, and she remained standing for a couple of moments longer, as if she were in agony and sitting down again would make it worse. Or if she sat down she would have to continue with her story, which was obviously causing her a great deal of pain.

"Perhaps getting it out in the open will help," McGarvey said. "At the very least we'll both get what we want. And that's stopping Liu."

"I think you'll have to kill him in order to accomplish that," she said, and she sat down, put her head back, and closed her eyes. "We flew back to New York Sunday afternoon, but I slept most of the way up, and when they dropped me off at my apartment, Liu came up to make sure that I'd be okay, because I was getting a little jittery. He gave me another shot to calm me down, and the next thing I knew it was later in the week. Thursday or Friday maybe."

"Do you remember how you felt?"

"At first when they gave me the shots I'd fall asleep, and when I woke up I'd feel like *merde*. But later, maybe after a couple of weeks, when I got a shot I'd be flying, I mean really flying up over buildings, or around the apartment like a balloon that's just been popped. All I wanted then was to have sex. But he'd never allow it, except that he brought me some things." Monique opened her eyes. "You know, sex toys. Dildos, a vibrator, stuff like that. Wanted me to experiment, find out what felt good." She shook her head. "I wanted him to make love to me, and he brought me toys. I tried to make him understand that I was willing to do *anything* for him. Anything he wanted."

"That's what he wanted," McGarvey said.

"That was just the prelude. Even going back to Mexico for six months was nothing but an extended prelude for the real score."

"You went back?" McGarvey asked. "Willingly?" It was a stupid question but he had to ask it. He wanted to keep her in the frame of mind in which she was so angry about what Liu had done to her that she wouldn't hold back anything, no matter how degrading it had been.

Monique laughed bitterly. "I was a heroin addict. The word 'willingly' had absolutely no meaning for me."

"Do you take drugs now?"

"No. But that's a long story, too." She fell silent again, lost in her own bitter thoughts.

"Mexico," McGarvey reminded her.

"Oui," she said, coming back. "All of a sudden he started being nice to me. One day he gave me something different, and although I was flying again, I was more in control. I was happy, and up, but not crazy. We went shopping, new clothes, some jewelry, nice stuff. Shoes, scarves, hats, even sexy underwear and little bikinis." She blinked owlishly. "I hadn't lost my figure yet, and with the right makeup and contacts it was nearly impossible to tell that I had become a junkie."

"Were you always with Liu, or were there other people around?" McGarvey asked.

"There were others, but don't ask me to give you any names. They were just faces. Sometimes young pretty girls, sometimes young pretty men, boys actually." She crinkled her nose. "And it must have been winter by then, because I remember this fur coat. Sable, I think. It was the most wonderful thing I'd been given."

"Did you go anywhere with Liu like you'd done at first? Parties, receptions?"

"Once I'd learned how to handle my addiction I was allowed to come to a couple soirees at Liu's apartment. But I'd never get to stay for more than an hour or two before I'd be driven back to my apartment."

"You were alone. Why didn't you just walk away? Try to find your husband?"

"Have you ever been a drug addict, Mr. McGarvey?" she asked, but she didn't wait for an answer. "You stay close to your source. Anyway, I was still in love with Liu. I still had hope."

McGarvey felt sorry for her, but burning her had been standard tradecraft. Every intelligence agency in the world had used sexual indiscretions and drug addictions as a means of controlling case subjects, what were called johns. It was the same term whores used for their clients, and for just about the same reasons.

"He took me to Washington the week before we left for Mexico, and this time it was a party at the State Department for the new secretary of state. She was an unattractive older woman, but she seemed to be very intelligent. I remember she had kind eyes, and she knew that something was troubling me. But she never asked, of course."

"Did you talk to anyone there?" McGarvey asked.

"Lots of people, but I don't remember any of the details."

"Did Liu introduce you to anyone specific? Maybe someone he wanted you to get to know?"

Monique shook her head. "I don't think so," she said. "That came later, after Mexico. I've already told you that all that shit, everything with Liu, was nothing more than a dress rehearsal. He had one specific job for me to do, and he spent more than a year getting me ready."

McGarvey wanted to ask: For what, or for whom? But he let her continue with the story in her own way. She was back there now, in living color, and the sharp pain was clear on her face, in her eyes.

"This time we flew directly to Chihuahua, where I was set up in my own apartment in one wing of Miguel's house. I remembered that I was worried because the arrangement looked a little too permanent for my liking. But when I said so, Liu promised that I would be staying for only a few months. He said it was terribly important for him. For us."

"How long was it before the first party?" McGarvey asked.

She laughed bitterly. "You don't miss much, do you?" she said. "The very next day the girls starting showing up around noon, then the caterers and barmen after them, and the musicians later, and finally the men. Gross, fat old pigs. And right from the start I understood what kind of a soiree this was going to be. The girls started shedding their clothes even before dark, and the pigs chased after them. Along the back of the pool patio were some cabanas where the pigs went to screw the girls. Everybody was having a grand time. A million laughs."

"You were Liu's star," McGarvey said. "What was your part?"

"I got a general. Ernesto something, I don't remember, except that he wasn't as bad as some of the others. And he was a gentleman, more or less. But when I refused to go to bed with the man, Liu took me aside and practically exploded. I don't think I've ever seen another human being lose control like that. I thought he was going to kill me." She shrugged. "Of course in the end I took the general back to my apartment, where we had sex. Afterward he gave me some money, which Liu said was mine to keep, but I didn't care about it. All I cared about was getting my next fix, which Liu promised would never happen unless I did as I was told. His message, and my plight, couldn't have been clearer."

"What else happened that night?"

"Nothing," Monique said. "I remember taking a very long shower after the general left and Liu had his little chat with me, but I can't remember drying off and going to bed." She averted her eyes. "A lot of nights ended that way."

The tradecraft that Liu had used on Shahrzad had been exactly the same with Monique. First he controlled them with money or drugs, and then he forced them to use their sex to target someone specific. It had been Updegraf with Shahrzad, and McGarvey wondered who it had been ten years ago—certainly not some Mexican general. Anyway, Monique had mentioned the real score, which apparently had come after Mexico.

"So you had sex with whoever Liu set up for you, and in exchange you got your shots every day," he said.

Monique's lip compressed. "Not much of a bargain, was it?"

"No it wasn't. How long did it go on?"

She shook her head. "I don't know exactly, except that I think it was winter when we went down there, and it was late summer by the time Liu brought me back to New York."

"Was he there in Mexico with you the entire time?"

"No, in fact he was almost never there. Most of the time it was the house staff that took care of me. If there was any kind of a problem, or whenever there was a party, Miguel would come up from Mexico City. Once in a while Liu would show up, but he never stayed for more than a day or two, no matter how much I pleaded with him."

"Until the summer."

She nodded. "By then I was a total mess. I never wanted to look in a mirror for fear that I'd have a heart attack. Near the end I was being given a lot of drugs and booze, and the parties got crazy. They were orgies. One night one of the girls drowned in the pool, but no one bothered to take her body out of the water until morning. That was the same party where they made me have sex with a dog, and I did it without fighting back."

She got up, stumbled into her bedroom, where she looked around for several long moments, and then came back and sat down again.

"It was the end," she said. "No matter how much I needed the drugs, I couldn't go on like that any longer. And I told Liu that I was finished."

"He was there at the party with the dead girl and the dog?"

"Yes," Monique said. "I wanted to kill myself. Nothing mattered to me any longer."

"But you still loved him?"

She laughed again. "As incredible as that may seem to you, yes, I was still in love with him. By then I'd started to think of him as my savior, and I told him that, too. The next morning he took me back to New York."

THIRTY-NINE

THE APARTMENT

This time Monique got to stay at Liu's apartment near the UN, though he was seldom there. The young doctor who came every day to see to her needs admitted at one point that the major had been temporarily called out of the country but phoned several times each week to see how she was doing.

"And how am I doing?" she'd asked.

"You're making remarkable progress considering the condition you were in when you first got here," the doctor told her.

"Do you remember his name?" McGarvey asked, but Monique shook her head.

"He had kind eyes, and even though his hands sometimes shook a little, he was always gentle."

"Was he an addict, too?"

Yes. That's one of the ways Liu controlled his mob. Anyway, the doctor was there to show me how intelligent people managed their addiction. The trick was to gradually switch from heroin by using methadone to control the pain of withdrawal. It wasn't very pleasant. The two or three weeks at the beginning were nasty, but the doctor was always there for me, day or night."

"But in all that time you never asked him what his name was?"

Monique shook her head. "Sometimes it's best not to pry too deeply, if you know what I mean. This guy was working for Liu, which meant he had his own problems, and yet he was there to help me. His name wasn't important."

"Eventually you broke the heroin addiction. Then what?"

"A little morphine sometimes when it got bad in the middle of the night, but mostly some high-quality coke. And let me tell you, it doesn't take very long to tell the good shit from the bad."

"I don't understand," McGarvey said. "You'd managed to break the one addiction. Why get hooked on something else? It was a second chance. Why didn't you just walk away when you could?"

"No, you don't understand," Monique said. "I wasn't a street person, a bag lady, someone sleeping in a cardboard box. I was living in luxury. The best clothes, the best food, the finest champagne anytime I wanted it. Jewelry, the sable. I didn't have to hustle for my fixes."

"But you were hustling for your fixes," McGarvey reminded her as gently as possible while keeping her on track. "You were Liu's whore."

"Everybody is someone's whore," she shot back. "And I began to like the feeling I got."

"When you were high."

"That too." She was becoming agitated. "But all men think through their dicks, and I was the one in charge."

McGarvey waited for a few moments to let her calm down. "Do you really think that?" he asked.

"You tell me."

"Did your husband fit that mold?"

She didn't answer, but it was clear that she'd been stung. She was on edge, and McGarvey wanted to keep her there, even though it was cruel of him.

"How long did that last?"

"I don't know. A couple of months, I guess. Maybe a little longer, because it was fall again when Liu showed up."

"Did he tell you where he'd been?"

Monique shook her head. "He'd come back for me, and that's all that mattered. He had one last job for me to do, and it was important. The real score. Afterward, he promised, things would be totally different between us."

"Did you believe him?"

She laughed. "What other choice did I have? I had nowhere to go. Not back to Pierre. Anyway, I didn't have any money. Even the clothes on my back didn't belong to me."

"What about the money you'd earned in Mexico?"

"Roaz took it all for expenses. A drug habit is expensive to maintain, but he told me that if I asked nicely Liu would probably give me as much money as I wanted." She shrugged her narrow shoulders. "I had no need for money. By then I never went anywhere unless it was with Liu or someone from the house staff, and they always paid for everything."

For Shahrzad the big score was to have been Liu, but that had been skillfully turned around so that in the end it was Updegraf who'd been burned. The man was every bit the master that Baranov had been, and apparently just as ruthless.

"Who was this target that it took an entire year to get you ready for?" McGarvey asked.

"Said his name was Joseph Schilling. He worked in the American delegation there at the UN, but Liu had him pegged as CIA, and he wanted to find out what was going on."

"There's always been a CIA presence there. What was so special about Schilling?"

"That's what I was supposed to find out," Monique replied dreamily. She was in the past, ten years ago.

"How?" McGarvey asked. It was another stupid question, but he wanted to bring her back on track.

"Seduce the poor bastard, of course," she said, looking up out of her daydream. "This time it wasn't a Mexican, it was an American. But it didn't make any difference. When Liu had his sights set on someone, the guy was as good as fried."

"What happened?"

"Schilling had set up as one of the diplomatic aides to the U.S. ambassador, apparently to spy on some of the other delegates—Liu's guess was the Russians. They were throwing a birthday party that Friday at the Grand Hyatt for one of the undersecretaries to the ambassador. A couple hundred guests, including some Brits, some Canadians, and a handful of others, had been invited, but Liu was sure that when it started to get late just about anybody could crash the ballroom.

"I got a room on the concierge floor Thursday afternoon, and that night the doctor came over and took me to dinner right there in the hotel. Afterward we took a stroll so that I could see the layout where the party was going to be held."

"How were you going to know it was Schilling? Did Liu show you pictures?"

"Videos from the UN, some inside, but some as Schilling was coming out to catch a cab." Monique smiled. "I remember that he looked sweet. He could have passed for a Frenchman, you know." She smiled again. "I felt a little attraction. It made seducing him a lot easier."

"How old was he?"

"That was the other thing. He was very young. Almost a *garçon*, in his early twenties."

"How did you feel about doing it?" McGarvey asked. It was the one aspect of both Shahrzad's and Monique's stories that he could not quite grasp. At some point in their relationship with Liu they had come to realize that they were on a downhill ride. There'd never been a way to climb out of the deep hole he'd lured them into, yet they had hung on until something catastrophic had happened. In Shahrzad's case it was Updegraf's murder. He expected that Monique would tell him the same kind of story.

"Liu had promised it would be my last job, and I believed him," Monique. "As it turned out he was telling the truth. It *was* my last job for the *salopard*."

"What'd you do all the next day before you crashed the party?"

"I indulged myself," she said. "For the very first time in more than a year I was alone. I had a little cash and a credit card, so I did a little shopping, had a massage and a facial, got my hair done, and had a room-service dinner in my room, including a whole bottle of Krug."

"You were doing coke then; I'm surprised Liu trusted you."

"He had no other choice. Anyway, I had my habit under control. In fact, I don't even think I had a line until just before I went down to the party, around ten thirty or eleven. I was in good shape. I think I looked better that night than ever before or since. The black dress I was wearing didn't leave a lot to the imagination. I was on the hunt to seduce a little boy, and he never had a chance. Not one chance in hell."

McGarvey said nothing.

"I was Liu's whore once again," she said. "And the funny part is that I was starting to enjoy it."

FORTY

THE APARTMENT

The transformation on Monique's face and in her bearing was startling. At the start of their conversation she'd come across as an old, tired woman too frightened to speak much above a whisper, but now that she was back that night at the Grand Hyatt stalking a young CIA field officer she was bright, animated, even happy, and she sat up straighter.

"Did you have any trouble crashing the party?" McGarvey asked.

She shook her head. "Not a bit," she said. "I just waltzed in, got a glass of champagne from a passing waiter, and looked around the room for Schilling. I found him over by the bar in the corner, talking with a couple of mousy women and some old man. They were all pretty drunk by then, except for Joseph. I remember telling myself to be careful with this guy. Everyone else was drunk, but he was fairly sober. Maybe there was more to him than Liu had told me. But as it turned out he was eas-ier than I thought he'd be."

"Were you sober?"

"I'd had too much champagne at dinner, but the line of coke I did just before I came downstairs to the party cleared my head. I felt as if I could see for a thousand kilometers, right through every man in the room. You know how it is?"

"Sure," McGarvey said, and she didn't catch the irony in his voice.

"He spotted me making my way to him, and just like about every other guy that night, his eyes were glued to my tits." Monique smiled. "As you say, I'd hit a home run first time at bat."

"How'd you handle the introductions?"

" 'Good evening, Mr. Schilling. I'm Monique Thibault, and I work as a pool translator at the UN. I've been wanting to meet you for the longest time.' " Monique's eyes were sparkling. "I thought the two women he was with were going to scratch out my eyes. One of them started to say something, but Joseph brushed her aside, took my arm, and led me away. 'I don't know how I could have missed you over there,' he said. 'I must be going blind in my old age.' "

"Did he ask if you'd been invited to the party?"

She shook her head. "I don't think he cared. From the moment he saw me he was trying to figure out how to get me to bed. It was as clear as the Frenchman's nose on his face, almost comical, actually. He was practically falling all over himself trying to impress me with his wit and charm, and it was all I could do to keep from laughing at him."

"I thought you said that you'd found him attractive," McGarvey said.

"I did," Monique admitted. "But it didn't stop me from thinking what an ass he was making of himself. We ended up dancing by ourselves across the room from the bar, and his hands were all over me, and I let him do it, even encouraged him. It didn't take ten seconds for him to get a hard-on, but instead of pulling away I rubbed against him, just like a cat. I think I might even have purred. 'Keep that up and they'll probably arrest us both,' he told me. I looked up into his big cow eyes, wet my lips like they do in the movies, and suggested that we could go to my room. 'Here in the hotel?' he asked. And for a moment there I could see that he was suspicious. Maybe he was thinking that I was too easy, and that he was being set up. Which he was, of course. But I nodded, and said something stupid like 'Perhaps you don't find me attractive.' And that was that. He was a puppy dog and I had him on a leash."

"Who saw you leaving the ballroom?" McGarvey asked.

"Probably everyone, especially the two women Joseph had been with. We made quite a spectacle of ourselves on the dance floor, and I think he had his hand on my ass all the way down the hall to the elevator. That would have been hard to miss."

"You managed to seduce the poor bastard and take him up to your room where you had sex," McGarvey said. "And that was the end of that, right?"

"That was just the beginning for Joseph. And it wasn't just sex. It was a lot more than that."

"Was Liu upstairs waiting for you?"

"Not until morning," Monique said. "We had a prearranged signal. Someone claiming to be from hotel security was going to bang on the door and tell us to quiet down or we would have to leave. It would be Liu. I was supposed to get dressed and get out of there."

"What about Schilling?" McGarvey asked.

"At that point he'd be in Liu's hands. I'd be gone and wouldn't be coming back."

"He wasn't just going to lie there and take it. Someone bangs on the door he'll get up to find out what's going on."

"Pas vrai," Monique said. "By that time he wasn't in any shape to know what was going on around him, let alone object."

"Drugs?"

Monique nodded. "Understand that I had been a serious addict for more than a year, but my habit was being managed. It made me a pro compared to Joseph."

McGarvey couldn't help himself. "And you were proud of what you were doing to the poor bastard?"

"Proud?" she said, turning the word over as if she'd never heard it before. "That was just as meaningless a concept then as it is to me this moment. I was giving everything to Liu. He wouldn't take my body, so all I had left to give was my pride, my cooperation, my sex for other men. I had become nothing more than a receptacle for Liu's plans."

"You had to realize by then that Liu was a spy for the Chinese."

"You still don't get it," Monique flared. "I wasn't a real human being by then. I'd played with fire and got my fingers burned. Nothing I could do would have turned the clock back. I wouldn't have cared if he was an alien from Mars."

"How'd you get Schilling to get high with you? He was supposed to be a trained CIA officer," McGarvey asked. It was another stupid question, but it seemed to be the day for them. Spies were very often notoriously unstable people.

"We had sex first. Probably took all of ninety seconds, and when I took out my stash he was right there snorting a couple of lines with me. Said he'd never tried coke before. He was like a kid with candy. He couldn't get enough, but for a few hours before he got stupid and went to sleep the sex was pretty spectacular. He had lots of stamina, and he was willing to do anything for me that I asked."

"What time did Liu show up?"

"I don't know," Monique replied. "It was still dark out. Maybe four thirty or five. But it was funny because Liu was out in the corridor telling us to shut up or we'd have to leave the hotel, while poor Joseph was so out of it he wasn't even snoring.

"Anyway, I opened the door for Liu before I got dressed. But he only had eyes for Joseph, spread out on the bed. 'You did a good job here,' he told me. He was all excited, like my brother was when he went hunting with my father and shot his first pheasant."

"Did you stick around to see how Liu was going to handle Schilling?" McGarvey asked.

Monique lowered her eyes. She wasn't as animated as she had been. "It had been fun to that point, but with Joseph lying there naked and vulnerable because of what I had done to him, I didn't want to see what came next, I put on my clothes and got out of there as fast as I could."

"Where'd you go?"

"Back to Liu's apartment," she said, looking up. "Where the hell do you think I would have gone?"

FORTY-ONE

THE APARTMENT

"Under Liu's direction you burned an American CIA officer, thus putting him into the hands of Chinese intelligence," McGarvey said, and when she started to object he held her off. "By then it wasn't your fault; you'd been conditioned by drugs and emotions to do whatever you were told to do. I understand that much."

"Thank you," Monique replied.

"But at the beginning you knew what you were doing. You had a husband, yet you let yourself be seduced by the bastard. It was the big leagues, money, power, connections, and you loved it all."

She nodded.

"Even if you'd known or suspected how it was going to turn out, you still would have gone along with him."

"Non. What do you take me for?"

"You've already established what you were, what you are." McGarvey gave her a hard look, even though he felt genuinely sorry for her. She'd been a young woman flattered by the attentions of an older, powerful, handsome man. It had been as easy for Liu to seduce her as it had been for her to seduce Schilling. They'd both been johns ready for the plucking.

Monique's eyes welled up.

"Save it for later," McGarvey said harshly. "I want to know the rest of it. What happened to Schilling, and what finally happened after Liu was finished with you, because surely after that night he no longer had need of your services."

Monique wanted to be angry, but she didn't have the emotional strength for it. "The hotel room had been bugged, of course, microphones and video cameras. Everything that happened from the moment I checked in on Thursday until a couple of Liu's people showed up and got Joseph out of there was recorded."

"Was he dead?"

"No. Liu spent a few hours in the hotel room with him, but it was never physical, just a hypo of something, probably heroin, and a little chat about the realities of life."

"Did he ask Schilling to spy for him?"

"Nothing like that," Monique said, her voice monotone. "He just told Joseph how they were going to be friends in the years to come. 'I've watched your career since the Farm, and I'll keep in touch with you. Someday we'll be able to team up, work together for our mutual benefit. But in the meantime we won't be seeing much of each other. You met a young woman, had some wild sex—if you want to admit that to your friends in Langley—but it was nothing more than a one-night stand.'

"Joseph wasn't so out of it that he couldn't realize what a terrible jam he'd gotten himself into. He tried to bluff his way out of it. Said that Liu was finished in the U.S. He was going to shut down the entire Chinese operation. By the time he got done, Liu would be working for the CIA. But when he saw the tapes he knew he'd lost. It wasn't the sex, it was the drugs."

"When did you see the tapes?"

"A few days later. And I was okay right up until the point that Joseph broke down and cried," Monique said. She shook her head in wonderment. "Liu had reduced a grown man to tears. It was an amazing, sad thing to see, and I couldn't understand it. 'The boy is ambitious,' Liu told me. 'He wants to go places, do big things, make great coups of intelligence gathering. And I will help him along the way.' "

"How'd it make you feel?"

She looked away. "I didn't care anymore. About anything. That whole year had burned everything out of me. That night Liu came to my bedroom and said that it was finally time for us to make love. He promised that it would be special. Something I'd never experienced before."

McGarvey thought that she looked like a woman at the end of her emotional life, that at any moment she was going to get up out of her chair, find a tall building, and leap to her death. Then again, maybe she'd already done that years ago, and she just didn't know that she'd been dead all along.

"I didn't care that he had the smallest, softest dick I'd ever seen. I would have laughed, but it didn't matter."

It was the same story Shahrzad had told at the Longboat Key house.

"But then he nearly killed me, and that did matter," Monique said, and she looked back at McGarvey. "What got him excited was strangulation. He even had me convinced that the only good sex was an orgasm at the point of unconsciousness. And I just lay there like an idiot with a death wish, letting him put his hands around my neck, cutting off my air until I was seeing spots and I tried to fight back. He got his erection and he fucked me, or at least I think he did, because I was mostly out of it."

The FBI reported that the young women found dead in New York and in Washington that Liu may have been involved with had been murdered that way.

"The next morning I packed an overnight bag, got my passport from Liu's desk, and, using the credit card he'd given me, bought an airline ticket to Paris. He didn't say a word, no one tried to stop me, and by Sunday afternoon I was in Lyon with my sister, who put me in a rehab clinic the same day."

Monique and Shahrzad had been damaged, probably beyond repair, by Liu, yet they were the lucky ones. "Why'd you come back to New York?"

"I like the States. Life is too restrictive in France, or just about anywhere else in Europe. Anyway, I made sure that Liu no longer worked at the UN, and I figured I had something to prove to myself. So I came back and got my old job translating."

"What happened?"

"At first it was good. About six months after I started back to work I met a man—he was one of the supervisors—and we moved in together. But he liked to smoke a little grass before we made love, and once I went along with him I was back to the races."

She absently tugged at a strand of hair above her left ear, her eyes vacant, staring backward in time; this set of memories was obviously just as painful as all the rest.

"I lived in a fog for a couple of years, spending everything I earned on drugs, and by then it wasn't the good shit. I was taking some raw stuff. It was a wonder I survived. I finally got fired, of course, and Jim Allison, my boss, finally had enough, so he sent me back to my sister in Lyon. But she'd had enough of me, too, so I was on my own at the rehab center."

"You got clean again and came back to New York," McGarvey said. "I'd have thought that by then you would have learned your lesson. This place is not very safe for you."

"I'm a stubborn woman," Monique admitted with a wan smile. "Always have been. I had to prove something to myself, so I came back again. This time of course I couldn't get my old job back, so I made my rounds of the publishers, finally getting a job translating a book from the French. Then there were a couple of Chinese books, though most of them are translated into English before they ever leave China. They have more control over the content that way."

"And you've been clean ever since?" McGarvey asked.

She nodded. "So far so good," she replied dreamily. But then she focused on McGarvey sitting across from her. "Is that what you came here to find out?" she asked.

"Yes, thank you," McGarvey said. "Will you allow me to leave you some money?"

She shook her head. "Just kill him," she said with sudden emotion. "As soon as you can. Put a bullet in his brain, like you did bin Laden."

Something lurched inside McGarvey's chest. He'd been on a freelance operation for the CIA last year, which had ended in tracking Osama bin Laden to a hideout in Karachi, where he'd put a bullet in the man's head. The mission had been kept top secret for fear of the blowback from Muslims across the world. Within a week a bin Laden double had sent a tape to the al-Jazeera, network, and the war against terror had continued without missing a beat.

"I don't know where you came up with something like that," he said.

"I don't work at the UN, but I still have friends who hear stuff," she said. "Diplomats never seem to notice their translators. We're like ghosts, and there's almost nothing a translator loves more than to share gossip."

It was a new wrinkle that McGarvey, and he suspected everyone else down at Langley, had never considered. "Whatever you think you know, I'd suggest you keep it to yourself."

She shrugged. "Kill him soon."

FORTY-TWO

□

UNITED NATIONS HEADQUARTERS

It was just about closing time for the public as McGarvey watched the replica of Foucault's pendulum ponderously swinging on its heavy weight, the tip scribing a series of lines in a circular pit of sand on the floor.

The device proved that the earth was turning on its axis, and here in the General Assembly Building it seemed an appropriate symbol because the UN, rightly or wrongly, had its missions and troops on just about every continent on the planet.

He hadn't known what he'd expected to learn by coming over here directly from Monique's apartment, except that he wanted to get a feel for the place where Liu had ensnared her as he had so many others. He suspected that Liu hadn't set out to kill any of his women; the deaths had been accidents during his rough brand of sex. Liu was confident enough to believe that none of them would go to the authorities to accuse him of being a spy for the Chinese. By the time they figured out that much, they themselves were in so deeply that no one would believe their stories. McGarvey hadn't completely believed Shahrzad until this afternoon listening to Monique's tale.

The pendulum was suspended from the soaring ceiling on about fifty feet of thin wire. Once it was set in motion the weight would continue to swing back and forth for a very long time.

Shahrzad had been tethered to Liu by her professed love for Updegraf, so she'd swung from one side to the other in a short time. Monique, on the other hand, had fallen in love with Liu, so her tether had been very long. It had taken her all of ten years to get to the point where she could talk about Liu.

The next step would be to find a new pendulum with enough weight to break the tether altogether. And it was this step that bothered McGarvey the most. People who tried to play in the general's league ended up dead or damaged beyond repair.

Loudspeakers announced that it was ten minutes until closing time as McGarvey walked back across the public lobby and outside. A small crowd of people had gathered in front of the gate, some of them holding signs protesting the latest round of sanctions against Iran, but they weren't being noisy, and the few cops on duty seemed bored as they leaned against their patrol cars. Almost every day some group demonstrated outside the UN; most of the time the crowds were small and peaceful, like this afternoon's, because people no longer seemed to care. In the past few years the UN had become a joke, and it had lost most of its effectiveness.

McGarvey made his way around the crowd, then crossed the street at Forty-second and walked the couple of blocks back up to the Grand Hyatt Hotel, where he'd stayed the previous night. It had been an odd bit of coincidence that Monique had come here to burn Schilling. Yet the hotel was near the UN, so it had been a convenient place to hold the party.

The soaring atrium lobby was busy with late arrivals, the cocktail lounge filled with the after-work crowd, but McGarvey found a spot at the far end of the bar. He ordered a Martell cognac neat and glanced over his shoulder, a tickling at the back of his neck.

He'd never trusted coincidences, but there'd been no reason for Monique to name the Grand Hyatt as the hotel where'd she'd burned Schilling, even if she'd been informed that McGarvey was registered there and would be paying her a visit.

That line of reasoning made no sense, yet her knowing that he'd assassinated bin Laden last year made no sense either.

He let his gaze drift across the lobby, looking for the one face that didn't belong, the odd man, neither checking in nor checking out, neither coming nor going. The one figure who shouldn't be there. After the incident yesterday north of the Farm he'd been having the feeling that someone was coming up behind him. But if anyone was here looking down his trail, McGarvey couldn't pick him out.

He paid for his drink and took it down to the next lower level, where he sat in an easy chair at a coffee table. He'd left his pistol up in his room, knowing that he was going over to the UN and wanting to avoid the security issue, but he felt naked without it now.

Rencke answered on the first ring when McGarvey called him. "Oh, wow, Mac, what'd you find out?"

"She confirmed Shahrzad's story, but Liu was in business here at least ten years ago, and maybe longer. Did you get a line on those two guys who tried to jump me outside Richmond?"

"Ex–Mexican special forces. GAFE. And you'll never guess where they got some of their training? Right here at Bolling Air Force Base."

"They're no longer in the service?"

"No, but their records are clean so far as I can find out. They resigned their commissions about six months ago, supposedly to work for a security consulting firm where they could make more money. Evidently no one blames them."

McGarvey looked up as a man came across the lobby directly toward him. "Hold on," he told Rencke.

There was something familiar about the face, but McGarvey couldn't place it, and before the man got all the way across he angled left toward the bar.

"False alarm," McGarvey told Rencke. But he wasn't at all sure it had been.

"You're in the hotel, but where?" Rencke asked.

"The lobby. I thought I saw someone I might have recognized, but I'm not sure." He glanced up toward the busy cocktail lounge but the guy had disappeared. "The French woman told me that she burned a young CIA field officer who worked at the UN."

"Did she remember a name?"

"Joseph Schilling. But it was most likely a work name."

"Hang on, I'll check," Rencke said.

McGarvey glanced again toward the busy cocktail lounge, but the guy he thought he might have recognized was nowhere in sight.

When Rencke came back he sounded out of breath. "You're not going to believe this shit, Mac," said. "Joseph Schilling left the UN mission a little over nine years ago. Wanted a transfer to our embassy in Beijing. Did a good job supervising a string of Chinese nationals working for us. Good product. Great fitreps. And you're right, Schilling was his work name."

It came to McGarvey all of a sudden. "Son of a bitch," he said softly. "Updegraf."

"Bingo," Rencke said. "Louis Updegraf worked for the Guoanbu for the last nine or ten years of his life. So why did Liu snuff him?"

"Updegraf probably tried to turn the tables and burn him. He came across Shahrzad and used Liu's weakness for women against him."

"Or tried to," Rencke said.

"No mention in his jacket about a possible problem with drugs?"

"There wouldn't be if he was turning in good product," Rencke said. "You sat on the seventh floor, you know the realities better than anyone else."

Alcohol, drugs, money, sex, the fast life. All those held the same kinds of allure for the right person as the act of spying did. The good field officer was the man or woman who lived outside the envelope, and a lot of the time way outside the letter of the law.

Updegraf had played with fire the first time, and got himself burned. The second time he got himself killed.

The timing bothered McGarvey. What was Liu doing in Mexico that Updegraf tried to interfere with, and that forced Liu to kill a man who'd probably been one of his star sources?

But something else bothered him, too. He glanced a third time toward the cocktail lounge. "Run a search on Liu's and Updegraf's assignments for the past nine years. I think they'll probably match. Updegraf probably got to each of his postings a few months before Liu, in order to pave the way."

"I'm on it," Rencke said.

"If that pans out, see what you can find in Updegraf's file for each assignment. Did something out of the ordinary happen to him or around him? Did he come up with something big? Or maybe the Chinese made big scores wherever Updegraf and Liu were stationed together."

"If there's a pattern I'll find it."

"I hope so, because I think we're going to need it to figure out what the hell Liu is up to down there that's so fully developed he didn't need Updegraf."

"What about the French woman?" Rencke asked.

"I'm going back over to her apartment to find out if she had any contact with Updegraf after that night. If he was trying to get something on Liu he might have tried to use her, like he used Shahrzad."

"I'm on that too," Rencke said. "Then what?"

"I'll let you know," McGarvey said, and he broke the connection, the tickle still at the back of his neck.

He finished his drink, pocketed his phone, and went up to his room to get his pistol. Just before the elevator door closed he looked across the lobby toward the bar one last time, but the man was nowhere to be seen.

FORTY-THREE

☐

THE APARTMENT

This part of the Upper West Side was a neighborhood of families. Traffic on Broadway was fairly light; most people were home from work, the kids were home from school, and supper was on the stove.

McGarvey buzzed Monique's apartment and glanced over his shoulder as a man carrying a load of dry cleaning over his shoulder walked past on the other side of the street. At the corner two men were involved in what appeared to be a heated discussion, and beyond them a woman carrying a bag of groceries entered an apartment building.

Nothing out of the ordinary. But he was spooked.

He turned back and hit the buzzer again. But after a full twenty seconds when there was no answer, he rang for the second-floor front apartment. A woman answered.

"Who is it?"

"Police," McGarvey said.

The door lock buzzed, and McGarvey went inside the dimly lit hall and held up his open wallet for the elderly woman who came to the head of the stairs. She seemed nervous. "What is it?"

"There's been a disturbance on the third floor," McGarvey said, starting up. Alarms were jangling in his head. "But Ms. Thibault does not answer."

"I've heard nothing," the old woman said, glancing toward the stairs up to the third floor.

"I'll just see," McGarvey said. "Go back into your apartment, please."

The old woman nodded uncertainly and went back into her apartment, from where she watched through the partially open door as McGarvey passed. He smiled reassuringly at her.

Monique did not answer his knock. If she was inside and had bolted the door, he wouldn't be able to get inside without making a lot of noise. But if she had merely stepped out, she would only have used her key. He used a credit card to fish around between the door and door frame to trip the latch, but it wasn't necessary—the door was not locked.

He stepped back, pulled out his pistol, and, standing to one side, eased the door open with the toe of his shoe.

"Monique," he called softly. "*Ici Pierre, encore.*"

The apartment was silent.

McGarvey slid inside, keeping low and moving fast, sweeping his pistol left to right.

Monique's body lay spread-eagled between the couch and her easy chair. Her T-shirt had been ripped open, exposing her small breasts, flattened in death, and her painter overalls had been pulled off and tossed into the kitchen. She had been strangled with her own panties, which were still twisted tightly around her neck. Her face had turned a deep purple, her eyes bulging, her tongue protruding from her half-open mouth.

McGarvey made a quick sweep of the apartment to make certain the killer was gone, then went back into the living room.

The door hadn't been forced, and it didn't look as if Monique had put up a struggle. Maybe she'd known her killer and had let him in. Maybe she'd even been expecting him.

Whatever the case, Liu was responsible for her death, there was no doubt about it. Nor was there any doubt that killing her was a clear message to McGarvey: Keep away.

He holstered his pistol and left the apartment, making his way down to the street and to the end of the block before he called Rencke on his cell phone. "The French woman is dead. I just left her apartment. It was meant to look like she was raped, which is possible, and then she was strangled to death with her own panties."

"Liu," Rencke said.

"Probably one of his henchmen," McGarvey said. "But it's a message."

"What do you want to do, Mac?"

"Get one of our teams over here to reduce it to a heart attack, and get an obit in the newspaper."

"That'll get his attention," Rencke said. "It's too bad about her."

"Yeah, I should have taken her out of there when I had the chance. We could have put her with Shahrzad in Longboat Key." It was a mistake that McGarvey would think about for a long time to come.

"I came up with something else on those two guys you offed near Richmond. They were ex-GAFE, but their records weren't so clean after all. They'd been forced to resign their commissions because they were probably involved in a drug-smuggling operation."

"No trials, no jail time?"

"Some money probably changed hands, so they walked," Rencke said. "Could be that Liu is working outside regular Guoanbu channels, and using drug cartel muscle to do his dirty work. It would explain what Alvarez was doing hanging around."

"Is Liu still in Mexico City?"

"Yeah, and he's making himself real visible all of a sudden. Makes you wonder what the prick is getting ready to spring on us."

"Whatever it is, it'll come soon, and it'll be something big that we haven't thought of yet."

FORTY-FOUR

☐

U. S. EMBASSY, MEXICO CITY

The day shift was just getting off work and leaving the building when Gil Perry phoned next door and asked Gloria to stop by. Word had come down from Langley this morning along with her package, which had been signed off by the DDO himself, but it had taken Perry until now to actually do what he'd been ordered to do.

He'd spent the day trying to figure out what the ramifications would be. He didn't want even the hint of any blowback coming his way. His shop was in enough disarray without Gloria raising some kind of hell.

The business with Updegraf's widow had been carefully swept under the rug, and Perry sincerely hoped that the same would be true in Gloria's case.

But he didn't believe it was going to work out so neatly. Trouble was, he had no idea yet what he could do about it, other than follow orders.

Gloria showed up a couple of minutes later, her purse on one shoulder, her laptop on the other. She was ready to leave for the day, and she seemed irritated that she'd been called to see the boss.

"It's been a long day, Gil," she said. "What do you want to see me about?"

"Close the door, would you? I don't think this needs to be announced for the entire building's benefit."

"Cristo," Gloria swore softly. She closed the door and sat down. "Couldn't this have waited until morning?"

"I'm afraid not," Perry said. Truth be told, he'd been itching to do this from the day she'd come to work for him. He passed the original message from McCann across the desk to her. "This came today."

Gloria set her laptop on the floor and quickly read the brief letter, which ordered her immediate termination from the CIA. She looked up in wonder. "Doesn't say why," she said. She tossed the letter back. "Have you been complaining to Howard about my short skirts?"

"No. And it's Mr. McCann."

"Howard or Mister, he's a prick just like you. And just like you he's wanted to get rid of me for a long time." She smiled, and got to her feet. "Well, good luck, Gilbert. But I will fight this. Maybe I'll bring a sexual-discrimination suit against the Company and a sexual-harassment suit against you."

"Of course those are your prerogatives," Perry said. "I want your identification card if you're carrying it, your weapon, and your laptop."

"I'm not so stupid as to carry a CIA ID card. The weapon is my personal property, and so is the laptop."

"You may keep your weapon, but until we can sanitize your hard drive the laptop stays here in the embassy. It will be returned to you when we're sure you weren't trying to carry secrets out the door."

"Fuck you," Gloria said, and she headed for the door.

Perry picked up the phone and punched a three-digit number. "Security," he said. "This is Perry. I want two men, with their sidearms, up here on the double."

Gloria turned back and looked at him with nothing but contempt on her face. She came back and laid the laptop on his desk. "Call when I can pick it up," she said evenly.

"Thank you," Perry said. "One last thing." He slid a Secrets Act statement across for her signature; it promised that she would never divulge anything of a classified nature she'd learned while in the employ of the CIA, under penalty of imprisonment for possibly as long as life.

She took the pen he offered, and signed it. "I'll keep my mouth shut," she said.

"I hope so, Ms. Ibenez," Perry said. "I think that you could have been a damned fine officer, but I think that you've been working some sort of a freelance operation. That's the sort of thing Louis was doing, and it got him assassinated. I won't have another death on my watch."

"A word of warning, Gil," Gloria said.

"Yes?"

"Watch your step. Something big is going down."

He started to object but she held him off.

"I'm not being shitty now, I swear it. But just tell all your people to watch their backs. I don't know what's going to happen, but whatever it is, it'll be big. I'm sure of it."

Perry didn't think that he'd ever despised anyone more than he did Gloria at this moment. But she was right. Something big was coming his way, and he still hadn't figured out how to handle it. It was Updegraf and his fucking meddling.

He handed Gloria a manila envelope. "It's your termination letter, something about the Secrets Act form you just signed, something about your hospitalization program and 401(k), and your severance check. The Company was generous."

"I'll bet," Gloria said.

Two marines in undress blues, their pistols holstered, showed up at the door.

"Hi, guys," Gloria said brightly. "Care to walk a lady to her car?"

"Ms. Ibenez is leaving," Perry said. "She is no longer authorized in any nonpublic area of the embassy. I want her pass before she clears Post One."

FORTY-FIVE

CIA HEADQUARTERS

Dick Adkins's secretary buzzed him a few minutes before seven as he was getting ready to call for his driver to take him home. Howard McCann was waiting in the outer office. For just a moment Adkins was a little irritated that his deputy director of operations had taken so long to answer the summons from earlier this afternoon, but everyone in the building had been running at top speed ever since Rencke's lavender warning.

"Send him in, Dahlia, then call Hank, and you may go home for the evening."

"Yes, Mr. Director. Have a good evening."

"You, too."

McCann walked in. "Sorry for the delay, Dick, but I've been slammed with meetings all afternoon." He glanced at his watch. "Fact is I have a Technical Means staff meeting next door in twenty minutes."

Adkins waved him to a chair across the desk. "I'm afraid I have another headache for you to deal with."

McCann sat down and nodded, darkly. "I figured as much. What's come up?"

"The president has changed his mind. Since we have assets inside Mexico, he wants us to launch a full-scale investigation into Congressman Newell's activities down there."

"Come on. That's a job for the Bureau and you know it. We have enough crap on our plate without chasing after some stupid politician who shoots off his mouth just before an election year." McCann shook his head. "Anyway, if it ever came out that we were bird dogging an elected official, you would have some tough questions to answer on the Hill."

It was about the reaction Adkins had figured he'd get. Dave Whittaker, his DDCI, had been a hell of a Clandestine Services director. And before him, of course, McGarvey had done the job brilliantly. He'd never been an administrator, but he'd run the DO with a lot of imagination.

McCann, on the other hand, was a great administrator, but he came up short on imagination. He was more of a bureaucrat than a spy.

"According to the White House, Newell also made a trip to Beijing four months ago. The president wants us to find out what he did when he was there. Who he saw, where he went."

"We can refuse this."

"Fred Rudolph's people are looking into his activities in Arizona and here in Washington."

McCann was stunned. Fred Rudolph had recently taken over the new FBI Division of Intelligence and Counterterrorism. Spying on Newell by Rudolph's people meant the president and FBI suspected the congressman had a connection with some terrorist organization. "If the media got onto to something like this it'd go ballistic. Because of 9/11, naming one of our politicians as a terrorist would be bigger than Watergate. Shit, it could bring down Haynes if he's wrong." He gave Adkins a hard look. "It could damn well mean Rudolph's job. And ours."

"Nonetheless, we've been asked to take on a job, and we'll do it," Adkins said.

McCann pursed his lips. "What's going on, Mr. Director?"

"We've been asked to check out Newell—"

"I mean what's really going on. First I'm told to fire Gloria Ibenez because she won't obey orders. And now I'm being told to help Fred Rudolph investigate an Arizona congressman who made a speech in Mexico City. Ibenez worked for McGarvey last year, and is in love with the guy, from what I hear. Rudolph and McGarvey are buds. And McGarvey was standing right there in front of the Chinese embassy while Newell was making his speech. So what's the connection?"

Adkins was careful not to let any surprise show on his face. He nodded. "Where'd you hear that McGarvey was in Mexico?"

"Come on, Dick. Gil Perry may be a pompous ass sometimes, but he didn't fall off a hay wagon last year. He's sharp, and he knows his people. And he also knows whom he's working for."

"Yeah," Adkins said. "Me." He shoved a thick file folder across to McCann. "This is the material on Newell that Dennis Berndt gave me. It's a start. Needless to say you have to keep tight control of the inquiries."

"I'll say," McCann agreed. He looked at the file as if it were an animal ready to pounce. "I'll follow whatever orders I'm given, of course, Mr. Director. I always have. But this time I have to ask that you put them in writing."

Adkins had anticipated that reaction as well. "You'll find my letter in the jacket. I'd just ask that you take care with whom you share it."

"Oh, yes, sir," McCann said. He got to his feet and picked up the file. "I'll take a great deal of care."

FORTY-SIX

□

EN ROUTE TO LA GUARDIA

McGarvey had checked out of the Grand Hyatt and caught a cab in front, the sight of Monique's strangled body sharp in his mind. Halfway to La Guardia his cell phone chirped. It was Rencke.

"Are you on the way out to the airport? I've got something on Liu."

"Yeah, I'm catching the eight clock to D.C.," McGarvey said. "What's up?"

"I missed it earlier, but one of my search engines picked up one of Liu's work names from an American Airlines flight to New York."

"He's here in the city now?" McGarvey demanded.

"No, he's on the Washington shuttle that left about ten minutes ago. Do you want me to have someone follow him?"

McGarvey thought about it for a moment. "I think it's already too late. He's finished what he came up here to do. Is he booked on a flight back to Mexico City?"

"First thing tomorrow morning."

"He'll most likely check with his embassy, although they probably won't be happy to see him. The FBI doesn't want him back, and his people won't want the possible hassle."

"I can give Fred the heads-up."

"No. Just make sure that he goes back to Mexico in the morning. If he misses his flight, give me a call."

"What else do you need?" Rencke asked. "Can I set anything up for you here tonight?"

"I want to talk to Dick, but I'll take care of that myself. In the meantime, pull up the dates of the rapes and murders that Liu was suspected of up here and Washington."

"What are you looking for?"

"I want to know if they match the times that he was with Monique Thibault."

"Okay, give me a minute," Rencke said.

McGarvey laid the phone on the seat beside him and opened his overnight bag to get his air marshal ID so that he could fly commercially while carrying his pistol. He came across the file that Liz had given him at the Farm. All this time he hadn't gotten around to reading it. He pulled it out and flipped through the pages.

This was material that Rencke had come across at the last minute, including a psych evaluation that had been completed just before Gloria had been assigned to Station Mexico City.

He picked up the phone. "Otto?"

"Thirty seconds," Rencke said.

McGarvey put the phone down again and started reading Gloria's psyche evaluation. When he'd become DCI, he'd required every field officer to undergo an evaluation by the Company's shrink before each posting. It was a notion that Jim Angleton had floated but that no one at the time had cared to do. The idea was to spot some indications that the field officer might be going off the deep end, or worse, going over to the other side. In the last couple of years the system had worked, to a degree, and the occasional drunk or nutcase had been weeded out.

But it had not worked to spot Updegraf's apparent maverick tendencies, or if it had neither Perry nor McCann had done anything about it.

The same thing seemed true for Gloria. She was a woman who had apparently been walking a very narrow line of sanity ever since her husband had been captured by Cuban intelligence in Havana, tortured, and killed. She had become a different person, even beyond what could have been expected because of the shock she'd gone through.

The main point of the psychological evaluation summary was that Gloria seemed incapable of feeling sadness or remorse. She was a good officer, and an otherwise stable person, but she had no regrets, and couldn't have them.

McGarvey looked up. She'd been broken up about the death of her partner during an operation at Guantánamo Bay last year. If this was correct, she'd been faking it. But why?

He picked up the phone. "Otto?"

"I ran the matches," Rencke said. "One of the murders in New York that Liu was suspected of being involved with happened before Ms. Thibault went to work for him. But she was on board during the times of the two others. Do you think she was somehow involved?"

"No," McGarvey said. One of the answers he had been looking for had just dropped in place for him. "I think he has two kinds of women. Ones like Shahrzad and Monique, whom he seduces and then uses to spy for him. And then he has party girls. His sex toys whom he has to end up killing."

"He's a disturbed man," Rencke said softly.

"He's all of that and more," McGarvey said.

"Dangerous."

"Yeah."

"You still don't want me to have him followed until you get here?" Rencke asked. "We could end this tonight."

"We still don't know what he's up to in Mexico. Just let me know if he doesn't go back in the morning."

"Will do."

"Do you know where Gloria's dad is living these days?"

"Miami, I think. Hang on."

McGarvey glanced at Gloria's psych evaluation summary again. If he was going to use her to take a run at Liu, he needed to know a lot more. Her life could depend on it. He didn't want her ending up dead like Monique, or broken like Shahrzad.

"I was right," Rencke said. "He's in Little Havana."

"Cancel my shuttle reservations, would you? And get me a seat on the next flight to Miami. I want General Marti's file waiting for me."

"Oh, wow, Mac. What're you thinking?"

"Has Perry fired Gloria yet?"

"It was supposed to happen sometime today," Rencke said. "I'll check on it. Are you going to use her to get to Liu?"

"I think so," McGaervey said. "But I still have some homework to do, and in the meantime I'll try not to get anyone else killed."

"Not your fault, kemosabe."

"Yeah," McGarvey said. But it *was* his fault.

FORTY-SEVEN

EN ROUTE TO MIAMI

Sitting at the very rear of the airplane, McGarvey had the last row of seats to himself. Since he was flying as an air marshal he couldn't have a drink, and no dinner was being served, so he used the two and a half hours to take a closer look at Gloria's psych evaluation.

The death of her husband had hit her very hard, as was to be expected. For the first couple of weeks she'd had trouble focusing, and she'd had frequent outbursts of temper, flying off the handle almost uncontrollably. When the assistant DDO, Chuck Bratton, suggested she take a leave of absence for a month or two, she'd become so enraged that security had to be called to get her under control.

The Company shrinks hospitalized her for seven days, but she'd bounced back and been certified fit for service, though none of her coworkers or her immediate supervisor on the Latin American desk where she'd been assigned believed it.

Yet she'd been assigned to Paris Station on the recommendation of Dr. Norman Stenzel, chief of the CIA's Medical Services Psychological Division, who'd written that leaving her at Langley could possibly damage her sense of self-esteem badly enough to make her nearly useless in future field assignments. But sending her back to a Spanish-speaking country would almost certainly cause even more damage, forcing her to relive the almost unbearable experience of her husband's arrest and the news that he'd been executed.

Three weeks after she'd transferred to the French section of the European desk to prepare for her assignment, she'd suddenly come awake, as if she'd been in a trance since Cuba. Her initial fitrep gave her absolutely top marks: "extremely intelligent . . . fast learner . . . positive attitude."

Six months later she'd gone to Paris to start her field assignment under Peter Avalon, who was a no-nonsense straight shooter who expected his people to be first-rate, or he'd kick them out.

Although Stenzel's psych evaluation that Rencke had managed to pull up and get to McGarvey made no mention of the types of assignments she'd been involved with in France, it did include glowing reports from Avalon. For the first eight months she was his rising star.

But then her father paid her a visit and everything changed.

It was the opening paragraph that had caught McGarvey's eye in the cab on the way out to La Guardia.

"Subsequent to General Marti's two-day visit with FO Ibenez, she asked for and was granted a fifteen-day leave of absence. The COS noted in her CIA 3467 that her father's visit 'apparently has brought back painful memories of her husband's death that she is having some difficulty dealing with.' "

She dropped out of sight for the two weeks, or at least no mention was made of where she'd gone, but when she returned she seemed to be a changed woman. Avalon's memos in her personnel file mentioned mood swings and an oftentimes sarcastic attitude, especially toward her immediate superiors; yet her work was first-class. She was a superior field officer with a lousy attitude, not such an unusual combination in the CIA.

Seeing her father had touched off something troubling inside of her. At her next psych evaluation, she'd explained that her father had come to Paris to talk her into quitting the CIA. He wanted her to get married again, settle down, and have babies. He wanted his daughter to have a normal life.

She'd refused, of course, which had caused a falling-out with her father. The two men most important in her life were gone: her husband killed in a Havana jail cell, and her father back in Little Havana drinking coffee and smoking cigars all day while he played dominoes with his cronies.

She told the Company psychologist that she would get over her funk because the Agency was her life now. She needed to get back at the kind of men who had killed her husband.

McGarvey looked up from his reading as they crossed the border into Florida, the ocean stretching off to the horizon out the left windows.

Katy wasn't very far away now, and thinking about her and their daughter gave him a deep sense of sadness for women like Shahrzad and Monique, and to a lesser extent Gloria. All of them had been damaged at some point in their lives, and they had ended up alone. Shahrzad had played the game for the big score, while Monique had been enamored with the glitter of wealth and power.

He could understand what drove those two. At least he could to some extent. But Gloria remained a mystery to him. He had a strong feeling that the Company's shrinks had got it wrong, most likely because she had skillfully lied. She had set herself up as a woman so troubled by her husband's death and her father's disapproval that she threw tantrums, had wild mood swings, and in Gil Perry's words was a "class A bitch."

Yet her work had not suffered. Through it all she'd never fallen into any sort of a depression that would affect how she operated in the field. Her intelligence had not been muted by her moods, nor had her courage been diminished. McGarvey had witnessed that part himself last year in Afghanistan. And according to all accounts she had not folded when she and her partner had come under intense fire down in Gitmo.

Even more curious, to McGarvey's way of thinking, was her reaction to her partner's death. If she'd been as psychologically scarred because of her husband and father as her psych reports indicated, she should have been out of it after Gitmo. She'd been upset, blaming herself for his death, but she'd picked herself up and gone right back into the field.

Gloria made no sense to him. Yet he was sure that she was the perfect tool to use against General Liu. He just had to find out who she really was from the only man left alive who might have the answers.

FORTY-EIGHT

MIAMI

The flight touched down a few minutes after nine at Miami International, more than twenty minutes early. McGarvey had only the one carry-on bag, so he didn't have to wait around to retrieve luggage. As he got to the aircraft door the pilot turned in his seat.

"Thanks for tagging along."

"My pleasure," McGarvey said.

"I hope they don't ax the air marshal program like they did in the seventies."

"Not this time," McGarvey said. He nodded to the copilot and flight attendants and headed through the jetway to the terminal. The program had eliminated aircraft hijackings, but he supposed that some congressman looking to get more votes by saving the taxpayers' money would make a move before long to cut the program, as had been done in the seventies. And it wouldn't take long after that happened for the bad guys to figure out that hijacking had once again become possible. He sincerely wished that he was wrong, but he didn't think so.

A short, slender Hispanic man with a pencil-thin mustache, wearing a Cuban guayabera shirt, who could have come direct from central casting, was waiting just outside the boarding area. He was carrying a fat manila envelope under his left arm. He stepped forward to intercept McGarvey.

"I have the material Mr. Rencke sent down for you, sir. Name is Martinez. Do you have any other luggage?"

"This is it," McGarvey said. "I'll need to find a hotel room and then locate General Marti. Tonight if possible."

"I've booked you a suite for two nights at the Park Central; we had no idea how long you'd be staying. And at the moment the general is at the Jugar Hasta el Fin, where he goes most nights. It's a small coffee shop with a big name where the regulars play dominoes."

They headed through the terminal toward one of the parking ramps, McGarvey paying attention to the people coming and going, looking for the face or faces that seemed out of place. Martinez noticed.

"The boarding area is clean—I made a sweep of it myself before you came in. And I've got a few guys cruising the terminal who'll give me a shout if they spot someone who shouldn't be here."

Because of Cuban intelligence activities amongst the émigrés, the CIA had a strong presence here, a fact that hadn't been much publicized since the Bay of Pigs fiasco.

Martinez's car was a pale yellow ten-year-old Coupe de Ville with spinner hub cabs and sheepskin seat covers.

"Do you want to go over to the hotel first, or see the general?"

It was a few minutes past nine. "How late does he usually stay out?" McGarvey asked.

"Midnight, sometimes later," Martinez said. "If you want, I'll drop you off near the coffee shop, then take your bag over to the hotel for you."

"Sounds good."

"Do you want me to hang around? I can pick you up when you're done."

"I don't know how long I'll be. If you have a cell phone I'll call if I need you."

Martinez gave him the number, and McGarvey programmed it into his cell phone as they headed south from the airport on Okeechobee Road toward the Orange Bowl, traffic fairly heavy.

The manila envelope that Martinez had brought out contained several dossiers on Gloria's father, former Cuban Air Force chief of operations General Ernesto Marti; a batch of articles from publications like the New York Times, the Washington Post, Aviation Week & Space Technology, and Jane's International Defense Review; a summary report from his CIA file; and a batch of photographs taken at various times and places including Washington, New York, here in Miami and at the Company's training site, and Cuban radio monitoring post in the Keys.

He was tall for a Cuban, dark skinned like his daughter, and husky, with broad shoulders and a square peasant's face, weathered by too much exposure to the elements. He was a distant cousin to the Cuban hero Jose Marti, which hadn't hindered his promotions.

He had decided to defect to the U.S. with his wife and their only child, Gloria, who was thirteen at the time, because of what Castro was doing to Cuba. With the help of the KGB the island had been turned into a police state with even tighter controls on its people than had been in place in East Germany at the height of the Cold War.

In Marti's own words, his country was "sliding into a deep depression that was sapping the life out of not only the people but of the buildings and infrastructure itself. Soon Cuba will be past hope for repair."

He was chief of air operations, so he'd had no trouble commandeering a light plane, picking up his wife and daughter, and heading the ninety miles north across the Straits of Florida directly to Key West before the alarm was sounded.

By then it had been too late not only for the Cuban government, but for Marti and his family. The plane had developed engine trouble within sight of Key West. He'd flown too low to make it land, and had to ditch in the ocean a hundred yards outside the reef in water more than five hundred feet deep.

His wife had been knocked nearly unconscious in the rough landing, and Marti had not been able to get her out of the plane before it sank. He and his daughter had watched her disappear.

The general had been extensively debriefed by the CIA and the Air Force OSI, after which he had become a paid consultant to the Company on Cuban military affairs. Times had changed, especially in the last couple of years with Castro's failing health, and the general had all but retired, only occasionally getting the call to come to Washington.

Like a lot of other Cubans living in Florida, he was counting the days until he could go home.

McGarvey was most interested scanning Marti's psychological profile, which had been conducted by Dr. Stenzel, the same man who'd done Gloria's. The general's was a strong personality. He had been deeply saddened by his wife's death, but understood that life was for the living.

After a period of mourning, he'd thrown himself into consulting for the CIA, giving something back to a country, he said, that had provided him and his daughter, and so many other tens of thousands of Cubans, a safe refuge.

"He is a man of strong convictions, and a deep sense of family and home," Dr. Stenzel wrote in his brief conclusion. "Leaving Cuba and turning informant against the Castro regime was the most difficult decision in his life to that point, a decision that he still ponders every day. He will never fully integrate into U.S. society, nor does he appear to desire U.S. citizenship. He is here to help bring about Castro's downfall so that he may return to his homeland."

Martinez got off the connector highway and took Southwest Twenty-seventh Avenue to Calle Ocho in the heart of Little Havana. This was an area of Cuban shops and markets and what were considered some of the best Cuban and Latin American restaurants anywhere in the world. The place was alive with activity, music blaring from open doorways, people strolling arm in arm, and the smells of good food in the air. It reminded McGarvey of how New Orleans's French Quarter used to be.

They circled back and pulled over at the corner of Southwest Seventh Street, one block up from Calle Ocho.

"The Jugar is in the middle of the block, on the upper side of the street," Martinez said. "Are you carrying?"

"Of course."

Martinez nodded. "The general's people are expecting you, and they'll want to take your piece before they let you inside. But you'll get it back later. Do you have a problem with this?"

"How does he know I'm coming to see him?" McGarvey asked, though it was about what he'd expected. Marti's CIA file also described him as a very careful man. Cuban intelligence agents had been trying for years to get to him. The fact that he'd survived for so long, especially here, was a testament not only to his caution but to the people he surrounded himself with.

"I told him," Martinez said. "It's not wise to try to sneak up on him. There've been a couple incidents."

McGarvey looked up sharply. "Lately?"

"I think somebody tried to get to him a few days ago, but we're not sure of the details," Martinez said. "He's agreed to see you, so you can ask him yourself."

"Thanks," McGarvey said, getting out of the car, leaving the envelope behind.

"Your suite is 501. They're holding your key for you."

McGarvey strolled up Seventh, taking his time, watching for anyone who might be taking a more than casual interest in a gringo by himself. But although the street was busy, no one seemed interested in him.

The coffee shop was in a narrow storefront on the other side of the street. The large windows were not covered, so the patrons inside could watch the comings and goings outside. The place was jammed.

McGarvey waited for a break in traffic, then crossed over. He was stopped at the door by a pair of beefy men in baggy black slacks and loose guayabera shirts.

"Your weapon please," one of them said politely, his accent heavily Spanish.

McGarvey unholstered his Walther PPK from beneath his jacket at the small of his back and handed it to the bodyguard, who stuffed it in a pocket.

"Straight back, there is a table in the corner. The general is expecting you."

Both men were professionals. They were pleasant but watchful, their eyes never resting on one spot for more than a moment. And when McGarvey had approached, they'd separated, so as not to present a single field of fire.

"Keep on your toes, gentlemen," McGarvey warned. "I expect they'll try to hit him again. Soon."

"Who?" one bodyguard asked evenly.

"An independent operator, I should think."

The bodyguard shrugged.

"From Mexico," McGarvey said, and he saw a brief flicker of interest in the bodyguard's eyes.

"Thank you."

McGarvey nodded and went inside the crowded, noisy coffee shop. A dozen tables were filled, mostly with men but also a few women, people playing dominoes loudly and with a lot of flourish.

In a corner at the back of the room, to the left of the kitchen doors, General Marti was seated with a half dozen men, who all got up and left when McGarvey approached. Like everyone else in the place they had been playing dominoes and drinking the strong *café cubano*. The place was thick with the haze of cigar smoke.

Marti looked up and studied McGarvey for a long moment.

"Good evening, General," McGarvey said.

"What are you doing here this evening?"

"I came to talk to you about your daughter."

"Yes," the general said. "She is in love with you."

"I know, but it's not about that. It's about her husband, Raul, and about you."

FORTY-NINE

LITTLE HAVANA

"Let's take a walk," Marti said, rising.

He escorted McGarvey out of the coffee shop, stopping at every table to say good-bye or make some small talk in Spanish. He was obviously well liked and well respected by these people.

Outside, the general took McGarvey's arm, and they headed around the corner up to Calle Ocho, which he explained was simply Spanish for Eighth Street. His two bodyguards fell in close behind, their heads on swivels.

Marti, like just about every other male in this part of the city, wore the traditional white guayabera shirt with lace trim, dark slacks, and shoes with pointed toes. He also wore a jaunty straw hat with a paisley band at the base of the crown.

"The Spanish-speaking people, especially us *Cubanos*, find it hard to completely integrate ourselves wherever we chance to land away from our homeland," Marti said lightly. He was smoking a very large cigar. "Have you been here before, Mr. McGarvey?"

"Once, briefly, ten or fifteen years ago."

"Yes, the Basulto business with the Bay of Pigs," the general said. "It was the Russian, General Baranov, whom you were after." He gave McGarvey a smile. "Relax. I, too, do my homework."

McGarvey nodded.

"Most of us count the days until we can return to Cuba and help re-build our country. But make no mistake, while we are here most of us be-have like loyal Americans." Marti shook his head. "There are only a few hotheads who find it necessary to blame someone for their troubles. And of course the DGI has its people everywhere here, stirring up trouble."

The DGI, Directorate General of Intelligence, was Cuba's secret service. Most of its officers had been trained by the KGB, and they were very good at what they did.

"Were they the ones trying to assassinate you a few days ago?" McGarvey asked, and the general gave him a sharp look, but McGarvey smiled. "I, too, do my homework."

"Probably DGI, like before, but we're not sure." Marti shrugged. "If it was Castro's boys, they changed their methods. Instead of trying to poison me, or run me over with a truck, or plant a bomb in the Jugar, they took a couple of shots at me from a passing car. A dark SUV. We're looking for it now, but nobody thinks it'll be found."

"A pistol maybe?" McGarvey asked. "Silenced?"

Marti gave him an interested look. "What are you trying to tell me?"

"They might have been independent operators from Mexico."

"GAFE?"

"Ex," McGarvey said. "I've already had a couple of run-ins with them."

"Interesting," Marti said. "Who is signing their paychecks?"

"That's why I came here to see you. I'm working on it and I need your daughter's help."

"But you're not sure of her, is that it?" Marti asked sadly.

"Something like that."

They had reached Calle Ocho, and Marti headed left, farther into Little Havana. If anything, traffic here was heavier than outside the Jugar. McGarvey glanced over his shoulder at the bodyguards, who seemed unfazed that their general was putting himself in danger. In these crowds an assassin would have very little trouble getting close enough for an almost certain kill.

"We call this place La Pequena Habana, how you say, Little Havana, because we can't stand to be away from our homes, and Havana is our capital city. But in fact this is changing too, as all things must. Now the Nicaraguans are coming, and a part of our Pequena is called Little Managua."

"Your daughter is working out of our embassy in Mexico City."

"She got fired recently," Marti said. "Did you have anything to do with that?"

McGarvey nodded. "I wanted her distanced from the CIA for what will be coming her way if she agrees to help me."

"If you ask her to help, your decision will be based in part on what you learn from me."

"That's right."

"My daughter's in love with you, and you want to know about her relationship with her husband, and with me. What's a father to think?"

"It will be a dangerous assignment, one that will not be officially sanctioned. She could get killed, or at the very least badly damaged."

Marti stopped and looked McGarvey in the eye. "What is your interest in my daughter, other than professional?"

"Nothing more than that, General. I have a wife and grown daughter of my own. And I'm almost old enough to be Gloria's father."

"But she's in love with you. Why?"

"I think she's a lonely woman, and I believe that she's probably in love with who she *thinks* I am."

Marti digested this for a moment, then turned and, arm in arm with McGarvey again, continued along Calle Ocho. "You are probably right on both counts, if I can still read my daughter correctly. She is a lonely woman, and eight months ago she told me that she was in love with a married man who was not in love with her, but she thought that he was a superman whom she was willing to wait for."

It wasn't quite what McGarvey had expected. "I thought you and she were not close."

"It's true. But we are still father and daughter, and she calls when she is troubled and needs me. It's sometimes a comfort."

"What happened, General?" McGarvey asked. "Was it because of your visit when she was in Paris?"

"Exactly why do you need this information from me?"

"I'm running an operation in Mexico, as I said, and I need Gloria's help."

"Sí, I understand this much, but what else?"

"I need to know if I can trust her."

"Ah," Marti said, more of a sound at the back of his throat than an actual word. "I was told that you were a blunt man."

They walked in silence for a minute, Marti apparently ordering his thoughts. By coming this far the general had tacitly agreed to answer some questions about his daughter. McGarvey hadn't believed Shahrzad's story until it had been confirmed by what Monique had told him. Nor, had he interviewed Monique first, would he have believed her without Shahrzad's confirmation.

"First you must understand how it was in Cuba before I decided to take my family away," Marti said. "By the time Gloria was born I was already in an important position with the military. Because of it we lived in a large house in the country, with servants, a very good cook, two gardeners, and a vaquero who took care of the horses and taught Gloria to ride. She had a nanny at first, and then tutors who were superior to the teachers in our schools. Our neighbors were either high-ranking military officers and their families, or ranchers and their wives and children. Gloria was never lonely, never bored, never unhappy, so far as I knew. She lived in a paradise. We shielded her from what was actually happening in Havana and elsewhere across Cuba."

"Being taken away from all that must have been a shock for her," McGarvey suggested.

Marti nodded. "Along with losing her mother the way it happened: do you know the story?"

"Most of it."

"Along with that tragedy, for which she blamed me, she had a difficult time adjusting to life in a new country. For the first time she realized that there were people living in poverty, and she couldn't understand why."

FIFTY

DOWNTOWN

At the edge of Little Havana Marti steered McGarvey into an eight-story apartment building. They took the elevator to the top-floor penthouse, where one of the bodyguards went inside first to make a quick sweep while the other bodyguard stood watch in the corridor.

"These procedures are tedious, but perhaps if you and my daughter are successful in Mexico the situation for me here will ease up somewhat."

The first bodyguard came to the door. "It's clear, sir," he said.

The apartment was large, more than four thousand square feet, modern, and luxuriously furnished. Thick rugs were scattered on marble flooring; soft white leather furniture, including a long sectional couch and huge easy chairs, faced a sixty-inch plasma television screen mounted on a wall. Shelves were filled with leather-bound books, and the inside walls were adorned with paintings, mostly showing Cuban scenery and life, while the outer walls were floor-to-ceiling glass doors, open now to an expansive wraparound balcony, equally well furnished in teak and glass, with tall potted plants and dwarf palm trees and water fountains.

The effect was spectacular with its view of Little Havana, and pleasant with the soft evening breezes, subdued lighting, and sounds of splashing water.

"Very nice," McGarvey said.

"Yes, it is," Marti replied. "But sometimes lonely."

"Will you be leaving the apartment this evening, sir?" one of the bodyguards asked.

"No," Marti said. "After Mr. McGarvey and I have concluded our business, I'll retire for the night."

"Very good, sir," the bodyguard said, and he and the other guard withdrew.

Marti invited McGarvey to have a seat on the balcony while he fixed them tall drinks with dark Cuban rum, lime juice, fresh mint, a little simple syrup, and seltzer water in tall glasses filled with ice.

They sat for a while sipping their drinks, the evening warm and pleasant. McGarvey had put thoughts about his wife in that special compartment of his mind, sealed away from his tradecraft, yet just now he couldn't help but think how close she was, and how normal she was compared to the three women he'd become involved with in this business. All of his life he'd had a tough time balancing his need for normalcy—an ordinary family, an ordinary job, an ordinary life—with an equally strong drive to fix things, make things right, figure out what had gone wrong, or was about to go wrong, and do something about it. Katy was probably right; he would never completely retire. Maybe in the end he would go up to the Farm from time to time to teach the new kids coming into the Company something of what he had learned being in the field for more than two decades.

"We only spent the day and that first night in Key West before the CIA sent a couple of field officers down with a jet to bring us to Washington," Marti picked up his story. "It was about what I had expected would happen, though I'd made a bet with myself that with the turf wars supposedly still going on between the FBI and CIA, it might be the Bureau who got to me first. I was wrong, but it didn't matter. I was willing to trade what I knew about our military for sanctuary, and the hope that I might be able to speed up Castro's downfall."

"How about Gloria?" McGarvey prompted.

"She missed her mother, of course, but gradually she started to come out of the shell she'd built around herself. That was in the first few months, at the safe house outside the city just above the Potomac. It was summer, the staff was pleasant, and our lives there weren't terribly different from what they had been in Cuba. During the days I was debriefed by a series of teams, but the afternoons and evenings were mine to spend with my daughter. It was more time than I'd ever spent with her. In Cuba I was a busy man. This was a luxury for me, and I think it was for her."

Marti fell silent for a bit, sipping his drinking, staring out over the city.

"The changes began when we finally moved to Washington. The CIA got us an apartment in Georgetown and hired me as a consultant to the Cuban desk, for a nice salary, which by itself allowed us to live quite comfortably. In addition, in the year before I defected, I had managed to transfer most of the money I'd accumulated in Cuba to a Cayman Islands account. We were not rich, but we were well off, even by U.S. standards.

"At first living in the city was a novelty for both of us, but especially for Gloria. I enrolled her in a high school run by Jesuits near Georgetown University's campus, and it was close enough so that she could walk there every day. The teachers were strict, but I knew she was getting a first-rate education, and I thought that a little discipline never hurt anyone.

"I bought a car, so on weekends we took minitrips to all the tourist sites at first, and then to some of the other neighborhoods in the city: Columbia Heights, Bloomingdale, Dobbins Addition, Eckington. For the first time in her life my daughter became aware that truly impoverished people existed. I didn't notice, because Havana has always been a city of slums. But Gloria had never been to Havana, not once, so she'd never been exposed to the things she saw in Washington. To her, Cuba was the land of milk and honey, while the U.S. was the land of black people who were kept poor by the white masters who worked in the important buildings downtown."

Marti looked at McGarvey, one father to another, searching for understanding. McGarvey saw it and nodded.

"The real world."

"Her mother and I had perhaps insulated her too much. She wasn't prepared to witness the seedier side of Washington, and it had a profound effect on her."

Marti shook his head.

"Then came winter, and the first cold temperatures and snow she'd ever experienced. The first week was okay. We went shopping for a winter wardrobe, and I drove her to school on most days, though the other children who lived as close as we did walked. But all of it was too much for her.

"That Christmas we flew down here to be with her mother's brother and his wife and four children. They'd come to Miami eight years earlier, which had caused me some trouble with the government. But I held an important enough position even then that my troubles didn't last."

"It must have been good to be with family again," McGarvey said. He thought about the years he'd been away from Katy and Liz.

"It was, and Gloria loved it. The weather was warm, the food was *cubano*, and everyone spoke Spanish." Marti shook his head again, his expression sad. "But then the next part was my fault. When we got back to Washington I became very busy working for the CIA. I hired a housekeeper-cook to take care of the apartment and Gloria, and sometimes I would be gone for days at a time. By spring she was beginning to rebel, and by summer break she had been caught twice shoplifting. In each case the charges were dropped when I paid for the little trinkets she'd stolen, plus a hefty bonus, which the shopkeeper called fines. But it was extortion against the family of a troubled girl."

Marti stopped again, lost in his thoughts.

"What did you do about it?" McGarvey prompted after a moment.

"The only thing I thought I could do. I sent her to live with her aunt and uncle here in Little Havana."

"Did it work?"

"In the beginning, although I was never there to witness anything firsthand. She was growing up and I was missing it, the same as I would have missed it had we remained in Cuba, because I was always busy there too."

Marti lowered his head, apparently unable to speak.

"What happened?" McGarvey asked.

"She got pregnant when she was fifteen, and without telling anyone she found a Cuban doctor to give her an abortion. Her aunt and uncle found out because when she came home that night she was bleeding, and they had to take her to the emergency room. They also discovered that she had stolen five hundred dollars from them to pay for the abortion.

"They're very strong Catholics. They couldn't accept what she had done, so they sent her back to me. I enrolled her in the Jesuit school in their program for gifted but troubled children, and she excelled. In fact she graduated at the head of her class."

Marti got up and fixed them new drinks at the sideboard.

Gloria had spent the first thirteen years of her life as an indulged but apparently happy and well-adjusted child. But the defection, her mother's death, and the shock of seeing the real world up close had unhinged her, so she'd rebelled. Her mother would probably have been able to do something to help, but she was gone, and Gloria's teenage years had disintegrated.

Marti came back to the table and handed McGarvey his drink.

"I'd lost her by then, though I'm not sure that I knew it yet. I was too busy. But I knew enough to understand that she had grown into a young woman, every bit as beautiful as her mother had been at that age, but without her mother's warm smile.

"She'd developed a hard attitude somewhere along the line. She'd become sharp-tongued, brittle, easy to anger. I despaired for her, but when I tried to talk to her she just brushed me off. 'Don't worry, Papá,' she told me. 'Life goes on.'"

⌐ I ⌐ T Ꮞ — ⊓ ⌐ ⋿

THE APARTMENT

She went to the University of South Florida in Tampa, where she graduated in three years with a B.S. in foreign studies, on the dean's list every semester.

"She never once came back to Washington to see me, or drive over to Miami to try to make amends with her aunt and uncle," Marti said. "I didn't even know where she was in school until I got a postcard from her inviting me to the graduation."

"She was just eighteen when she left Washington," McGarvey said. "Didn't you wonder where she'd gone? She might have been kidnapped and brought back to Cuba to be used against you."

Marti shook his head. "I still have contacts in and around Havana. I'd have known if something like that had happened."

"Maybe she was dead. Killed in a car crash. Run over by a bus."

Marti said nothing.

"The CIA or the Bureau would have found her for you if you'd asked," McGarvey said. "But you never did. Why?"

"By then my daughter had become a resourceful woman."

"She'd just graduated from high school—"

Marti held up a hand. "I'm a lousy father. Without Maria—my wife—

I was nothing except for my work." He looked away for a moment. "Unlike my daughter, or my wife, I knew about poverty firsthand, because I was born and raised in one of Havana's barrios. My father died when I was just a baby, leaving my mother to care for seven children. We lived in a cardboard box covered with a tin roof and tar paper. The floor was dirt, and when I got older it was my job to bring our drinking water from the open sewer.

"By the time I reached high school age, my mother was dead along with everyone else except for an older sister who went away to the other side of the island, to San Francisco, where she worked as a nanny.

"I never saw her again. She was raped and murdered by the man of the house, who was later shot to death by his wife." Marti shrugged. "I was alone, but my scores in the boarding high school were good enough that I was sent to officers' school outside Havana, Antonio Maceo, where I studied mechanical engineering, business administration, and English."

"An odd combination."

"Yes, but Cuba has always needed everything."

The man had been driven to succeed at all costs, as many young men coming from his situation might have been. But it made no sense to McGarvey why he had apparently turned his back on his daughter when she may have needed him the most.

"Why didn't you try to find her? At least to make sure that she was okay."

"I did fine on my own; now it was Gloria's turn. It was up to her if she took hold of her own life and did something with it."

"How did she pay for college? How did she live?"

"I don't know. But she never asked me for money."

"I'm sorry, General, but you were even less than a lousy father," McGarvey said strongly, in part because he had abandoned his wife and daughter. But he had come back.

Marti nodded. "That's what she told me a few years ago, and both of you are right, but still she calls from time to time when she needs something."

McGarvey could see at least one very good reason for Gloria to have attitude. Who wouldn't with her background?

"Did you go to her graduation?"

"Of course."

"Was anyone else there? Her aunt or uncle, or any of the cousins?"

"Only me, and some of her friends who were graduating with her."

"Did she introduce you to them?" McGarvey wanted to know. He was having a tough time comprehending the relationship.

"No, though I told her that I wanted to meet them. But they all had family with them, and right after the ceremony Gloria and I went to a little seafood restaurant in St. Pete Beach for an early dinner."

"How was she toward you?" McGarvey asked.

"Pleasant. Distant. I hadn't expected anything other than that."

"Were you proud of her?"

An odd expression came over Marti's face. "Proud that she was finally standing on her own two feet, yes, of course. But I think I was a little worried too. She was leaving with some friends to spend the summer in Europe, and when she got back she was enrolling at Stetson Law School, right there, near Tampa."

"I saw that in her file," McGarvey said. "Did you go to that graduation?"

"I wasn't invited."

"Christ," McGarvey muttered.

Marti looked at him coolly. "I want you to understand something, Mr. McGarvey. Our family have been strict Catholics. It was Maria's doing. Gloria's pregnancy was a sin that she made worse by the abortion. But what hurt the most was when she turned her back on us. We were willing to forgive and get on with our lives, but she wasn't."

If you're going to tell a lie, tell a very big one, and chances are someone will believe it. But in this case McGarvey wondered if the general even realized what he had just said.

FIFTY-TWO

☐

THE APARTMENT

After that everything changed. In late September she showed up in Washington and telephoned her father to have lunch at the Watergate. She was already at a table overlooking the Potomac when he arrived, and she got up and embraced him warmly.

"Hola, Papá," she said.

She was dressed in an obviously expensive, fashionable dark suit and medium business heels, with her hair done nicely and her makeup minimal but perfect. She had transformed from a rough-and-tumble young woman with attitude to a beautiful grown woman with a million-watt smile.

"You look marvelous, sweetheart," Marti told her. "But what has happened to you? Where have you been? We've heard nothing for three years."

"I know, and I'm sorry, but I've been a busy girl," she said. "I graduated in June from Stetson and sat for my bar exams in Florida and here in D.C., and then a bunch of us spent the summer skiing in Chile."

"I thought you hated snow."

She brushed it off. "Hate's a little too strong a word," she said. "Anyway, I'm a full-fledged lawyer now with a job at the Navy's JAG office in the Pentagon. How about that?"

Marti nodded. "How about that," he said. "When do you start?"

"I started two weeks ago. I wanted to get settled into the new job and my apartment before I saw you." She reached out for her father's hand. "It's been too long, Papá. I've missed you."

Marti started to tell her that he had missed her too, but she held him off.

"I blamed you for uprooting us from our wonderful life in Cuba, and for mother's death. For a long time I was sure you had done it on purpose to get rid of us, so I rebelled." She lowered her eyes contritely for a moment. "I was horribly wrong," she admitted. "And I'm truly sorry. It's all I can say."

"It's enough," Marti told her, his heart swelling.

Marti had made them another drink, and when he came back to the table he gave McGarvey a wan smile. "You asked if I had been proud of my daughter. I was on that day. She had disappeared as a troubled girl and had returned in triumph."

"That must have been a relief for you," McGarvey said.

Marti nodded. "It was, at first," he said. "For a while it was like the old days when we'd first come to Washington, after she'd gotten over her mother's death. At least outwardly. We had lunch a couple times a week, even though she was very busy. Some weekends she'd come over and bunk with me. We'd go to movie, maybe have a pizza afterward. I'd bought a new barbecue grill, and we had a few cookouts on the balcony of my apartment."

"Did she ever bring any of her friends or co-workers over to introduce you?" McGarvey asked.

"No. She always said that she wanted to make her mark with the JAG before she branched out with personal issues."

"Her words?"

Marti nodded. "More or less."

"No boyfriends?"

"Not until her husband, Raul," Marti said. "Or at least none that she ever mentioned."

"But she was still up, happy, pleasant to be around?"

"For the most part. Once in a while if she was tired, she might snap at me, but she always apologized immediately. She'd tell me that she was 'working on it.' She was busy in those days, more often than not putting in seventy- and eighty-hour weeks."

"How about you?" McGarvey asked.

"Oh, I was scaling back, the calls out to Langley were getting less frequent and certainly a lot less urgent, so in the spring I packed up, sold the Georgetown apartment, and moved down here." Marti smiled suddenly. "Gloria took the better part of a week to help me pack. It was great." He looked away. "I'd held the hope, even though I knew it was utterly impossible, that she would quit her job, move down here, and open a law practice in Little Havana."

"Did you ever mention it to her?"

Marti shook his head. "In the fall I learned that she had been recruited by the CIA, and for the first time I was frightened for her safety."

McGarvey knew the answer but he asked anyway. "Why?"

"She was going to be sent back to Cuba—it would have been a waste of a valuable resource otherwise. But she was the daughter of General Marti, a traitor to Uncle Fidel. The DGI would have moved heaven and earth to get its hands on her. I would have been forced to return."

Would you have returned? McGarvey wanted to ask, but he didn't. He figured that whatever answer Marti gave him would be a lie. The relationship between the general and his daughter was as complex as it was odd. It wasn't as if they simply disliked each other; there was something deeper than that going on, but McGarvey didn't know what it was yet.

"In the end there was nothing I could say or do that would have had any effect on her decision," Marti said. "She had turned into a thoughtful, pleasant daughter, but she was still headstrong—if anything, more than when she was a difficult child. So in the end I said nothing to her, and decided to do nothing until she was sent to Cuba."

"How long was it after she'd joined the Company before she was sent to Cuba?"

"About a year, maybe a little longer, but by then she was married and I was a little less worried."

His name was Raul Ibenez. He was an instructor at the Farm when Gloria took her training. Within the first two weeks they had fallen head over heels in love with each other, and Gloria blossomed like never before.

"She called me every time she could to tell me about him," Marti said. "His parents had defected when he was an infant, so he had no direct memory of Cuba, only what he'd been told. And she said that's all they ever talked about at first. He wanted to know everything about her life as a kid, and together they were going back to help topple Fidel's regime.

"When she graduated from the field operations course, she was assigned to the Cuban section of the Latin American desk, which was no surprise. But within three months she and Raul were married in a civil ceremony in the Falls Church courthouse."

"Did you approve?" McGarvey asked.

"Of course. It was at least half a dream come true. She was marrying a nice Cuban boy. I checked him out. He was three years older than Gloria, he had his degree in foreign studies right there at Georgetown University, and his supervisors all gave him top marks.

"His father was a tailor and his mother a seamstress, and in fact they're still here in Little Havana. But they closed their shop after their son was killed. I do what I can to help."

"Does Gloria ever come to see them?" McGarvey asked.

"Just the once when she got out of Cuba, but since then, no."

"Did you go to the wedding?"

Marti shook his head. "I didn't know anything about it until two weeks later when they came down to Miami and invited me to lunch. They'd gone to Monaco for their honeymoon, and they looked like they had the world by the tail. They were young, beautiful, intelligent, and invincible." Marti smiled with the memory. "They were something to behold. I didn't even ask them about a proper church wedding. If I had, Gloria would have told me that they were too busy to fool with anything like that."

"What about his parents?"

"They'd already broken the news, so they were going back to work the very next day."

"To get ready for Cuba," McGarvey said.

"Yes," Marti said. "They divided their time between the Cuban desk at headquarters, and advanced tradecraft training at the Farm. They were working seven days a week by then, so after lunch that day I didn't hear much from them."

"You knew they would be assigned to go back."

"As sure as the sun rises," Marti said.

"When did it finally happen?"

"Not for a whole year," Marti said. "I was even beginning to hope that maybe it wouldn't happen. But they showed up here one night, all excited.

They were on their way, and pumped up. They even refused to speak any English, although Raul's accent wasn't right, and I told him so. His controllers had built a legend around a small-town boy from up around Santa Clara. They all talked funny up there, so he figured he'd be safe in Havana."

"Then what?"

"They left that night," Marti said. He got up and went into the living room, brought back a humidor of cigars, and offered one to McGarvey.

"No thanks," McGarvey said. "What happened in Havana?"

"Nothing much for maybe six months. My contact at Langley wouldn't give me anything, in fact he wouldn't even admit where they were. But I was sure that if anything were to happen, or if they were in any grave danger, he would have let me know."

"What about the people you knew in Havana?"

A pained expression came into Marti's eyes. He was lighting a cigar, and looked up. "I asked some friends to look out for my daughter, I'll admit that, though Langley ordered me not to do it."

"And?" McGarvey prompted.

Marti finished lighting his cigar. "In retrospect I'm sorry I did."

"Why?"

"I learned something about my daughter that I wished I'd never learned."

FIFTY-THREE

THE APARTMENT

Marti smoked his cigar in silence for a minute, looking out across the city. He was a man who was obviously wrestling with a difficult decision, but McGarvey couldn't find much sympathy for him. He was worried about his daughter. That much was obvious. But he'd never had any idea of what it was to be a father.

"What was it that you learned?" McGarvey prompted.

Marti took a moment before he turned his attention back to McGarvey, and he suddenly seemed ten years older than just a minute before. "Would you like another drink?"

McGarvey shook his head, and Marti looked away again.

"I found out that they had been made by the DGI within the first day or two after they got to Havana," the general said. "But the word didn't get out to me until six months later, and by then there wasn't much I could do."

"How did you find out?" McGarvey prompted.

"I have friends there."

"Yes, I know. But exactly how do you hear things from Cuba?"

"From Mexico. We have an organization here in Miami to collect money for our friends and relatives. We can't send it from the States, so we fly people over to Mexico City once a week with cash for Havana or wherever.

"But it's not a wire transfer. The Cuban government would take a hefty share as import duties if we went through normal channels. The money is given to a banker, who sends a message to a friend in Managua perhaps, or Bogotá, where U.S. dollars need to be laundered, with the amounts he has collected, and the people to whom they are to be delivered.

"Our banker in Mexico City distributes the cash in trade for a bagman from Bogotá to fly into Havana with the money he needs to launder and delivers it. The books are kept in balance that way."

It was a method of transferring cash all over the world without having to use legitimate banks or mechanisms such as Western Union. Its use was widespread because it worked.

"I understand how the cash gets from Miami to Havana. But how do you get information back?"

"Lists of needs in code," Marti said. "Let's say a friend of mine working in the Air Force wants to send me a message. He will hand a personal letter for the Bogotá bagman to take out of Cuba. The letter is a list of items he needs money for. Maybe a special medicine for his parents that he can't get in Cuba. Or money for building supplies, or to fix his car.

Things like that. If the Cuban authorities discover the letters, and they do from time to time, they look like nothing more than innocent requests for help. Which most of the letters are. Not all of them contain codes."

"Does the CIA know about this?"

Marti laughed. "They can't help but know, but I'm told they don't, or at least they claim not to know. So far as I can tell, no one in the DO has ever acted on any intel that was handed to them. 'Unsubtantiated rumors. Local gossip. Unreliable information. Probably DGI disinformation.' "

"How long has this been going on?"

"Since after the Bay of Pigs," Marti replied.

"I never knew," McGarvey said.

"At first no one down here trusted the CIA. Not after that disaster. Later the CIA trusted no one down here because every second refugee was a DGI agent or informant."

"You said that you learned something about your daughter that you wished you hadn't."

"When I got word that Gloria and Raul had probably been made by the DGI, I flew to Mexico City with five thousand in cash to be sent to one of my old Air Force friends. It was some serious money, so nobody objected when I told them I wanted to get a message inside. Two words: 'Get out.' "

"What happened?" McGarvey asked.

"Nothing," Marti replied tiredly. "I don't know if they received my message; if they did, they ignored it."

"The DGI might have picked it up. If you were infiltrated here in Miami, it's likely that they were watching the Mexico City money operation."

Marti nodded. "Sí, I thought of that, so I flew up to Washington and went out to Langley to talk to Don Nealy, my contact on the Latin American desk. He made a couple of phone calls while I was sitting in his office, and when he was finished he promised to see what he could do."

"I'm surprised he even acknowledged the fact that your daughter and her husband were in Cuba," McGarvey said. Nealy had risen to chief of the Western Hemisphere Division because he was a bright, capable officer who knew how to play by the book. He would not have divulged that sort of information even to a man such as General Marti.

"He didn't," Marti said. "Or at least not in so many words."

"But he promised to help."

"He promised to see what he could do. He looked me in the eye and told me that he had no idea where my daughter was stationed. It was possible that she was somewhere in the States. Maybe even in Little Havana. But wherever she was, he would see about getting a message to her."

"What was the message you wanted him to deliver?"

"I wanted the Company to order her and Raul out of there because the DGI knew about them."

"Did Nealy want to know how you came by your information?"

"He never asked."

"And you didn't volunteer."

Marti was irritated. "Don knew the situation. Everybody on the Latin American desk did. It was an open secret. So long as the money going into Cuba stayed reasonably small and out of the public's eye, and so long as it didn't interfere with the CIA's operations, everyone looked the other way. It was a humanitarian thing to do, so I was told. In fact, during my consulting days my contact officer never delved too deeply into how I was getting my information. Not after the bulk of what I'd handed over had been verified."

"You sent a message to your contact in Havana, and you let the Company know that a pair of its field officers had probably been burned. What did you do next?"

"I flew down here, picked up some more money, and went back to the banker in Mexico City. Every day I sent one thousand dollars in, with a query for word about my daughter and her husband."

"How long did it take before you heard something?" McGarvey asked.

"I started getting bits and pieces within a day or two. Their address in an apartment building. The old Dodge they were trying to buy. The jobs they supposedly worked at. She was a waitress at a small music club, and Raul was an electrician for the state. It was their cover, of course, because it would have been impossible for either of them to actually get a job. They were visible for their neighbors' sake, but below the radar as far as official Havana was concerned."

"But you never found out if they had been warned?"

"No," Marti said. "But of course I continued to send the same message every day: Get out. And I continued to hear back about them. They had been spotted dancing at a street party. They had been spotted on the beach."

"All of which could have been DGI-engineered messages to you."

"I considered that possibility as well. But it made no difference. I had to try to get the word to them."

Traffic on the street below had begun to quiet down, and a wet blanket of humidity had descended over the city, as it did most evenings in Miami. McGarvey had to wonder if Marti had played the part of the worried parent in Mexico City because he'd been concerned for the safety of his daughter and her husband, or because he'd been concerned about his own safety. If Gloria had been arrested by the DGI, they might have tried to use her as a lever to bring the general back to Havana.

McGarvey didn't think that Marti would have returned to Cuba, even to save his daughter's life. But he must have been worried that his image would have taken a serious hit had he not sacrificed his freedom for his daughter's.

Marti was a big man down here in Little Havana. A star among his people. A man to be looked up to, a man to be respected. He stood to lose that position if his daughter got into trouble in Cuba and he did nothing to help.

"In the end it didn't matter if my messages got through or not. Raul was arrested one night at their apartment about twenty minutes before Gloria was supposed to come home from her job.

"She disappeared, and three days later Raul was shot to death while trying to escape from a DGI interrogation center. Three days after that Gloria showed up right here in Miami, and before I could get back from Mexico she'd flown up to Washington."

"You never saw her," McGarvey said.

"I never even talked to her," Marti said. "But I tried. I think she was hiding out at the Farm while she was being debriefed. But nobody would tell me."

"You must have been relieved that she got out after all."

"It was a father's comfort."

"I imagine it was," McGarvey said, but Marti apparently did not catch the sarcasm. "What did you learn about your daughter?" he asked again.

FIFTY-FOUR

THE APARTMENT

The question hung in the air, and it didn't seem as if Marti was going to answer it. He finished his drink, and snipped the glowing end off the cigar with a silver cutter. "Good cigars have become hard to find, even for me."

"That'll change when Cuba finally opens," McGarvey suggested.

"It's time to go," Marti said, getting up.

McGarvey got to his feet. "I still don't know about your daughter."

"Neither do I," Marti said, and he ushered McGarvey to the front door, where one of the bodyguards was there with his pistol.

"I'd hoped that you would help me."

"Why?"

"Because I don't want to make a mistake with her. A lot of lives could be at stake."

"Yours?"

It was the sort of question McGarvey had expected from a man such as Marti. He nodded. "Yes, mine, and Gloria's and some others."

"It wasn't long after she'd gotten out that I began to hear things from my friends in Cuba. At first I didn't believe any of it. As you suggested, I thought the rumors were nothing more than the DGI's crude attempt at disinformation. They knew I was getting the messages, and maybe they wanted to discredit my daughter in my eyes."

"For what reason?"

"I truly do not know," Marti admitted. "But it became a moot point when a man claiming to be a former DGI case officer showed up here at my door. My people came close to killing him, until he convinced them that he had escaped from the island, and that he had something I needed to see. It was a document he'd smuggled out."

"Something about your daughter?"

Marti nodded. "It was a signed confession that she and her husband were a CIA team. In exchange for her freedom, she promised to come back to the States and either convince me to return to Cuba or kidnap me and bring me back. The guarantee was to be her husband, who would be placed in 'protective custody.' But no one counted on him trying to escape."

"It was probably a forgery," McGarvey said. "I can't imagine her signing something like that, or for the DGI to let it walk out the door with a defector. Did you recognize her signature?"

"I don't know my daughter's signature."

"Did you bring it up to Langley?"

"No one had been willing to help get them out of there, and I didn't think they'd changed their thinking even if one of their officers had been shot to death in Havana," Marti said. "In any event, by the time I got the confession Gloria had already had a chance to tell her own story."

"You could have brought the DGI defector up to Langley."

"He was shot to death out on the street not fifty feet from my front door," Marti said.

All of it was too convenient, yet there was a certain symmetry to Marti's story, and to Gloria's psyche reports after Cuba. "Was that why you went to Paris? To confront her with the story?" McGarvey asked.

"Sí."

"What did she say?"

"She looked at her confession and handed it back to me. 'Is this why you came to Paris, *Papá*?' she asked me. If she'd been angry, or sad, or confused—anything like that—I would have understood. If she had denied that it was her signature, I would have believed it. Her husband had been shot to death, and her father was asking her if she was a spy for the

Cuban government, and she was neutral. We could have been discussing the weather."

"What did you say to her?"

Marti shook his head. "I don't remember. Maybe something like, 'What is a father to do?' I had dinner reservations for us at the Restaurant Jules Verne, but she couldn't make it. She was too busy. The next day I flew back to Miami."

For the first time this evening, McGarvey saw a genuine sadness in the general's eyes, and in the set of his shoulders. He was carrying a burden, and because of the lateness of the hour, or because of McGarvey's probing, the weight had become almost too great to bear.

"I didn't know the woman my daughter had become," Marti said. "She was a total stranger to me."

"And now?" McGarvey asked.

"You came here wanting to find out if you could count on my daughter. If you could trust her," Marti said, his voice softened by emotion.

McGarvey had come to hear a father's assessment of a daughter. But Marti admitted he didn't know her as a woman, which was not surprising, since he hadn't known her as a child.

"Whatever happened in Havana, she managed to save her own life," Marti said. "That in itself doesn't make her a bad person, merely a survivor."

McGarvey held his silence, though there were a few dozen points he could have made.

"She's been involved in at least one operation with you. What's your read?"

"I think she's confused."

Marti shrugged. "She's not confused about you. Unrealistic, now that I've met you, but not confused."

"Do you trust your daughter?" McGarvey asked.

Marti took a moment to answer. "I love her with all my soul. I'm sure of that much, although since my wife's death, perhaps my definition of love and yours may be different."

"Do you trust her?"

Marti lowered his eyes after a beat. "No."

FIFTY-FIVE

☐

EN ROUTE TO SARASOTA

After an uneasy night at the Park Central Hotel, McGarvey had Martinez arrange for a rental car under a work name, and he checked out and headed across the state on Alligator Alley. Traffic was almost nonexistent on the divided highway that ran straight through the Everglades; no curves, no hills, only the sawgrass in every direction out to the horizon, and showers falling out of a few small clouds in the distance.

He'd not called Katy to tell her that he was on his way back to Sarasota, and he felt a little guilty about it. But he was in full swing, and he needed to stay focused.

He had almost all the pieces now to find out what Liu and the Chinese had been doing in Mexico for the past ten years. Very soon being around him would get dangerous, and he wanted to insulate his wife as much as possible by keeping his distance from her.

Later he would explain it to her, but for now he was on the hunt, and the next steps he was going to take would not be pretty.

First came Gil Perry.

A few miles outside of Naples, McGarvey used his cell phone to call the Mexico City chief of station. Perry's secretary answered on the first ring and immediately put him through, as if they were expecting his call.

Mexico City was an hour earlier, which put it a few minutes after ten in the morning. When Perry answered he sounded out of breath, as if he had just run up a flight of stairs, or as if he were girding himself for bad news.

"I'm on the way to see the woman," McGarvey said.

"Are you there now?" Perry demanded.

"I'm a couple hours away. She's your mark, so I thought you should know what's going on, and give the house the heads-up that I'm on my way."

"Thank you," Perry said. "I'll give the detail a call right away. Have you come up with something? I mean, do you have some more questions for her?"

"I want to nail down a couple of loose ends," McGarvey said. "I'm doing a little research, and I've turned up a few inconsistencies."

"Anything we can do from this end?" Perry asked. "I mean, for heaven's sake, we're part of the team. It was our field officer who was assassinated."

"Her family in France is rich. Any idea what she was doing in Mexico trying to earn money to get to the States?"

"She was never quite clear on that point. And believe me, I pressed her when she first walked in, and again when we arrived at Tommy's house."

McGarvey looked up. "Do you know Tom Doyle?"

"Not to sit down and have a chat, but everyone in the Company knows of him. And it was damned decent that he offered the use of his house."

"How was that arranged?"

"Mr. Adkins made the call."

"Not McCann?" McGarvey asked.

Perry hesitated for just a moment. "I imagine he was in on the initial conversation, but I believe it was Mr. Adkins who actually asked for the favor. Is there a problem about the arrangement that I should know about?"

"No, none whatsoever," McGarvey said. "I was just curious." Perry was apparently trying to cut his boss, Howard McCann, out of the operation, but why lie about it now? And why had he lied about not knowing Updegraf was fluent in Mandarin? The man had his own agenda, which he expected would land him in the number two spot at the Agency, so it was possible he was trying to protect himself. But from what?

"I'll see what I can dig up about her family background. Maybe there'll be an answer there. Could be we'll have to query Paris Station."

"It's not important for now, but I'll leave it up to you."

"I'll find an answer," Perry said. "What else are you looking for?"

"I want to know the real reason she left all her money behind when she walked away from Liu. And I want to know what she thinks Updegraf was doing up in Chihuahua."

"I expect she doesn't know," Perry said. "And we may never know. As I said, Louis left no records. Not a mention in his computer. Not even a veiled reference in cipher."

"We'll find out what he was doing up there," McGarvey promised.

"How will you do that? Louis is dead."

"I'm going to ask General Liu."

F I F T Y — S I X

LONGBOAT KEY

Working as an intelligence officer meant that you had a suspicious nature. Probably nothing was as it seemed, no one was telling you the truth, and if you were given three ironclad facts, the one that would do you the most harm was almost certainly a lie.

Good tradecraft meant listening to your inner voices, and driving onto Longboat Key, McGarvey's sixth sense was roaring like a Concorde coming in for a landing.

The opposition had come after him the moment he'd left the confines of the Farm. And a few days ago someone had tried to hit General Marti. Coincidence? He thought not.

Traffic was light on the only north–south road on the key, and McGarvey was able to take his time, keeping a constant check on his rearview mirror as well as a peripheral view. He was looking for the out-of-place car or van that seemed to be taking too much of an interest in him; the hint of a movement from the upper windows or the rooftop of a condominium tower; the pair of men, who didn't belong, walking on the sidewalk, maybe wearing khakis or jeans instead of shorts; perhaps a low-flying airplane or helicopter with a real estate firm's logo that seemed to be taking more of an interest in traffic than in properties. But there was nobody.

The house was about two thirds of the way up the eleven-mile island, and screened from the road by a tall wall and thick vegetation. Passing the house, he could make out little more than the roofline. Nothing on either side of the house or across the road would give a watcher a vantage point to look down onto the property, or give a sniper any sort of a shot.

Tommy Doyle was a very private person, and he had picked the location with a great deal of care. The house was exposed only to the Gulf.

McGarvey drove past the place, pulling off the road at a public beach access one hundred yards to the north. A narrow path from a small unpaved parking area cut from the palms, palmettos, and sea grapes led over the low sand dunes to the broad white beach. No other cars were parked in the lot, nor was there anyone on the beach.

Just at the rise McGarvey held up. A sailboat was hull down on the horizon, slowly making its way to the south. Well to the north, a large commercial ship was heading for Tampa Bay, and a small plane towing an advertising banner for a restaurant headed south along the beaches.

About one hundred yards directly off the beach in front of Tommy Doyle's house, a large motor yacht, at least ninety feet on deck, was heading north. Even from here McGarvey could make out several people aboard, including a couple of women in bikinis on the forward sundeck.

He could also see the glint of at least one pair of binoculars from inside the wheelhouse. Someone aboard the yacht was taking an interest in the house.

McGarvey stepped back a few yards so that he would be screened from view as the yacht slowly cruised past. He could hear the low thrum of the diesels, and some music playing, and the sounds of laughter. Someone out for a day of fun on the water. Nothing sinister. Yet the insistent voice was shouting at the back of his head: coincidences were to be treated with great respect and suspicion.

The name on the stern was *Ocean Mistress*, Miami.

He watched the yacht until it disappeared around the headland at the north end of Longboat Key, then waited for a full half hour to make sure that it wasn't coming back, before he returned to his car and telephoned Rencke at the Building.

"Oh, wow, Mac, you're back in Sarasota. But you're not home and you're not at the college. Longboat Key?"

"I'm pulling Shahrzad out of here."

"Trouble?" Rencke asked.

"Could be, but I'm not sure," McGarvey said. He told Rencke about the yacht. "Someone aboard was taking an interest in the house."

"Could have been a sightseer."

"She was the *Ocean Mistress* out of Miami."

"Stand by," Rencke said. He was gone for less than a minute. "No coincidence, kemosabe," he said. He was excited. "It's a documented vessel registered in the name of Connie Newell."

"The wife of Congressman Newell?"

"Bingo," Rencke said. "But right now it's in charter service out of Fort Lauderdale."

"See if you can find who has it."

"I'm working on it," Rencke said. "Place called Boat Dreams in Paradise Inc. Hang on."

It would be too much to expect that the congressman or his wife were aboard, or that General Liu or some of his henchmen had sailed up here to find out where Shahrzad was hiding.

"You ready for this, Mac?" Rencke came back. "The *Ocean Mistress* is supposedly down for maintenance. Not expected to be back in service until next week. No one has her."

"Ninety feet, white hull, blue trim."

"Ninety-four feet, white hull, blue trim, double stripe just below the coaming."

"That's the boat," McGarvey said.

"Do you want me to give the Coast Guard the heads-up?" Rencke asked.

"No. I don't want to push back yet. I'm getting Shahrzad out of here anyway."

"You bringing her up here?"

"I'm going to leave that up to McCann."

After just a moment's hesitation Rencke chuckled. "She'll come as a surprise. Do you want me to keep tabs on him? I'd just love to stick it to him."

"I just want to know if and when Gil Perry calls him," McGarvey said.

"And what they say to each other?"

McGarvey had to laugh. "Play nice, Otto. McCann may be a jerk, but I don't think he's one of the bad guys."

"One can always hope," Rencke replied, a vicious edge to his voice. "Are you coming up here?"

"Tonight," McGarvey said. "Tell Dick that I'm ready to get started. I just need to have a word with him."

"You've got it," Rencke said. "How about Mrs. M.? You going to let her know you're in town?"

"No."

FIFTY-SEVEN

THE DOYLE HOUSE

The CIA detail at the house was expecting McGarvey. He stopped at the gate, identified himself, and was buzzed through immediately. The day was already hot, but a pleasant breeze from the Gulf filtered through the trees and riot of subtropical vegetation.

McGarvey parked in front and Toni Dronchi was waiting for him at the open door when he walked up. She was dressed in white shorts and a T-shirt, over which she wore a shoulder holster for a Beretta 9 mm. No shoes.

"Welcome back," she said, smiling.

"Everything okay here?" McGarvey asked.

"A big yacht cruised by a half hour ago. I think somebody aboard might have been interested in us. We're working on finding out who it was." She stepped aside to let him enter, and before she closed the door she glanced out toward the driveway.

"Belongs to Congressman Newell's wife," McGarvey said when she joined him in the sweeping entry hall. "But it's supposed to be over in Fort Lauderdale for maintenance until next week."

Toni grinned. "You saw it?"

"From a public access just up the beach. Otto ran it down for me. Has there been anything else?"

"Except for her constant bitching about everything, it's been quiet. Thanks for sending the extra help."

A large-boned woman in her early thirties, dressed in jeans and a T-shirt, a big Glock in her shoulder holster, appeared at the head of the stairs. "Good morning, sir," she called down.

"Karen West," Toni said. "She was one of my instructors at the Farm."

"Tell me you're getting us out of here, and you'll make me a happy woman," Karen said.

"That's exactly what I'm doing here," McGarvey said. "But first I want to talk to her. Then you can arrange something with housekeeping. I want her in one of our Washington area safe houses by this time tomorrow, if not sooner."

"She's in her room," Karen said. "I'll get her."

"Mr. McGarvey, you're a lifesaver," Toni said. "Believe me."

He followed her out to the veranda. "What's she been complaining about?"

"Just about everything. The food, the house, the weather."

"But not about being cooped up here under house arrest 24/7?"

"Not that," Toni said. "I think she realizes that she might not be safe anywhere else. Can you tell me why we're moving her out of here? Is it because of that yacht?"

"Could be the opposition has found out she's here," McGarvey said. "I don't know for sure, but I don't want to take any chances."

"She's that important?"

McGarvey nodded.

"I see," Toni said. "Would you care for something? Iced tea, a Coke?"

"A beer."

"Yes, sir," Toni said, and she went to get it for him just as Karen appeared from upstairs with Shahrzad, who was dressed in a bright yellow bikini with a flower print silk wrap around her slender waist. She pulled up short when she saw who it was.

"Care to go for a walk on the beach?" McGarvey asked.

"I don't think so," Shahrzad said. "Didn't they tell you about the yacht?"

"It was probably nothing."

Shahrzad laughed disparagingly. "Don't count on it. I'm sure that by now Liu knows where I am. He'll send his people."

"How do you know?" McGarvey asked.

"I know Liu," Shahrzad said. "And no matter how well you think you know him, you don't. Believe me."

She was frightened, he could see that much in her eyes. But she was defiant, obviously working the angles to figure out how she could come out of this mess on top. She was in the U.S., which was one of her goals. All that was left was her freedom, and some money.

"We're moving you out of here, tonight if possible. If not, tomorrow sometime. Pack your things."

"Where are you taking me?"

"You'll find out when you get there."

She stamped her foot. "I don't have to take this, you know!"

"Okay," McGarvey said.

She glanced at Karen and then back at McGarvey. "Okay what? What are you talking about?"

"You're free to leave, if that's what you want," McGarvey told her. He glanced over at Karen. "When she's packed, take her into town and check her in at the Ritz. I'll take care of the bill for the first week."

"What are you trying to do to me?" Shahrzad demanded. "Are you trying to get me killed?"

"I'm trying to save your life long enough to bring Liu down."

"All right."

"You're being moved to someplace that might be safer for the moment. You have no need to know where it is. We'll take care of that."

Shahrzad nodded warily. " 'For the moment'?"

"That's right. And if you complain again, about anything, I'll dump your ass on the nearest street corner so fast you won't have time to blink." McGarvey waited for that to sink in.

Shahrzad wanted to argue; it was clear by her attitude, by the look on her narrow face, by her posture. Finally she lowered her eyes and nodded. "I'll do whatever you say."

"Yes, you will," McGarvey assured her.

"I just want it to end," she said softly. She looked up, her eyes wide. "You don't believe me, I know that. And I can't blame you. But I *was* in love with Louis. Maybe he was the only man I was ever in love with."

McGarvey softened his manner. "Then help me bring Liu down."

"I will."

"No more bullshit."

She nodded. "No more bullshit. I promise."

McGarvey took one of the photographs he'd lifted from Gloria's personnel file and showed it to Shahrzad. "Do you know this woman?"

She studied the picture for a second and looked up. "I don't know who she is, but I've seen her once or twice."

McGarvey held himself from showing any reaction.

"Who is she?" Shahrzad asked.

"I don't know," he said. "I want you to tell me. Where did you see her?"

Shahrzad shrugged. "I don't know. I'm telling the truth. Her face is familiar, I remember seeing her somewhere, but I don't know where."

"At Liu's house?" McGarvey prompted.

"Maybe."

"At the compound in Chihuahua?"

"It's possible, I just don't know." She looked at the photograph again. "She's not Mexican. Part *negra*. Does she work in your embassy? I think I might have seen her there."

It was not likely that Gloria had met Shahrzad at the embassy. Perry would have mentioned it. According to him, he'd kept the woman isolated until he could hustle her out of the country.

"You wouldn't have seen her at the embassy," McGarvey said.

Shahrzad handed the photograph back. "Then it was at one of the clubs, or at Liu's house. I never went anywhere else."

FIFTY-EIGHT

□

WASHINGTON

McGarvey flew commercial Delta to Atlanta and then on to Dulles, arriving just before seven in the evening. He left the details of getting Shahrzad to Washington and set up in a safe house to Toni and Karen, knowing that word would get to McCann and Gil Perry. He felt like a Vegas act, balancing a half dozen spinning plates on long, slender rods. Disaster was a single misstep away. And when one plate spun out of control it would cause a chain reaction, bringing the entire act crashing to the ground.

Rencke was waiting for him at the terminal and led the way to his car in the short-term parking garage. "Dick Adkins is expecting you in his office at eight."

"Good."

"I think he's asked Carleton Patterson to sit in."

Patterson was the Company's general counsel. He was called into these sorts of meetings only when legal troubles seemed possible.

"Has Perry called yet?"

"No," Rencke said as they reached his battered old Mercedes diesel. He was tight-lipped. Something was bothering him.

"What's happened?" McGarvey asked.

"Plenty," Rencke said, but he didn't elaborate until after he'd paid the parking fee at the gate and they were on their way back into the city.

Traffic was steady despite a light rain that made the highway slick.

"There's no order in any of this," Rencke said. "No one-two-three, but my lavender has never been deeper. Heading toward violet unless we do something." Rencke glanced over at McGarvey. "I shit you not, Mac. I'm scared." He shook his head. "I just don't know what's going down. I can usually figure this shit out, but not this time, ya know?"

"Tell me," McGarvey said.

"Gloria's dad, General Marti, is dead. Supposedly a suicide. His body was found early this morning in his bed, a pistol in his hand, a gunshot wound to the head. Dave Whittaker is making sure that the Miami cops are cooperating with us to keep this quiet for as long as possible. Things might get crazy in Little Havana because everyone will suspect it was a DGI hit, not suicide."

"It was a hit," McGarvey said. "But not DGI. Has Gloria been told?"

"I don't know," Rencke said. "But it's going to hit her right between the eyes when she finds out. And I don't know how you're going to be able to use her."

"Liu had him killed because he talked to me," McGarvey said. "And it's possible that she's somehow involved with him."

"Oh, Christ," Rencke said softly. "I'm starting not to believe any of this shit. It's just gotten so goddamned weird."

"It's going to get worse."

"Don't I know it," Rencke said.

"Where were Marti's bodyguards?"

"They said they left the apartment just before dawn because something was going on down in the street. A fight. When they got back Marti was dead."

"I'll bet just about anything that at least one of them is on someone's payroll. See what you can find out."

"Will do," Rencke promised. "In the meantime, we've got two other problems: Newell and Perry."

"Let me guess: the good congressman is on the take," McGarvey said. He'd expected something like that to surface sooner or later.

"Yeah, but he's been slick about it. He's been taking soft money from several political action committees for the past few years. Nothing new in that. There's any number of congressmen who've got their hands out. But in Newell's case at least two of the PACs have ties with a couple of dummy corporations in Hong Kong, supposedly with business interests in the States. His wife's yacht, the *Ocean Mistress*, is almost never chartered by anyone except a few guys from the dummy corporations."

"Any connection to Liu?"

"None that I've been able to come up with so far, but I'm still working on it. At the very least Newell is raking in the money working some sort of a private deal with the Chinese."

They got on Interstate 66 in Arlington and headed toward the Roosevelt Bridge over the river into the city. The rain got a little stronger.

"What other good news do you have for me?" McGarvey asked. None of what Rencke had come up with was very surprising just now, but it did complicate the issue.

"Gil Perry is almost certainly dirty."

McGarvey watched the streaks left by the windshield wipers for a moment or two. "Who isn't?" he asked rhetorically. He turned back to Rencke. "What did you come up with?"

"As of nine months ago Perry was in debt up to his ass—credit cards mostly. His wife likes to shop, and they both like the good life. His monthly bills just at the wine shop he uses were a couple of grand until they cut off his credit. But two months ago he and his wife moved into a new luxury condo right downtown. Seven weeks ago he bought a new Mercedes AMG55. That was about the same time the wine shop started delivering again, and he began buying his suits from Armani."

"Fits fairly well to when Liu showed up in Mexico City," McGarvey said.

"Something's going on down there that's got Newell's and Perry's hands dirty, got Updegraf's head cut off, scared the shit out of a belly dancer, and has my programs going crazy."

The Building was fairly quiet at this hour of the evening. Most of the activity was in Operations, where a watch was kept on what was going on worldwide, 24/7.

Adkins and Patterson were waiting for him in the DCI's office on the seventh floor, while Rencke went down to his own office.

"Welcome back, Mr. Director," the seventh-floor security officer said. "Are you carrying, sir?"

"Yes," McGarvey said. He surrendered his pistol and walked back to the director's expansive office.

Patterson, his tie knotted correctly and his suit coat properly buttoned, was seated on the couch, across from Adkins, whose tie was off and jacket was loose. Before coming to work for the CIA, Patterson had been a senior partner in a prestigious New York law firm. His stint at the CIA was to have been temporary. That had been nearly ten years ago. Although he never professed to being a spy, he liked working in the Building for much the same reason a lot of people enjoyed working for the CIA: he liked knowing what was going on in the world, having an inside track.

"Good evening, Mr. Director," Patterson said. "Nice seeing you again. Mrs. McGarvey is well?"

"She's just fine," McGarvey said. "I'll tell her you asked." They shook hands. "I'm surprised to see you here."

"I thought that we could use a little advice, especially since this might concern Congressman Newell," Adkins said.

"He's up to his ears in it," McGarvey said. He took a seat in one of the leather easy chairs between them.

"Tell us," Adkins prompted.

McGarvey quickly summarized almost everything he'd done and learned, from when Rencke had taken him to meet Shahrzad to right now, leaving out only the possibility that Gloria was involved somehow, and the mystery man at Liu's compound.

"Jesus," Adkins said. "What the hell kind of a mess is this?"

"From what you're saying, it would appear that a U.S. congressman and a CIA chief of station are in collusion with the Chinese," Patterson said.

"That's what it looks like," McGarvey said.

"Our entire operation in Mexico is compromised," Adkins said. "Their intel guys must be laughing their asses off at us."

"I don't think it's Chinese intelligence," McGarvey said. "Or at least this may be an operation not of their design. It's General Liu's. Something he's apparently been developing over the past ten years. Here and in Mexico."

"Since you've started poking around, he's been tidying up," Patterson said.

"Something like that."

Adkins was shaking his head. "I still don't understand what the hell is going on."

"Could be that Updegraf somehow found out about Perry's involvement with Liu, so he went after the general. He'd probably come up with the proof in Chihuahua and was assassinated before he could get back to Mexico City. Either that or Shahrzad was lying about seeing Updegraf there so that we would protect her until we nailed Liu."

"But he was there, after all," Adkins said.

"Yes, but it could have been information she had been fed."

"By whom?" Adkins asked.

"Perry," Patterson answered. "But that would mean—or could mean—that Perry has more than one agenda." He spread his hands. "A falling-out among thieves?"

"That's another possibility," McGarvey agreed.

"Nailed Liu for what, exactly?" Adkins asked.

McGarvey had been asking himself the same question at every juncture for the past week. "I don't know," he admitted. "But whatever Liu and the Chinese are doing in Mexico has nothing to do with a U.S. partnership to pump oil."

"What do we do next?" Adkins asked.

"I'm going back to Mexico to ask Liu just that," McGarvey said. "I suggest that in the meantime you brief the president. Otto's programs are starting to go off the scale."

"A word of caution," Patterson interjected. "I'm assuming it's why I have been included this evening. Going up against an elected official is a risky business, especially now, since Newell sees himself running for president. And from where I sit he's got a credible chance of at least getting his party's nomination. Which puts him in a very powerful position."

"I'm going after Liu," McGarvey said. "I'll leave Newell to Haynes."

"What about Ms. Ibenez?" Adkins asked. "Perry fired her, but she's still one of ours, and she deserves to know that her father was shot to death."

"He was assassinated on Liu's orders."

"Why?"

"I don't know yet. It's something else I'm going to ask Liu when he and I have our little chat."

FIFTY-NINE

□

ANDREWS AIR FORCE BASE

In the car out to Andrews, McGarvey told Rencke everything he intended to try. It wasn't going to be pretty, and when it was over a lot of people would probably end up damaged and most likely even killed.

"It always ends up this way, doesn't it," Rencke said. He'd called to arrange for a CIA Gulfstream jet to Mexico City, no questions asked.

Although the flight would be listed as IFR with a destination of San Antonio, it would cancel its flight plan somewhere over the Midwest and switch to VFR, sneaking under the border radar into Mexican airspace. It was a little trick of putting an agent into place in secret that CIA pilots were well familiar with.

"We didn't invent the game," McGarvey said. "But since they want to play it, I'll change the rules." He grinned humorlessly. "They think Americans are bound by some code of ethics. Innocent until proven guilty. Bring the bad guys in for trial. Give them their rights."

"That's what separates us from them," Rencke said.

"Not this time."

McGarvey had left the files on Gloria and her father and all the other material he'd carried around back at the Building. He was stripped for fieldwork. He was bringing only his go-to-hell kit, including a diplomatic passport and some cash, and his weapon. The aluminum case Rencke had sent down to the Hotel Four Seasons was still there, checked with the bellman, and McGarvey meant to leave it there, where he could get to it in a hurry if need be.

"Mrs. M. calls me nearly every day," Rencke said, breaking into McGarvey's thoughts.

"Do we have people keeping an eye on her?"

"Yes, but she's already spotted them," Rencke said. "What am I supposed to tell her?"

"Nothing," McGarvey said.

"But—"

"Keep her out of it, Otto."

SIXTY

□

CIA HEADQUARTERS

It was late, but Adkins was still in his office. His wife had died of cancer a few years ago, and his daughters had gone to college and moved on with their lives, leaving him alone in a house that was vastly too large for one man.

He had nothing or no one to go home to, and he could do his thinking just as well here as in an empty house.

Adkins was a frightened man. When he had risen to deputy director under McGarvey he'd thought that he wanted to sit behind this desk someday. But the moment he'd gotten his wish, he'd realized that he'd never really wanted it in the first place. He was an administrator, not a field officer, not a spy. And the job of DCI had for too long been the sole property of the politician, unlike almost every other secret intelligence organization in the world, which professional spies headed.

Ever since 9/11 a new world order had emerged. It was the same holy war between Islam and Hindus, between Islam and Jews, and between Islam and Christians that had been going on for fifteen centuries. Only this time the soldiers were Muslim radicals, jihadists who were filled with such holy zeal that they were willing to sacrifice their own lives for a cause that most of them could not name, let alone understand.

Education was often all but forbidden for girls. And for boys, who were taught mostly religion, the situation wasn't much better. Islamic fundamentalists were sliding into the abyss of ignorance and, like wild, unreasoning animals that hunted in packs, struck wherever the group leaders told them to strike.

The division between right and wrong, innocence and guilt, and especially between male combatants and women and children no longer held any meaning. The jihadist's only mission was to kill and keep killing until he, and in some cases she, lost his or her own life.

Reason was an unknown factor. Courts of law meant nothing. Codes of conduct were a joke.

Since 9/11 a terrible passion had gripped the world. It was like road rage only more widespread and certainly deadlier. No place was safe. No country, including China, was without its own brand of terrorist who was mad at the world.

In the morning he would go over to the White House to brief the president, but standing at the window in his office looking down toward the Potomac, Adkins had no idea what he would say except to report the bare facts and speculations. He had no idea what to recommend. He didn't even know what the president might want to hear. Nor did he hold much hope for the director of National Intelligence, whose job, it seemed, had devolved almost from the beginning into a purely political entity whose only function was to study and collate.

The only solid thing that he could give to the president, he decided, was a warning that something terrible was coming their way, this time apparently from a different direction than 9/11. As certain as the sun rose and set the U.S. would be hit again unless McGarvey could stop it.

PART

THREE

The next day

SIXTY-ONE

□

MEXICO CITY

It was still a few hours before dawn when the CIA's Gulfstream IV touched down at Benito Juárez Airport and taxied over to the VIP terminal.

McGarvey had managed to get a few hours' sleep in the six-hour flight from Andrews, but he'd dreamed about Gloria and about what this assignment would probably do to her. She had her own agenda, one that he hadn't gotten a handle on yet. It was possible that she was working Liu in the same way Updegraf had. And it was possible that she had become freelance, offering her services to the highest bidder.

It sometimes happened that the burned-out field officer went looking for enough money to pay his or her way out: the "big score" Updegraf had told Shahrzad about.

He didn't know where Gloria fit, but he would find out in the next few days, and he knew it wouldn't be pleasant. She was in love with him; that was a certainty. And he was going to use it against her, whether she was innocent of being a double or not.

McGarvey gathered his hanging bag as the male attendant opened the hatch and lowered the stairs. A lone Mexican official in a dark uniform came out of the terminal and walked across to the jet. He looked half asleep.

Once they had entered Mexican airspace up around Tampico the pilot had announced their intention to fly directly to Mexico City with a U.S. diplomat aboard. No special services were required other than an early morning customs and passport check. The aircraft would require refueling, and would depart for Miami immediately.

The door to the cockpit was open when McGarvey went forward. The attendant stepped aside, and the pilot and copilot looked up.

"Good flight. Thanks, guys," he said.

"Glad to be of service, Mr. Director," the pilot said.

"You sure you got all your things?" the attendant asked.

"Yes, thanks."

Outside, McGarvey handed his diplomatic passport to the official, who flipped it open, glanced at the data, then looked up to compare the photo with McGarvey's face.

"Do you wish me to stamp your passport, señor?"

"It's not necessary," McGarvey said.

"Welcome to Mexico. Your rental car is waiting in front."

The kerojet truck was just pulling up to the Gulfstream when McGarvey went through the deserted terminal. A light gray Volkswagen Jetta was parked just outside. A bored cop sitting behind a glass booth looked up when McGarvey tossed his bag in the backseat, then looked away.

The fact that an American diplomat had arrived in the middle of the night with no one to meet him raised no eyebrows. But this was Mexico. Almost no one would have taken notice if he had flown in from Colombia, or from Mars. In many respects Mexico was a perfect place for a man such as Liu. Almost anything was possible here for the right amount of money.

Traffic on Boulevard Puerto into the city was almost nonexistent, and in less than forty minutes he was downtown, where he parked on a side street a couple of blocks from the Hotel Catedral on Donceles, then went back on foot.

The city center was normally a busy, dangerous place to be after dark. But this time of the morning was too late for the pickpockets and thieves. In an hour the first deliverymen would begin their rounds, but for the moment it seemed as if the D.F. were holding its collective breath. It was a city asleep.

The night clerk at the old but still respectable hotel, which very few Americans and certainly no businessmen or diplomats ever used, came out to the front desk when McGarvey rang and checked him in, under another work name.

"Do you wish for the services of a bellman, señor?" the young, pimply-faced kid asked, handing over the old-fashioned room key.

"No," McGarvey said.

"Do you wish for a wake-up call?"

"No."

"Welcome to Mexico, señor," the clerk said, still half asleep, and he disappeared into the night office before McGarvey got halfway across the marble lobby to the elevators.

Upstairs in his fifth-floor room facing the spires of the Catedral Metropolitana, McGarvey stopped a moment to look out. He had a sense that rough beasts were slinking around in the dark, and that whatever solutions he found, the answers would be anything but simple, anything but easy.

He broke the diplomatic seal on his hanging bag, finished unpacking, and retrieved his pistol, holster, and spare magazine of ammunition. He dressed in jeans, low-topped sneakers, a short-sleeved pullover, and a dark nylon windbreaker against the morning chill. Mexico City could be blazingly hot during the day, while at night it often cooled down to near freezing.

Downstairs he crossed the empty lobby and walked back the couple of blocks to where he'd parked his car. It had not been disturbed yet, but he would have to find a secure parking place before it got dark again. At the very least thieves would strip the wheels, smash the windows, and steal anything inside.

He drove the few blocks over to the U.S. embassy on the Paseo de la Reforma, the streets just starting to come alive with the first trucks and vans, but cruised past the front entrance without stopping. If Perry had put the embassy on emergency footing because of Updegraf's assassination, no outward signs of it were visible from the street; no heightened security measures such as a sandbagged entry, no guards on the roof.

Next he went out to the Chinese embassy in Colonia Tizapan San Angel and cruised slowly past its front entrance. He had no real idea what he was looking for, but if he'd expected that the Chinese had done more than the Americans to prepare for the coming troubles, he was disappointed. So far as he could see it was business as usual.

A storm was gathering, and there were people in both places who knew it, yet the castle gates had not been closed nor had the moat been flooded.

Finally, he drove over to Colonia Lomas Altas, past the Iranian embassy, also quiet this morning, and up the hill to Gloria's apartment complex, where he parked next to her Mini Cooper.

He sat thinking about the other times and places he'd holed up waiting for dawn to come, and for the battle to begin. Most of the time he'd gone into the field alone, no one to help or hinder him. He'd always preferred it that way.

But now he was going to have to juggle a dancer and a spy against a consummate, dangerous player in the new world order.

Just as the eastern sky was beginning to lighten, McGarvey got out of the car and headed down the path to the park bench that over looked the city, deciding once and for all that there would be no more nightmares and regrets.

Since last year, when he'd put a bullet in Osama bin Laden's brain, a weight had been lifted off his shoulders. He'd finally begun to accept himself for who and what he was. In that he was a step behind Katy and a couple of steps behind his daughter, but now that he had made the transition he was ready to go to work with a clear conscience.

The legendary spymaster Lawrence Danielle, his mentor in the early days, had once told him that he was a kid with the fire in his belly.

"So long as it doesn't end up consuming you in flames, you'll make one hell of an opponent for the other side."

Danielle's battle had been with the OSS against the Germans during the war, and then with the newly formed CIA against the Soviets at the start of the Cold War.

He had died in his bed years ago, but he would easily have recognized the new war for exactly what it was: a conflict with an order of fanatics bent on nothing less than the destruction of modern civilization. Such a thing could never happen, short of the result of a global thermonuclear war, but that wouldn't stop the jihadists, who had to be destroyed. It was this that Danielle would have understood with a clarity that seemed to have gone missing just about everywhere.

"You came back," Gloria said from over his shoulder.

McGarvey looked up. Gloria, dressed in a track suit, a towel around her neck, her hair plastered with sweat to her forehead and the sides of her neck, was grinning. "You're out early," he said.

"Have to keep in shape," she replied. "Is it time now?"

McGarvey nodded. "But it's going to be tougher than I first thought. Especially for you."

She had been moving from foot to foot, keeping warm so that she wouldn't stiffen up in the morning chill, but she stopped, the smile fading from her lips. "You've come to tell me something."

"It's about your father."

"What about him?"

"He's dead. He was shot to death yesterday in his apartment."

Gloria held McGarvey's eyes for a long beat, but then turned away and looked down toward the city. "¡Hijo de puta!" she said half under her breath. "It's the DGI. They were going to get him sooner or later." She turned back. "The old fool wouldn't take care of himself."

"I think it was Liu," McGarvey said.

She didn't believe it. She shook her head. "But why? It makes no sense, unless he somehow knows that I'm working with you again."

"I went to Miami to see your father. That night after I left he was hit."

Her eyes narrowed. "What did you want from him?"

"I wanted to know how the DGI got to your husband. Somebody probably fingered you. I thought he might have had contacts down there who might have known something."

She shook her head again. "It was a coincidence, your being there."

"A few days ago I talked to a woman in New York, one of Liu's girlfriends from when he worked out of the UN. Within a couple of hours after I left her apartment she was murdered."

Gloria's eyes were filling, but she was angry. "Why didn't you warn him?"

"I warned his bodyguards."

She looked away again, trying to assimilate what she was being told. "It still doesn't make sense," she said. "If Liu wants to stop you, why go after the people you talk to? Why not you?"

"He's tried twice, three times if you count the night I went out to his compound."

A wan smile returned to the corners of her mouth. "My father always knew that he would never make it back to Cuba. He knew that he'd be hit either in Washington or most likely in Little Havana. But he never really took any precautions."

"We think that one of his security people might have been in on it. Otto's checking it out."

She straightened her shoulders. "Now we know Liu figures you're too tough to screw with, at least directly, so he's going after the people you get close to. I'm next."

"Something like that."

"Okay," she said. "How do we start?"

SIXTY-TWO

THE WHITE HOUSE

At nine in the morning Adkins was chauffeured over to the White House, where Dennis Berndt met him at the corridor into the West Wing.

"What news of McGarvey?" the president's national security adviser asked.

"He's back in the field," Adkins said. "He came out to Langley last night and we talked. He brought me up to date, and I don't think the president is going to like what I'm going to have to tell him."

"From the look on your face, I don't expect he will."

They went down to the Oval Office, where President Haynes, already in shirtsleeves, was just ending a phone call. He hung up and waved them in. "Good morning, Dick."

"Good morning, Mr. President," Adkins said. "I'll take only a few minutes of your time this morning."

"This is about McGarvey and the business in Mexico, I presume."

"Yes, sir."

"The situation may be changing," the president said. He motioned for Berndt to close the door and for him and Adkins to have a seat. "I'm going to Beijing in two weeks to discuss a number of trade issues, among them this business about Mexican oil, which I think is nothing more than a damn fool stunt that Walt Newell got himself mixed up with. But Hu is bound to bring up the arms-for-Taiwan deal that's on the table, and that could cause us serious trouble down the road."

Selling antimissile defense systems to Taiwan was nothing new, except that China had been rattling its sabers with increasing frequency and intensity over the past six to eight months: missile drills on the mainland, naval maneuvers in the strait, and mass demonstrations in Tiananmen Square.

"I understand, Mr. President," Adkins said. "But the problem in Mexico will not disappear on its own."

"We can't afford to jeopardize our trade relations with China. Not now. Possibly not for another ten years, until South America is brought online."

One of President Haynes's goals was to provide enough aid and direction to countries like Brazil and Chile, where labor was much cheaper than in the U.S., so that manufacturing jobs lost to China could be brought back to the Western Hemisphere. It was a long-range goal that had bipartisan support, although no one had a clear-cut vision of how such a thing could be accomplished.

"Yes, sir," Adkins said.

Haynes glanced at Berndt, then nodded. "You understand the situation we're faced with, so tell me what's happening in Mexico. Have we identified Updegraf's assassins?"

"McGarvey is convinced that Updegraf was killed on General Liu's orders. We'll probably never find the contract killers, but most likely they work for one of the drug cartels. We think that Liu is using them for his fieldwork, and probably financing."

"Financing what?" Berndt asked.

"That's what McGarvey is trying to find out," Adkins said.

"Are you saying that whatever it is Liu is up to may be an independent operation?" the president asked. "Something without the sanction of his government?"

"At this point it looks that way."

Again Haynes exchanged a glance with his NSA. "I may bring it up with the premier."

"I wouldn't advise that, Mr. President," Adkins said.

"Why?"

"In the first place, we don't have all the facts. McGarvey could be wrong."

"That's not likely," the president said.

"Liu's background and position have to be considered," Berndt said. "It would be like the Chinese trying to convince you that one of the Kennedys was a traitor."

"What does McGarvey think Liu is doing?" the president asked sharply. He was getting frustrated. "Is the man a terrorist? Is he mounting an attack on us? Because if that's what you're saying, I can't buy it. The Chinese are trying to squeeze our balls on trade issues to give themselves leverage on Taiwan. But you sure as hell can't convince me that one of their top spy agency generals is another Osama bin Laden with a holy grudge against the West."

"We haven't come to that conclusion, sir," Adkins said. "But one of our field officers was assassinated, and coincidence or not, he was targeting Liu for some reason, and he was seen at a party hosted by Liu. The same party that Representative Newell attended. At the very least we need to find out what the connections are."

"I agree," the president said after a moment. "We're not going to let an American's death go uninvestigated. I promise you that much. But the timing is wrong. Whatever Liu has as his agenda does not involve World War III. So I think it's safe to suggest that we rein in McGarvey until I return from Beijing."

"I don't know if that's possible, Mr. President," Adkins admitted.

"We've been down this path before," Haynes said angrily. "I don't intend doing it again. Get word to McGarvey to back off, just for now."

"Yes, Mr. President," Adkins said. "What about our ongoing investigation of Mr. Newell?"

"So far as it doesn't involve the Chinese beyond the oil deal, you may proceed."

"He's been to Beijing, and he's taking soft money from a pair of PACs in Hong Kong that do have a connection with Liu. We've come up with that much so far."

This was unexpected news to both the president and Berndt. "Christ," Haynes said softly. "How long has this been going on?"

"I'm not sure we know that yet, but we're working on it from this end."

"Does the son of a bitch actually think that nobody will find out?" the president asked rhetorically. "If the *Post* or the *Times* gets wind of this they'll have a field day. Which is fine with me. But not yet. Is that clear?"

"Yes, sir."

"No leaks. Not so much as a hint. Is that also clear?"

"Perfectly, Mr. President," Adkins said.

Haynes let it hang for just a moment, then softened. "Is there anything else this morning?"

"Just one, Mr. President," Adkins said. He'd debated with himself bringing this up, but ever since McGarvey had been DCI, the CIA always told the White House the entire, unvarnished truth, whether or not it agreed with the president's policies. "Our special-projects director believes that the threat level to the U.S. is very high."

This was something the president definitely did not want to hear. "Are you talking about Otto Rencke?"

"Yes, sir."

Haynes nodded. "I see," he said. "Keep me posted. All I need is two weeks of McGarvey not killing someone. Two weeks."

SIXTY-THREE

COLONIA LOMAS ALTAS

The horizon to the east was just starting to brighten when they got back to Gloria's apartment. The television was tuned to CNN in Spanish and the only lights on were in the kitchen and the master bath. The city outside the sliding glass doors was just beginning to awaken with the dawn. It seemed to McGarvey to have been a long night.

"I'm going to take a quick shower. There's coffee in the kitchen, but it might be a little strong for you. It's Cuban."

"That'll be fine," McGarvey said.

She looked at him for a long time, her eyes alive, her dark skin glowing. "It was you who had me fired, wasn't it?"

McGarvey nodded. "I wanted you to have the freedom to operate independent of the embassy."

"I knew it," she said. "The only part that grates was Gil's attitude. He loved every second of it, the officious prick."

"What's his problem with you?"

"He's never been in control. Drives him nuts."

"He was your boss," McGarvey suggested.

Gloria laughed. "What's the plan for today? What should I wear?"

"Blue jeans. Nothing is going to happen until tonight."

Her expression darkened. "The clubs?"

McGarvey nodded. "We're going hunting."

She smiled. "I don't suppose you'd care to wash my back."

"Behave, and I might take you to lunch," McGarvey said.

The coffee was extremely strong but very good. McGarvey had opened the sliding glass doors and sat outside on the balcony and was watching the city come alive when Gloria came out to him. She was dressed in designer jeans and a sleeveless white turtleneck, and was barefoot.

"This is the best time of the day," she said. "But I was going a little crazy with nothing to do, wondering when you would come back."

"I'm sorry about your father."

She started to say something, then changed her mind and looked away. It was impossible for McGarvey to gauge her mood, to guess what she was thinking, what she was feeling just then, but he felt instinctively that he was missing something important.

The odd pause lasted just a moment, and then she was back. "I'm making breakfast. Do you want some?"

"I'll have whatever you're having," he said.

He got up and followed her into the kitchen. He sat on a stool at the counter, and she poured him another cup of coffee.

"Unless you're used to it, you should drink this only in the morning," she said. "In the evening it'd keep you glued to the ceiling all night."

She took out eggs and bacon and butter from the refrigerator and started breakfast, her movements swift and efficient, as if she were a short-order cook. But then everything McGarvey knew about her from firsthand experience and from her fitreps was of a woman who was highly competent.

"What did my father tell you about me, or aren't I supposed to know?"

"That he loved you, but didn't understand you."

"He never did," Gloria said. "But it wasn't his fault, not entirely. I was a difficult kid, and never got better. I got worse."

"He said that, too."

"What'd he tell you about Raul? Havana?"

"He liked your husband, thought it was a good match. But he didn't know what happened in Havana. He had only some secondhand opinions and guesses. But he was proud of the fact that you were enough of a survivor to get out in one piece."

A brief look of pleasure crossed Gloria's face. "He said that?"

"Yes."

She finished cooking and served McGarvey his eggs, bacon, and toast at the counter. She sat down next to him.

"I would have thought you'd make huevos rancheros," McGarvey said.

"That's Mexican. Cubans eat this if they can get it."

They ate in silence for a minute, CNN in the living room little more than background noise, the sounds of traffic outside rising.

"What do you want me to do?" she asked finally.

"I want you to become a dancer for General Liu."

Gloria fell silent again, finishing her breakfast. When they were done she rinsed their plates and silverware in the sink and loaded the dishwasher. McGarvey figured it was busywork, to give her time to think.

She turned back to him. "For you, darling, I'll do anything," she said. "Even that."

"It's not like that," McGarvey said.

She nodded. "Yes it is. It'll always be like that. I love you."

"You know that nothing will ever happen."

She nodded. "Doesn't change how I feel," she said. "But hey, listen, it's not your problem. It's mine, and I'll deal with it."

"We start making the rounds of the clubs tonight to get you established," McGarvey said. "This won't be pleasant, but it's the only way I can think to get to him."

"He has a weakness for women."

"He hates them, for whatever reason. And he's already killed at least three and probably more, so you're going to have to be extremely careful."

"But not so careful that he gets suspicious from the start."

"Something like that," McGarvey said. "First you'll need the right clothes."

"I thought that we would probably be going in this direction, otherwise you wouldn't have taken me to the Wild Stallion," she said. "Hang on a second."

She went into the bedroom, leaving McGarvey sitting at the kitchen counter. Two minutes later she was back, dressed in a fluorescent white cocktail dress with almost no back, a neckline that plunged to her navel, exposing all but her nipples, and an uneven hemline that was well above her knees. The effect against her dark skin was stunning.

"Something like this?" she asked, doing a slow turn.

"You're a beautiful woman. If any men in the clubs aren't turned on, they're dead above the neck."

She smiled. "I'm only interested in turning on one man."

"Yeah, General Liu," McGarvey said.

SIXTY-FOUR

THE APARTMENT

"I'll do whatever it takes to get close to Liu," Gloria said after she'd changed back into her blue jeans and turtleneck top. "Anything. But first you're going to have to level with me. If I'm going to stick my head—my entire body—into the lion's mouth, I want the whole story."

"I agree," McGarvey told her. "But it'll have to be a two-way street. You'll have to be straight with me. No bullshit. If I find out that you've lied to me, you'll be outside looking in."

"And if this plan of yours works, and I get to Liu, what then?"

"Whatever you want," McGarvey said. "At the very least back in the CIA with McCann off your back."

"Fair enough," she said. "What are we looking for exactly? What has the general done that has the CIA so interested?"

"And got Updegraf assassinated," McGarvey said.

An odd expression came into her eyes and the set of her mouth, as if she were doing everything within her power not to let her anger show.

"What?" McGarvey asked.

"It was so stupid, getting himself killed."

"What do you mean?"

"He wasn't trying to burn some code clerk, that much was obvious from the start. But he didn't do his homework."

"How do you know?"

"I said it was obvious," she snapped, all but dismissing the question. "Are you going after Liu because Louis got himself killed? Or do you have something else?"

McGarvey could not tell if she was lying. She was not as transparent as Shahrzad or as Monique in New York. But if she was holding something back, as her father suggested she'd done all of her life, then she was a master.

"One of Otto's research programs was starting to show lavender when the National Reconnaissance Office came up with a couple of satellite shots of Liu here in Mexico City, and the threat level started to go ballistic. He ran a quick background check on the general and stumbled across a couple of old FBI files naming Liu as a principal suspect in a series of murders in New York and Washington."

"But that wasn't enough for them to call you out of retirement. There had to be something else."

"It looked like the Chinese might be up to something down here, and when Updegraf was assassinated after supposedly going after a clerk in the Chinese embassy, Liu's presence began to raise some serious question marks, at least in Otto's programs."

Gloria was shaking her head. "I still don't get it. Why didn't McCann send a flying team down here to find out who killed Louis and why?"

"Nobody wants to upset the Chinese just now," McGarvey told her.

"Trade issues."

"Something like that. But it's possible that Liu is running his own operation for a reason or reasons unknown to his own government."

"So they sent you," Gloria said. "Still doesn't make any sense."

"We think it's possible that Perry is dirty."

They had gone out to the teak chairs and table on the balcony to talk. Gloria sat back. "Cristo!" Her eyes were wide, and for the first time McGarvey thought that he could see fear in them. It wasn't the reaction he'd expected.

"Did you have no idea?" he asked.

She shook her head. "I suppose I should feel glad or something, but I don't. He's a prick and I don't like him, but I would never have guessed he was anything but a Boy Scout. He wanted to be the deputy director someday."

"Tell me about him," McGarvey prompted.

She took a moment before she answered. "He was a crappy manager, I can tell you that much with certainty. He has no people skills." She shook her head again and laughed. "I'm telling you, Mac, this is hard for me to accept. I would have thought he was too chickenshit to work for the opposition."

"We're not sure about him; could be he just has a lousy memory," McGarvey admitted. "Did you know that Updegraf was fluent in Mandarin?"

Gloria nodded. "It was a weird kind of hobby for him. When he was a kid he started tinkering around with the language. He'd wanted to be an artist, but he had no talent. The next best thing was reading and writing the Chinese pictographs. He was pretty good at it, but he used to joke that it was a good thing his Spanish was lousy, otherwise he would have ended up in China."

"Would Perry have known that?"

"I would imagine so."

"Perry told me that he wasn't aware of it," McGarvey said.

"You met Gil, you talked to him?"

"Yeah."

"Here?"

"No," McGarvey said. It was plain that she wanted to know more, but he didn't volunteer anything and she didn't ask. "Tell me about working for him."

Gloria took a moment to gather her thoughts. She shrugged. "One thing he was a stickler for was our day sheets and encounter records. Everything we did and anyone we met had to be logged, and no one was supposed to see our logs except for Gil. We weren't supposed to co-op information without his approval. He was in charge and he made no bones about it.

"But he wanted to be pals. I think he sometimes fancied himself everyone's dad, or uncle or big brother, something like that. Of course everyone was laughing their asses off behind his back."

"But you got work done. The station reports I read looked pretty good," McGarvey said.

"Oh, the work got done all right, despite Gil's best efforts. And some of the embassy staff seemed to like the attention he gave them. After all, he was the CIA chief of station, and that's a big deal. He used to throw after-work wine parties for the people who worked the comms center, and I know for a fact that he had a hand in getting Sam Eggert her new apartment not too far from his. Sam was his secretary, and rumor was that they were having an affair. I wouldn't put it past him, but I'd also thought Sam had better taste than that."

"Did he ever hit on you?" McGarvey asked.

"Practically from day one. He wanted to get me an apartment down-town. I think he was probably trying to set up a harem for himself. I just laughed in his face, which pissed him off. After that I did just about everything I could to irritate the little prick."

"Did he give up that easy?" McGarvey wanted to know.

"No. And you had to give him marks for trying. But after a while, maybe three or four months after I got here, something changed." Gloria looked away for a moment, choosing her next words with care. "It was almost like he was running scared."

"When was that?"

"Oh, I don't know. Last year sometime. But then about seven or eight months ago he perked up. Like it was almost an overnight change. He was still a jerk, but he went from a nervous jerk to a happy jerk." Gloria laughed. "I don't know which was worse."

"What were you doing all this time?" McGarvey asked.

"My job," Gloria shot back.

"Would you care to be a bit more specific?"

Gloria stared at him for a long time before she averted her eyes. "Actually I wasn't getting much of anything done. Gil blocked me every chance he got." She turned back. "I joined one of the downtown Rotary clubs that was big with some of the top guys in the attorney general's office and the LE people, including the Seguridad idiots. Figured I could get something going, but when Gil found out what I was trying to do he told me to back off. Said he had those guys covered, especially the intel types in the Seguridad."

"That doesn't make any sense."

"None whatsoever. You jump at any chance you have of getting close to the opposition. The more roads to Cibola the better."

"What do you suppose Perry's chances are of becoming deputy director?"

Gloria looked to see if McGarvey was kidding, and then she laughed out loud. "If he's dirty, then he'll go to jail, I hope. If not, he'll probably make it. He's kissed way too much serious booty not to make it."

"According to you this station is a mess. But from the reports I've seen, Perry's doing a good job."

"Come on, Mac," Gloria said. "Who the hell do you think writes the bloody reports? The whole operation down here has been a mess, and still is."

"Sour grapes?" McGarvey suggested.

"You're damned right, but it doesn't alter the fact that Perry is a fuck-ing idiot. It's a wonder he's come this far. But if going after Liu will help burn Perry, then it'll be a fringe benefit for me."

SIXTY-FIVE

THE APARTMENT

Morning traffic was in full swing. In the distance they could hear sirens, a sound common to every large city 24/7. And already the haze of auto-mobile exhaust had begun to build. By afternoon the air over Mexico City would be unfit to breathe because of the air inversion against the mountains that trapped the dense smog.

"Did you know Updegraf very well?" McGarvey asked. "You worked together; maybe you held Perry as the common enemy."

Gloria laughed again. "Indeed we did," she said. "Louis was a nice guy who tried to live down his midwestern blue-collar upbringing. Perry was East Coast Ivy League, and he was forever dropping little unsubtle hints about how differences in backgrounds and education could influence a man's perception of reality."

"Perry pissed you off from day one, but how did Updegraf handle the situation?"

"It didn't seemed to bother him most of the time. He was doing his job, and he knew that if he kept his nose clean he'd eventually be reassigned, hopefully with a better COS to work for." Gloria shook her head again. "It's why I can't understand how he got himself into that kind of a situation up in Chihuahua. He was a lot smarter than that."

"Apparently not as smart as Liu," McGarvey said. "On the surface, how did he and Perry get along? There was tension between them, but was there any outright animosity?"

"Only once," Gloria said. "And strangely enough, the incident seemed to clear the air between them."

"Tell me about it."

"It was in the spring, maybe six or seven months ago. I was out in the courtyard behind the embassy having my lunch, a sandwich and a Coke from the commissary, when Louis came out and sat down next to me. 'Do you mind?' he asked, which I didn't. I thought he was a bright guy, sort of attractive in an odd way. Maybe it was his eyes, or his smile. He was almost always smiling about something. . . . So we starting talking."

"Shop talk?" McGarvey asked.

"God no," Gloria said. "The usual stuff, you know, the weather, movies—he was a movie buff—things back in the States."

"Skiing?" McGarvey prompted.

She gave him a sharp look but shook her head. "I hate the snow," she said. "What made you ask that?"

"I thought I saw a note somewhere in your file that you took a summer leave and went skiing in Chile," McGarvey said. "I must have been mistaken."

"You were," Gloria said. "Anyway, Gil evidently spotted us together, and he practically ran across the courtyard to where we were sitting and demanded to know what we were talking about.

" 'We're talking about the Yankees. Any law against that?' I asked him. He went ballistic, called me a goddamned liar, and said that he would fire off an e-mail to McCann that I was unreliable unless I fessed up." Gloria smiled. "He actually used the word 'fessed.' It was a new one on me, I had to look it up later, but I understood what he was telling me."

"How did Updegraf take it?"

"Not very well," Gloria said. "He jumped up and went eyeball-to-eyeball with Gil. 'What we were discussing is none of your fucking business,' Louis told him. Perry was almost having a heart attack. 'Everything in my shop is my business!' he shouted.

" 'Even baseball, you moron?'

" 'Even baseball.'

" 'Don't be such an asshole,' Louis said. All of a sudden Gil got super calm. 'That's exactly what I mean when I talk about upbringing and education,' he told Louis. 'How we've been educated to perceive reality determines how we will react. There's never a good reason to overreact and become crude.' "

"Was that the only time you ever saw something like that between them?" McGarvey asked.

"Just the once," Gloria said. "But then the oddest thing happened. Wasn't more than a couple of months afterward that Louis and Gil became the best of pals. They even went over to Acapulco a couple of weekends with their wives. I never understood what had changed, or why."

"Did you ever ask Updegraf about it?"

"Once, but he just laughed at me and said I was making a mountain out of a molehill. We all had to work together, so we might as well make the best of it."

"Did you go to bed with Updegraf?" McGarvey asked.

Gloria flared for just an instant before she managed to control herself. He had hit a nerve and it was painfully obvious.

She nodded. "He was nice, and he defended me that day in the courtyard. I thought he was sweet, and I was lonely."

"When was that?" McGarvey asked.

"I don't know. I didn't write down the date like a schoolgirl with a crush. I found the man attractive and I had sex with him. No big deal."

"The next day after he'd told off Perry? The next week? One month later?"

"It was several weeks later, I think," Gloria said, and this time McGarvey could tell that she was holding something back.

"Or was it after Updegraf and Perry became the best of buds?" McGarvey pressed.

She nodded. "It might have been."

"You wanted to know what was going on. Why the big switch in attitudes. You went to bed with him and that's when you asked."

She looked away momentarily. "Perry had just about cut me off from most of the day-to-day operations. He had me clipping and translating articles from a dozen Spanish newspapers and magazines."

"It was driving you crazy not knowing what was going on," McGarvey suggested.

"They were working some operation, at least that much was obvious."

"Do you think that whatever they were working on involved Liu?"

"I don't know," Gloria said. "I don't think so."

"You didn't want to go to Perry, so you went to Updegraf. Did he move in with you?"

"It wasn't like that," Gloria said. "We went to bed only the one time."

"So you could find out what was going on."

"I'm a spy, goddamn it," Gloria shot back. "I was trained to come up with answers whatever it took. And it's in my nature because of the way my father treated me when I was growing up."

Gloria's story so far was about what McGarvey had expected to hear. No surprises, except that Perry and Updegraf had apparently become so close. "When he wouldn't tell you anything, you dumped him, is that about right?"

"That's right," Gloria said. "I never loved him, and I certainly wasn't interested in making him leave his wife, although it would have been easy."

She wanted to say more, so McGarvey didn't reply.

"If that makes me a whore, then so be it," she said. "Not much different from what you've come here to ask me to do."

"I'm not asking you to sleep with him, just dance."

"Right," Gloria said.

Another thought occurred to McGarvey. "Were they still buddies when Updegraf got killed?"

"No. The lovefest between the two of them lasted only a couple of months, and then it was back to business as normal."

SIXTY-SIX

THE APARTMENT

Most of what Gloria had told him had the ring of truth to it, but there were little bits and pieces that didn't add up in McGarvey's mind. Why had she lied about skiing? Why her almost indifferent reaction to her father's murder? And most important, her lousy relationship with Gil Perry: She was a manipulator. Perry should have been an easy mark for her.

The evening chill was gone, and already the morning was warming up. By noon it would be in the high eighties or low nineties, with rotten air.

"How did you find out that Updegraf had been assassinated?" he asked.

"Gil told me. Said he had no idea what Louis had been doing up in Chihuahua, but his body had turned up in front of the hospital, and Tom Chauncy was taking care of things up there. He wanted me to backtrack Louis's last couple of months."

"Did he mention Liu?"

"No, just that Louis had apparently been trying to burn a communications clerk in the Chinese embassy," Gloria said. "Was he going after Liu?"

"Liu was probably up in Chihuahua that night," McGarvey replied, looking for a reaction. But there was none.

"He never said anything to me, and there was nothing in the file Gil gave me."

McGarvey let it rest for a moment.

"Would you like some more coffee?" she asked.

"No thanks, I'm flying as it is," McGarvey said. "How did you feel when you heard Updegraf was dead?"

"Shocked."

"Saddened?"

"A little."

"Surprised?"

"Not really," Gloria said. "Louis was something of a loose cannon. He was looking for what he called the 'big score.' When it happened he was going to write his own ticket straight to the top." She smiled. "Sometimes he could be melodramatic."

"But you understood what he was saying."

"Oh, sure," Gloria said. "What field officer doesn't?"

"Is there any reason you can think of that Liu would know your face?"

"Not unless the Guoanbu has access to embassy files," she said. "Do you think that's possible?"

"Everything's possible. I'm just trying to eliminate the improbabilities."

SIXTY-SEVEN

THE APARTMENT

Gloria took their cups into the kitchen and rinsed them in the sink. McGarvey followed her inside and waited until she had closed the sliding glass doors and the window in her bedroom, and turned on the air conditioner.

"It's not so much the heat, it's the air pollution," she said. "By noon it's impossible unless you seal everything up. It's like being on Venus or something."

"Do you want to go for a walk before it gets too bad out there?" McGarvey asked.

"Sure, why not," she said.

McGarvey left his jacket in his car and they headed down the path, past the park bench, silent at first, lost in their own thoughts. Like Shahrzad, Gloria had lied about a number of things. McGarvey was reasonably sure of it. What he didn't know was why.

Last year he and Gloria had been on a mission that took them from Guantánamo Bay in Cuba to Karachi in Pakistan. Several times during that operation he had stopped suddenly to look over his shoulder at what had just happened. Each time he did it he came up with a question about her. He hadn't known then if he could trust her, and talking with her father hadn't helped. Nor did seeing her now give him any confidence.

They had gone a couple hundred yards down the path in silence when she looked at him. "I still don't get why McCann didn't send a flying team down here to find out who killed Louis and why."

"Because Perry had a walk-in who told a wild story that Updegraf had been using her to get to General Liu."

"I never heard anything about it."

"Perry pulled the woman out of Mexico City in secret and brought her up to the States so that I could talk to her."

"You've completely lost me," Gloria said, and she seemed sincere.

"Her name is Shahrzad Shadmand," McGarvey said. "She's an Iranian belly dancer. Do you know her?"

Gloria nodded tentatively. "I think she may have been someone Louis knew. She might have danced at one of the clubs that he and some of the other staffers used to go to, but I don't remember ever meeting her."

"She was Louis's mistress."

"I don't find that hard to believe."

"She was also Liu's mistress," McGarvey said. "Louis sent her to spy on him."

Gloria pulled up short, obviously trying to remember something.

"Louis let it slip at one point that he was onto something important. I knew it didn't have anything to do with some minor clerk." She shook her head in wonderment. "I don't blame him for not wanting to share it with Gil. But it got him killed in the end."

"That's the point," McGarvey said. "I think he did share it with Perry. In fact I think that Perry probably pointed him toward Liu."

Gloria was startled. "Is that what that girl told you?"

"Not exactly."

"Anyway, why did Perry want you in on the operation? What in heaven's name did she say to him?"

"She didn't trust anyone. Louis evidently told her about me, and I was the one she insisted on talking to. The only one."

Gloria nodded. "Louis was trying to cover his bases in case everything went south," she said. "Which it did." She thought of something else. "But if Louis told her about someone like you, it must have meant that he was afraid he'd be burned. By someone who was supposed to be covering his back. Gil?"

"It's possible," McGarvey admitted. He was watching her reactions very carefully. But he was unable to read anything from her facial expressions or her tone of voice, or by the questions she was asking and the conclusions she was drawing.

"But why? What was Gil trying to hide? I mean, if he'd sent poor Louis on a mission, why didn't he admit it? Why'd he whip the whole staff into a frenzy to find out what the hell happened up there? He could have blamed Louis for the operation falling apart, or he could have kept his mouth shut and waited for McCann to send down help."

"He had to deal with the woman."

Gloria laughed harshly. "He could have tossed her out on her ear. She was a slut, who was going to believe her? Not you of all people." She looked at McGarvey and her eyes narrowed. "But you do believe her."

"I think that Perry somehow found out something about Liu and he was shaking down the general for a lot of money," McGarvey said.

Gloria was startled again. "Found out something, like what?"

"That Liu likes to kill young women while they're having sex with him," McGarvey said. "It happened a couple of times up in New York and again in Washington."

"Did Gil actually get money from Liu?"

"If I'm right about everything, then yes," McGarvey said. "But Liu probably tried to put a stop to it somehow, so Perry sent Louis after him. But when that backfired he sent the entire station on a fishing expedition."

"Wouldn't he have worried about exposing himself?"

"He pointed his people, including you, in the directions he wanted them to go," McGarvey said. "He had no other choice. One of his people had been assassinated, so his back was against the wall. He even started making noises about the Chinese up to no good down here in order to divert attention away from him."

"Congressman Newell," Gloria said softly. "Holy shit, Liu set him up with the Mexicans and with the Chinese, as a countermove against Perry. The oil thing is just a sham."

"Again, I'm just guessing," McGarvey admitted. "But it all seems to fit."

They walked a little farther in silence. They could smell the acrid odor of car exhaust building now with the rush hour. It wasn't pleasant.

"Shahrzad must have come as a shock."

"He wants to use her to put more pressure on Liu."

"He's playing a dangerous game," Gloria said.

"I think he's desperate for enough money to get out in case things start to fall apart," McGarvey said.

Gloria shrugged. "Okay, so what we've got is a blackmail scheme that got out of hand. Arrest Gil and lay it out for him. He's the kind who'll crack from the get-go. Why come down here to send me after Liu? It'd be dangerous and nothing more than a waste of effort."

"Because there's more," McGarvey said.

"Like what?" Gloria asked.

"That's the part I don't know yet," McGarvey admitted. "Louis was partially right. The Chinese are up to something down here, and were setting it up maybe as early as ten years ago. Or at least Liu is up to something. Perry was just an irritant, but Updegraf probably got too close and had to be eliminated, his death made to look like a drug cartel hit."

"Newell was a countermove on Liu's part, but what do you think Perry will do next?"

"He's done it by getting me involved. Liu thinks that I'm here under Perry's direction, which is exactly how I want to keep it."

Gloria's brow knitted. "I don't understand."

"I want Liu to think that I'm part of the scheme to shake him down," McGarvey said.

"In the meantime you're going to get close enough to find out what he's really up to," Gloria said. "And that's where I come in. I'm to be a part of the diversion."

"You and Shahrzad."

Gloria was visibly shaken. "What?"

McGarvey let the question hang as they started back to Gloria's apartment. He had come to her hoping that he would be able to tell something from her reactions. But if he'd expected to get a read on her, he was disappointed. It was possible that she was nothing more than a pain in the ass, as Perry had called her. Or it was possible that she was an expert actress who might have worked with Updegraf on the shakedown. Or it was possible that she had her own agenda, something that none of them could guess yet. But in a day or two, when all the players were in place, the next move would be Liu's, and it would be large.

SIXTY-EIGHT

THE APARTMENT

McGarvey didn't go in with her. She stood in the doorway looking at him, an odd, troubled expression on her pretty oval face.

"I don't work very well with anyone unless they're professional, and even then I don't like it much," she said.

"You won't be working with her," McGarvey said. "I want you to get into his inner circle. Shahrzad will be nothing more than a distraction for him."

"When she shows up he'll know something is coming his way."

"I hope so."

"He might even guess what I'm really up to."

"Possibly not," McGarvey said. "It'll depend on what Perry's next move is."

She started to say something, but then held it off for a beat. "Don't you want to come in?"

"No."

She shook her head. "You're a devious bastard, do you know that?"

He had nothing to say in reply.

Again she hesitated for a beat. "All right, I'll do it. When and where do I start?"

"I'll pick you up tonight around ten. Get some sleep."

"Then what?"

"We'll go hunting," McGarvey said. He brushed a kiss on her cheek and turned and walked back to his car, even less sure of her than when he'd first got here before dawn.

SIXTY-NINE

HOTEL CATEDRAL

McGarvey found a parking place with a taximan a couple blocks from the hotel, and walked back. It was a workday and the streets were crammed. Whatever problems Mexico had, its capital city was bursting at the seams with prosperity. In the distance all around the city, where there should have been mountains, was only a thick brown haze, the result of too much prosperity.

The lobby was busy but no one paid him any attention as he crossed to the elevators and rode up to his room on the fifth floor. So far as he could tell no one had tampered with his door; nevertheless, he drew his pistol before he went inside. Moving fast he slid to the left, covering the room and the open door to the bathroom, then the closet and the ledge outside his window, keeping well out of the line of sight of a sniper on an adjacent roof.

If the opposition knew that he was in town, either they'd not found this hotel, or they were keeping it low-key, waiting to see what his opening moves would be. He suspected the latter.

He ordered an American coffee, a brandy, and the local English-language newspaper from room service, then took a quick shower. He was gummy from the flight down, and felt faintly dirty after his morning with Gloria.

He put on a T-shirt and a pair of jeans, and turned the television to the English-language CNN. A minute later the room service waiter arrived. McGarvey signed the check and gave the man a decent tip.

When he was alone, he downed the brandy and telephoned Rencke at Langley. For better or worse he knew what he was going to try. He suspected that some people were going to get banged up before he was done, but he had not invented this game, and the bastards who thought that they could get away with assassinating an American intelligence officer were in for a rude awakening.

Rencke answered on the first ring, as usual, all out of breath. "Oh, wow, Mac, I was just going to call you."

"Let me guess: someone in Washinton has gotten cold feet," McGarvey said. He'd seen this coming a mile away.

"Yeah, the prez. He's going to Beijing the week after next, and he wants you to cool it until he's back."

"You tried but you couldn't make contact with me," McGarvey said.

"He's worried about the trade issues with China, and especially about the Taiwan missile sale."

"This has nothing to do with the Chinese," McGarvey said. "Just Liu. Perry was blackmailing him over the issue of the murdered women in New York and Washington, and he'd sent Updegraf to put on some pressure."

"It's gotta be more than that," Rencke said. "My program has slid solid violet. That's not blackmail."

"I know. Liu is into something else. I don't know what it is yet, but it has something to do with the drug cartels and money laundering, and possibly with the Iranian intel guy you picked up in the shadows."

"There's a lot of shit going on."

"It's mostly white noise, I think."

"Well, Newell is no longer our problem," Rencke said. "He met with Haynes this morning, and about an hour ago he anounced his resignation because of ill health." Rencke chuckled. "I would like to have been a little bird in the corner."

"It probably wasn't pretty."

Rencke laughed harder. "Nope." He loved sticking it to pompous people.

"Have you come up with anything else?"

"Louise is lending a hand. She managed to redirect a couple of birds to focus on northern Mexico, where the Chinese and Pemex are supposedly drilling exploratory wells. It looks like that's exactly what they're doing."

"No possibility of a cover-up for missile silos?"

"None. It's not going to be like the nineties with the Russians. Whatever the Chinese and Mexicans are up to, it's not about nuclear missiles. And that's the sixty-four-dollar question."

"Could the oil deal be real?" McGarvey asked.

"Could be," Rencke said. "I hacked into Exxon's top secret oil-exploration site, where they've pretty well mapped out every likely reserve anywhere on the planet. Where the Mexicans and Chinese are drilling is not on Exxon's map."

"Could mean that Mexico is in on whatever Liu is doing."

"Either that or they're just grateful for the money the Chinese are spending," Rencke said. "And who knows, maybe the Chinese oil geologists know something that the Exxon guys don't. Wouldn't be the first time a big oil pool that no one knew anything about was discovered. And the Chinese do want to gain a foothold in this hemisphere."

"Has the president been told about the drilling?" McGarvey asked.

"I don't think so."

"Pass it upstairs to Dick, and make sure that he informs the president," McGarvey said. "It'll give him something else to think about other than me before he heads to Beijing."

Rencke chuckled. "Devious, Mac. I like it."

That was the second time this morning that someone had called him devious, and he didn't know if he liked it. "I need you to do two things for me."

"Shoot."

"I want Shahrzad here first thing tomorrow morning."

"I'll have Toni and Karen bring her down," Rencke said. "Where do you want her?"

"I'll pick her up at the airport," McGarvey said. "But listen, Otto, no one is to know about it. Not Dick, not Dave Whittaker, and especially not McCann or Gil Perry or anyone in the station down here. I want the babysitters to keep their mouths shut, no leaks."

"Are you going to need them to help babysit her down there?"

"No, just get her here and I'll do the rest."

"Okay, a cover story'll be easy," Rencke said. "Are you getting set to make your move?"

"Tonight."

"What else?"

"I want you to talk to Jared, see if he can come up with something for me." Jared Kraus was the sometimes eccentric genius who headed the Company's Directorate of Science & Technology. His was the shop that came up with the James Bond gadgets.

It took only a minute for McGarvey to explain what he wanted and what he planned to do with it.

"I'm pretty sure that we've already got something like that," Rencke said. "But if not, I think Jared will come up with something. I'll send it down with Toni, unless you need it for tonight."

"Tomorrow morning will be fine," McGarvey said. And when he hung up he called room service and ordered another brandy.

SEVENTY

☐

THE ROAD FROM XOCHIMILCO

From the Fuentes Botanical Park outside Tlalpán it was almost exactly ten miles to the center of Mexico City. McGarvey had driven up from a spot a couple of miles away from Liu's compound in Xochimilco to get the timing right.

He sat at the entry road to the park, the Jetta's engine turning over, the dome light on as he studied an English-language map of the downtown area. It was a few minutes before eight, and the night had cooled down. Traffic on the highway was only moderate, which was a plus for tonight to work.

Only one road came north from Xochimilco, but less than two miles from the park, the highway split, and from there, several routes could be taken into the city. McGarvey wanted to conduct his first encounter with Liu tonight. He didn't think he had the luxury of making the rounds of all the clubs on the chance that on any given night Liu would be at a specific place. He was going to force the issue. Perhaps if Liu felt rushed he would make a mistake.

If Liu left his compound tonight with a mob, as Shahrzad and Monique had described, he would most likely head to either the Wild Stallion or the Doll House. It was a chance McGarvey was willing to take. He figured it would be no good to follow the general all the way into the city. His people would most likely spot a single tail sooner or later, even if they weren't expecting it.

Without a team to switch off with, McGarvey was forced to guess about the two clubs, and as soon as it became clear which direction Liu's entourage was heading, McGarvey could use an alternate route and get there first.

Just about everything could go wrong: a lousy guess, Liu might change his mind at the last minute, or McGarvey could be stopped for speeding by a traffic cop.

He put the map aside, turned off the dome light, and headed into the city, looking for the spot where Liu's driver would have to turn left or right: left to the Wild Stallion, right to the Doll House.

Fifteen minutes later he found the likely spot, where the broad Avenida a Chapultepec made the turn to the east, around the wooded park. Liu would follow it to get to the Wild Stallion, or turn left through the park up to Paseo de la Reforma, just north of which was the Doll House.

If it was to be the Doll House, McGarvey wouldn't be able to turn off until the Melchor Ocampo Causeway, and he would have to hustle to reach the club before Liu did. He needed to be only a minute or two ahead. Just long enough for Liu to think that he hadn't been followed.

No one made the downtown club scene until ten, and from what Shahrzad had told him, Liu usually had parties at his compound in the evenings, not getting downtown sometimes until after midnight.

McGarvey headed first up to the Wild Stallion, where he let the valet parker take his car. The pretty hostess at the front desk looked up and smiled when he came in.

"Good evening, Mr. McGarvey," she said, her smile dazzling. "Will you be alone tonight, or will your friend be joining you?"

McGarvey had been here only once with Gloria, but the young woman remembered them. It was a professional touch.

"She hasn't arrived yet?"

"No, sir."

"Well, let me get a table, near the dance floor, and if she's not here in the next few minutes I'll go get her."

"Of course," the receptionist said.

Immediately a hostess, dressed in the skimpy costume of a French maid, appeared and led McGarvey to a nice table in the front. Very few other tables were occupied yet.

"I'm expecting someone any minute," McGarvey told the hostess. "Bring me a bottle of Dom Pérignon and two glasses. A nice year."

"Yes, sir."

A jazz combo was playing onstage, the music mellow. A minute later a female sommelier brought the champagne, opened it, and poured a glass for McGarvey. "Will your guest be joining you soon, señor?" she asked.

"I hope so," McGarvey told her. "But she may be late, so make sure the wine remains cold, and have another bottle ready in case I have to find out where she's gotten herself to." He handed the woman an American Express card in his own name.

"It's not ncessary, Mr. McGarvey, we have your information on file."

"Very good," McGarvey said. He sat back and sipped his champagne as he listened to a couple of songs. A few others came in and sat at tables or at the bar, and McGarvey kept looking up impatiently and checking his watch.

Finally he got up and went back out to the hostess. "The stupid bitch is late," he muttered.

"We'll hold your table, Mr. McGarvey," the woman said pleasantly.

By the time he got ouside to the curb, a valet parker was bringing up his car. He gave the young man a tip and headed over to Polanco, where ten minutes later he pulled up in front of the Doll House, which had been built to look very much like the Moulin Rouge in Paris, only the windmill atop this club was garishly lit with pink lights.

He bought a membership for two from the young woman at the front desk, who could have been a carbon copy of the girl at the Wild Stallion except she was Oriental; she had the same pretty round face, slight body, and pleasant, almost syrupy manner.

A guitarist playing Spanish classical songs was onstage, and only a few of the tables were occupied. McGarvey was seated near the front, and ordered a bottle of Dom Pérignon and two glasses with the same explanation about his date that he had given at the Wild Stallion.

This club was more expensive than the Stallion. The few men already here were older than at the other place, and the party girls sitting with them were even younger than at the Stallion.

Because McGarvey had mentioned he was waiting for his date, none of the club girls came over to bother him, and after a couple of glasses of champagne he charged back out to the lobby.

"Save my table," he told the receptionist. "I'll get her."

"We can easily arrange pleasant company for you this evening, Mr. McGarvey," the girl suggested.

"I told the bitch to be here tonight," he said harshly. "And she will be here! Hold my table."

The valet parker brought his car, and McGarvey peeled rubber until he was around the corner, then headed over to Gloria's apartment, keeping well within the speed limit.

The downtown streets were starting to come alive with the evening, and it was past nine thirty by the time McGarvey reached Gloria's place.

When she came to the door she was dressed in a silk robe, her feet bare and her hair done up in back. She'd already put on a little makeup, and wore a thin gold chain with a tastefully small diamond pendant around her neck.

"Is it time?" she asked, letting him in.

"You'd better get dressed. I'd like to get down to Xochimilco as soon as possible," McGarvey told her.

"Is there time for a drink?"

"No."

She nodded tightly. "Okay, give me just a minute."

She padded back into her bedroom, leaving McGarvey waiting in the vestibule, and when she returned less than sixty seconds later, McGarvey's jaw dropped.

The dress she wore was fluorescent white, like the one she'd modeled for him this morning, but this one was not whorish. It was low cut, and off one shoulder, but the effect, with tall heels and extremely pointed toes in black alligator, made her look like royalty. A dark-skinned Princess Di.

"The other dress was cheap," she said. "I didn't think Liu would go for something like that."

"You're probably right," he said.

"Is it okay?" she asked, almost shyly. "Do you think it'll get his attention?"

"It has mine," McGarvey said.

She brightened. "No time for that drink?"

"No."

SEVENTY-ONE

XOCHIMILCO

A couple of miles down the road from Liu's compound McGarvey pulled over in a scenic overlook blocked from the road by thick willows. From here they could see the compound across the lake, the lights on the walls reflecting in the dark water.

McGarvey doused the car lights, shut off the engine, and got out and walked to the lake's edge. Even from this distance he could hear the sounds of a party: music playing, people laughing, girls shrieking.

Gloria got out of the car and joined him. "They're having a good time over there," she said.

"Sounds like it."

The night was silent except for the noises from across the lake.

"What do you suppose he's up to?" she asked.

"I don't know," McGarvey admitted. He and Rencke had discussed it, and neither of them had come up with anything concrete. Whatever it was had occupied Liu for at least ten years, and that was a very long time for anything lightweight. People, especially men of Liu's character, did not spend that extraordinary amount of time on nothing more than parties or sex games. He was into something serious, and Rencke's program had picked up on it.

It was the shadowy Iranian or Middle Eastern figure who worried McGarvey, because he couldn't figure out a scenario that would explain such a man's presence here in Mexico.

McGarvey went back to the car and got the pair of image-intensifying binoculars he'd retrieved from the aluminum case he'd checked at the Hotel Four Seasons. From the water's edge he could make out the compound and the first hundred yards of the road. At least a dozen cars were parked outside the compound, many of them Mercedeses or Jaguars or BMWs. A group of chauffeurs stood around smoking and talking.

The general was having a big party over there, and it was possible that he wouldn't bother going into the city tonight. If that turned out to be the case, they would return tomorrow night, and again the next night, and the next, until they got lucky.

McGarvey lowered the binoculars. Gloria had returned to the car and was sitting back against the hood. She took a cigarette from her purse and lit it with a narrow gold lighter.

"Want one?" she asked, offering him the pack.

He shook his head and leaned against the hood next to her. "What's the best thing you remember about growing up in Cuba?" he asked.

She offered him a wry smile. "What is this, another psyche eval?" she asked. "Did I hate my mother? No, I was afraid of her. Did I hate my father? No, I didn't know him. Next?"

"My daughter was just a few years old when I was assigned to an ops outside Santiago, Chile," McGarvey said. "It went bad almost from the beginning, and when I finally got back to my wife I was a mess. But she gave me a choice: her or the CIA."

"What'd you choose?"

"Neither," McGarvey said. "I was young and couldn't handle it, so I ran away." He shook his head. "But the best thing I remember, still to this day after all the hurt, and finally the reconciliation, was my daugher just after she was born. I got to hold her, and smell her breath on my cheek, and feel her fragile little body against mine. And there was a moment, just one out of ten million, when I looked into my wife's eyes and without words we told each other that we had a daughter, that we'd done good."

Gloria was watching him, but she said nothing.

"We all have those moments," McGarvey said. "Name one."

Goria was silent for a long time. When she finally spoke her voice was low and filled with barely suppressed emotion. "My mother and I never got along. At first I didn't know I was supposed to be a girl. I was having too much fun to bother thinking about it. Later I began to realize what I was, and I thought that boys were pretty stupid in general. Whenever I talked to my mother, or tried, we never got anywhere. It was like we were from different planets. We knew that we were supposed to love each other, but I don't think I ever felt it from her. And I know she never felt it from me."

A burst of laughter and then a cheer came from the compound, and they both looked that way for a moment.

"When Daddy, my father, took us out of Cuba and flew us to Key West it was an adventure at first. I don't think I had any real conception of what was happening. What the consequences would be. And when we crashed in the sea in the deep water outside the reef, all I could think of was getting out of the airplane. I didn't want to drown."

Gloria looked directly into McGarvey's eyes, almost pleading for him to understand.

"I was treading water and I could see my mother trapped in the airplane as it started to sink. I knew that she was going to drown, and I knew that there was nothing I could do to save her. That entire side of the airplane was crushed. We could not get to her."

Again Gloria hesitated, her eyes filling. "I looked into her eyes, and I could see that she wasn't unconscious. She could see me, and understand. And for just that moment, that second or two, I knew that she loved me, and I could see that she finally knew that I loved her."

The story was as sad as it was revealing, yet McGarvey couldn't help but wonder if Gloria had lied about even this, thinking that such a story was what he wanted to hear.

He turned away and stared at Liu's compound. If this had been nothing more than unraveling a ten-year-old murder mystery or uncovering a blackmail scheme, he would have dropped it, as the president wanted him to do, and go home. He missed Katy and their life in Sarasota. He even missed teaching.

But there was more here. If nothing else, Rencke's threat-assessment program could not be ignored. And there was something else, something nagging at the back of his head, something about the guy in the shadows at Liu's compound, that he couldn't put his finger on. But it was important.

Gloria tossed her cigarette into the lake and pushed away from the car. "I have to pee," she said. She looked brittle. She picked her cocktail purse off the hood of the car and walked off into the thick willows.

"Don't get lost," McGarvey called after her.

She was gone for a couple of minutes, and when she came back she laid her purse back on the hood of the car. She was grinning, and even in the starlight her eyes were bright. "How long are we staying here?"

"If Liu hasn't made his move by midnight we'll head back into town," McGarvey said. He picked up her purse, and she tried to grab it away from him, but he held it out of reach.

"What do you think you're doing?" she demanded.

"Just curious," McGarvey said. He opened the purse and took out a Walther PPK in the 7.65 mm version and a silencer, which he laid on the hood of the car.

"Don't you trust me?" she demanded.

"I don't trust anybody," McGarvey replied. He took out a package of Marlboros and a small gold lighter, and laid them on the hood. All that was left was an American Express credit card, a couple hundred U.S. dollars, a house key, and a large gold compact.

She watched as he laid the purse down and opened the compact. The inside of the lid was a mirror. One compartment held a one-hundred-dollar bill rolled into a straw and a single-edged razor blade. The other, large compartment was filled with a white powder. Some residue was dusted on the mirror.

"This is a tough business," Gloria said. "Especially for a woman alone."

McGarvey closed the compact and handed it and the purse back to her. "How long have you been on the stuff?"

"Since after Raul was killed," she said. She gathered up her cigarettes, lighter, pistol, and silencer and stuffed them back in her purse along with the compact. "It's under control."

"How do you get past the Company's random drug tests?"

"Just like everybody else."

"There's a lot of this going around?" he asked.

"This and worse," she said. "More than the suits care to admit, which is why the random tests aren't so random. They're usually posted on one of the confidential in-house Web sites."

This was news to McGarvey. When he'd been the director of operations and finally the DCI, he'd relied on his staff, especially Dick Adkins, to watch out for these kinds of things.

"It's no worse than booze," she said defensively. "And we all know that there are a lot of drunks out in the field, and even a fair share in the Building."

"I'd rather have a drunk than an addict watching my back," McGarvey shot back harshly.

"Why's that?"

"It's a lot harder to get a drunk to sell out."

Gloria flushed. She opened her purse, took out the compact, and held it out to him. "Take it. I don't want to make you feel uncomfortable."

"You keep it," McGarvey told her. "If you think you can hold yourself together, I want you to make a show of using it from time to time."

She nodded.

"Even offer to share it."

"It's one way of making instant friends," she said, putting the compact back in her purse. "Don't worry. I can handle it. I never go overboard."

SEVENTY-TWO

DOWNTOWN

A few minutes before midnight the music over at the compound suddenly stopped and the noise level of conversations and laughter began to decrease. McGarvey got the binoculars from the car and walked back down to the water's edge where he could see the main gate and the cars parked along the road. Gloria came up behind him.

"Is this it?" she asked.

"We'll know in the next few minutes," McGarvey said. He raised the binoculars as the gate to the compound swung open, and a dozen men and a few girls came out and headed up the road.

The drivers hurried back to their cars and snapped to at the rear doors. None of them was dressed in uniform, and most of them looked like professional bodyguards. Mexico was a dangerous country for anyone, including high-ranking government officials, especially men like these, who were playing games with a Chinese intelligence officer.

"Maybe he's staying put tonight," Gloria suggested. "Could be the party is just breaking up early."

"Has that ever happened before?" McGarvey asked.

Gloria gave him a sharp look. "How would I know?"

"You might have heard something," McGarvey said. "Maybe Louis let it slip."

"I told you that I didn't know anything about Liu." Her eyes narrowed. "What the hell are you getting at?"

McGarvey continued to study the activity on the road. "I don't know," he said. "The son of a bitch is up to something, but I can't figure it out and it's driving me nuts."

"Is it worth all this trouble?"

It was an odd question. McGarvey lowered his binoculars and looked at her. "A CIA field officer was assassinated. I'd say that makes this worth an effort."

"I suspect it was more of a warning than an assassination."

"Well, I'm not giving a warning," McGarvey said. He raised the binoculars again as the cars on the road started to leave. "Start the car, but don't switch on the headlights."

She walked back to the car and started the engine. Moments later two BMWs and a Jaguar emerged from the compound, followed by a big Mercedes Maybach and a black Mercedes AMG55.

Two other cars that had been parked on the road took up the rear as McGarvey raced back to his car and jumped into the passenger seat.

"Drive," he told Gloria.

"Is it Liu?"

"I think so."

Gloria pulled up onto the road out of the parking area in time to see the last set of taillights disappear around the bend a hundred yards away. She switched on the headlights and sped up.

"How do you want to play this?" she asked. She was suddenly hyped up.

"Get in close behind the last car, as if we belonged there."

"Then what?"

"I'm betting he's going to either the Wild Stallion or the Doll House. As soon as we know which, we're going to get there ahead of him."

"Cristo," she said softly, but she paid attention to her driving, and in a couple of minutes they had caught up with the big BMW at the rear.

Once they were away from Xochimilco and on the Avenida Insurgentes Sur, which was the main highway back into the city, they encountered some traffic, more than they had seen on the way down a couple hours ago. The city was starting to get its second wind.

"So what do we do when we catch up with him?" Gloria asked.

"Make him notice us," McGarvey said. He had turned the exterior rearview mirror on his door so that he could see if anyone behind them was taking an interest. But so far as he could tell they were clean.

"Then what?"

They could see the skyscrapers downtown in the distance, and traffic started to pick up.

"The next move will be his," McGarvey said. "But he knows that I'm here, and he'll want to find out who you are when you show up with me."

"He'll realize it's a setup."

"But he won't know why, and that'll drive a man like Liu around the bend," McGarvey said. "He'll have to try to get to you."

"Which I'll make difficult."

Twenty minutes later Liu's choice became clear when the Maybach and his entourage of a dozen cars turned left off Avenue Chapultepec through the park, near Los Pinos.

"He's going to Polanco," McGarvey said.

"What's up there?"

"The Doll House."

"Do I follow them?" Gloria asked.

"No," McGarvey said. He watched as they passed the exit of Avenue de los Constituyentes, until the last BMW had made the turn. "Do you know the way?"

"No."

"Turn at the causeway, but you'll have to hustle if we're going to beat them," McGarvey told her.

She glanced at him. "Why did you have me drive?"

"You know the city better than I do," McGarvey said. "Just get us to Polanco. The club is on Avenida Horacio."

"I'll find it," she said, and she sped up, threading through traffic as if she had been doing this sort of thing all of her life.

They pulled up in front of the Doll House a few minutes later, and the valet parkers opened the car doors for McGarvey and Gloria. There was a great deal of traffic now. The action inside had picked up in the last couple of hours and there was a line outside the door. A pair of beefy bouncers was letting only a few people inside. The rest were not important enough for the moment. If the club did not fill up by one, more of them would be allowed to pass.

"Welcome back, Mr. McGarvey," one of the bouncers said. He opened the velvet rope to allow McGarvey and Gloria inside.

The same hostess as before led them inside. McGarvey's table had been held for him, and at the same time that he and Gloria sat down, the sommelier brought over a bottle of Dom Pérignon in an ice bucket as their waitress brought them fresh glasses.

"Thank you," McGarvey said.

"You were here before," Gloria said when they were alone. "When?"

"A couple hours ago," McGarvey said, his eye toward the entry from the reception area.

The classical guitarist had been replaced by a very good combo playing American soft jazz. The dance floor was nearly filled with couples, mostly old men with young women from the club. The lights were lower than before, and the atmosphere had come alive. The night was just starting to get interesting.

Two wine stewards and several waiters were hurriedly setting up a round table, large enough for a dozen or more people, just off the dance floor fifteen feet from where McGarvey and Gloria were seated. Several of the scantily clad club girls hovered nearby.

Gloria nodded toward the table. "Liu?"

"Looks like it," McGarvey said. "And unless I've missed my guess, he should be showing up any minute."

A short Mexican man with a round, pretty face, wearing an Armani tuxedo, appeared at the entry from the reception area. Rencke had identified him as Miguel Roaz from the pictures McGarvey had taken at the Xochimilco compound. He was the owner of the club. He stepped aside with a flourish as General Liu came in at the head of the entourage from the compound. The Chinese intelligence officer was a movie-star handsome man, and tall for an Oriental. He wore an obviously expensive sport coat over an open-collar white shirt.

Most of the people in the club looked up as Roaz led Liu and his party across the room to the large table.

They passed within a few feet of McGarvey, who raised his champagne glass in salute.

Liu was startled. It showed on his broad face and wide, dark eyes, for just a moment, along with something else; maybe fear or perhaps anger, it was difficult to tell. But then the moment was gone, and he nodded.

Roaz had noticed the exchange, and as Liu and the others were taking their seats, he bent to say something into the general's ear. Liu shook his head and waved off whatever Roaz had said.

"Well, he knows we're here," Gloria said.

McGarvey smiled and sipped his champagne. "Indeed he does."

SEVENTY-THREE

THE DOLL HOUSE

By two the club was in full swing, all the tables filled, the bar area crammed to overflowing, and the dance floor so packed that it was nearly impossible for anyone to move, and still people kept arriving. The jazz combo alternated with strip acts, the dancers all very young, very beautiful, and extremely talented, most of them Oriental, probably from Bangkok or the geisha schools of Japan. Dozens of club girls, some of them dancers, circulated around the floor from table to table until they found customers, whom they led to a curtained doorway into the back rooms. Roaz had a thriving business.

Gloria had gone to the ladies' room and when she came back she was bright and animated, her eyes sparkling. She'd obviously done another line of coke. "This is fantastic," she told McGarvey, taking her seat, her back toward Liu's table. "Did he notice me?"

"He spotted you, and so did half the guys in the club," McGarvey said. "But you'd better pace yourself with that shit if you're going to be any good for me tonight."

"I'll handle it."

"Did you meet anyone in the bathroom?"

"No one from his table," Gloria said. "When one of them heads that way let me know. I'll see what I can find out. But so far they don't seem to give a damn that we're here."

McGarvey had been watching Liu's table for the past hour and a half, making his interest obvious. But neither Liu nor anyone else had glanced his way. "It'll happen sooner or later," he said.

"Does he know who you are?"

"I'm sure he does. But I told his people that I was here looking for my girlfriend, nothing else."

"Shahrzad," Gloria said. "Do you think he bought it?"

"Probably not. But he has to be curious."

Roaz, who'd been working the room, stopped at the big table. Liu, a young girl on his lap, kissing him on the cheek and neck and his perfectly shaved head, looked up and said something. Roaz nodded, then came over to McGarvey's table.

"Good evening, Mr. McGarvey," he said pleasantly. He turned to Gloria. "Ms.—?"

"Ibenez."

He nodded. "The general is wondering if he could offer you and your lady a bottle of champagne. We have a very good Krug. His favorite."

"It's vinegar," McGarvey replied coolly. "I've always preferred Cristal, or when I'm slumming, a decent Dom, which, as you can see, I already have."

Roaz's features darkened. "The general is a generous man, but he has his limits."

McGarvey sat back and smiled. "Are you asking us to leave, Señor Roaz?"

"I'm begging you to take care, Mr. McGarvey. For your sake as well as for Ms. Ibenez's."

"You might ask him about a friend of mine. She's disappeared and I'm worried about her."

"I'm sure we know nothing about that."

"Her name is Shahrzad Shadmand."

Roaz returned the smile. "Never heard of her," he said. "Enjoy your evening." He nodded politely to Gloria, then turned and went back to Liu.

"That'll get his attention," Gloria said. She was loving it.

"Go to the powder room now," McGarvey ordered. "I want to see if he sends someone after you."

"What do you want me to say?"

"That I'm an asshole. A macho bastard who likes to beat up women."

Gloria laughed lightly. She got up, gathered her purse, and sauntered past Liu's table on the way to the ladies' room, giving the general a pretty smile.

Almost immediately Liu said something to the girl on his lap. She jumped up and headed after Gloria. He turned and gazed at McGarvey, a calculating look on his face. He was a man who was used to giving orders and having them followed. This was the third time McGarvey had sidestepped him, and it was apparent that he was getting irritated.

The stripper onstage finished her act for an audience that was mostly indifferent, caught up in their own sexual fantasies. As soon as she was gone the jazz combo came out and began playing a Stan Kenton piece, and more couples went out onto the dance floor.

Gloria was gone for nearly ten minutes, and when she returned she was flushed and unsteady on her feet. She slumped down on her chair and knocked back her glass of champagne. "Relax," she said sweetly. "This is mostly an act."

"Fair enough," McGarvey said. "Did you find out anything?"

Gloria shook her head. "The girl's a fucking idiot. Liu doesn't know who I am or what I'm doing with an old guy from the CIA, but he wants to know. She's his main girl at the moment, and she warned me off. Said she'd send her friends to get me."

"She doesn't look more than fourteen or fifteen."

"Try twenty-three," Gloria said. "She just looks young. She's been in the business since she was ten. Mostly German tourists in Bangkok. Liu, she told me, is a gentleman."

McGarvey had seen stuff like this in 'Nam, especially Saigon. It had sickened him then as it did now. "All this in ten minutes?"

"I gave her a couple lines of coke. Her name is Sally, and she has a small tattoo of a red and green dragon on her inner left thigh."

"Okay," McGarvey said.

Gloria shrugged. "The kid is sexy," she said. "Anyway, I suspect that if at some point you mention the dragon to him it might piss him off. Could be he'll make another mistake."

McGarvey made a mental note of it, but he wondered what she meant by *another* mistake. Coincidences were starting to pile up around her like dirty laundry.

"Let's dance," he said, getting up. He held her chair and they walked out onto the dance floor.

"Are we going to give him a show?" she asked as he took her in his arms. Her smile was wide and she was obviously enjoying herself. They began to dance.

"Just don't give me a heart attack," McGarvey said lightly.

She molded her body closely against his. "God, I hope you know how good you feel," she said huskily, and she started moving her hips against his.

McGarvey felt himself responding, much sooner than he'd hoped. But she was a beautiful, desirable woman.

She looked up at him, a secret smile on her lips. "It's okay, Kirk," she whispered. "You do care, but I won't make the first move. Honest Injun. It's your call."

She laid her head on his shoulder and they danced the next two songs without speaking. McGarvey had wanted to give Liu a show, and that's exactly what Gloria was doing. She was acting like a woman in love, which in fact she was. It made her a prime target. Liu would have to figure that if he got to her, he would be striking back at McGarvey. And maybe through her he could put himself in a position to find out what the retired director of the CIA was doing messing around down here.

When the set finished, Gloria went to back to the ladies' room and Liu's girlfriend got up and followed her again.

A stripper came out onstage and began her routine to a nice rendition of "The Four Seasons" over the club's sophisticated sound system, as the waitress came over.

"Would you care for another bottle of champagne, Mr. McGarvey? Compliments of the house."

"Tell the general that I'm not interested in his hospitality."

"No, sir, this is from Señor Roaz," the girl said. "He told me to tell you that it was a peace offering. He wants you and your lady to have a good time this evening."

He gave her a cool look. "That's exactly what I intend doing," he said. "Have my car brought up. We're leaving."

The girl started to say something.

"Now, if you please," McGarvey told her.

She left, and McGarvey got to his feet as Gloria came back to the table. She was even more glassy-eyed than before, and a little unsteady on her feet. This time he didn't think it was an act.

"We can't dance to that," she said, glancing at the stripper.

"We're leaving," McGarvey told her. "We've done enough for tonight."

"Good," she said tightly. "The son of a bitch sent his whore to invite me to a party at his house sometime. But she had the balls to warn me not to show up or I'd be sorry." She chuckled. "I think I broke the bitch's jaw. She won't be giving any head for a couple of months."

At the reception desk McGarvey signed his tab, adding a generous tip.

"We hope that you will join us again very soon," the young hostess told him.

"Count on it," McGarvey told her.

The crowd waiting to get inside had thinned out somewhat, but McGarvey suspected there'd be people standing in line until nearly dawn. He gave the valet a big tip and drove directly over to Gloria's apartment up in Lomas Altas.

She was messed up, sometimes not very coherent. "Did we do good?" she asked.

"Very good," McGarvey assured her. He felt rotten about tonight and what was still to come for her. "But tomorrow will be even better."

"We'll get the son of a bitch," she said. "He and Roaz's muscle killed a good man. He'll pay through the nose for it."

When they got to her apartment she was half asleep. He helped her out of her car and had to carry her down the walk, where he fumbled in her purse for the key.

Inside he took her back to the bedroom, threw back the covers, and laid her down. She'd been mumbling something, but as soon as her head hit the pillow she passed out.

McGarvey looked at her for a very long time, hating what he was about to do to her as much as he hated the necessity of it. Liu was an accomplished master of manipulating people, especially women, into believing in him. Unless Gloria was convinced in her own mind that a real relationship existed between her and McGarvey, Liu would almost certainly see through the deception.

He took off his jacket and laid it on a chair. Then he took off his tie, tossed it aside, and ripped his shirt open, popping most of the buttons, and pulled it off. Sitting on the bed beside Gloria, he wiped her lipstick on the front of his shirt and dropped it on the floor. Finally he took off her dress and tossed in on the floor on top of his shirt. She was naked beneath, and her breasts were perfect, her stomach only slightly rounded, and her dark complexion flawless. A tiny white rose was tattooed just above her shaved vagina.

"Kirk," she suddenly called out, her eyes closed.

"I'm here," he said softly.

He covered her with the sheet and comforter, put on his jacket, and let himself out of the apartment, the night very st-ll and very dark under a sky that had clouded up.

SEVENTY-FOUR

▢

BENITO JUÁREZ AIRPORT

The same Gulfstream bizjet and crew that had brought McGarvey down from Andrews showed up a few minutes after nine on a gray overcast morning. McGarvey was waiting for it in the VIP hangar leased to the U.S. embassy. Rencke had assured him that the flight would be logged as a training mission, the crew and passenger list lost in DO red tape.

The aircraft pulled even with the main doors, and once the engines spooled down, the passenger door popped open, deploying the boarding stairs, and Toni Dronchi appeared in the hatch, brightening when she spotted McGarvey.

"Good morning, sir," she said, stepping down. She looked around. No one else was in the hangar. "What about customs?" She was dressed in khakis and a dark blue windbreaker.

"This is a training flight. No one will be leaving the aircraft."

"Yes, sir."

"How was the flight down?"

"Long," Toni said. "She bitched the whole way, especially when she realized where we were taking her. She's scared."

"I don't blame her," McGarvey said. "Get her out here and you can get back to Washington."

"Are we done babysitting?" Toni asked hopefully.

McGarvey nodded. "For now, anyway."

She took a small padded envelope from her jacket pocket and handed it to McGarvey. "Mr. Rencke said you wanted this."

"Thanks," McGarvey said.

"I'll just go fetch her," Toni said.

"You did a good job," McGarvey said. "Thanks."

She flushed with pleasure, and nodded. "Yes, sir."

She went back to the aircraft and returned with Shahrzad and a hanging bag of clothing and toiletries that Toni had provided her with in Sarasota from a nonaccountable CIA fund. So far the woman was a nonentity as far as the official Company database was concerned, and McGarvey wanted to keep it that way for now.

"I'm telling you, I don't like this one goddamned bit," she complained, stepping down from the hatch. She was dressed in a short black skirt, a white frilly top.

"You came to us," McGarvey told her coolly.

"What if I decide not to cooperate?" she demanded. "I could get killed. My life's not worth it."

"Well then, we'll just get out of here," Toni said. "Good luck."

McGarvey took Shahrzad's bag and loaded into the backseat of the Jetta as Toni got back aboard the aircraft and closed the door. The Gulfstream, its engines spooling up, headed to the taxiway. The pilot waved from the window, and McGarvey waved back.

"The bastards wouldn't give me a drink," Shahrzad said. "The least they could have done was—"

"Yes, you could get killed," McGarvey interrupted. "But if you pay attention and do as you're told, you'll probably come out of this in one piece."

She looked at him, a hand on her hip, her eyebrow arched. "Probably?"

"Yes," McGarvey said.

She turned away and said something under her breath in Farsi. "I didn't expect it to turn out like this, you know. Louis dead, and me alone."

"It's the hand you were dealt. Now you either play it or walk away."

"What if I walk away?" she asked. "What do I get?"

"At this point it's either Liu or us," McGarvey said. "If it's us, we'll take care of you when it's over."

"I've heard that before," she said bitterly.

"Your choice," McGarvey said.

"I don't want to be here," she said plaintively. "I want to go back. I want Louis here. I want to move to the States. He promised me."

"I'll set you up at the Four Seasons for a week. I can get you a few thousand in cash and an airplane ticket to wherever you want to go. I'd suggest Paris, back to your family."

"I can't go back," she cried. She looked at him. "I can never go back."

"Why?"

"Because I'm a goddamned whore," she whispered. "I'm what my father made me. And for an Iranian girl it means no forgiveness. Never. You're all I have."

McGarvey's heart softened. She'd never had a chance after her father had used her to seduce Baranov. Better one wayward son than a dozen devoted daughters. In places like Iran women were a burden, only to be used and then discarded if a husband willing to take on such a burden couldn't be found.

"Then we'll do this together," he said. "And you won't be alone."

She thought for a few moments, but then nodded. "I don't really have much of a choice, do I?"

"No."

"Okay. What do I have to do?"

"I'll tell you on the way," McGarvey said.

SEVENTY-FIVE

MEXICO CITY

On the Avenida Rio Consulado into the city, McGarvey called Gloria's apartment on his cell phone. Surprisingly, she answered on the second ring, and she didn't sound hungover.

"Good morning," he said. "How are you feeling?"

"Lousy," she replied crisply. "Next question?"

"It was a difficult night."

"Yeah," Gloria said. "Maybe I'm in over my head, you know?" She hesitated. "Look, I'm sorry as hell."

"About what?" McGavey asked.

"You know."

"You finally got what you wanted," he said harshly. "Don't apologize."

"But I didn't want it that way."

"What way is that?" he asked. He felt like a heel. But it was the business. He glanced over at Shahrzad hunched against the door. It was the season for that kind of thing.

"I don't know," she said miserably. "I don't remember a thing except for the club, and then waking up in my bed—"

"Just leave it at that," McGarvey cut her off. "You did a good job last night, and tonight we're going to up the ante."

"I don't know."

"Yes you do," McGarvey said. "Don't fold on me now. I need you."

Gloria was silent for a long time. When she came back she sounded contrite. "All right, darling."

"We're going out again tonight, only this time you'll have some help."

"What do you mean?"

"I'm on my way to your place now from the airport."

"It's not one of McCann's people, is it?" she asked.

"No," McGarvey said. "Just hang on, and I'll explain everything when we get there."

"Whatever you say, Kirk. But I think that I'm afraid."

"I know," he said, and he broke the connection. Christ, what a lousy way to do things. This was something that he knew he could never explain to Katy or to their daughter, Liz. But then even Liz had no real idea what tradecraft was all about.

McGarvey glanced in the rearview mirror to see a dark blue BMW SUV switch lanes and tuck in behind a shuttle bus about five car lengths back. He was reasonably sure he'd spotted the beemer at the airport VIP terminal, but he hadn't gotten a look at the tag numbers or the driver, so he couldn't be sure it was the same vehicle.

When he had the opening he pulled over into the left lane and gradually began to slow down, letting traffic in the right lanes pass him. He glanced again in his rearview mirror.

Shahrzad realized that something was going on. "What is it?" she asked. "Are we being followed?"

"It's possible."

She started to turn, but he stopped her.

"Don't," he said, laying a hand on her shoulder. "I want to see what they do."

The beemer did not switch lanes, and when it passed McGarvey, the driver, a Hispanic man in a white shirt and tie, did not look over. No one else was in the SUV with him.

"Well?" Shahrzad asked.

"It was the blue BMW," McGarvey said. "I spotted it at the airport." He checked his rearview mirror but could see nothing unusual, simply ordinary weekday morning traffic. Yet he would have bet almost anything that after last night's performance Liu would have put a tail on him. He'd parked the car at the hotel, so it wouldn't have been difficult to find him and follow him out to the airport this morning.

Unless Liu was playing some other game, almost as if he knew why McGarvey had gone out to the airport.

"Who was that person you called?" Shahrzad asked.

"An old friend."

"CIA?"

"Yes, she is."

Shahrzad didn't seem surprised. "I'm supposed to help her with what, exactly?"

"You're going to help each other bring Liu down, and for just about the same reasons."

SEVENTY-SIX

□

LOMAS ALTAS

McGarvey turned onto the broad Paseo de la Reforma a few blocks from Gloria's apartment, and Shahrzad suddenly sat straight up and gave McGarvey a wide-eyed look.

"What the hell do you think you're trying to do to me?" she demanded.

"I don't know what you mean," McGarvey said.

"You damn well do," she said, her voice rising. "This is the way to the Iranian embassy. If they get their hands on me they'll send me back to Tehran for trial."

"You're here on a French passport."

"It doesn't matter," she practially shrieked. "If I'm recognized they might not bother sending me home. They might put a bullet in my brain right here in Mexico City and dump my body in some back alley."

It wasn't the reaction McGarvey had expected. If the Middle Easterner lurking in the shadows at Liu's compound had been a regular, she would have met him. Possibly he wasn't an Iranian after all. "Recognize you as what, a friend of Chinese intelligence? That should be no problem."

"Recognize me as my father's daughter," she shot back. "They killed him, and they want his family, too."

"Is that why you don't want to go back to France to be with your mother and sister?"

Shahrzad looked at him, naked fear on her face. "They're already dead. I'm supposed to be next. It's the real reason I want to get to the States. I can lose myself there." She looked out the window as they approached the Iranian embassy. "Don't you see? God, you can't do this to me!"

When they passed the embassy without slowing or turning in, her relief was immediately replaced with anger. "You bastard," she said. "You drove me up here just to see how I would react."

McGarvey glanced over at her. There it was again, the same nagging at the back of his head. If her fear had been real, her sudden relief and then anger didn't ring true. There was no reason for her to be angry. Anyway, what did she think her reaction would reveal?

"You're wrong," he told her. "This happens to be the way to my friend's house. She's just a couple blocks from here."

She looked out the window as they passed the shopping center. "I've changed my mind. You can take me to a hotel, and I'll make my way from there."

"You've already accepted the CIA's help," McGarvey said. "How will you explain that to your friends?"

"What friends?" she practically shouted. "I don't have any friends. Can't you see, you fucking idiot? Louis is dead and I'm alone."

McGarvey turned at the street up to Gloria's apartment, the morning gloomy, the air thick. "Louis is dead and maybe you don't have any friends, but you're not alone." He looked at her. "What you're going to have to do won't be easy, but I'm not going to walk away from you. I promise."

"That's what Louis said."

"We're both after the same thing," McGarvey told her. "You'll have to trust me."

"More than you trust me?" she asked.

"It's the nature of the business. I don't trust anybody."

"Neither do I," she replied bitterly.

When Gloria came to the door she was dressed in jeans and a white T-shirt, with no bra and bare feet. Her smiled faded when she saw whom McGarvey had brought with him. "One of your girlfriends?" she asked cattily.

"Don't you know each other?" McGarvey asked.

Gloria stepped aside to reveal the pistol she'd hidden behind her back. "Never seen her before."

McGarvey and Shahrzad entered the apartment, and Gloria closed and locked the door after first glancing up at the parking area. She turned back to them and laid the gun on the hall table.

"Is this the one from the photograph?" Shahrzad asked, eyeing Gloria.

"Yes. You said you'd seen her somewhere," McGarvey said.

Shahrzad pursed her lips and shook her head. "I was mistaken," she said. "I've never seen this woman in my life."

"Does either of you want to tell me what's going on?" Gloria said.

"This is the woman I told you about," McGarvey said. "Shahrzad Shadmand. She was working with Louis just before he got killed."

"Louis's mistress," Gloria said coolly. They hadn't moved out of the entry hall.

"I was working for Louis," Shahrzad flared.

"I'll bet you were." She glanced at McGarvey. "And now you're working for him."

"I don't have to listen to this—" Shahrzad said.

"Yes you do," McGarvey interrupted. For just a moment he considered saying the hell with it and turning his back on the whole mess. A CIA field officer had tried to work some deal on his own and got burned for his effort. Such things happened, not often, but they did happen. But Otto's threat assessment had gone from lavender to violet. Something bad was coming their way.

"Your call, Kirk," Gloria said.

They went into the living room and sat down, the women on opposite sides of the room, as if they were trying to insulate themselves from whatever they were going to be asked to do. It was an odd moment for all of them, but especially for McGarvey, whose fault was that he was from the old school. He was an anachronism who still thought that women were special, that they were to be put on a pedestal, that they were to be given special treatment, protected, honored, respected. He'd gotten those values from his father and mother, and they ran deep inside of him. He didn't like bullies. And he especially hated men who treated women badly. His father's rule from day one was simple: No hitting. Especially not those weaker than you.

"General Liu is a Chinese intelligence officer who has gotten himself in over his head because he likes to strangle women to death while he's having sex with them," McGarvey began.

"Cristo," Gloria said softly.

"I think that he's also in over his head because the Chinese government is not paying him enough to maintain his lifestyle. He's run through his father's small fortune, and all he has left in Beijing is his family name, and some outstanding accomplishments, especially in industrial and military-technology espionage.

"But most of that happened ten years ago or more. In the meantime he's run out of money, and now he's running out of options. He's a desperate man who's sold out his own government for money."

"How do you know so much?" Gloria demanded.

"Gil Perry evidently stumbled across some old FBI files naming Liu as a suspect in a series of rape-murders in New York and Washington and was apparently blackmailing the general."

"If the FBI did nothing, why would Gil's threat have carried any weight?"

"Because to this point all the FBI's suspicions have been kept private. There's been no hard proof. I think Perry threatened to make the files public. Liu would have been disgraced and would have been recalled to Beijing."

"You said that Liu had run through his father's fortune," Gloria pointed out. "He was broke. How was he coming up with the cash for the blackmail?"

"Laundering drug money," McGarvey said. "At least on the surface. He's probably pumping money back home through his father's old business and manufacturing interests. Senior was a lawyer, but he held majority interests in a number of manufacturing companies that did business with the West, especially the U.S."

"On the surface?" Gloria asked.

Shahrzad followed the exchange, but she remained silent.

"Otto did a rough spreadsheet on Liu's spending and the likely profits he was earning from the drug business. Even without the pressure from Perry, Liu wasn't making enough money. Not by a long shot."

"Who's Otto?" Shahrzad asked.

"Guesswork," Gloria objected.

"On the exact numbers, you're right," McGarvey admitted. "But overall the numbers don't lie. Liu has dug himself a hole and he's desperate to get out of it."

"How desperate?" Gloria asked.

"That's what we're going to find out, because Otto's programs have gone violet."

"Who's Otto?" Shahrzad asked.

McGarvey turned to her. "He's the man who brought you to see me in Florida."

"There's something wrong with him. He's a retard, I think. But you trust his judgment?"

"You'd better hope he's right. If not, all this will be for nothing."

Shahrzad just shrugged, but again there was something in her attitude that didn't sit quite right with McGarvey. But for the life of him he couldn't put his finger on what was bothering him. She was a liar, that much was clear. But he couldn't make out what she wanted, beyond the vague wish to immigrate to the States. Once she got there, what then? Maybe even she didn't know.

"I understand what we were trying to do last night," Gloria said. "What's next?"

"The two of you are going after Liu," McGarvey said.

"He's got all the women he needs," Gloria said. "The only reason he'd be interested in me is to find out what you're up to." She glanced at Shahrzad. "But what about her?"

"She's going to help you."

"Not a chance," Shahrzad protested. "If he finds out that I've gone to the CIA he'll kill me."

"I don't think so," McGarvey said. "First he'll want to find out what I'm doing here. Maybe I'm part of Perry's blackmail scheme. Maybe I'm here for something else."

"Right," Gloria said. "You didn't come to Mexico to investigate Louis's death, or to find out if Perry is running a scam. So what exactly are you doing here?"

"Liu has been coming down here for ten years. I want to know why."

"If we go after him he's bound to smell a rat," Gloria said. "Honestly, I don't think he'll give either one of us the time of day."

"I've told everybody that Shahrzad was my girlfriend and I was looking for her," McGarvey said. "After our little show on the dance floor he's got to be curious about you. And tonight when I show up with both of you he'll have to ask himself what game I'm playing."

"He'll still suspect that it's a setup."

"Not after Roaz kicks me out of the club, and his people try to kill me," McGarvey said.

"What are you going to do?" Shahrzad asked, wide-eyed.

"I'm going to get pissed off when the two of you leave me for each other."

Shahrzad didn't get it at first, but Gloria did and she laughed.

"That'll get his attention. But seeing a couple of dykes going at it in public won't make him suddenly tell us all of his dirty little secrets."

"No, but it will get him to invite you to one of his parties," McGarvey said. "Either down here at his house, or up in Chihuahua where Louis was killed."

"And then what?"

"I'll tell you when the time comes," McGarvey said. "First we're going to get the two of you noticed."

Gloria was intrigued, but she shook her head. "A dozen things can go south with a plan like that," she said.

"A hundred," McGarvey replied. "Are you in?"

"You know I am," she said.

"What about you?" he asked Shahrzad.

"Do I have a choice?" she asked.

"No," Gloria answered before McGarvey had the chance.

Shahrzad looked at both of them. "Bastards," she said softly.

"If we're going out tonight we'll have to get some sleep," Gloria said. "And we'll have to get her some party clothes unless she has something in the bag."

"I left everything behind," Shahrzad said.

"In that case we'll definitely have to do some shopping," Gloria said. "What about you?" she asked McGarvey.

"I'm going to try to draw out the opposition, see if they're still interested."

"Are we in any real danger yet? Should I carry a piece?"

"You should be okay," McGarvey said. "And I'll be around if you need help. Anyway, Liu's people won't let you get close if you're armed."

"Same time as last night?" Gloria asked.

"Yeah," McGarvey said. "I'll pick you up around midnight."

SEVENTY-SEVEN

☐

THE CITY

McGarvey drove over to San Angel and got lucky with a parking space across from the Chinese embassy on Avenida Rio Magdalena. As soon as he pulled up, the security officer at the embassy's front gate picked up a telephone and called someone.

A minute later two uniformed security officers came out of the main building and walked out to the gate, where they exchanged a few words with the guard, then looked across at McGarvey.

One of them pointed what was most likely a video camera at McGarvey's car, but none of them made a move to come across the street to ask what the hell he thought he was doing here.

While they were watching him, McGarvey made a show of making a call on his sat phone. The embassy's roof bristled with at least a dozen types of antennae and satellite dishes. He figured at least one of them would be picking up his call. But it would be an exercise in futility. The phone's encryption program was unbreakable.

Rencke answered on the first ring. "Oh, wow, Mac, someone's trying to bust your algorithm. Sloppy, sloppy. They're leaving a trace. Where are you?"

"In front of the Chinese embassy. They've taken an interest, but no one's made a move so far."

"You picked up Shahrzad with no trouble?"

"I thought I might have attracted some interest at the airport, but if we were tailed they were damned good."

"Where is she now?"

"She's staying with Gloria," McGarvey said. "I'm sending both of them out tonight. In the meantime I want you to find out about her family in Paris. According to what she's told me the Ministry of Intelligence had her mother and family killed, and she's next."

"If they're still alive they shouldn't be too hard to find," Rencke said. "Did you believe her?"

"I don't know anymore," McGarvey said. "One minute I want to toss her back on the street, and the next I'm feeling sorry for her. But if Iranian intel has a price on her head, then who the hell is the guy in the pictures?"

"My program is chewing on it, but I need another head shot, something I can use to compare. As it is I've run through all the images we have of every intelligence officer from Saudi Arabia to Iran and back."

"No matches yet?" McGarvey asked hopefully. Any near misses?"

"A half dozen that have risen to a forty percent confidence level," Rencke said. "But that's less than fifty-fifty, kemosabe. Nothing you could take to the track with your rent money."

"What's your gut feeling, Otto?"

"This time I don't know," Rencke replied without hesitation.

The two uniformed security officers had come out of the gate and were looking for a break in traffic so they could cross the street.

"Looks like I'm going to have some company," McGarvey. He started the car and put it in gear with one hand. "Call me as soon as you have something."

"Take care," Rencke said.

The security officers were just starting across the street when McGarvey caught a break and pulled out. He glanced in the rearview mirror in time to see one of them take a photograph of the Jetta's tag. As soon as they got to a computer they would find out that the car had been rented in the name of Martin Saint, a low-level American diplomat who was not on the roster of U.S. embassy personnel here in Mexico City. It wouldn't take long for them to identify McGarvey from the photos they'd snapped, which would leave them with a question: What was the former director of Central Intelligence doing snooping around their embassy in a car rented to a nonexistent person?

With any luck word would get back to Liu, and perhaps the ambassador might ask some embarrassing questions of the general.

It wouldn't do much, but it might add just a little extra pressure.

He drove toward the U.S. embassy, taking a roundabout route to make it difficult but not impossible for someone to tail him. A few blocks out, he suddenly sped through an orange light just as it changed to red. Traffic with the green surged through the intersection, making it impossible for anyone to follow him. But if he had picked up a tail, they would report to their handlers that McGarvey had apparently gone directly over to his embassy.

His attempt at misdirection was purposely crude, but if it was noticed and word got back to Liu, it might give the general a small measure of false confidence that he was dealing with an amateur, or at least with a man whose tradecraft was rusty.

McGarvey got back to Lomas Altas a little before noon. He found a parking spot and walked two blocks back to a sidewalk café in the shopping plaza that faced the Paseo de la Reforma. He was between the Iranian embassy and the street up to Gloria's apartment. From where he was seated under a bright green market umbrella he could see both ways up the street. When the girls left the apartment to go shopping he couldn't miss them, nor would he miss seeing if they'd picked up a tail.

He ordered a Dos Equis, an enchilada, and rice and beans and settled down to watch and wait.

It didn't take long before Gloria's bright yellow Mini Cooper flashed around the corner at the end of the block. Instead of heading away, it came straight past where McGarvey was seated. Gloria was behind the wheel, intent on her driving, but he got the distinct impression that Shahrzad had spotted him but then had looked away at the last second as if she didn't want to be made.

If he hadn't known better he would have suspected the woman of practicing a bit of tradecraft just then.

He waited until they were out of sight, lost in the traffic, before he paid for his lunch and headed back to where he had parked his car. So far as he'd been able to tell, no one had followed them.

That situation, he expected, would change after tonight.

SEVENTY-EIGHT

THE DOLL HOUSE

McGarvey had gone back to his hotel for a few hours' sleep, something he thought was going to be in short supply over the next couple of days. It was dark outside when the sat phone buzzed softly, but he was awake instantly, even though he'd been deep into an erotic dream.

He was back at the club and Gloria was all over him, as she'd been last night, and he was responding even though he knew that something very bad was going to happen. Suddenly Gloria's image morphed into that of Marta Fredricks, the Swiss federal cop he'd lived with during his self-imposed exile in Switzerland. He kept trying to push her way, but she wouldn't let go of him. She was clinging around his neck, kissing him, rubbing her body against his, telling him that she loved him, that she would never leave.

When he was finally able to pull free, he was standing at the end of a runway watching a commercial jet take off. He could see her face in one of the windows, and he tried to wave good-bye. He wanted to tell her that leaving was for the best. But before he could raise his hand the airplane exploded in midair, and someone was calling to give him the bad news.

He got out of bed and reached the phone on the second ring. "Yes."

"Are you okay?" Rencke asked. He sounded worried.

"I was catching a few hours' sleep," McGarvey told him. "It could be a long night." He looked at his watch. It was a few minutes before ten. He'd slept nearly eight hours. For the first time in years he wanted a cigarette, and he realized how jumpy he'd become. "What did you find out?"

"Plenty," Rencke said. "But I'm telling ya, Mac, it beats the shit out of me what's going on."

"Tell me."

"You were right about Shahrzad. She's lying through her teeth. There's apparently no reason for her to be in Mexico City trying to raise money to come to the States. Her father's dead, that part she told the truth about. But her mother is still alive. She's in a mental institution outside of Versailles, and has been there for eight years, ever since she and her four sons moved to Paris to live with her parents. Her father was a pioneer in the French computer industry and is worth something in the low billions. He's sorta the Bill Gates of France, only with hardware, and on a much smaller scale."

"Did Shahrzad move to France with them?"

"Apparently she did, seventeen years ago. But five years ago she quit her job with her grandfather's company and moved to London, where she lived in an expat neighborhood of mostly Muslims off Queen Street near the river."

"What'd she do there?"

"Worked as a secretary for a small insurance company."

"Iranian intel?"

"That was my first guess," Rencke said. "But if it was a front it was damned good. I haven't turned it. Thing is, they could have learned a lesson from Mossad. Remember during the Eichmann operation? The Israelis set up a series of travel agencies across Europe to funnel their agents into Argentina for the kidnapping. Afterward they kept the agencies open because they were making a profit. Some of them are still up and running. Could be that the Iranians have done the same thing. Could be the MOIS has set up insurance agencies in Muslim communities, wherever."

"Which would make Shahrzad an Iranian intelligence agent."

"Yeah. But what the hell was she doing in Mexico screwing around with one of our guys so that she could get to Liu?" Rencke asked.

"Unless Liu was working some sort of a deal with the Iranians, and they didn't trust him," McGarvey suggested.

"They might have sent one of their people to check on him," Rencke finished it. "What the hell is he up to?"

"It's worth risking some assets to find out," McGarvey said. "But her being here in Mexico City could be for something entirely innocent."

"Poor little rich girl out to prove herself?" Rencke asked.

"Something like that."

"Mac, do you really believe it?"

McGarvey walked over to the window and pulled the curtains aside. "I don't know what I believe anymore."

"If that's all it is, she's got herself in over her head and she's lying her ass off to try to figure a way out," Rencke said. "And it's definitely going to get worse for her."

"So why doesn't she just run?" McGarvey asked.

"The sixty-four-dollar question."

A short, slender man stood in the shadows of a doorway across the street. McGarvey pushed the curtain farther aside, and the figure suddenly stepped out of the doorway and headed down the street.

A mistake? he wondered. Or had he just been sent a message?

"We need to start eliminating the variables," McGarvey said. "Let's start with Gil Perry. I want him recalled to Washington to give Dick an update on the situation down here. Have Howard sit in on it. And have Dick put some pressure on both of them."

"How long do you want him held up here?"

"Forty-eight hours," McGarvey said. No matter what happened, he didn't think the situation would remain stable much longer than that.

"Will it be that fast?"

"I hope so," McGarvey said. "In the meantime I want a cleanup crew down here asap. But under cover. I don't want to raise any flags."

"What have you got in mind?" Rencke asked.

"I think Perry is blackmailing Liu over the murdered girls in New

York and Washington, and I think Updegraf was in on the deal. The pictures Shahrzad took for him in Liu's compound, and maybe up in Chihuahua, might have ended up on Perry's desk. I want his office and his apartment tossed, and I don't care if they leave any traces."

"I'll send them down first thing in the morning," Rencke said. "Soon as Perry clears out, they'll move in."

"Send them down tonight," McGarvey said. "And have the jet standing by. Could be that Liu will take the girls up to Chihuahua. I just don't know how this is going to play out. But I want to keep my options open."

"I'm on it," Rencke said. "Anything else?"

"Yeah. Call Katy and tell her that you heard from me. I'll be home in two days tops."

Rencke laughed. "Oh, boy, that's one call I'm going to enjoy making."

SEVENTY-NINE

☐

THE APARTMENT

McGarvey left the hotel a few minutes after eleven and headed over to Gloria's apartment in Lomas Altas. He took care with his tradecraft to make sure that he didn't pick up a tail. Traffic was steady downtown, and it was relatively easy for him to make a number of last-minute turns, and switchbacks to see if he was clear.

Twenty minutes later he pulled into the driveway of the complex and parked next to Gloria's Mini Cooper. She and Shahrzad were flawed women. Whether it was because of their troubled childhoods, or simply the luck of the genetic draw, they had chosen a world that was destroying them.

Yet if they had been normal women, with nothing more than the garden variety of weaknesses and self-indulgences, they would be of no use against Liu. Gloria was in love with him, and Shahrzad wanted a ticket to the States. But that was just on the surface. What either woman really wanted was still a mystery to him. It was enough at the moment that they had agreed to cooperate with something that had every reason to fail.

Whatever their reasons, both of them had been doing their little dances, Gloria around Gil Perry, and Shahrzad around Updegraf. Now they would have to dance with Liu, and McGarvey would try to make sure he didn't get them killed.

Gloria answered the door. She was barefoot, but her hair had been done up, and she wore some light makeup, a revealing red dress slit up the side almost to her hip, and a small gold chain around her neck.

"You look nice," he said, following her into the apartment.

She smiled with pleasure. "Give us a minute. We're just about ready. You know where the drinks are," she said, and she disappeared into the bedroom.

McGarvey went to the window and carefully pulled the blinds aside just far enough to see out to the driveway and parking area. Nothing moved for the moment, yet he couldn't shake the feeling that someone was there.

When he turned away, the women had come out of the bedroom. Shahrzad was in a short strapless dress made of some satin material in gold that was crumpled. Her hair had been piled up in back, and she wore a stunning diamond pendant around her long, slender neck. Both of them wore open-backed spike heels.

"You're going to turn some heads," McGarvey said. "Both of you."

Shahrzad smiled and looked away for a moment. "Thank you," she said softly.

Gloria brought a bottle of white wine and three glasses from the kitchen. She poured for them, and offered up a toast. "Success," she said. Her eyes were bright, her moves animated. She'd taken a hit.

Shahrzad had calmed down from this morning, and she no longer seemed angry or frightened. It was likely, McGarvey thought, that she'd taken a line of coke, too.

He raised his glass, and they all drank.

"How are we going to play this?" Gloria asked.

"Like I said this morning, you're not going in there armed," McGarvey started. "Liu's people would never let you get close to him. And if it came to a situation where you needed deadly force, you'd probably be outgunned."

"I don't like it, but I understand," Gloria said.

"I'm taking Shahrzad over to Roaz's club first. We'll have a couple of drinks, and make a show on the dance floor."

"I used to work there, you know," Shahrzad pointed out. "Everybody knows me. And Miguel knows that I walked out on Liu. Could be they won't even let me in the place."

"I think they will," McGarvey said. "Liu's curiosity is going to be his downfall. He'll want to know how this is all going to play out. He has no idea what I'm up to. So he'll figure on using you and Gloria to get to me. And we're going to make it easy for him."

"How long before you want me to unexpectedly show up?" Gloria asked.

"Fifteen or twenty minutes," McGarvey said. "I don't think you'll have any trouble getting in. They've seen us together twice now."

"Okay, I'm with you so far, Kirk. Then what?"

"You and I are going to make a big scene. I'm a son of a bitch, a bastard, a typical man interested only in a piece of ass."

Gloria was grinning.

"I'm going to tell you to go to hell. You're going to slap me in the face and I'm going to knock you to the floor."

"You'll have to make it convincing," Gloria said.

"Bite your lip on the way down," McGarvey told her. "I'm going to try to kick you, but Shahrzad is going to be all over me, screaming, scratching."

"I can do that," Shahrzad agreed.

"At that point I'm hoping that Roaz will kick me out of the place."

"It's more likely he'll tell us to take our fight outside," Shahrzad said. "I've seen it before."

"Then I'll tell you two to go to hell and I'll walk out," McGarvey said. "I'm hoping that either Roaz or Liu will send someone after me, and this time I'm going to lean on them to see what they think is going on."

"What about us?" Gloria asked.

"None of this will be worth anything unless Liu is there," McGarvey said. "After I'm gone I want you two to be all over each other on the dance floor. I don't think it'll take long before he invites you to his table."

"If it gets that far he'll want us to come down to his house," Shahrzad said. "Especially if I come across as hard to get. I walked out on him once. He might want me back to prove something to himself."

"Either that or he'll fly you up to the compound in Chihuahua," McGarvey said. "Tomorrow's Friday. He might have something planned for the weekend."

"He usually does," Shahrzad said.

"I assume that you're going to be lurking in the shadows somewhere," Gloria said. "What happens after we get down and dirty at one of his parties?"

"Does he ever do drugs?" McGarvey asked Shahrzad.

"I've never seen it," she said. "Everything with him is all about control."

"It'll be up to you two to get him alone someplace, after the party's over and the guests have left. He's going to want to talk about me, and you're going to tell him everything you know. No lies, only the truth."

Gloria's eyes narrowed. "I don't understand. You want us to tell him that you sent us to get to him?"

McGarvey nodded. "He won't believe anything else. But I'm betting that his ego will convince him that he's outthought me. That's the easy part." McGarvey took out the compact that Toni Dronchi had brought down with her from Langley and handed it to Gloria. "You have to get him to take a hit from this."

Gloria opened the compact, which was nearly a twin of hers, except it was silver and hers was gold. It contained a mirror, a single-edged razor blade, a small straw, and a compartment filled with a white powder. Gloria dipped a fingertip into it and started to bring it to her mouth, but McGarvey stopped her.

"It's coke, but it's laced with something you don't want to take right now."

Gloria's eyes were wide. "What is it?"

"An LSD derivative. Soon as it hits his bloodstream he's going to be pretty well out of it for thirty minutes, maybe a little longer."

"So?"

"He'll be highly susceptible to suggestion," McGarvey said.

"A truth serum," Shahrzad said softly.

"Something like that," McGarvey said. "He won't take a hit unless he's seen both of you doing it, so he'll think it's safe." He took an aspirin bottle out of his pocket and handed it to Gloria. "Both of you will have raging headaches, because you've mixed champagne with this shit. So you'll take these all night."

"What is it?"

"Ordinary aspirin, so far as I've been told. It's supposed to make you immune."

Gloria nodded. "I'm still with you, Kirk. But how do we get him to take a hit? He's straight."

"That'll be up to you two," McGarvey said.

Shahrzad started to object, but Gloria held her off.

"We'll figure out something," she said. "Then what?"

"Where will his bodyguards be?" McGarvey asked Shahrzad.

"He usually dismisses them when he takes one of the girls to bed. Except for the guy in the surveillance room everyone will be asleep."

"Gloria will take care of him, and you'll let me in through the back gate," McGarvey said.

"Why don't I just kill Liu and be done with it?" Gloria asked.

"Because I want to talk to him first," McGarvey said.

"What if he takes us up to Chihuahua?"

"I'll be there," McGarvey said.

"How do I signal you to come in?" Gloria asked.

"As soon as you've taken out the guy on surveillance, switch off the lights on the wall and open the main gate," McGarvey instructed.

Shahrzad was looking at them. She shook her head in wonderment. "Both of you are crazy. Do you know that?"

EIGHTY

□

THE DOLL HOUSE

If the receptionist at the front desk thought it was unusual to see Shahrzad back, and with the American from last night, she didn't give the slightest sign of it. She smiled at them both.

"Good evening, Mr. McGarvey," she said. "Would you like the same table?"

"Yes, please." He slurred his words as if he were slightly drunk.

The hostess, a young Japanese girl, gave Shahrzad a double take but said nothing as she led them into the club, which was packed this evening, threading her way to the table at the edge of the crowded dance floor.

McGarvey spotted Liu and his party at the big table, and as he held Shahrzad's chair their eyes met. The general nodded, but McGarvey just smiled and sat down.

"Bring us a bottle of Krug," McGarvey told the hostess. "Make it a good year, and make sure it's very cold."

"I'll send a sommelier over immediately," the girl said, and she left.

"Do you know her?" McGarvey asked.

"Her name is Kiko," Shahrzad said. "She used to be one of Liu's regulars. She's only fifteen."

A five-piece band was playing easy dance music, and the lights on the main floor were low. From time to time, however, a baby spot in the ceiling picked out one of the couples and followed them around the floor.

"They sell the videos," Shahrzad explained. "Something for the old bastards to show their friends."

"Do they do the same in the back rooms?"

"Yeah. For souveniers."

"Any of Liu?"

Shahrzad laughed. "Back at his house, but never here."

Roaz came over with the sommelier. "Welcome back, Mr. McGarvey." He gave Shahrzad a warm smile. "Nice to see you again, Ms. Shadmand. We wondered where you'd gotten yourself to. You're well?"

"Never better," Shahrzad said.

"You might want to go over to say hello to the general. He was worried about you."

"I imagine he was." Shahrzad shrugged indifferently. "I'm sure he'll want to have a word, but later."

The sommelier had the champagne opened and he poured for them.

"Compliments of the house," Roaz said. "Have a pleasant evening." He and the wine steward left.

Shahrzad gazed at his back and shook her head. "It's like I was just away on vacation," she said. "Evidently they haven't made the connection between me and Louis."

"Maybe they don't think you're a threat," McGarvey said.

She looked back at him. "They know that you're CIA, or at least ex-CIA, and they'll have to wonder what the hell I've told you and what I'm doing here with you."

"That's your safety net," McGarvey told her. "Until Liu finds out just that, he can't afford to hurt you. He'll play nice, at least at first."

"It's the later I'm worried about. The man is insane."

An attractive blonde came out onstage and, accompanied by the band, began to sing "La Paloma," her voice pure, the melody haunting.

"Showtime," McGarvey said, and he led Shahrzad out onto the dance floor.

At first he thought that she wasn't going to play the charade, but then she got into the music and molded her body to his, her legs straddling one of his, rubbing herself against his thigh.

Gloria had been good on the dance floor, sexy, seductive, with all the right moves, but this girl was a pro. She had worked as a high-class whore, after all, and McGarvey found that he had to fake a response to make it look good for Liu.

Almost immediately the ceiling spot was on them, and somebody at one of the tables let out a cheer. Shahrzad's face was flushed, and she was panting, her lips parted, her eyes half shut.

The singer came onto the dance floor to them, her voice low and throaty, no lights other than the spot, no sounds other than the band and her voice.

Just as the song was ending, Shahrzad brought herself to orgasm, rubbing against McGarvey's leg. She threw her head back and let out a deep moan of pleasure, then looked up into his eyes and smiled.

The house erupted with cheers and applause as McGarvey and Shahrzad went back to the table.

"Do you think I convinced him?" Shahrzad asked as they sat down.

"You sure as hell convinced me," McGarvey said. "You were faking?"

She nodded. "All women know how it's done, and there isn't a man alive who can tell the difference. Not even the former director of the CIA."

"I guess I've led a sheltered life."

"I guess you have," Shahrzad said, and she suddenly looked up. "Here comes Gloria."

The music had started again, an American big-band piece, when Gloria arrived at the table, her face screwed up in a mask of anger.

"What the fuck do you think you're doing to me?" she demanded at the top of her lungs. Her complexion was splotchy, as if she had run all the way over.

McGarvey looked up indifferently. "I didn't expect to see you here to-night."

"I guess not!" Gloria screeched. "You motherfucker!"

"Take it easy," McGarvey told her. Whatever else Gloria was or wasn't, she was a damned fine actor.

"Fuck you!" she shouted, and she hit him in the face with a closed fist, holding nothing back.

He saw stars for just a moment, but then he jumped up. Roaz was coming across the floor with a couple of bouncers dressed in dark turtlenecks and loose-fitting blue blazers. They were carrying.

"Bitch!" McGarvey shouted. He backhanded her and she went down hard, her lip split where she'd bit it.

"Okay, folks, everybody settle down," Roaz said. He motioned for the band to resume playing, then helped Gloria to her feet.

"The son of a bitch," she muttered.

One of the bouncers came around behind McGarvey while the other planted himself next to Roaz, his eyes never leaving McGarvey's.

"If you don't mind, sir, we'd like you to settle your argument outside," Roaz said. He shrugged. "We don't want to upset the other patrons."

Shahrzad had gone around to Gloria and was dabbing a napkin on her cut lip. She glared at McGarvey. "Bastard," she said.

"Fuck you both," McGarvey said to them. He turned back to Roaz and spread his hands. "Look, I don't want any trouble here. They can stay, for all I give a shit. I'm out of here."

"Would you like to close out your account for this evening, sir?"

"No," McGarvey slurred. "Let 'em have a ball. My nickel."

McGarvey lurched away from the table. One of the bouncers held out a hand to help him, but McGarvey batted it aside and charged across the club and out to the curb, the sounds of cheering and applause following him.

The line of people waiting to get in was still long. One of the valets came over. "Would you like your car, Mr. McGarvey?"

McGarvey shook his head, stuck his hands in his pockets, and headed down the street on foot in the opposite direction from the queue. He crossed the street and headed in the general direction of the park and the Paseo de la Reforma.

He would have bet almost any money that Liu would have him followed and either roughed up or killed. Within a block he'd picked up a tail, two of them, large men, possibly the bouncers from the club. He suspected that Liu didn't use his own Guoanbu personnel down here; instead he relied on ex-GAFE muscle. He figured that Roaz was supplying him with the warm bodies, financed by Alvarez with drug money.

It was something he intended to find out tonight.

He came around a corner a couple blocks from the club and ducked into a cobblestoned alley down which was a small mall of fashionable shops, pulling up short just inside the doorway of a women's resort-wear boutique.

Sixty seconds later the two bouncers from the club hurried past the entrance to the mall, and McGarvey stepped out of the doorway and walked back up to the street. He pulled out his pistol, thumbed the safety catch off, and held it partially concealed at the side of his leg.

The men realized they'd lost their quarry, and they turned to come back just as McGarvey stepped out of the shadows.

"Looking for someone?" he asked.

"You should have minded your own business," the one on the left said, and he reached inside his jacket as the other one stepped to the right.

McGarvey raised his pistol. "I wouldn't advise it," he said.

"Puta," the one on the right said, starting to draw his weapon.

McGarvey switched aim, fired one round into the man's knee, and as he cried out in pain and crumpled to the sidewalk switched aim back to the first man.

"As I say, I wouldn't advise it. I might aim high and shoot off your balls."

The first man moved his hands away from his jacket. "We just want to talk," he said, but his eyes flicked for just an instant to his partner on the ground, who despite his wound had pulled out his pistol and was bringing it up.

McGarvey turned and put one round into the man's forehead, killing him instantly, and again turned back to the first man.

"You want to talk, so do I," McGarvey said. "Who sent you to come after me?"

The man was impressed. "The police will be here soon. I have a permit to carry a weapon, but I doubt that you do. And now my friend is dead. You are in some serious shit, señor."

"They can't hang me twice if I kill a second man," McGarvey said. "Who sent you?"

"Miguel."

"Roaz?" McGarvey asked. "What's he got against me?"

"I don't know. He just sent us to rough you up and warn you to mind your own business."

In the distance they could hear a police siren. Someone must have reported the sounds of gunfire.

"Are you talking about Alvarez?" McGarvey took a stab in the dark. "I'm not interested in his drug money."

"Alvarez is dead. He's got nothing to do with us. Like I said, you're in deep shit here, señor. You fucked up."

Updegraf had been eliminated and now Alvarez. Where were the connections other than Liu, and the fact they'd both been at Roaz's compound in Chihuahua?

The siren was getting closer.

"I suggest you take your friend's ID and get out of here," McGarvey said. "I don't think you want to answer questions by the police any more than I do."

"How do I know you won't shoot me?"

"I won't, unless you follow me again," McGarvey said.

He turned and headed down the street, toward the park. The bouncers who'd followed him were Roaz's muscle, there was little doubt about that. Nor was there much doubt about who was actually pulling the strings. But Liu had apparently been working with Alvarez to raise money. Eliminating Alvarez made no sense.

The connection that worried him the most was the Iranian figure in the shadows. Too many strings led back to Tehran, and nothing was making any sense, especially now that Alvarez was dead.

One thing he knew for certain was that the two men tonight had been sent not to talk, but to kill him. He was starting to worry Liu. The fallout from assassinating a former DCI would be immense. It wasn't something the Chinese government would be interested in. It meant that Liu was definitely working on his own.

EIGHTY-ONE

OUTSIDE THE DOLL HOUSE

The same crowd was still lined up outside the club when McGarvey made his way back. He stood in the shadows across the street for several minutes to make sure that the bouncer who'd come after him wasn't hanging around out front.

He waited for a truck to lumber by, then stuck his hands in his pockets and staggered across the street. The two valet parkers looked up, their jaws dropping open for just an instant when they recognized who it was. He was supposed to be dead by now, and evidently everyone on the staff knew it.

The doorman, a big guy in a white blazer, came over. "Mr. McGarvey, we don't want any more trouble here tonight. I can't let you back inside. Mr. Roaz's orders."

"I came back for my car," McGarvey said.

The doorman motioned for one of the valets to get it. "Would you like us to drive you back to your hotel?"

"It's all right," McGarvey said. He shrugged. "Just give Mr. Roaz my apologies. Won't happen again."

"Yes, sir," the doorman said. He was just as surprised to see McGarvey as the valet parkers were, but he managed to hide it a little better.

"I didn't expect both bitches to be here on the same night."

"I know how that goes, sir."

The valet brought up the Jetta, and McGarvey got behind the wheel and lurched off down the street, nearly hitting a parked car before he rounded the corner at the end of the block.

Looking in the rearview mirror as he drove away he'd seen the doorman walk back to the front door, a cell phone to his ear. He expected that a reception committee would be waiting for him if he ever showed up at his hotel.

McGarvey circled around the block, finding a parking spot in the service area behind a large apartment building. Anyone passing on the street would have no chance of spotting the car unless he drove down the delivery alley.

In ten minutes McGarvey was back, standing in the shadows of a doorway to an office complex. A tall free-form aluminum sculpture loomed overhead, and in the middle of the entry plaza a fountain that could have come directly from Madrid splashed softly. The contrast between the modern and the ancient was typical of Mexico City.

He hunched up his coat collar against the late-evening chill and leaned a shoulder against the wall, prepared for a long wait.

By now the cops had found the body, but unless McGarvey missed his guess the other man had taken his suggestion and removed all traces of identification from his partner. Sooner or later the dead man would be identified from his fingerprints, and it was a fair bet he was a former GAFE operator. His killing would raise a few eyebrows, but not many. Mexico had been a land of death from its beginning.

The crowd in front of the club was finally beginning to thin out when two of the valet parkers brought up Liu's Mercedes Maybach and the AMG55 and opened the doors.

First out of the club were two of Roaz's bouncers, along with Liu's two bodyguards and his driver. They fanned out, scrutinizing the crowd, watching the traffic, which had finally died down, and scanning the opposite side of the street.

McGarvey moved a little farther back into the shadows.

Minutes later Roaz and Liu emerged from the club. They stopped at the curb and said something to each other. Gloria and Shahrzad came out, arm in arm, laughing loudly and weaving all over the place. They were drunk, high, or pretending to be both.

Roaz and the doorman helped the women into the rear of the Maybach. Liu said something else to Roaz, they shook hands, and he climbed into the backseat.

Keeping in the shadows, McGarvey hurried to the end of the block, then sprinted to where he had parked his car. They were either going down to Liu's house outside Xochimilco, in which case they would take the route through the park, or they were going to the airport, in which case they would head downtown past the U.S. embassy on the Paseo de la Reforma.

McGarvey reached his car and raced down to the intersection of the Paseo and the park road, weaving in and out of traffic, just making a couple of red lights, and crowding a delivery van halfway onto the sidewalk.

He pulled over to the side of the boulevard and doused his lights, watching in his rearview mirror for the Maybach and AMG55.

Two minutes later both cars showed up and headed directly into the park on the Chivatito Causeway.

They were going to Liu's house in Xochimilco.

"Gotcha," McGarvey said to himself.

He switched on the headlights and headed over to the Hotel Four Seasons, where he'd left the aluminum case, as he speed-dialed Rencke's number in the Building.

His friend answered on the first ring. "I've been waiting."

"The girls are with Liu and they're going down to Xochimilco."

"That was quick," Rencke said.

"I'll tell you about it someday, but the way they were operating, I don't think he had a chance," McGarvey said. "I found out that Liu's drug-money connection, Thomas Alvarez, was assassinated. Find out what you can."

"That's number two on my list of things for you. His head was found last night up in Chihuahua outside the same hospital where Updegraf's head was dumped. They haven't found his body yet, but the Mexican Drug Enforcement Agency called our DEA guys with the news. Scratch one on our most-wanted list."

"They're trying to tell us that Updegraf was involved in the drug trade."

"That's what it looks like."

"What's number one on your list?" McGarvey asked.

"Perry has disappeared."

"Did he get the recall?"

"Yeah. Apparently after he hung up from talking with Dick, he got his coat and walked out the door. No one's seen him since. Embassy security is on it, and so is the assistant COS, Tom Chauncy. But so far there's been no word."

"He was dirty after all."

"Looks like it. Unless you think Liu had him taken out."

"I don't think he'd bother at this point. Not until he knows what I'm up to," McGarvey said. "Find out if Perry has any bolt-holes. Anyplace where he'd likely go to ground. And have Dick send someone senior from the Mexican desk to act as temporay COS."

"What about Chauncy?"

"I don't know, Otto," McGarvey admitted. "It's possible the entire station has been compromised. Perry and Updegraf were working their own agendas with Chauncy in the middle. He must have known or suspected something, but he didn't do anything."

"I'm on it," Rencke said.

"I'm going down to Xochimilco to have my chat with the general. Maybe tonight we'll find out what the hell is going on that has your computers going lavender."

"Violet," Rencke corrected. "Take care."

EIGHTY-TWO

EN ROUTE TO XOCHIMILCO

Gloria had overdone it with the shit McGarvey had brought in the silver compact. Strange things were starting to happen inside her head, and she found that her feelings were flipping back and forth between euphoria and deep depression.

She smiled at Liu. "It's good to be back."

"It's good to see you again," Liu said. "Though I'm not so sure about the circumstances."

Shahrzad had taken several hits at the club and she too was flying, and it was obvious that she was confused about what was happening now. "What do you mean?" she asked, her voice small.

Gloria patted her knee. "The general and I are old friends." Her tongue was thick and it was a little difficult for her to form words properly.

"McGarvey sent you?" Liu asked.

"Yes," Gloria said dreamily. She laid her head back for just a moment. She could feel him in her arms, feel his body against hers, feel him making love to her. He was a man unlike any other man she'd ever known. Better than her father, who had been nothing more than another Cuban dissident after all; better than her husband, Raul, who'd never known the real Cuba. Giving him up to Cuban intelligence so that she could get back to the States had been surprisingly easier than she'd thought it would be. He was just a boy, filled with Cuban male machismo, but with no sophistication to soften his hard edges. He'd been anything but worldly, nothing like the kind of men she found attractive.

Especially not Kirk.

"Why?" Liu was saying in her ear.

She opened her eyes.

"What does he want you to find out?"

"What you're doing here in Mexico. He knows about the drug money, but he thinks there's more."

"Just like that stupid Updegraf," Liu said angrily. "He got in over his head, even though I'd warned him."

"Kirk knows that Perry was blackmailing you," Gloria said. "And he knows that you've run out of money."

"I can't be touched here in Mexico."

Gloria laughed. "Do you know what his real job for the CIA has always been?" she asked. She wanted to taunt the bastard, hold McGarvey up for him so that he could know what a real man was supposed to be.

Liu was becoming irritated. "He started out as a field officer, just like you."

Gloria laughed. "He's an assassin, and he's come here to kill you. What do you think about that?"

"I think that he probably won't see his home again."

"You're right," Gloria said. "I'm keeping him here with me."

Liu caressed her cheek with his fingertips. "You're going to kill him for me," he said. "If not tonight, then very soon."

Gloria started to laugh, and after a little while she realized that she couldn't stop. She nodded. "Sure," she managed to promise, the lie easy for her. Kirk had instructed her and Shahrzad to tell Liu the truth, but she had lied all of her life. Sometimes she thought that she was even able to lie to herself and believe it.

When she'd been stationed in Paris she had earned perfect fitreps even though she was spying on the CIA for French intelligence. It was

only after her father had come to visit and and seen in her eyes something of what she'd been doing that she'd gotten spooked. She'd run
away to be alone so that she could get her head on straight, but after that
confrontation nothing had seemed right any longer. Nothing had seemed
worth the effort.

Here in Mexico she had stumbled across what Perry and Updegraf
were up to, and she'd driven down to the compound in Xochimilco one
morning, and rung the bell at the front gate, for the first of her little
chats.

No sex. Liu didn't interest her, nor was she interested in the money,
or the parties, or the power.

"What is it that you do want, my dear?" Liu had asked her that morning. She could still see the amused look on the prick's face.

"China," she'd said.

"Nothing modest about you," he'd said. "In exchange for what?"

"Perry and Updegraf, and protection for whatever else it is that
you're doing here," she'd replied. "Sooner or later you're going to attract
the wrong sort of notice, and Langley will send someone who actually
knows what he's doing. When that happens I'll run interference for
you."

"What if they send a woman?"

Gloria had shrugged. "Won't make any difference to me."

"How can I be sure this isn't just another scam?" he'd asked.

"Because I'm not asking for anything right now," she'd told him.
"Sooner or later you'll finish and you'll return to Beijing. I'll get reassigned as soon as possible, and then you and I will do great work."

"To what end?" he'd asked. "You must want something for yourself."

"I want to be the first woman to sit on the seventh floor in the Building."

His eyes had widened momentarily. "You want to become the first
woman director of Central Intelligence?"

"Why not?"

"Why not indeed."

That had been then. Now what she really wanted was within her
grasp. Becoming DCI had never been anything more than a pipe dream.

In fact, until she'd met McGarvey she'd never known what she actually wanted. It would be a trade, but not Liu's safety for China. It would be Liu's head on a platter for McGarvey, the only man she'd ever loved.

Shahrzad had been mostly quiet on the ride out of the city, staring out the window, but as the driver turned onto the dirt road that led back to Liu's compound she turned to Gloria. "I thought I'd seen you out here once," she said.

"That was a mistake on my part," Gloria admitted. "Why didn't you say something to Kirk?"

"I want to go to the States, and I don't want to screw it up."

"Fair enough," Gloria said. Her head was beginning to clear again. Each time she took a hit from the doctored coke Kirk had given her, it took longer to come back to reality. And that was with the antidote.

What effect it was going to have on Liu was anyone's guess. But none of this was going to work unless she could induce him to take a hit.

XOCHIMILCO

The compound seemed deserted and strangely quiet when they arrived. The house staff and bodyguards buttoned up the place and then discreetly disappeared.

"We won't be disturbed," Liu said. "We have the entire night ahead of us."

"Champagne," Gloria said as they walked out onto the pool deck.

"Of course," Liu said pleasantly. He went across to the bar, where he set up three crystal flutes and opened a bottle of Krug.

Liu's private suite was open to the left, gauze curtains in the sliding glass doors billowing in the soft evening breeze. It was chilly, but several electric heaters sprouting like overgrown toadstools around the pool had been switched on, and the air on the patio was almost balmy.

Gloria took a hit from the compact, then cut a line on the mirror for Shahrzad. She laid the works on a chaise longue as the drug hit her brain in a rush, and she was floating again, dreamy, out of focus, as if she had jumped from an airplane and was flying weightlessly through the fantastic clouds.

Shahrzad had a stupid grin on her face, her eyes glassy, as Gloria kissed her deeply on the lips. "Ever do it with a girl?"

"No," Shahrzad answered huskily.

Gloria undid the zipper on the back of Shahrzad's dress and helped her step out of it. She kissed the woman's erect nipples and caressed her ass, before she slipped off her own dress.

"Nice," Liu said.

Gloria led Shahrzad across the patio and into Liu's bedroom, where they lay down together on the big bed.

Shahrzad was mostly out of it, in her own world, just barely responsive to Gloria's touches.

Liu had followed them into the bedroom, and he stood at the open doorway, a smirk on his lips.

"Why don't you join us?" Gloria said, looking up. "But first bring me my stuff."

Liu hadn't bothered with the champagne. He went outside and brought the compact back. "What happened to your gold one?"

"This is some new shit. A lot better."

Liu raised the open compact to his nose and delicately sniffed. "Where'd you get it?"

"I have my own sources. Be my guest."

He cut a thin line, came over to the bed, and held it for her. "Take another hit," he told her. "I want to watch."

She held one nostril closed as she took the line through the straw. She looked up into his eyes as she handed him the compact, and then the drug hit her. "Jesus, Mary, and Joseph," she said softly. The room was in soft focus, but orange and green and yellow sheets of light shimmered on the ceiling and in the air like the southern lights she'd seen once in Chile.

"Kill her," Liu said.

Gloria couldn't help but smile. "No shit?"

"She's an Iranian intelligence officer sent here to spy on me."

"Why?"

"They don't trust me," Liu said. "Kill her and we'll make love."

Gloria turned and looked at Shahrzad, who was mumbling something incoherent, her eyes dilated. Liu's seductive words came from a long distance, yet his voice seemed to be coming from inside her head. She could think only of Kirk, his strong arms holding her, whispering in her ear what to do.

"Kill her," Liu whispered sweetly.

Gloria pulled Shahrzad's nearly inert form to a sitting position and without hesitation clamped her left arm around the girl's neck and with her other pulled the girl's head sharply to the right, the neck bones breaking with an audible pop, the spinal column instantly severed.

Shahrzad's body went limp and the light went out of her eyes. Gloria shoved her aside, then lay down on her back, her legs spread.

Liu cut a big line of doctored coke from the compact and took the hit in his left nostril. He set the compact aside, then got undressed and joined her on the bed.

"This is how I like it," he said, putting his powerful hands around her neck and squeezing. "It's the only way I like it."

Almost immediately Gloria began to see spots, and she tried to pull his hands away, but he was too strong. Somehow he was immune to the doctored coke, and she thought that it was such a stupid way to die, but there was nothing she could do about it; his body held her down, and his grip was unbreakable.

"Kirk." The word exploded in her brain like a billion stars, and she began to black out.

EIGHTY-THREE

ZONA ROSA

Before Mexico City Gil Perry figured that his career and life had only one direction in which to go: straight to the top. He was well connected in the Building; his last three duty stations, in Madrid, Caracas, and Bogotá, had gone well; and even his short stint in Baghdad had earned him high marks.

Station Mexico City was his reward for a lot of years of dedication, hard work, and especially loyalty.

Standing naked in front of the eighth-story window of the luxury tourist Hotel Four Seasons, a 9 mm Beretta autoloader in his right hand, he was saddened by what he knew his co-workers would say about him. But then, the blame wasn't theirs; it was entirely his.

It had started to go bad within his first year down here, when he began to realize that the lifestyle he had carved out for himself and his wife was costing more than he was making.

They'd tightened their belts in an effort to economize, but the heavy social scene was a part of his cover. He'd picked it, so he had to pay for it. No slush fund existed for these sorts of expenses, though for a brief period he managed to siphon off some off his discretionary funds, money used to pay informers. But when he couldn't report any decent product for the money he was spending he had to stop the fraud.

Standing now looking down at the sparse early morning traffic on the Paseo de la Reforma, he could trace the exact steps that he'd taken to bring him here to this hotel.

He'd met General Liu at a cocktail party held for the new Chinese ambassador to Mexico at their embassy. Something had bothered Perry from the moment he'd laid eyes on the man, but it had taken him several weeks of digging through old CIA files to find that Liu had a history not only with Company, but with the FBI, which suspected him of rape and murder.

In two days he had a friend at the Bureau send him a hard copy of the FBI's files, and his problem had been solved. He would blackmail Liu for some serious money. If the general refused, Perry planned on burning him. His stock within the CIA would rise, and he could claim a decent amount of money in expenses for what he would manufacture into a major operation.

Of course, that extra money would have been only a Band-Aid on a hemorrhage, but his tradecraft was good; he would have found another source.

It hadn't been necessary, because Liu had agreed at once. He had even agreed each time Perry had raised the amounts. Only later did Perry realize that the general might have been only too eager to go along because he had something else, something even more important, to hide from the CIA.

Involving Louis was a terrible mistake, but by then Perry was beginning to understand that all good things came to an end sooner or later. And when this operation went south he'd wanted to be insulated. He hadn't thought Louis would actually get himself killed. And when he tried to point his staff in directions that would lead them to believe that Louis had been shaking down the general, he never suspected that Adkins would send somebody like McGarvey to figure everything out.

But that's exactly what had happened, what was happening. The message recalling him to Langley was proof that it was over.

Perry smiled wryly. He would have liked to live in Washington as one of the players. He would even have enjoyed the confirmation hearings, which were often brutal. He would especially have liked the respect that he would have earned.

"Fuck it," he mumbled.

He flicked the safety lever off, raised the muzzle of the pistol to his temple, and without hesitation pulled the trigger.

EIGHTY-FOUR

XOCHIMILCO

McGarvey, dressed in black, night-vision glasses hanging by a strap around his neck, waited in the willows at the side of the road twenty-five yards from the compound wall. He'd driven over to the Four Seasons to retrieve his equipment in the aluminum case and had gotten down here less than a half hour behind Liu and the girls.

Nothing moved in the night, and no sounds marred the stillness. Even the light breeze that had rustled the leaves had calmed down.

Everything depended on Gloria. If he was right about her he would be walking into a trap, but other than house staff he didn't think there would be many of Roaz's people over there this morning; and there would be Liu's driver and the two bodyguards who had followed in the AMG.

He sincerely hoped he was wrong about both of the women. But he suspected that Shahrzad worked for Iranian intelligence and that Gloria had become an independent operator even before she'd gone back into Cuba with her new husband.

Too many coincidences had accumulated around both of them to be merely coincidences.

What he couldn't fathom was what all the pieces added together could possibly mean. If it weren't for Otto's programs turning up lavender and now violet he would have bet almost anything that this was nothing more than a shakedown operation that had gone sour. Updegraf was assassinated when he and Perry pressed too hard. Shahrzad was a walk-in at the embassy to put the pressure back on Perry, and the congressman's oil deal between the Chinese and Mexican governments was nothing more than a smoke screen.

But to hide what?

The lights along the top of the compound walls suddenly went out.

McGarvey got to his feet, slung his small pack over his shoulder, made his way to the water's edge, and headed along the shoreline in knee-deep water. In addition to his Walther PPK, Rencke had sent down a suppressed version of the Steyr AUG assault machine gun that fired subsonic 9 mm ammunition, making it deadly and silent.

Gloria was expecting him to come up the road, where she was supposed to open the main gate. If it wasn't a trap, she would be waiting alone for him. Otherwise Liu's bodyguards would be there.

McGarvey wasn't going to risk his life to find out that way.

He reached the wall on the west side of the compound, facing the lake, in ten minutes. It was plaster painted white over concrete block, and was twelve feet tall. Lights rose from short stanchions every twenty-five feet. Closed-circuit television cameras were mounted at the corners and above the front and rear gates. The motion detectors and infrared sensors that Rencke's ESMs receiver had picked up when McGarvey had been here last were hidden from view. If this was a trap, whoever was manning the surveillance equipment knew that he wasn't coming through the front door.

The countdown clock was ticking now.

McGarvey took from his pack a grapnel with big padded hooks attached to one hundred feet of nylon line, made sure the line was coiled properly, and tossed it up and over the wall.

It caught on the first throw, and after a moment to listen for an alarm to be sounded, he clambered to the top of the wall and eased his head high enough to see down into the compound.

A slightly built figure stood in the shadows by the front gate about seventy-five feet away. Nothing else moved in the compound.

McGarvey took a couple of turns of the rope around his left arm, and pulled the night-vision glasses up to his eyes with his free hand.

Gloria's figure fluoresced dark green in the glasses. He scanned the parking area and the front of the house, but as far as he could tell no one else was there.

He lowered the glasses, pulled himself up and over the wall, retrieved the grapnel and line, and dropped soundlessly to the ground on the inside.

He pulled the Steyr from its sling on his back, charged the weapon, and switched the safety to the off position. With his finger outside the trigger guard, he straightened up and started across the compound, all of his senses superalert for any sign that this was a trap.

The night remained silent. No shots were fired from somewhere inside the house. No lights suddenly blazed, no sirens blared.

He got within a few feet of Gloria before she sensed something and turned around. Her hand went to her mouth and she stumbled backward against the partially open gate.

"Mother of God," she blurted. "Kirk." She was dressed in a pair of blue jeans and a white T-shirt.

McGarvey stepped into the shadows, his back to the wall. "You came here in a party dress," he said.

"Oh, for Christ's sake, I don't know whose shit this is," she shot back. She was wired. "If we're going to run I needed something better than a dress."

"Where's Liu?"

She hesitated for just an instant. "In the master bedroom."

"What about the guy on surveillance?"

"He's down, but I didn't have time to take out Liu's driver and body-guards."

"Did you give him the coke?"

She nodded. "It didn't work. He didn't tell me anything."

"Take me to him."

"Goddamn it, he's out of it. Won't do us any good."

"Now," McGarvey said. He was getting an itchy feeling between his shoulder blades. No trap had been set at the front gate, but he still didn't trust her.

"You're playing with fire," she said. "We're outgunned." She turned and padded off in the dark.

McGarvey followed her into the house, keeping within the deeper shadows as they crossed the expansive living room. They went out onto the pool deck and then through the open sliding glass doors into the master suite.

Liu was lying on his back in the middle of a very large bed with black silk sheets. He was naked, one muscular leg crossed over the other, his eyes fluttering. Shahrzad lay crumpled, half bent over, next to him. Her head was twisted at an impossible angle, her neck obviously broken.

"He killed her," Gloria said from behind him.

"Why?"

"He said she was an Iranian spy."

"I thought the coke didn't work," McGarvey said. He crossed to the bed and felt for a pulse at Liu's neck. It was strong but irregular, as if he had a heart murmur. It was what the fact sheet Kraus had sent with the compact had said to expect.

"We have to get out of here before someone checks with surveillance," Gloria said. "The people around Liu don't sleep through the night. Never."

"Where's your weapon?"

"I didn't bring it. Remember?"

McGarvey took out his Walther and tossed it to her. "Watch my back."

"What do you think you're doing?"

"What I came here for," McGarvey said.

"The son of a bitch doesn't know anything."

"Go," McGarvey ordered. "I'll just be a minute."

Gloria looked at Liu's figure on the bed. "He's not worth it," she said. For just that moment she sounded like a feral cat ready to pounce, a low rumble at the back of her throat.

She turned and left, disappearing around the corner back into the living room.

McGarvey looked down at the general, who was still out of it, then quickly searched the suite, finding a laptop computer on a desk in an adjacent alcove. He laid the Steyr on the desk and turned the computer on. When it booted up, a message prompt in Chinese script dropped down with a blank box. It was asking for a password.

He turned it off, closed the lid, picked up the gun, and turned around.

Liu, still naked, stood in the doorway, a SIG-Sauer pistol in his hand, no signs whatsoever that he had taken the doctored coke.

"You have a heart murmur," McGarvey said.

"Since I was a child," Liu replied pleasantly.

"My people know that I'm here."

"I'm sure they do, but I'm curious to know why you have come here like this. What do you want, Mr. McGarvey? Surely not to arrest me for some trumped-up charges of rape and murder back in the States. I won't go back with you."

"Not that."

"Fair enough." Liu nodded. "Gloria tells me that you are an assassin. Did you come here with the intent to murder me?"

"That's part of why I'm here," McGarvey admitted. He held up the laptop. "This is the rest of it, unless you want to tell me what you've been doing down here for the past ten years, and what it has to do with Iranian intelligence."

"Poor Shahrzad?" Liu asked. "I didn't kill the girl. Gloria did it."

"I meant the intelligence officer who was at your party here, hiding in the shadows."

For just a moment Liu was nonplussed, but then he laughed. "You got a photo of him that night. But it mustn't have been a very good one if you thought he was Iranian."

"Middle Eastern."

"No, his mother was a Siberian, I think. He was an intelligence officer, but he worked for the FSB."

"Russian," McGarvey said, surprised. "What the hell are you doing with them?"

"Yes, Russian. But you did manage to get part of it right. Viktor was freelancing, this time for Iran, which is why Shahrzad came here to keep an eye on me."

"And Updegraf?"

"That was her idea, to keep me on the straight and narrow. And by the way, it was her idea to have him eliminated when he started to get too close. I turned him, and it was easier than you think, him and that utter fool Perry."

"It still brings us back to Iran," McGarvey said. "They were paying you a great deal of money, but why? What have you been doing for them right under the noses of your own people?"

"That's something you'll never know," Liu said, and he raised his pistol. "Put my computer back on the desk, please. Even if you managed to get out of here with it, the machine would be of no use to you. One wrong keystroke and the hard disk will fry itself. But that's a moot point after all, because you're not getting out of here."

EIGHTY–FIVE

□

THE COMPOUND

Gloria appeared in the doorway behind Liu. She was out of breath, her lips parted, her nostrils flared. Her eyes were on McGarvey's.

"I never meant for it to come to this," she said.

"Very touching," Liu said. "Kill him."

"You can't kill a former DCI."

"We had no idea who he was, just some intruder with a grappling rope coming over my wall. One of my men shot him to death. Sorry. But he should have knocked on my front door. I would have met with him. In fact, it is I who'll telephone the authorities, as soon as his body is put in place and you're out of here."

"By tomorrow morning they'll come down on you so hard even your own government won't be able to bail you out," Gloria said. "You won't be able to run."

"I don't intend to go anyplace," Liu said mildly. "Either kill him or get out of here."

"He can't let you leave alive," McGarvey suggested.

"I know," Gloria said, and she jammed the muzzle of the Walther into the back of Liu's head. "Nobody has to die tonight," she said. "Put down the gun."

"It's a little late to switch sides again, my dear," Liu said. "The man isn't stupid. He knows that you're a double. You either take your chances with me, or return to the States and go on trial for treason. If you're lucky you'll get life in prison."

"Fuck you," Gloria said, and she pulled the trigger, the hammer slapping on an empty chamber.

Liu was distracted for just a split instant, time enough for McGarvey to bring the rifle up to his hip and squeeze off two rounds, catching Liu in the middle of his chest and under his chin as he staggered backward, the second bullet spiraling up into the general's brain, killing him instantly.

He went down hard, his head bouncing on the tile floor, blood pooling like a halo.

Gloria was staring at McGarvey. "You knew all along," she said. "The gun was empty."

"I wasn't sure until just now," McGarvey said.

She was figuring her options—he could see it in her eyes.

"What if I just turned around and walked out of here?" she asked.

"I'd stop you."

It was the answer she'd expected. She nodded. "I would have killed him, you know. For you."

"Why?" McGarvey asked.

"Why was I working with Liu?"

"Why were you working for everybody except us?"

She shrugged. "I couldn't very well go back to Cuba—my father took care of that for me nineteen years ago. And the States was never home. Nobody there, including my father, gave a shit about me. My mother was gone. My aunts and uncles and cousins were in their own little worlds. And it looked as if guys like Perry and poor, stupid Updegraf were going to end up on top. Talk about the dumbing down of America. You have no idea."

"So you decided to work for yourself," McGarvey prompted.

"Me is all I've ever had," she said. "Until you."

"What was going on?" McGarvey asked. "What was Liu doing?"

"I don't know," she said. "But you have his computer. If you can get it out of here tonight and up to Otto, he'll figure it out."

"How many men are in the compound?"

"Six, I think," she said. "They know you're here. They're just waiting for Liu to call them in, or for you to try to get out." She looked down at Liu's body. "I thought he would kill you, and it drove me crazy. It's why I came back." She looked up. "I love you. That part's never been a lie."

McGarvey took out his sat phone and speed-dialed Rencke's number.

"It won't work inside the compound," she said.

The no-signal indicator came on.

He looked up. "You can come with me or stay," he told her, though for the life of him he didn't know why he had changed his mind about taking her back. It certainly wasn't love.

She was surprised. "There's nothing for me back at Langley," she said. "I won't sound the alarm or try to stop you. But if you get out of here in one piece I'll disappear."

"And if I don't?"

She looked away. "I don't want to think about it," she said softly. "No matter what happens I'll never see you again."

McGarvey felt a genuine sorrow for her. Almost everything that had happened in her life after her father had defected had been her fault. Yet she'd done some good work for the CIA, and she had a lot more to give.

But there was no chance for her now, which put him between a rock and a hard place. He couldn't take her with him. As she said, there was nothing but prison for her back home. Nor could he kill her.

"Someone will probably be coming after you."

"I know," she said.

He stuffed the laptop in his backpack.

Gloria held out his pistol. "Do you want this?"

McGarvey reached into his pocket, pulled out two magazines of ammunition, and handed them to her. "You might need these."

She nodded tightly. "Thanks."

As he stepped past her back into the bedroom, she reached up and kissed his cheek. "Good-bye, Kirk," she said. "Watch your left."

McGarvey passed through the bedroom and held up just at the open sliding glass doors. He pulled the night-vision glasses up to his eyes and searched the deeper shadows around the pool. One man, holding what appeared to be an AK-47, was hiding in one of the cabanas. A second, also armed with a Kalashnikov, was crouched behind a stack of pool chairs and chaise longues. Neither weapon was equipped with a suppressor. Evidently they didn't care how much noise they made.

He raised the Steyr, the sighting awkward because of the bulk of the night glasses, and squeezed off one shot, taking down the guard behind the chairs. The man's body pitched backward, his gun clattering on the pool deck.

The one in the cabana stepped around the corner to see what the noise was all about and McGarvey double-tapped him, once in the chest and the second time in the head, and he crumpled to the deck.

Gloria suddenly appeared out of the darkness behind him, and before he could pull off his glasses and turn around, she was at his left shoulder, the Walther in her hand.

"I'm getting out of here with you," she said. "His people will kill me if I stay. Anyway, I think my chances are better on the outside."

"Probably a good call," he said. "I've taken out the two on the other side of the pool. But no one's reacted."

"As long as you're in the house they won't risk hitting Liu. They're pretty good."

"Ex-GAFE?"

She nodded. "They'll be waiting for you to try for the front gate or go over the wall on the same side you came in."

"What about the back gate?"

"They've got claymores back there, tied to motion sensors," she said. "But I don't think they'll be expecting you to go over the wall behind the cabanas. It's probably why they put only two of their guys back here."

"Okay, cover me," McGarvey said.

"No, you're a better shot," Gloria said. "And I don't think they'll open fire on me, not at first."

Before McGarvey could object, she stepped out onto the pool deck, the pistol at her side, and headed toward the cabanas.

She got halfway around before someone in the darkness to the left called out something to her. McGarvey couldn't make out what it was, but Gloria suddenly ducked down and sprinted for the cabanas, firing over her shoulder as fast as she could pull the trigger.

McGarvey was out the door, laying down a line of fire in the same direction in which Gloria was shooting, as he followed her in a broken-field run.

The guards hiding in the shadows of the east wing of the compound began returning fire, first at Gloria and then at McGarvey when they could see that he hadn't brought Liu along as a hostage.

Gloria just made it to the end of the last cabana when she was hit and went down, scrambling the last couple of feet on her hands and knees around the corner.

McGarvey emptied the magazine toward the east wing just as he reached the last cabana and ducked around the corner.

The side of Gloria's T-shirt was covered in blood, but she'd managed to swap out magazines in the Walther.

"Are you hit bad?" he asked as he dug a spare magazine out of his backpack and reloaded the Steyr.

"I'll live," she said tersely.

"Can you make it over the wall?"

"I think so."

The compound had fallen silent. McGarvey stuck his head around the corner for just an instant, and drew immediate fire from the house. He ducked back, held the Steyr around the corner, and fired off a quick burst in the direction of the shooter.

When he looked down, Gloria was grinning up at him. "You're damned good," she said.

McGarvey laid his rifle aside, pulled the grapnel out of his pack, and tossed it up over the wall. Like before it caught on the first try.

"On three, go," he told her, snatching the rifle.

She got painfully to her feet, stuffed the pistol into the waistband of her jeans, and grabbed the rope. She nodded. "One . . . two . . . three," she said, and she started up.

McGarvey held the rifle around the corner and fired a continuous burst as Gloria scrambled up the rope and disappeared over the top.

The return fire came immediately, most of it over the top of the cabana or into the lintel. Their angle from the east wing was all wrong, making it impossible to hit anyone on the wall. It was a weakness in the compound's security, and Gloria had known enough about the place to understand what it meant for them.

But by now Liu's men would understand they had made a mistake, and would be changing their tactics.

McGarvey switched out his last magazine, and peered around the corner just long enough to see two men sprinting across the pool deck in front of the open sliders to the living room. He took them down with two short bursts, then emptied the magazine on the east wing.

Slinging the weapon over his shoulder, he reached the wall in three steps, grabbed the rope, and started up, more fire coming from the east wing. But then he was over the top and on the ground on the other side.

Gloria was trying to struggle to her feet, the left side of her T-shirt soaked with blood, and some black fluid.

McGarvey helped her up, but she tried to push him away.

"I'll cover you," she said, her voice weak.

"We're getting out of here together."

"I'm not going back to stand trial."

"I'm pretty good at coming up with cover stories," McGarvey said. "Been doing it all my life. I'm taking you home."

She winced in pain when he gathered her up in his arms, but she didn't cry out.

"Watch my back," he told her as he started down a shallow slope to the edge of the road, trying his best to jar her as little as possible.

At the bottom he searched the top of the wall, but nothing moved, nor had anyone come out of the main gate.

"Anything moves, shoot it," he said.

Holding her as gently as possible, he sprinted across the road to the thick willows at the water's edge.

Halfway across, Gloria started shooting, squeezing off one methodical shot after the other, emptying the magazine by the time they reached the lake and the cover of the willows.

But they'd taken no return fire, which bothered him.

Gloria's body went slack and she almost slipped out of his arms. He went down on one knee and laid her on the damp ground. Her eyelids were fluttering, and when he checked her pulse at the side of her neck, it was weak and rapid. He pulled up her T-shirt to check the wound, which was leaking a thick, dark fluid. She'd been hit in the liver. The pain must have been brutal, and she had to know she was already as good as dead. Even if she had been on an operating table her chances would have been slim.

She stopped breathing with a little sigh, and her body went totally slack.

"Goddamn it," McGarvey said softly.

He put much of the blame on her father's shoulders. There'd never been any love between them, and he'd never bothered being there for her when she'd needed him the most after her mother's death. The only question left in his mind was who had ordered him taken out and why. Either it was Liu, to stop him from saying anything more about Gloria, or it was Cuban intelligence that had finally gotten to him. Either way didn't really matter, because even at the end he hadn't stepped up to the plate for his daughter. He hadn't defended her, as most fathers would have done for their daughters, when McGarvey had come calling. All he could say was that he didn't trust her.

McGarvey took his pistol from Gloria's dead fingers and checked the load. It was empty, and there were no more magazines for it or for the Steyr.

At that moment someone shouted something from the road in front of the compound, and a car came out of the gate, its headlights flashing on the road above.

EIGHTY-SIX

XOCHIMILCO

No doubt they had found his car by now and the route he had taken approaching the compound. And they would realize that he and Gloria were trapped in the willows.

What they couldn't know was that Gloria was dead, and McGarvey was totally out of ammunition. They would be cautious, which gave him a slight advantage.

He speed-dialed Rencke, who picked up on the first ring. "I lost your signal for a while. Were you inside?"

"Yes," McGarvey said, keeping his voice low. Someone had entered the willows and was heading his way. "Liu is dead, but I got his laptop. If I can get it to you, we should be able to find out what the hell he's been up to down here. In the meantime I'm in a corner. I'm going to even the odds, but I'll be needing an extraction real soon." He explained the situation on the ground.

"A DEA chopper is standing by. I'll have it to you in under ten minutes," Rencke said. "It's a gunship, but this'll be a real quiet drug bust."

"I don't know how many of Liu's people are closing in on my position, but it sounds like five or six of them," McGarvey said. Gloria had lied to him about the number of armed men in the house.

"Soon as you hear the helicopter, call them in on your position through this connection. I'll patch it through," Rencke said. "Are the girls with you?"

"They're both dead. Liu killed Shahrzad, and Gloria took a hit helping me out of the compound. I have her body with me now."

"Oh, wow, she was clean after all?" Rencke asked.

"Yeah, just a little confused," McGarvey said. Something moved in the brush less than ten feet away. "Gotta go," McGarvey whispered. He shut off the sat phone, laid it and his backpack beside Gloria's body, and slithered the few feet into the lake's ice-cold water.

He swam twenty feet along the shoreline in the direction of the compound before he came ashore. He quietly made his way into the thick willows and headed back toward where he'd left Gloria.

Someone called out from the general direction where he'd hidden his car, but there was no answer.

It took only a couple of minutes to get back to where he'd started. Two of Liu's men were there. One of them was bent over Gloria's body. He'd found the sat phone and backpack and was examining them while the other one watched. Both of them were armed with AKMs.

McGarvey stepped into the narrow clearing. "That's my property. I'd like to have it back."

Both men spun around, bringing their weapons to bear.

"You should have kept running," the one farther from Gloria's body said. "You're not going to enjoy what's going to happen next."

"Liu is dead. Who's giving the orders now?"

"You'll see," the ex-GAFE operator said.

The other one held up the cell phone. "Nobody's coming to help a CIA gringo. Mexico belongs to us."

"It that why you two were drummed out of the army, because you're patriots?"

"Hijo de puta," the nearest man swore. His finger tightened on the trigger at the same moment that McGarvey snatched the end of the gun barrel and twisted it out of his hands.

"Roberto," the man by Gloria's body shouted.

The weapon fired one short burst into the trees just as McGarvey shoved the man's body backward off balance toward his partner, who'd also opened fire. Three rounds slammed into the ex-GAFE operator's back.

McGarvey stepped to the left as he flipped the AKM end over end, catching it by the pistol grip. He squeezed off one round and hit the operator in the middle of the face, destroying his nose, blowing off the back of his head, dropping him backward on top of Gloria's body.

The night fell ominously silent.

McGarvey pulled the man's body off Gloria's and found two spare thirty-round magazines between the two of them, plus the bullets left in each weapon. He figured he was going to have company homing in on this position any minute now, and he would need all the firepower he could gather.

He transferred the remaining bullets from one of the weapons to the other, stuffed the spare magazines in his pockets along with the sat phone, and slung his pack over his shoulder.

Gloria's body was covered in her own blood plus the blood from the ex-GAFE operator who'd died on top of her. He lifted her body in his arms, awkwardly picked up the AKM, and headed up toward the road, and at that moment he thought he heard a cyclic noise in the distance to the northeast.

He pulled up short and held his breath to listen, but the sound was gone. It came back almost immediately, and this time knew it was the DEA helicopter Rencke had sent for him. The U.S. Drug Enforcement Agency had maintained a presence here in Mexico for the past several years, working alongside the local authorities in drug-interdiction raids. This flight would supposedly be logged as a routine drug bust. When Liu's body was found in the compound along with the bodies of the ex-GAFE muscle, the incident would be reported as a shoot-out between rival drug lords.

Whatever names were on the arrest report, McGarvey's would not appear. Nor would Gloria's name show up on the list of KIA.

But first he had to get out of here in one piece with Liu's laptop.

He gently laid Gloria's body on the ground, took out the sat phone, and speed-dialed Rencke's number.

"Gotcha," Rencke answered. "What's your situation?"

"Two bad guys are down, and the chopper's inbound."

"I'm patching you over now," Rencke said. "Just keep your head down. They're going to take out anything that moves."

"Do it," McGarvey said.

He left the sat phone on and dropped down beside Gloria's body to wait.

Within twenty seconds the pitch of the helicopter's blades changed, and suddenly it was screaming at treetop level just above the road, firing its 7.62 mm machine guns.

It was past in seconds, making its turn just above the compound. McGarvey could see it above the trees, its side hatch open, as it fired at someone inside the compound's walls, then came back over the road.

In under a minute the one-sided fight was over and the Seahawk 60F settled down for a landing on the road, the willows bent over to the ground in a large circular swath.

Rencke was on the phone. "Mac, it's clear now. They're waiting for you."

"We need to get out of the country asap."

"The Gulfstream is warming up at the airport," Rencke promised. "But you gotta hustle—Seguridad is taking an interest."

"On my way," McGarvey replied tersely.

He lifted Gloria's body in his arms and made his way up to the waiting helicopter, leaving the AKM behind.

"It's McGarvey!" he shouted. "Coming out."

Gloria's head was lolling back as he hurried up the shallow slope through the trees, her eyes half open, her slack-jawed mouth moving as if she were trying to tell him something. Tell him that everything would turn out for the best now, because in the end she had done something good for the only man she had ever loved.

"Goddamn it," McGarvey said again. "Goddamn it to hell."

EIGHTY-SEVEN

□

CIA HEADQUARTERS

Twelve hours later when McGarvey entered the DCI's office on the seventh floor of the Building, Adkins, Whittaker, McCann, and the CIA's general counsel, Carleton Patterson, were seated around the large coffee table at one side of the room, having afternoon coffee.

"Here he is finally," McCann said.

"We're glad to see you, Kirk," Adkins said, and it was obvious he was relieved.

"Where's Otto?" McGarvey asked. "Is he having trouble with Liu's computer?"

"He called just a minute ago, said he's on his way up," McCann said. "Have you heard about Gil Perry?"

"Did you find him?"

"I should say. With his head blown off. Self-inflicted." McCann glanced at Adkins and Whittaker. "Couldn't take the pressure."

"He was dirty," McGarvey said. "And so was Updegraf. They were shaking down Liu for a lot of money, threatening to go public with proof that he'd raped and killed some young women in New York and here in Washington."

"But there never was any proof," Patterson said. "At least none that the FBI could find. And wouldn't it be likely that Liu knew this?"

"Almost certainly," McGarvey said. He was sitting across from McCann, who was giving him a speculative look. Perry had been one of his rising stars, and it was clear by his expression that he put some of the blame on McGarvey.

"Then why pay the blackmail if that was the case?" McCann demanded. "It makes no sense."

"Because Liu was up to something else, something big that was apparently earning him some serious money. Whatever it was, Otto started picking up the signs six months ago, and his programs started going lavender."

"Which is why we called you," Adkins said.

"Don't keep us in suspense," McCann said. "What was the man up to that had Rencke all in a twitter? Beyond his usual eccentricities, that is."

"I don't know," McGarvey admitted.

"Good heavens, you assassinated a Chinese citizen without knowing if he was guilty of anything other than sexual indiscretion?"

"That's right," McGarvey said. He was starting to get tired of the DDO, who in his estimation was an idiot, very much like another man who'd sat in that same chair a number of years ago. They were wannabe spies who hadn't a clue what they were doing, or how to run what on a good day was the best clandestine service on earth.

McCann turned to Adkins. "What the hell are we going to say when the Chinese government starts asking questions?" he demanded.

"It's us who should be asking Beijing to explain why they didn't put Liu away years ago," Rencke said coming through the door. He looked like hell, his long hair flying everywhere, the shoelaces on his dirty sneakers undone, his eyes bloodshot. He looked as if he hadn't slept in a week.

"Did you crack Liu's laptop?" McGarvey asked.

"Piece of cake," Rencke said. "And I'm telling you guys right now that we're in some serious shit. There's trouble right here in River City."

"You're putting credence in what you got off some laptop computer that McGarvey stole, without any corroborating evidence?" McCann asked.

"Shut up, Howard," Adkins told his DDO. He turned back to Rencke. "What have you come up with?"

"Liu got himself into a financial bind, big-time," Rencke said. "So big, in fact, that his own government was trying to figure out what the hell to do with him. His family and his connections are solid gold, and the intel he was gathering for Beijing was nothing short of stellar."

"We know all of that," Whittaker interjected. "Which is why he was connected with the drug people. He was helping launder a lot of money for a percentage, wasn't he?"

"Exactly. But it wasn't enough money by a long shot, and he was heading toward enough trouble on that score alone that he was starting to back out of the business. But he had developed another operation that was even better for him."

"Is that what he started to work on ten years ago in Mexico City?" McGarvey asked.

"No, he was working the drug trade then," Rencke said. "This shit didn't start until six months ago, when he turned up down there again."

"Tell me," McGarvey prompted.

"There were two guys in the shadows at the compound the night you took the pictures, and Liu wasn't lying, one of them was an ex-KGB officer by the name of Viktor Sheshtakov. The other one was Iranian intel, just like we thought, by the name of Mohammed Nuri."

"Wait a second," Whittaker broke in. "Wasn't Sheshtakov one of the guys involved with the hit on the Russian in London last year?"

"Bingo," Rencke said. "Alexander Litvinenko. They poisoned him with polonium-210, which they put in his drink."

McGarvey had a bad feeling that he knew what was coming next, and if Rencke's programs were correct, it was far worse than lavender.

"The KGB has been using that stuff for years," McCann said. "Are you saying that Liu was being supplied with it by this Sheshtakov?"

"Exacto mundo, Howie," Rencke said.

"Who was he planning to kill in Mexico?"

"No one," Rencke said. "You see, the nifty thing about this shit is its versatility. You can use it to lace a cigarette. You can put it in an aerosol can of underarm deodorant or room freshener. You can put it in someone's lunch or in his drink. You can spray it from an airplane, let's say over Los Angeles. Put it in a reservoir of drinking water. Hell, you could even put a couple ounces of it into someone's gas tank, and as he drove around town he'd be killing a lot of people, or at least making a bunch of them sick. And once it's in your system, it's all over but the dying."

"Odorless, colorless, tasteless," Whittaker said. "We worked with MI6 on the Litvinenko thing. It scared the hell out of them. They found radiation traces on at least two commercial jets that flew in from Moscow, but worse than that, they found traces all across London."

"If not a Mexican, who was General Liu planning on killing, and how was that going to make all this fabulous money for him, as you claim?" McCann asked.

Adkins waved him off. It was obvious from the worry in his expression that he had figured it out, too. "Let him finish."

"Iran was supplying the money not only to buy a lot of the stuff from Sheshtakov, but to pay Liu millions for his part in the Hezbollah scheme," Rencke explained.

"Hezbollah in Mexico?" McCann asked. "Give me a break—" But then he too understood. "Son of a bitch."

"Liu arranged for Hezbollah to get into the country, and from there up to Chihuahua, which was the staging area for the rest of the trip north."

All the air seemed to leave the DCI's office.

"Was?" Adkins asked.

"Liu's part in the operation is a done deal," Rencke said.

"How can you be sure?" Patterson asked.

"His Swiss account was credited with one hundred million dollars seven days ago," Rencke said.

"How much of the material got into Hezbollah's hands?" McGarvey asked.

"More than one hundred pounds," Rencke said. "And it took just a trace to kill Litvinenko."

"Well, then we can work with the Mexican Seguridad and close Chihuahua down," McCann suggested.

"Too late," McGarvey said, sick at heart. "It's already here."

Rencke was nodding. "As of last week, it had already been brought across our border. All one hundred pounds of it."

"I need to brief the president," Adkins said, his voice soft.

"And we need to pass this along to Homeland Security and the FBI," Whittaker added.

"We'll need to generate a National Intelligence Estimate immediately," Adkins said. "Otto, can you help?"

"I'm here for the duration, boss," Rencke promised.

Adkins turned to McGarvey. "Mac?"

"You can handle it from here," McGarvey said, getting to his feet. "I'm going home." He headed for the door.

"Hold on just a moment," McCann called after him. "What about Ms. Ibenez?"

"She deserves a star on the wall downstairs." Stars, not names, were inscribed on a wall in the lobby for field officers who'd fallen in the line of duty.

"I thought she was a traitor."

"She saved my ass last year in Karachi, and she saved it again last night in Mexico," McGarvey said. "Give her the star."

"Say hi to Mrs. M.," Rencke said at the door.

"Good luck," McGarvey said. "To all of us."

EIGHTY-EIGHT

CASEY KEY

It was early evening when the cab dropped McGarvey off at his home. The Florida air was soft, a light breeze off the Gulf pleasant. It was good to be home, except he felt dirty, and he didn't think a hot shower would ever take care of it.

He'd phoned from the Sarasota airport that he was home but that he would cab it, and she understood. Now that he was back on the ground, back to his life, he needed the extra time to come down, to return from the place where his tradecraft was all that mattered, the only thing that could preserve his life, and his sanity.

He dropped his bag in the front hall, took off his jacket and pistol and laid them on the bench, and went back to the kitchen. It was a full moon, and he could see Kathleen's silhouette in the gazebo down by the water, where she was waiting for him.

For a long time he just stared at her, and it began to dawn on him that he wasn't some freak of nature after all. He wasn't some psychopath whose mission in life was murder. He was a soldier, and what he did was for her, always and forever for her.

When he came down the lawn, she turned around, a huge smile on her pretty oval face, her eyes lit up like a billion stars.

"Hello," he said.

"This is the part I like best," she said, the words coming from the back of her throat. "When the boy finally comes home and gets the girl."